FORLORN HOPE

BY STEPHAN GRUNDY

TLS

CHAPTER ONE

The stink was the first thing Lieutenant Wolfram noticed, even before he opened his eyes. Stale spirits, vomit, dung and piss, unwashed bodies, a prison reek. He moved his head slightly, eyelids slitting to let a dazzle of light in. His stomach twisted; he retched feebly, and the motion sent a brutal ache pounding through his skull. His clothes lay clammy and damp on him. His armor was gone, and when his hand went to where his sword should be, he found nothing, not even his belt. No sword, no dagger, not even his belt-pouch.

I've been captured, he thought. By whom, how? Wolfram closed his eyes again, trying to lie still and think. He had been assigned to command the midnight watch by the building where the pay-chests were kept. Obrist Helmuth preferred to give night sentry duties to the soldiers who could see in the dark: the very few Elves or Elf-blooded, Dwarves, or the occasional man with a touch of orc or goblin in his ancestry. Wolfram had seen nothing but stars and trees and the setting crescent moon, heard nothing but the wind in the branches and the footsteps of his fellow sentries and then, blackness and awakening here, wherever here was.

The hammering pain in Wolfram's head eased a little as he tried to think of who could have attacked him. Eichendorf was a small village in one of the quietest parts of the Empire, a good place for the Silver Eagle to wait for a new contract while their wounded healed and their smiths repaired the armor and weapons damaged three weeks ago in their last battle. There were two or three Landsknecht regiments that held a grudge against them, but there was no way for something the size of a mercenary company to approach Eichendorf without being noticed days in advance.

The pay chests themselves were protected, not only by soldiers, but by magic. Granted that most powerful mages preferred studying in the College of Magics or in reclusive privacy to risking their tender hides in battle, Provost Alberich was one of the best mages to be found in any Landsknecht unit, and his seconds, Marshal Gudrun and Marshal Wilhelm, were no slouches either.

An attack on the Silver Eagle's finances would have to be very desperate - or very well-planned and backed up by major power. That someone had managed to conceal themselves from the Lieutenant's half-Elvish senses well enough to sneak up and hit him on the head; that, he thought, argued for a serious professional attempt. So why did they capture me? Ransom?

Do they know that no one in the Companies knows about that. If I had been traced from my father's home, surely there would be no reason for anyone to think that Graf Ulric's, his, Wolfram's mind shied away from completing the thought. To the best of anyone's knowledge, he had left a home that had no place for him; that was enough.

"Slept long enough, Beauty?" A raucous voice inquired. Wolfram recognized the speaker without looking. Black Joachim, one of the company's worst troublemakers - cheater at dice, suspected petty thief, and, in Wolfram's opinion, all-around scum. What in the name of St. Hildebrand is he doing here?

"Glad I'm not in your place - you screwed up big-time, Elf-boy. It's a whirl on the wheel or Forlorn Hope for you, so I hear."

Wolfram's slitted glare dimmed the worst dazzle of light in his eyes. Painful as it was, he raised his head to look at his tormentor. Black Joachim, for sure, greasy dark hair standing up in spikes on his head, three days of stubble on his long face, his missing front tooth a black gap in his malicious grin. Joachim was hobbled in irons, chained to the sturdy log wall of the barn; the heavy clink when Wolfram moved his own foot told him that he was restrained likewise.

"What are you talking about?" Wolfram asked. His tongue was thick from the head-blow; he had to speak slowly and carefully to get his words out slurred.

"Is the pay-chest safe?"

"No thanks to you, I hear."

"What happened? I was on duty, when..."

"When you fell down dead drunk!" Joachim chortled.

"I may have gotten ratted for being on the piss in camp at the wrong time once or twice, but at least I know better than to slug down the spirits on watch - and I'm not even an officer." His voice lowered to an oily false sympathy.

"What was the matter? Delicate Elvish sensitivities get the better of you at last? Couldn't stand remembering how we waded in blood and guts at our last battle? They say Elves can't take being soldiers for long."

I will kill him, Wolfram thought, the anger washing away the worst of the pain in his head. Laying hands on a sworn companion was one of the hanging offenses of the Landsknechts' Orders, along with desertion in battle - and drunkenness on duty - but right at that moment, only his own weakness when he tried to rise and the galling bite of the iron on his right ankle kept him from going for his fellow soldier's throat.

Joachim laughed gleefully. "Or was it a woman? Are you pining for Big Katy, maybe? She's used to handling a pike; I don't think your little half-breed dagger will do much for her."

"Shut up!" Wolfram said furiously. "Just shut up!"

"Going to come over here and make me? Of course," the other prisoner added thoughtfully, "if you hadn't drunk everything you had on you, I bet a few swigs would put your temper to rights again. When they carried you in here, you were sleeping so deep even a good kicking didn't rouse you."

Wolfram breathed slowly and deeply, trying to calm himself. His ribs throbbed harshly in spots; he knew exactly where the purple lumps of bruises would show beneath his stained uniform. The soldiers of the Silver Eagle were not gentle with men who got drunk on duty: that could endanger all their lives, and it was generally considered that death was a fair enough penalty for the offense. But I wasn't drunk! I've never had more on duty than a few sips of water with a quarter-part of wine against the bowel-flux, and the healers said the streams around here were clean. There's no way.

Joachim's dirty scarred face seemed to float in the dusty air of the barn, grinning in malicious joy. Wolfram knew there was nothing to say that his unwelcome companion would not make mock of. On the other hand, he should have nothing to fear, either. Wolfram felt the back of his head gingerly. Bolts of pain shot through his skull as he touched the swollen lump that proved his innocence - for, once he was knocked out, anyone could have poured spirits over his clothes and face, perhaps even into his canteen.

The Zauberobrist or one of his Marshals would simply work a
spell of truth-telling to clear him, without even the need to bring
the matter to trial. Then it would only be a question of seeking
out who had tried to frame him, and why. Still, the sense of fear,
and the deeper pit beneath of knowing himself betrayed, would
not leave Wolfram. The Silver Eagle had been his second home - a
rough, smelly, and dangerous home compared to the first; but,
Wolfram had thought that among the Landsknechts, whose Orders
acknowledged no race or birth-rank and where few men had spoken
pasts, he would never be at risk of losing his place. Yet he had
believed the same thing in the home where he was born.

The Lieutenant set his teeth, steeling himself not to answer
any more of Black Joachim's taunts. After a while, frustrated by
Wolfram's silence, the other prisoner gave up and settled down to
entertaining himself by picking through his clothes for lice, which
he cracked between his fingernails with noisy commentary on each.

"Ho, there's the bastard Hauptmann who had me whipped for
being late to duty. That's an Obrist, thinks because he can tell
poor soldiers what to do that it doesn't stink when he craps. A
bloodsucker, like all the rest. Yes, there's a Lieutenant who got
drunk on watch. Snap, he's dead! It happens to all of them, sooner
or later, but so much sooner for him."

The faint daylight showing through the chinks between logs and
around the edge of the roof began to dim after a couple of hours.
The barn door banged open, and four guards came in with torches.

Moving swiftly and efficiently, one of them set a wooden bowl and
tankard down by Wolfram, while the other three tied Joachim's
hands behind his back, unlocked his leg manacle, and led him out.

Joachim looked back at Wolfram and called, "They're taking me
for a few lashes now. But don't worry, I'll be fit enough to drink a
last health to you while you're dying up on the wheel!"

CHAPTER 2

By the next morning, Wolfram's nausea and the pain in his head had eased, though his body was even more stiff and sore from the beating he had taken while unconscious. Still, as the slivers of daylight brightened on the filthy straw, Wolfram's hopes rose. It would not be long before Alberich, both Zauberobrist and Provost, able to determine the truth of his statement and order him freed, arrived, then he would be free. The day passed slowly. Wolfram had only been able to eat a little of the gruel the guards had given him at dawn, though he had drained the water quickly.

There was no pot, he had to void in the straw, as far away as the chain on his leg-iron allowed, but the stink of animals and former prisoners was so bad that even his keen nose hardly noticed the additional stench. It was nearing sunset again when the Provost, accompanied by two torch-bearing guards and one of his seconds, Marshal Gudrun, entered the makeshift jail.

Provost Alberich was a tall man, thin-limbed but round-bellied, though his wide-skirted, gold-embroidered black brocade doublet was tailored to disguise his ungainly shape as well as possible, and his black silk hose were discreetly padded. A hood of black brocade concealed his short gray hair. His blue eyes glared piercingly down his narrow aquiline nose, as though he had already weighed Wolfram and found him lacking. The Lieutenant had to remind himself that the Provost always looked as though he were about to pronounce someone guilty.

Perhaps it was the rigors of his duty, as the one man in the company who was beyond the chain of command, entitled to examine and prosecute even the Obrist, if circumstances required it. Or perhaps, as the general opinion among the soldiers was, Alberich was simply a sour old mage who had taken the post of Zauberobrist and then accepted the office of Provost with the Silver Eagle as well because it gave him a place to spread his sourness equally from the lowest ranks to the highest without fear of risking his position in the College.

It was not uncommon for the same man to hold both offices in a Landsknecht regiment, precisely because he could both determine the truth and make judgments.

"Lieutenant Wolfram," Alberich said abruptly. "You were in command of the night watch, and found at your post drunken to unconsciousness. Do you deny that you flouted the Orders of this company?"

Wolfram braced to attention, as well as he could with the heavy iron cutting into his leg. "I do deny it, sir. I did not knowingly or willingly become drunk before or on my watch. Sir, I ask that you cast a spell of truth-reading on me to prove my words."

"You are entitled to this examination. Marshal Gudrun, please note the prisoner's defense and his request for examination."

"Yes, sir," the young woman answered quietly. Her fine-boned face was pale inside its frame of deep auburn braids. She would not look directly at Wolfram, but concentrated on the piece of parchment in her left hand as she scratched quickly on it with a quill, something of a feat of juggling. Wolfram wondered how she managed to write legibly like that.

"Hold your position," Alberich ordered. He drew his wand from the gold-embroidered sheath at his waist as if it were a dagger, pointing its tip straight at Wolfram's heart. A thin line of colored fire ran out of it, tingling unpleasantly in Wolfram's chest. "State the events as you remember them."

Wolfram quickly summarized, watering his evening wine to one-tenth lest it make him sleepy, taking his watch sober, the silence until near-moon set, then awakening in prison.

"There is a painful lump on the side of my head. I believe I was struck there and that whoever felled me also poured spirits over me so that I would be taken for drunk."

"You assert that you had nothing stronger than heavily watered wine?"

"I do so assert sir."

The mage dropped the tip of his wand. The tingling in Wolfram's chest spread and eased, like the tingling heralding the return of life into a limb that had been slept on too long.

"Gudrun." The Marshal started, pressing her lips tightly together as though to bite back a curse. "Mark down that at this date and time, I examined the prisoner according to his right and request regarding the events of his watch two nights ago. That he was proven to have lied regarding his sobriety and his suspicions of an undetected attack upon himself. The trial may take place no sooner than tomorrow morning and no later than two days hence."

The secondary mage's quill flew, her eyes fixed firmly on her writing. Alberich waited until she stopped, then continued. "The penalty for drunkenness on watch is death or assignment to Forlorn Hope, at the malefactor's choice."

The Provost's fierce brisk posture relaxed fractionally, his voice softening until Wolfram could almost hear a human note of compassion in it. "Lieutenant, it may seem better to you to fall fighting than to be executed. I can assure you that you are wrong.

Beheading is a quick and clean death. The former, you could undergo any manner of suffering before you perish. Seven men of ten choose the Forlorn Hope; do you know how many of those have survived five battles to be reinstated?"

Wolfram shook his head.

"Since I became Provost of the Silver Eagle, twenty-four years ago, eleven. Less than one every two years. For the virtual surety of being slaughtered, you will remain chained off the field, responsible for the vast majority of the punishment duties. You will be forced to associate with the most inveterate thieves, drunkards. Those who cannot restrain themselves well enough to follow the Orders, though their lives be at stake. You have no family name to defend or clear your honor for. Therefore, should you be found guilty by the court and Marshal Gudrun has witnessed clear proof of your guilt. I strongly recommend you to take the easy way out."

"Sir!" Wolfram protested. "Sir Provost, I have heard that even the mightiest mage may foul a spell. Meaning no disrespect, Sir Provost, I would ask that Marshal Gudrun also cast the spell of truth reading on me. I know I am innocent. Therefore there must have been a fault in the spell."

Gudrun's gray-green eyes opened wide, her face lighting. She took a step forward, but Alberich shook his head in disgusted amazement, gesturing her back.

"Surely you cannot believe that a magician of my stature would not recognize a spoiled spell? Either you are the most brazen liar I have yet come across, or." He shook his head again. "Your request is denied. Your trial will occur tomorrow. Do you wish a defender, or will you speak for yourself?"

"I would have a defender sir," Wolfram stammered. If it had truly been a matter for trial, he could have spoken for himself. But now, the only thing that seemed important to him was convincing someone - anyone! - That he had not passed out drunk on watch.

"One will be shortly be sent to you to prepare your case. I personally suggest that you prepare yourself to go before the gods." Alberich turned and marched out, followed by Gudrun and the two guards.

Gudrun half hesitated at the door, as though she meant to turn back to look at him or speak, but then she hastened out in a quick rustle of robes. Wolfram sat down, gasping. How could the Provost's spell have gone so badly wrong without Alberich noticing? He knew that he had not knowingly gotten drunk. Even if spells of compulsion and forgetfulness had been placed upon him, the spell should have revealed only what he believed himself. He knew the difference between the nausea of a head-blow and the lingering sickness of a hangover.

I will wait for my defender, the Lieutenant thought.

He may be able to win me a second examination. For a moment Wolfram considered what Graf Ulric had said to him when he left Burg Löwenstein. Though forever exiled from the place that had been his home, Wolfram knew that he could still appeal to the Graf for aid and be sure of receiving it. Except that he cannot help me here. The Landsknechts' Orders were carefully written so that, at least in theory, even the Emperor could not interfere with their justice.

No more could their own Obrists: Wolfram had heard the stories of how the Obrist of the Crossed Swords, upon taking a third of a campaign's plunder for himself, had been accused by the Crossed Swords' Provost, tried like any common soldier that had filched a few extra coins or a pair of boots from the company's hoard - beheaded like one. As for Forlorn Hope, the unit that Alberich had advised him so strongly against...the Provost had told nothing but the truth: Forlorn Hope was death almost as certain as a chop of the Katzbalger to the back of the neck, but with no surety of a quick or merciful dying. But I am innocent. This attack, the Provost's error - surely there is justice enough in the Orders to overcome them. Gudrun walked silently back to the mages' main pavilion with the Provost. She could not stop thinking of how Wolfram had looked when Alberich pronounced his tale a lie.

Even stained and stinking, pale with pain or sickness, and his fair hair a tangle of matted straw, the half-Elf had held himself proudly as he spoke. The certainty in his melodious voice had made her sure that he would go free, and glad. She had hardly believed that one of the Elf-blooded would have gotten drunk on duty; even had he been a Man, she would have been convinced by his noble bearing. Then his almond-shaped eyes had gone huge and dark with shock, mouth dropping open in dumb denial, as though the Provost had ripped a dagger through his bowels.

"Sir," she said - carefully, lest Alberich think that she was doubting his magic, "are you certain that the Lieutenant's story should not be checked a second time, just to make sure? It is a small spell, and even my power would hardly be wasted in doing it."

Alberich stopped in his tracks, turning to glare down at her. Gudrun's heart froze, then thumped hard again beneath his gaze. In the torch lit darkness, she could see the faint shimmer of blue glowing from his eyes, like grave-light playing over buried gold.

"Are you questioning my skill?"

"Never sir!" Gudrun said desperately. "But you yourself have warned us so often of the risk that the least unknown thing may foul a spell. If Wolfram were touched by some powerful magic? Who could sneak up on one of the Elf-blooded in a clear space at night?"

"You're gibbering," Alberich said sternly. "How often have I told you that a mage must always have thought and word neatly arranged and controlled?"

"I'm sorry, sir."

"A little further thought would have proven the prisoner's guilt to you. He was set to command the night guard, despite his rank, for that very reason. Are we to believe that someone had sufficient power to conceal themselves from an Elf's keen eyesight and hearing, someone who took the time, not only to attack a sentry, but to thoroughly discredit him then, having made a clear path through our outer defenses at the most difficult point to breach, either did not bother to take advantage or was thwarted by the magical protections within? It is a ridiculous story. I thought better of your wits than that, Gudrun. I am grievously disappointed. Further- " Alberich's gaze pinned her like a pike nailing a man to a wooden wall.

"The prisoner is known for not behaving like one of the Elf-blooded. There is no telling how deeply his anomalies run, nor do we know why he chose to join us. Granted that the Orders forbid taking account of a Landsknecht's race in any matter other than gross physical difference, if you intend to speculate, your speculations must take into account all relevant factors, not merely the ones that please you."

"I'm sorry, sir," Gudrun said again. "I did consider the problem of the failure to press an attack, and it seemed to me logical that - if the Lieutenant were attacked successfully with no further disturbance. That the intent to harm was directed against himself, rather than what he guarded. It is also possible that someone meaning to simply get close enough to examine our protections before making more preparations would have discredited a sentry to hide the fact that an effort at entrance was made. However, I think it more likely that he has an enemy outside the Company, since you, Wilhelm, and I are the only mages here, and a common soldier could hardly have afforded the spells of concealment that would hide sight, smell, sound, and the very traces of magic from an Elf, mixed-blood or otherwise."

Alberich shook his head. "Why would this hypothetical enemy not simply have killed him? If the attacker meant to disguise his action, he could simply have knocked the Lieutenant's head in and put a rock under the injury before covering him in spirits. There would have been no investigation, merely 'Death as a consequence of dereliction in duty'. No, the case is simple enough. Granted that, as mages, we learn early that Peter's Blade cuts too indiscriminately to over-use in our art, I think this is one case where it is our best tool."

Gudrun bowed her head. "Yes sir."

Peter's Blade, formulated by one of the great theoretical sorcerers of two centuries past, stated that the simplest explanation which fit all the facts was usually the correct one. Mages were taught to look beyond that, for magic was the art of shaping Chaos to order, and in the Chaos of life and power, there were too many little things flouting the neatness that the human mind tried to force on reality.

But here, as the Provost said, there was one simple and inclusive explanation to be balanced against an unlikely host of possibilities and coincidences.

"Write up the account neatly for the trial, and then you may go to bed. Put the prisoner from your mind. He will not be there for you to worry about much longer." With those words, the Provost departed for the farmhouse where he was billeted together with the Obrist and his wife.

Enchanted glow-lights kept the Provost's pavilion bright enough to read or write easily in. Wilhelm was still in there, his lips moving silently as he committed words from a grimoire to memory. Careful not to disturb him, Gudrun sat down and arranged her writing materials. The torchlight and lack of a solid surface to write on had fouled her handwriting to a near-illegible scrawl, but it seemed to her that the words were burned on her memory.

Reaching the end of his passage, Wilhelm put his book down. "Heyla, Gudrun, what's wrong?" He asked, his wheezy voice light and cheerful. "Don't tell me Alberich has you writing punishment lines?"

"No."

"Did something go wrong with Lieutenant Whatsisname? Come on, tell me, your aura's so dark you're making it hard to read in here."

The other mage's watery blue eyes blinked at her. Sometimes Gudrun wondered what madness had driven the frail young man to join a mercenary regiment where he slept in a real bed less than one day a month unless they took a city contract but then, sometimes she wondered the same thing about herself.

"Nothing went wrong, as such. But," She looked at Wilhelm, wondering how far she could confide in him. He and she often shared their grumbles about Alberich, and neither had tattled on the other yet, but this was a more serious matter. Still, he was as close to a confidant as she had in the Silver Eagle. Anyway, he might find a way to be helpful. "Alberich says the truth-finding spell showed he was lying when he said he hadn't knowingly gotten drunk. When Alberich said that, his face. That was a man who'd had the world yanked out from under him. I'd swear it on the High Altar of Donmar in Mannerheim, Wolfram believed he was telling the truth."

Wilhelm shook his head slowly, dishwater-blond ringlets flopping about his cheeks like the long ears of a scent-hound. "The Provost didn't have you do a secondary check, just to be sure?"

"The Lieutenant requested it. Alberich refused."

"Hmm." Wilhelm thought for a few moments. "I can see why, actually. It's not good policy to raise doubts about the Provost's magic. Any mage can foul a spell, but there are too many times when he'd better not. He might have thought you wouldn't be totally disinterested."

"What do you mean by that?"

"Well, I'd give, oh, a significant body-part to be as good-looking as Lieutenant Wolfram, or as good with sword and lance and horse, or, what I mean is, I think you've got a crush on him that a blind man could see. The Provost may be a dried-up old bastard who never looked at a woman in his life, but he certainly isn't blind."

"I do not have a crush on Wolfram!" Gudrun declared indignantly. To her horror, she could feel her cheeks flaming, tears stinging in her eyes.

"Damn it all to Darkness, Wilhelm! Don't enough people already think I'm a whore, just because I'm a woman in a Landsknecht regiment?"

"Hey, hey," Wilhelm said gently. "I didn't say that. No one thinks you're a whore. You're not even subject to the Hurenweibel." He gave a little dry laugh: the title "Whores' Sergeant" for the officer in charge of the large noncombatant train was a running joke among the Landsknechts.

"My parents..."

"I know, I know. Your parents are nice, well-off burghers who only sent you to the College when they found out that suppressed magic leaks, and they expected you to take a nice comfortable job casting horoscopes for one of the cities after you graduated, or marry a well-off mage and settle down to have children and mix the occasional philter. Damned few in the Company had parents who understand them, Gudrun, or if they did once, their parents are dead now. You can't let it get to you, or you'll go Chaos-shit. All I'm saying is that the Lieutenant seemed like the kind of man you could appreciate, maybe even love, and it's upset you to find out that he could piss it all away by getting drunk on duty."

"But I don't really think, oh what's the use?" She dipped her quill into the ink pot, cursed as she splattered black droplets across the parchment. "As Alberich said, he won't be here for me to worry about much longer. I just wish I knew why."

"I doubt he'd have been here if he didn't have a wobbly rivet or two in the first place. I think they just came loose at the wrong time, is all. We have some kind of drunk-and- disorderly case practically every week. The threat of the wheel keeps them from doing it on duty, mostly, but it does happen."

"Alberich offered him a quick beheading," Gudrun said numbly. "He advised him to choose that, rather than Forlorn Hope."

Wilhelm cocked his head to the side, thinking. "That was kind of him, actually. I think if it were me, I'd rather have it over with than spend a month digging latrine trenches while I waited to get chopped up in a battle where I knew I was getting sent in to die. What do you think he'll do?"

"I don't know. I can't help thinking that he might have a chance. If his defender can get him tested again with the truth-finding spell, by one of us."

"Probably me, considering. No, don't get mad at me again. You know how Alberich thinks, he doesn't trust anyone who shows they have personal feelings. I think you should sit down and meditate for a while before you finish writing up the transcript, or the accounts of this case will consist entirely of, 'scribble, illegible, blot, text uncertain.'"

It was not long before Wolfram's defender arrived. Hauptmann Heinrich, the captain of the Golden Bear Fähnlein – the division in which Wolfram himself fought – was serving this month as the Gemeinweibel. He had been elected to that position a number of times, and always proved to be an excellent advocate for the common soldiers, whether in individual cases such as this, or when a general complaint was raised. There were rumors that he had studied to be a lawyer in Mannerheim, until some disgrace - some said gambling debts, others said a woman, or a duel with the wrong man - had forced him to seek a home among the Landsknechts.

Heinrich was a small, neat man with a huge dark mustache, who shunned the colorfully-slashed garb of most Landsknechts in favor of sober doublets and gowns, such as might indeed have suited a lawyer or well-off burgher. Laughter-lines cracked out from the corners of his brown eyes, but now his gaze was dark with disappointment, his mouth set angrily under the outstretched raven-wings of his mustache.

"Provost Alberich has informed me of the results of your examination," the Hauptmann said. "It is my duty to stand for you as best I can, but truthfully, at the moment I find it hard to see how I can help you." The formal mask cracked; his mustache quivered in rage. "Before Donmar and Alagrith, Wolfram! If you were going to get drunk for the first time in years, could you not have waited a few hours?"

Wolfram's guts churned with his own anger – the anger and the deep, seething, sense of betrayal that had been with him since he left home. Like a fire-drake in a flimsy cage, sometimes it slept, sometime it roused; now it had burst free, feeding its flaming wrath on everything in and around him to double and redouble the old fury with the new. Yet he had expected something like this and was able to keep his voice steady as he answered,

"Herr Hauptmann, I see the problem, but I can maintain honestly that the fault must have lain in the Provost's spell, I have at least some physical evidence to support that, wait! Have you looked in my canteen? I know I filled it with heavily watered wine. If the remains are still in there, and no flasks were found near me."

Heinrich sighed deeply. "I have already examined it. There was a small quantity of rough spirits in the bottom."

"Sir, someone has gone to great effort to frame me," Wolfram insisted. "But if you examine my skull, just here, so, you will find the lump left by the blow that laid me out. No one bothers to cosh a man who is dead drunk."

The captain's careful fingers probed the lump, sending streaking pain through Wolfram's skull. "Hmm. That could raise some doubt. However, the Provost will say that you could have struck your head when you fell, and I understand that the guards were not notably careful when they brought you in."

"Sir, you must believe me!" Wolfram insisted. "I don't know why anyone would want to be rid of me, or why they would go to such trouble rather than killing me on the spot - as they assuredly could have, if they could sneak up unseen to strike me. But you know I have never offended against the Orders, and never gotten drunk even off-duty since I joined up. Will not, would not have. Because I am afraid of what it might unloose, afraid of half myself."

Heinrich looked carefully at Wolfram. The Lieutenant was uncomfortably aware of the stains of vomit and stink of old spirits on his clothes. His Elvish blood did not let him raise beard-stubble, but aside from that, he knew that after a full day in the prison-barn, he must look and smell like a drunk hauled out of the gutter.

"You have been with the Silver Eagle, what, four years?"

Wolfram nodded.

"There are men who strive for abstinence so long and when they fail, are the worst of drunks. Yet, while dry, they usually remain abstinent. Lest one drink turn out to come in a thousand flasks. Whereas, though I have never seen you drunk, I have certainly shared plenty of wine with you myself." The Hauptmann's musing voice became brisk again. "You have no enemies in the Company?"

"No real ones. Black Joachim dislikes me, as do a few others, particularly men I have had to discipline."

The captain laughed. "Aye, they do grumble over discipline. If Black Joachim ever liked anyone in the course of his scummy life, I have yet to hear of it. But no quarrels over women? No forsaken lovers in the company?"

"No, sir." Wolfram had not been able to bring himself to lie with a woman for fear of passing on his own tainted blood. The whores had propositioned him until they gave up, spitefully accusing him of being a boy-lover. Sometimes he had felt Marshal Gudrun's eyes on him as he passed, or found himself turning to watch the sway of her firm-curved body beneath her robes, but they had never spoken for more than Company business or pleasantries.

As a mage and a woman, Gudrun kept her distance from the male soldiers in general.

"You share an every-man's-wife with, let me see, three of your men. But none of you sleep with her?"

"No, sir. Gretel just does our cooking and washing. Looks after whoever gets wounded."

"Well. We both know men of the Landsknechts have no past before the day they joined up, and just as well for most - eh?" One side of Heinrich's huge mustache twitched over a wry, humorless grin. "But those outside our Orders have not always seen it that way. Is there anyone from...someone else's former life, that might think they had reason to want you out of the way?"

Wolfram thought about that. Graf Ulric's heir Rudiger might have reason. If he had grown to fear Wolfram's return or had discovered some truth behind the old secret that had driven Wolfram away, some knowledge that his once-brother's very life posed a danger to Löwenstein, or even the Empire itself.

I cannot believe that Rudiger would change so in so short a time. If I, even here, may truly be the vehicle of harm - he had but to inform me: I would drive the blade into my own heart. Still the gnawing rat of doubt crept in. Rudiger had not seen him in four years, and a boy's shocked willingness to die at need might easily have become a man's will to live at any cost after several years in a mercenary company.

"Possible," Wolfram said after a time. "Possible, but I doubt it." Donmar protect Löwenstein, and the Empire, if I am wrong!

"I fear it will be almost impossible to clear you if you cannot provide a reason for such an elaborate set-up. Remember Hohenzauberer Peter von Magdenburg, our courts cut with Peter's Blade as often as those of the Empire."

Then another thought came to Wolfram. If someone had
discovered the full truth behind his departure from Löwenstein,
someone who had not known him all his life and had no reason
to trust him as Graf Ulric and Rudiger did. Such a person might,
with all good will, have thought they had excellent cause to seek his
death. But he could not bring himself to tell Captain Heinrich why
that might be.

It was said that there was no race, nor station of birth, in the
Landsknechts. Save for the odd jibe, Wolfram had found that true.
True for a half-Elf or a Dwarf, true even for those men whose ugly
faces and rough strength suggested Orc or Goblin blood; but, in his
case alone, that rule might change in a heartbeat.

"Do what you can sir. I have told you all I can."

Heinrich raised an eyebrow. "Not all that you know? If you are
keeping some secret - is it worth being broken and left to rot on the
wheel, or dying in Forlorn Hope, to hold it?"

"Provost Alberich advised me to choose death," Wolfram said
bitterly. "He said it would be quick, beheading, rather than the
wheel."

The captain unhooked the leather canteen from his belt and took
a deep swallow, then offered it to Wolfram. It held red wine, mellow
and good, if slightly earthy from the container.

"I..." Heinrich drank again. "In truth, I would not know which is
the worst. Save that Forlorn Hope offers at least a chance of life and
freedom. Whereas, unless a beheaded man fall into a necromancer's
hands - Donmar forfend! - He will never stand up again. If the name
you have made among the Landsknechts matters to you at all, a
chop of the blade will leave it defiled forever, whereas Forlorn Hope
will clear it whether you live or die." He gave Wolfram the canteen
for one last drink, then stoppered it and hooked it back into place.

"I will send someone in the morning to clean you up and give
you fresh clothes. At least your appearance need not help make the
Provost's case for him."

CHAPTER 3

As promised, Wolfram was able to clean up and change clothes before his trial. He spent his last hour in prison standing, trying to keep the filthy straw from touching anything more than his broad-toed shoes and hoping that the stink of the barn would not cling to his clothes. The maximum length permitted for a trial was three consecutive days. Wolfram hoped that his would be long enough to acquit him in spite of what seemed to be overwhelming evidence. *But if they will only let one of the Marshals check the Zauberobrist's truth spell, I could be cleared in moments!* At last two guards arrived, unfastening his manacles and marching him roughly out. He submitted without resistance, walking as proudly as he could to the clearing beneath an oak tree where benches and tables had been set up for the trial.

Provost Alberich sat flanked by his fellow mages Gudrun and Wilhelm; Schultheiss Otto, the officer responsible for the Company's laws, sat as the chief judge, with a half-circle of twelve judges behind him. The Schultheiss was as impressive a figure as any civilian judge, a heavyset, gray-haired man dressed in rich robes of deep blue velvet banded with gold brocade and a chain of office made of heavy gold plates enameled with the sword and scales of Donmar's Justice. As if to set himself apart from the fighting men with their fashion of clean-shaved chins and large mustaches, Schultheiss Otto wore a full gray beard which hid much of his expression, though his little square spectacles gave him a look of intelligent severity.

Behind Alberich stood Freimann Martin, the company executioner in his blood-red cloak and beret with its blood-red feather, hangman's noose and beheading sword at his waist. The Freimann was scowling, a common expression on his rough-angled face, but there was a gleam in his pale eyes that Wolfram unliked. It took a particular sort of man to hold that office, one who was not disturbed by his fellows drawing away from the emblems of his duty as he walked through camp or enjoyed his duty too much to care. Four more soldiers, resplendent in their most colorful slashed doublets and puffed trousers, sat along one of the benches, together with Black Joachim, his greasy hair slicked down and the stains on his doublet.

Almost hidden by the bright patches that proudly proclaimed how it had been hacked about in battle. One of the men, Little Kai, had been on watch with Wolfram that night, it must have been he who had found his Lieutenant. Wolfram was somewhat relieved at that. Little Kai was an ugly hulk of a man, with a good deal of Orcish blood, perhaps as much as half. But he was painfully honest, peasant tidiness and good manners ingrained, he had said, by a heavy-handed and sharp-tongued grandmother who was determined that, though her grandson might look like an Orc, he would not act like one. Further, Kai was not only Fähndrich, flag-bearer, of Wolfram's Fähnlein, but was one of the six men in the half-Elf's own Rotte: they had fought side-by-side for the last two years. Little Kai would tell the truth. The only question was what he had actually seen. The Schultheiss banged his gavel on the table for silence.

"Bring the accused forward," he ordered. "Are you Lieutenant Wolfram, called Wolfram Longsword?"

"I am, sir," Wolfram answered steadily.

"Let the charge be read."

Marshal Wilhelm lifted a piece of parchment close to his face, his watery gray eyes squinting at it for a moment. His voice carried clearly through the clearing; Wolfram suspected a touch of magic, since normally the young mage never spoke above a whisper.

"Lieutenant Wolfram called Longsword is accused of dereliction in duty which might have endangered lives of the Company, to wit, drunkenness on night watch."

"How plead you, Lieutenant?" The Schultheiss asked, staring at Wolfram through his little square spectacles.

"Innocent, sir," Wolfram answered.

"The witnesses may be called."

One by one, the witnesses stood and told their tale. Little Kai, when he had not heard Wolfram's counter-signal on the quarter-hour, had alerted the rest of the sentries. More guards had been called, they went looking for Wolfram, to find him lying beneath a bush asleep, with a strong smell of spirits about him. The sergeant in charge of the guards had performed the arrest. When the last of the men who had taken Wolfram in had spoken, Black Joachim rose, but the Provost waved him down.

"As is our custom in such cases, a magical investigation was carried out to determine whether trial was necessary. Gudrun, read the account."

Gudrun stood, the shifting leaves of the oak casting dappled shadows across her pale face. Her clear voice was utterly expressionless as she read, "The accused plead innocence and requested to give his account under a spell of truth-telling. The Provost of our Company performed the spell, during which the accused claimed his innocence of the charge laid against him and stated that he believed he had been knocked unconscious, with the physical evidence of drunkenness produced upon him afterwards. The Provost did state that his spell registered these assertions as knowingly untrue. The accused repeated his insistence of innocence and requested that the spell be cast by a second mage. The Provost asserted the integrity of his spell and refused the request. He then offered the accused the chance to have a defender speak for him, which the accused accepted."

Schultheiss Otto nodded to Gudrun and she sat down, staring straight ahead. "Hauptmann Heinrich, do you accept the charge of speaking for Lieutenant Wolfram?"

"I do sir," Heinrich replied. "Sir, I have spoken with the accused and can state that in all apparent ways, he seems to believe firmly both that he is innocent of wrongdoing and that the spell of truth-telling was in some way faulty. I should like to repeat his petition for a second mage to examine him. This will cost the court a minimal amount of time and power, and may serve to save the life of a fine soldier and innocent man."

"Hauptmann, do you think it necessary to have a lesser mage repeat the work of a greater?"

"Anyone, however good, may stumble sometime," Wolfram's defender answered steadily. "There is no harm or loss that is risked by this, and considerable good to gain."

Otto looked at Alberich. The mage glared back. The Schultheiss' gaze clouded, as though he were turning his sight inward. Finally Otto said. "Your petition is granted. Marshal Wilhelm, please cast the spell."

Wilhelm repeated the process that Alberich had performed the previous night. The tingle Wolfram felt from his magic was not nearly so strong, the foxfire glow almost invisible in the sunlight but it was there and he felt a rush of hope. Of course the Provost had no grudge against him. The older mage had fouled his spell by chance, but it was a simple can trip; Wilhelm would be able to announce the truth without further delay. Wolfram finished triumphantly, unable to keep the grin of relief from his face. Certain of what would happen, he almost did not hear the pale young man's weak voice, "He lies."

"No!" Wolfram cried in shock. "No, it cannot be, you!"

Alberich's dry voice cut across his words. "Restrain the accused."

The guards took a rough grip on Wolfram's arms, hauling him back as Wilhelm sat and hastily began to scribble the court account once more. Despite Hauptmann Heinrich's best efforts, the rest of the trial went quickly. Little Kai said that Wolfram had been lying with his head on a rock; he had examined the injury himself before the soldiers had taken the Lieutenant in.

When the captain asked why a surgeon had not been called, Kai said, "I've seen head-bumps like that before, sir. We couldn't rouse him and I thought nothing would do for it but rest. I told the men to be careful with him, but I think one or two put the boot in anyway, sir."

Black Joachim stood to describe gleefully how Wolfram had vomited in his stupor and spoken in a slurred voice when he awoke, "as drunk as I've ever seen a man, sir, I should well know it." Wolfram hardly heard him. A horrible suspicion was beginning to rise in his mind. Had the taint of his birth somehow distorted the magic of the Zauberobrist and his second? If he spoke of it, could they alter the spell so that it would work properly to prove his innocence? Or, would they take the chance to rid themselves of one who might be a danger to the whole regiment? Both men were Empire-born. Would that loyalty, in such a delicate balance, override the Landsknechts' law of ignoring race and birth?

At last the Schultheiss stood to pronounce his judgment. "Lieutenant Wolfram, we have heard all the evidence set before us, in accordance with the Orders of the Landsknechts and the customs of the Silver Eagle. I have no choice but to pronounce you guilty. In awareness of your previous good record and service to the regiment, despite the heinousness of your crime, I am willing to offer you a swift death by beheading, rather than a slow death by breaking on the wheel.

The Orders also permit you the choice of entering the unit Forlorn Hope, with your rank suspended until you are slain or your crime is expunged by five battles in that unit. How do you choose?"

"Sir - I choose Forlorn Hope."

Alberich's mouth tightened. Otto blinked, staring at Wolfram. "Have the obligations of that choice been explained to you?"

"Yes sir, they have. I would prefer to die fighting, rather than as a common criminal."

"So be it. Will you give your oath and parole, not to attempt escape from the Company until you have expiated your crime by death, by forced resignation at quarter-pension from a crippling wound, or by surviving five battles in Forlorn Hope?"

"I will, sir."

"As you have expressed doubt concerning the spells of this nature formerly cast by both myself and Marshal Wilhelm," Alberich said, his voice acid-dry, "I shall permit Marshal Gudrun to establish the truth of your oath. Marshal?"

Gudrun rose and went through the spell. The touch of her magic hit Wolfram like a shock to his breastbone. He could not help staring into her gray-green eyes. Gudrun's dark lashes were wet and spiky as if from tears and she swallowed hard twice as he spoke his oath.

"He speaks the truth," Gudrun said when Wolfram had done.

"Well enough," the Schultheiss declared. "Wolfram, you may go to join your unit. Your gear and possessions shall be returned to you there. May Donmar aid you, for it is certain that you are beyond mortal help."

Gudrun watched Wolfram walk away, his graceful step broken to the stumbling gait of a defeated soldier making his way back from the battlefield. She had seen the flare of hope in his face when Alberich had agreed to let Wilhelm retest him; she had been certain, absolutely certain, that he would be proved innocent. It was almost impossible that two mages - one a Magister of thirty years' experience, one a talented graduate of the Colleges - could both have failed on such a simple spell.

Perhaps, she said to herself, Wolfram thought he had a charm or amulet which could deceive a weaker mage than Alberich. She found that hard to believe, as hard as thinking that both her fellow enchanters could have fouled the can trip in the same way. If her own effort had failed, she might have wondered if some error had crept into the spell as the three of them performed it. It had happened before: a mistake of copying, a slip of one magician's mind, could ruin a charm for a whole group, particularly one as close-knit as Alberich and his two students.

Gudrun knew that she had worked it correctly; she had watched Wilhelm closely, both with the outer eye and the Inner. Wolfram must be guilty. I would never have thought it of him! He had sounded so certain. Gudrun could not guess what Chaos within could have driven him to drink that night, heedless of his duties or the inevitable punishment.

She could almost feel two hearts thumping in her breast: one fluttering the desperate desire to run to him, offer comfort and hope and healing; the other pounding out her rage at his blind stupidity. By all the demons of Darkness, there are plenty of times when soldiers can drink themselves into a stupor and have no worse than a hangover, or at most a few lashes. That piece of scum Black Joachim, he will live while Wolfram dies, because the tiny sodden scrap of brain in his greasy skull is large enough for him to know not to piss up on duty.

Even in Wolfram's defeat, his - deserved! - Disgrace, Gudrun could not stop looking at him. The sunlight-halo burning off his shining golden hair; the breadth of his upper back in the light blue doublet with its dark blue slashing, puffed over his broad shoulders and tight-fitted on his body to show his trim waist and hips. His sturdy thighs and calves in their particolored black and blue hose, curving solidly down to ankles as fine-boned as her own, the fairness of an Elf with the muscled strength of a Man, the best of both sides of his mixed heritage.

She knew he had been considered the best of the Company's
Lieutenants, rising to that rank in less than four years, with further
promotion in the near future hinted at. Angrily Gudrun scrubbed
the back of her hand over her traitor eyes, forcing herself to turn
away.

"Hey," Wilhelm said, touching her shoulder lightly. "It's over now.
This way, he still has a chance - would you rather have seen him
beheaded?"

"Some chance," she muttered. "Sent out to die. I've seen how we
use Forlorn Hope."

"It's saved the whole Company, more than once. Besides, there's
usually some of them survive. Three Gods of Darkness, Gudrun,
there are men who join Forlorn Hope on purpose! Sascha the Mace,
for instance. He went in by choice and he's been fighting with them
almost a year."

"Sascha got thrown out of Kievia because he was too mad even for
them. He wants to die, you can see it on his face. Whereas Wolfram
wants very much, I think, to live."

"Does he?" Wilhelm asked softly. "If he did."

He would never have gotten into that kind of trouble. Alone, with
no one to urge him to be stupid or betray him - what else could it
be but a kind of suicide? There must be something wrong with him,
why else would an Elf-blooded have joined the Landsknechts?

But there are other Elf-blooded - two full Elves! In the regiment,
though they never say why they are here. Wolfram never seems to
spend time with them, where the rest stick together as much as they
can as Alberich said, he doesn't behave like an Elf, either. There
must be something deeply wrong with him, something that just
came out that one night.

"I don't know."

"He wouldn't have been good for you. Gudrun, why do women
always seem to go for the men who are the worst trouble? The
fighters, the drinkers, the ones who run off after adventure with
never a thought to anyone else - while the good, sensible men
get left in the dust?" Wilhelm's pale eyes stared closely into hers.
Despite the light breeze, Gudrun suddenly felt the heat stifling her.

"I don't know. Anyway," she added, "that's not always true. If it were, Black Joachim wouldn't be able to move for the ladies hanging on his arms."

Wilhelm laughed and the tightness in Gudrun's lungs suddenly evaporated. An iron gong clanged in the distance and from the other side of camp they heard one of the sutlers shouting, "Trough's full! Fodder up!"

"Come on," Wilhelm said. "Let's go see whether today's stew is horse, rat, or battlefield butchery."

CHAPTER 4

The soldiers of Forlorn Hope camped under guard - a guard strengthened by archers and pistoliers. They had ceased to be men and companions: they were only weapons now, tended for their use in war - for there were often times in battle when a suicide unit was needed to break a staunch defense or blunt the worst of a charge. Any man condemned to Forlorn Hope leaving the camp without permission would be shot without warning, under the assumption that he had chosen to forsake his oath to save his life. Only the rare volunteers were allowed to go in and out freely.

The numbness of shock was wearing off as Wolfram silently pitched his tent. Save for Sascha the Mace and Fredrik the Tired playing dice in the shade of a tent's awning - the two madmen who had chosen to join the unit because they wanted to be in the heaviest fighting - its inhabitants were off digging latrine trenches or carrying out other distasteful tasks. He was grateful for that: it meant that he could close the canvas tent-flap behind him and sit alone in the dimness.

However, Wolfram could not shut away his own thoughts. Despite their cost to him, he usually enjoyed his half-Elven senses to the fullest. But not only were his sight and hearing keener than those of humans, he had inherited some part of the Elven memory: the trick of mind that could make the past as real as the present, a country not to be merely remembered, but revisited with all the vitality of living experience. Now displaced again from what had seemed unshakeably his, betrayed again by others for reasons unknown, the memories of Wolfram's first loss overwhelmed his mind, until, instead of canvas and cot and fighting-gear, his eyes looked on his first home, and he was there.

Wolfram von Löwenstein, second son of Graf Ulric von Löwenstein, was hunting by himself in the woods south of his father's castle. The day was clear and bright as only the cool spring of the Empire's northernmost lands could be. It seemed to him that he could hear the rustling of every new green leaf overhead, scent each of the tiny woodland flowers beneath his feet, so that their beauty would almost have drowned him if he could have borne to stand still. Instead he ran lightly through the forest, springing over fallen tree-limbs and little glimmering creeks. He felt wholly at one with the woodlands, as much a part of them as deer or wolf.

Though he had brought bow and arrows, he gave little thought to his prey: he would find something, or he would not, and he could not bring himself to care much either way. Then Wolfram heard the two sets of footsteps crashing through the forest, heedless as a bears, but not as natural. For a moment, a surge of anger struck through him. Those were not the steps of noblemen used to stalking deer or boar, or even his father's skilled gamekeepers. If there had been anything worth shooting nearby, the sound of clumsy feet would surely drive it away now.

With an effort of will, Wolfram got control of himself. He could not hear horses. If these were intruders, they were probably not noblemen, hence untrained to battle. Armed with both bow and sword, he thought he could easily take the two men. But they were coming from the direction of Burg Löwenstein, and considering that and the hurried urgency of their movements, he suspected it was more likely that they were his father's servants, sent to find him with some important message. Quietly Wolfram wove through the trees towards them, until he saw the bright red and gold tabards - his father's men, certainly. Then he recognized the voices: old Peter the Gamekeeper and his younger assistant Martin.

The older man was saying, "By all the little demons of Dark and Chaos, how could he have come through here and not left a trail?"

"Would he have walked in a stream like a stag hiding his scent, if he were tracking one?" Martin suggested diffidently.

"He could have, but curse it, we looked both up and down the only real stream we've crossed. He's eighteen: that's too old to be playing silly hiding games, especially by himself."

"All right, all right. I don't know."

"Are you looking for me?" Wolfram called. "Here I am."

He saw the gamekeepers blink as he stepped out of the woods, as though he had drawn a green curtain aside to reveal himself. For a moment they simply stared at him, then Peter coughed uncomfortably. "Ah yes. Here you are."

"What's wrong?"

The two men looked at each other, then back at him. He could see the puzzlement on Peter's wrinkled brown face, Martin's dark brows drawn tight. Then the expression faded to set sorrow and Peter said softly, "Lord Wolfram, your mother is dead."

The words seemed to wash over his ears like gurgling water. For a moment Wolfram thought that surely the silk of his hood had distorted them into the impossible. He had seen his mother just that morning, her slim figure radiant in the sunlight on her gold-brocaded white dress and sparkling ducal coronet. She had laughed and wished him good hunting. "What happened?" He whispered.

"She fell," Peter answered. "Tripped coming down the staircase, there where the steps are uneven, she hit her head against the wall. Smashed her skull."

Wolfram shook his head. As in most castles, Löwenstein's spiral staircase had been built irregular and left-spiraling: the defenders would know each gap with their feet from childhood and have their right arms free to fight, if a foe ever entered the keep. But his mother had been walking those stairs two years longer than he had been alive and she was the most graceful woman he had ever seen. She could not have tripped.

"She did," Peter murmured. Wolfram realized that he had spoken aloud. He still could not comprehend, could not picture his mother lying dead, but the deep sorrow was already settling on his heart. How far into the woods had he come? Far enough that he could not hear the sea that beat against the cliff-walls beneath his father's castle. He could not remember his path, nor gather his wits to find the way out again.

"Take me home," he said.

The courtyard of Burg Löwenstein was abuzz with activity, but all the voices were muted to whispers, leaving the rumble of wooden wheels on cobblestones, the creaking as a servant girl cranked a bucket of water up from the well and the constant rumble of surf against the rocks below strangely loud in Wolfram's hooded ears. The brightness of the open yard dazzled tears into Wolfram's eyes.

He blinked them away, looking about for his father. His sight seemed unnaturally sharp. The tiny rivets in a guardsman's chain mail coif, the wen by the nose of the old man scrubbing the cobbles, the feathers spreading in the wing of a gull circling above, all stood out keen as the edges of a drawn sword before him. But he could not see his father, nor his elder brother.

"They're in the chapel," Peter said softly. "Shall I..."

Wolfram shook off the old gamekeeper's supporting hand. At the chapel door he paused, taking off his hood in respect before he entered. A play of colored light from stained-glass windows filled the vaulting arches of the Graf's chapel, the deeds of gods and heroes turned to living brightness. Color splashed across the carved wooden panels showing the miracles of Saint Hildebrand, panels carved recently by Tilman Lindenschneider in the new style where the stark detailing of the wood itself made up for the bright paints over gesso detail of earlier days. An image of Hildebrand himself, the warrior's patron, stood above the altar with his ax raised, proof in stone that Men could drive Dark and Chaos back with weapons and will and strength. The Gräfin' body lay on a bier before him, tiny and fair. A white silk headdress like a bride's hid her death-wound, but it seemed to Wolfram that, despite her ladies' best efforts, he could see the slight distortion of her skull, like the first warping under Arioris' twisted hand.

Chaos is here, as everywhere, he thought. That moment of ill chance, turning all that ordered and supported our lives into broken sorrow.

Wolfram stepped forward to where his kinsmen waited by his mother's body. He heard the gasps and the scrape of steel together; then his father's hand was on his brother's arm, holding the younger man's sword halfway out of the scabbard.

"Hold, Rudiger," Graf Ulric whispered. Then, louder, "Who are you, come to visit unannounced in a time of such grief?"

Wolfram gasped himself, trying to make sense of the words. Has his sorrow driven him mad? "Father?" He said. "Father, what?"

"Stay where you are," the Graf ordered.

Wolfram could no more have moved than have flown, as his father walked cautiously closer, looking him carefully up and down, staring into his face. Then Graf Ulric straightened, settling his thick shoulders as though to balance the burden of rule on them again. "A spell, some creature with a strange sense of humor," he said firmly. "Rudiger, go fetch Magister Arnwald. Tell the guards that no other is to enter or leave here until I give the word."

Wolfram waited until his brother was gone. Then he said, "Father, what is the matter?"

Ulric looked aside at the bier where his wife lay. His heavy features tightened, as if he were fighting back a sob. Gruffly he cleared his throat.

"My son, I trust you are, though if this is some trick, be aware that I still have my sword and we stand in a hallowed place. There is no mirror here; but, touch your own face and see if it is as you remember it."

Wonderingly, Wolfram raised his hands. Even before he felt the delicate lines of tilted brows, the sharpened edge of a jaw that had always been blunt as his father's, he could see how the solid bones of his wrist had thinned, stubby hands lengthened to a grace he had never possessed, though still calloused from years of riding and fighting. Last, for final confirmation, he touched his ears. Not as up-swept as a true Elf's, nevertheless he could feel the pointed tips and dropped his hand - his stranger's hand - as if he had touched hot coals.

"An illusion," he said. From the momentary flash of hope on his father's face, Wolfram knew he had spoken wrongly. "A very real illusion, to touch as well as see. Or a shape-shifting cast on me, though I met no one in the woods."

"Has anyone else seen?"

"The gamekeepers looked strangely at me, but I still had my hood on."

"You are still recognizably yourself, though changed somewhat. Never mind. Magister Arnwald will sort it out and this tasteless joke, or whatever it was meant as will pass without harm. But on the day of Tilde's death!" Wolfram looked away: the raw croak of pain in his father's throat was not meant for him to hear, nor any other save the gods.

Master Arnwald hastened in ahead of Rudiger. The mages neatly tailored dark robes flapped about his slim body, his dark hair, usually immaculate, was wild as though he had been tearing at it.

He bowed to the Graf, made as if to bow to Wolfram and stopped, uncertain. "My liege, you wish me to determine what has happened?"

"Aye, and break the spell if you can." Ulric's voice was firm now, only a faint ragged edge remaining. "Do we need to go elsewhere for this?"

Arnwald shook his head, unsheathing his wand from the leather case on his belt. "It will help that we are in the chapel, for we seek the light of Truth. Stand still Wolfram."

Wolfram stood still as the mage scribed a circle about him. It seemed to him that he could see a glimmer of foxfire where the tip of the wand had passed.

A tingling rush of power rose over him as the circle closed, raising the little hairs of his arms in a prickle of goose-flesh. Arnwald began to chant, pausing every now and then as if to listen to an answer only he could hear. With each pause, the mages lively face grew grimmer, tightening at last in a grimace that might have been either anger or pain. At last he struck the circle with his wand. Wolfram jerked involuntarily as the power flashed over him and away.

"My liege," Arnwald said, his voice soft and grieving. "I would have given my life to have spared you this on this day."

"Spit it out, man!" Ulric growled.

"Wolfram is, this is Wolfram, no trickery. He is Gräfin Mathilde's son and hence cannot be yours. His appearance before was a deception: he is truly half of Elvish blood."

"She..."

"Betrayed you, yes."

"With an Elf." Wolfram could not look at his father's face. But Graf Ulric shook himself, as though emerging from deep water. "I have heard that there are nights when, if a mortal woman goes abroad in the forest, she cannot resist, or protect herself from the magics of seduction. If such happened and she feared to tell me...O Mathilde, I would have understood, and forgiven you!" His last words were a bare whisper; Wolfram knew suddenly that no one else in the room, save himself, had heard them.

"No, your Grace," Magister Arnwald said sadly. "Wolfram's - other blood - is not from the Fair kindred, neither High Elf nor Wood Elf. It is...if there is any truth to my magics at all... of the Fallen kind, of those who worship the Queen of Night."

"Dark Elf." The Graf's words fell on the chapel's air with a leaden clang. "She was raped. Or, if not, then she truly betrayed me, and yet, why? How was it hidden so long?"

"To the latter, I can at least guess. The amulet your Wolfram has worn around his neck since his birth, that the Gräfin claimed was a family gift to keep him safe from evil spells. I respected her word, never looked further at it, but now the power is gone with the life of her who enchanted it."

Wolfram touched the pendant that his mother had given him. A small silver fleur-de-lis, a simple trinket, but on a chain that would not break or come off, no matter what.

"As to why?" The mage shrugged. "It might yet have been rape, or magical seduction, or accident. But, my liege, I would fail in my duty if I did not suggest that it might also have been a plot. If you died, Rudiger, Wolfram would rule. Who knows what might have been planned for then, if one of the Dark Elves' own blood came to power over a land whose shores they have plagued so long?"

The Graf turned back to the bier where his wife lay, white and still. Gold glimmered in the hollows beneath her brows; but if her face had shown fear as she fell, pain when she struck the stone, her women had gently massaged it away, so that she seemed to sleep serenely. He reached out a hand towards her, pulled it back.

"Tilde," he whispered. Then, "Could you restore the illusion?"

"I could," said Arnwald reluctantly. "But not near so well. From the style and strength of the enchantment, what lingering traces I could glean from it, I believe that those who caused the difficulty also helped the Gräfin to conceal it. Which, in turn, leads me to more suspicion. The magic of the Dark Elves is beyond the skills of men, recognizable as much by its strangeness as by the taint of the Queen of Night. But even if you were willing to put that aside - and I would counsel against it with all my heart, not only for your sake and Rudiger's, but for all your folk - my illusion would be imperfect. If a woman were to caress his face even, well, I am no warrior, but I trained as every boy of proper family does. A shield-push, a breaking or throwing hold with bastard swords, any skilled fighter would recognize the difference in weight between what he saw and what he felt. It would take a true shape-change and such spells can be." The magister paused, searching for the correct word. "Problematical. Even unpredictable, at times."

"There would always be the question. Thank you, Magister. It is a good counselor who will not try to soften uncomfortable truth, or silence needed doubts."

"I'm sorry, your Grace."

"No. You have done your duty by me and my people. Rudiger, Wolfram, we shall go up to my chambers. Wolfram, put your hood back on, and keep your face averted. With luck, it will be thought only that you are overcome by sorrow." Ulric's voice hitched slightly on the last word, but he strode off with the confident step of a much younger man.

Graf Ulric's chambers were at the top of the castle, with no other rooms to share a wall with them; the creaking of the oaken staircase would betray any would-be eavesdropper and generations of mages had warded the rooms against scrying. Wolfram and Rudiger followed the Graf in. Ulric stared at Wolfram for a long moment. For the first time, Wolfram noticed that the Graf's hair and beard were almost wholly gray, the marks of age graven deep into his face like scars. Wolfram had always thought of his father as immortal, unchanging; now he saw that Ulric was old, on the downward curve towards death.

"What can I do with you?" The Graf asked softly, as if speaking to himself. "Before the gods, I believe that you knew nothing of this - that you are betrayed as surely as I. Yet."

"You cannot let me stay," Wolfram finished. He felt dazed, as though he were standing outside himself, watching actors in a play.

"If we could, if Magister Arnwald could..." Rudiger's voice trailed off. Wolfram saw the tears standing in his brother's eyes. Half-brother, in truth, no, he reminded himself. No blood-kin at all. Rudiger's mother had died in childbirth; Ulric had married Mathilde a couple of years later because he felt his infant son needed a mother to tend him.

Looking at the other youth's features - broad-cheeked and blunt-jawed, so like to the Graf's that Rudiger could have been a shadow of his father thirty years past; so like to what he remembered of his own. Wolfram felt a stab of envy and felt guilty immediately. The more so, because he could see the pain on Rudiger's face: was it his own tainted blood arousing bitterness where he should feel love? Thinking that, Wolfram was certain of what he must do.

"You cannot let me stay," he repeated, thinking slowly aloud. "If my birth was part of some deep plot, I know nothing of it. I would not knowingly betray you, or Rudiger, in any way. Magister Arnwald admits that he cannot match the magic of the Dark Elves. Something could be hidden within me that he cannot find. Or there could be some plan that only needs for me to be here as I am, disguised by illusion or not. Löwenstein wards the coast against Dark Elves as well as northern pirates: how could I risk endangering this bastion by my presence." He went on, "what if, the gods forfend, some accident befell Rudiger? You could never know that I had no part in it, nor I know that it had not happened because of me."

Ulric shook his heavy head. "This never occurred to you before, simply because you were the younger and he the elder?"

Wolfram's eyes widened in shock at the thought, even as Rudiger's mouth opened in surprise. The Graf laughed painfully. "How rare is it, that the heirs to a realm never think that the second might find a way to supplant the first? True brothers in heart. With every word you speak, Wolfram, you prove it unjust to send you away. Wolfram, whatever the blood of your birth, I took you from your mother's arms and named you my son. I have watched you for eighteen years, and seen you grow into a good man, a man of whom I am proud.

Donmar help me, I have never been prouder of you than now! By my own wish I believe, by Rudiger's, " his son nodded vigorously - "I would keep you here. But sooner or later, as Magister Arnwald said, the secret must be discovered. Then, not only you, but all of us, would earn the mistrust of both the commons and the Emperor. However good your counsel to your elder brother might be, some would say it was meant to deceive. They would be convinced - forgive me for saying it - that either we were fools or enchanted, or we had turned to evil ways ourselves. That would be disaster for every man and woman in the care of the Grafs of Löwenstein."

"It would," Wolfram agreed. "When I took a man's weapons, I swore my fealty to you, not only as my father, but as my Graf. If the best way for me to serve you, and Löwenstein, is for me to go away, then I am prepared to go."

In truth, Wolfram's legs were trembling with nervousness. Though he had served as a page in a neighboring Graf's castle, and traveled about all the nearby duchies as part of his father's retinue, he had never tried to make his way alone. But he kept his voice steady, and tried to show nothing but resolution on his face.

"Perhaps, as some say, the gods delight in irony. I raised you to care more for our folk and lands than for yourself, that you might give your brother good counsel and aid - or rule yourself, if the gods so willed it. Now they have brought us to this, that you must prove the worth of my teaching in your departure." Clear water pooled in the Graf's brown eyes, but did not spill. "So be it. But you will go as befits the son of the Graf von Löwenstein. Rudiger, choose the best of our horses: a destrier, a riding palfrey.

Hmm, if you are traveling alone, as you must at least for a time, I fear that more than one packhorse would make you too tempting a target of brigands. One packhorse, then. Clothes suited to hard travel, and a set for dressing well." Ulric looked appraisingly at Wolfram.

"Your armor should still fit you, I think. That, and a full selection of weapons, the best we have. The blade Löwenzahn must pass to the eldest son of Löwenstein; but, I may give you Treuherz, as I had meant to when I grew too old to wield it in battle any longer.

I have carried it often in the defense of our lands; as you leave for that sake, I would see you bear it now. Rudiger, please see that it is all made ready. I would talk to Wolfram alone now."

"Yes, Father," Rudiger said, his voice choked. He turned to Wolfram. "My brother." Words failed him. He embraced Wolfram tightly for a moment, then tore himself away. His footsteps clattered outside, fading swift as if a nightmare chased him down the stairs.

"Now," Graf Ulric said, "I would give you the advice I would rather no other heard. I think you will do best to seek out one of the Landsknecht regiments. Many speak ill of mercenaries; but I myself hired such a regiment before your birth, when the Dark Elves sought to invade us, and they fought valiantly and well. Among the Landsknechts, a man is judged solely by his abilities, not his birth or blood. I have heard of one company led by a peasant Lieutenant – commanding the whole regiment while the Obrist was leading several – and I myself once met a half-Orc - if you can believe it – who was the Hauptmann of a Fähnlein. No one will so much as ask after your heritage or past." The Graf paused, frowning.

"It may be that we will never know why Tilde did...what she did. If it was foolishness or accident or enchantment - it will always prey on my heart that she did not trust my love enough to tell me.

If she meant harm to me all along." He sighed. "Perhaps that thought hurts less than the fear that it was some fault in me that made her think I would not forgive her, that some word or act of mine made her choose to live in fear for herself and you all those years.

I, ah, you are old enough to have lost your heart once or twice, but you have never been wedded, never known what it is to believe you held a woman's trust so completely." He straightened his shoulders, setting his jaw firmly. "I am old enough to ramble. Go with my blessing and my love, Wolfram. If you are not my son in body, you are nevertheless the son I made you through all the years of your life. If you are ever in need, send to me and I shall give you every help I can. Even if it means revealing yourself: I would sooner that, than have you harmed when I could have prevented it."

Wolfram moved forward to embrace the old man, then stopped as another thought came to him. "Am I likely to be recognized if I meet someone whom I had known before?"

The wrinkles on the Graf's forehead furrowed deeper beneath his coronet. "Truth be told, I do not think so. It is not that you are so much changed," he added hastily. "But, when I saw you in the chapel - I, who have known you near as well as I have known myself, all your life - I thought first of the heritage you show, and looked past that only when you called me 'Father'."

"Could I could I look in your mirror?" Wolfram asked hesitantly.

The Graf opened the door to his bedchamber. As children, Wolfram and Rudiger had capered and pulled faces before the large mirror on the wall. Now Wolfram approached it slowly, as if some monster of his childhood fears lurked beneath its glassy surface. An Elf, he thought. The delicate cast of feature, slanted green almond eyes, pointed ears - it took Wolfram a second glance to recognize his own face. Not so much changed, after all, as the Graf had said, it was more a trick of the mind, that noticed the race first of all, and only then looked at the individual shape of features. A closer gaze revealed his mother's human blood, the green of his eyes tinged richly with blue, blunter-faced than a true Elf, ears lower-peaked, shoulders broader and heavier.

Wolfram understood now why his mother had always encouraged him so to do anything that would build his weight of muscle, from sword-work to lifting stones: the more closely his true shape conformed to the illusion she had wrought, the easier it must have been to maintain. But half an Elf, a Dark Elf! He could see no sign of the taint of evil on his face, and yet.

Then Wolfram realized the most telling thing of all. The wooden shutters were closed, and no candle or lantern burned within the chamber. The outer room was dimly lit; this one was dark, save the faint glimmer through the half-open door. Yet he could see as well as if he stood in the full light of the sun.

"I have heard that the Lion Rampant is an honorable regiment," he said numbly. "I think I shall go to them first, to see if they have a place I can fill."

CHAPTER 5

The sounds of scuffling outside his tent aroused Wolfram from his daze as the center pole lurched dangerously over suddenly slack canvas. "Hey!" He shouted. A burst of laughter answered. Wolfram dived out the door in a long low roll, the tent collapsing behind him. Coming to his feet, he looked at the four men surrounding the heap of fallen fabric over his belongings. One of them was bringing a thick branch back to his shoulder - a branch that had just, Wolfram realized, swung where his head would have been if he had scrambled out upright instead of rolling. The man with the club, a red-haired bruiser with a huge matted beard and stained ribbons drooping all over his puffed pantaloons and sleeves, smiled falsely at him. "Are you all right?" He asked. "You really should take more care how you put your tent up. A man can get some nasty bruises if his center pole falls on him."

Wolfram eyed him grimly. The half-Elf knew what the redhead and his comrades had planned. A game known as Badger-in-a-Bag.

Wrapped in his tent, helpless and unable to see his attackers, they could have beaten him senseless with fists and feet and sticks without retribution falling. Certainly he could never have known who to accuse, and who, in the Forlorn Hope, would bother turning in their fellow condemned for their rough amusement? When the Graf's son had first joined the Landsknechts, he would have been stricken helpless by the simple brutality of these men - had been at first, indeed, by the roughness of far better soldiers who bore him less ill will. Wolfram had learned a great deal since, and one of his first lessons, when facing several together, was: make the ringleader pay.

"I'm indebted for your help," he said coldly. "Come, shake my hand on it."

Grinning, the red-haired man switched the branch to his left hand and stepped forward with his right extended. Wolfram reached out. In a single motion before the other could react, Wolfram grabbed his left wrist, twisting it as he dropped to his knees. His own left hand shot up between the other man's legs, crushing his testicles; Wolfram turned his body hard to the right and pulled, sending the redhead flying over his shoulder to land in a moaning heap on the ground.

Thank you, Father, he thought, for hiring an arms-master who would teach young nobles more than the skills of chivalry and dueling! Wolfram was on his feet at once, looking at the other three. Deliberately he scuffed at a rock.

"Bad ground for putting up tents is generally bad ground for walking over, too. Your friend should have watched where he was going."

The three men stared at him without speaking, moving apart, and Wolfram knew that they were going to try to jump him together. He let out a long slow breath, poised for the first one to move as he instinctively sized them up. The short, dark-haired boulder of a man to his left - a lanky, long-armed blond in the middle, shuffling his feet slightly - the one on the right was of middling height and build, with close-cropped brown hair, but the cold professional look on his face worried Wolfram more than the eager aggression of the other two. As Wolfram had expected, the lanky one stepped in for a kick as the short one charged low to shoulder-ram him.

Wolfram whirled, sidestepping the short man's rush and catching the taller one's leg in the same motion. He twisted the kicker's foot, flinging him bodily at the third man, who had hung back to let his comrades occupy Wolfram's attention. Wolfram caught the dull gleam of a metal weight in the man's hand as he dodged his companion's flailing body. Then the short man closed again, grabbing for Wolfram's arms - meaning, the half-Elf guessed in the flashing half-thoughts of combat, to hold him while the other ones worked him over. Wolfram spun away, his leg hooking as part of his movement to catch the grappler behind the knee.

The short man did not fall, but in the moment while he regained his balance, Wolfram had gotten well out of range. The first attacker was on his feet again, but all three were moving more cautiously now, shuffling slowly about as they considered their next move. Wolfram's breathing came more quickly. He would have to incapacitate at least one of them in the next rush; he might have the advantage of a young lifetime's training with one of the best wrestling masters in the northern part of the Empire, and of Elvish agility together with human strength, but he had also been very lucky that the three of them had not simply rushed him at once. Sooner or later they would realize it, or one would slip behind him while another distracted him.

"What are you turd-brains doing?" Came a voice from the trees to the right. Wolfram did not turn to look until he saw his attackers' stances sag; even then, he only afforded himself a flicker of a glance.

His heart thudded hard with relief. The two men walking towards him were Fredrik the Tired and Sascha the Mace. Sascha's size - six and a half feet tall, and near four hundred pounds of muscle and meat, exaggerated by the puffs and slashing and ribbons of his clothing - was enough to intimidate even the hardest case. Although Fredrik was slender, if well-muscled - he and Wolfram could have traded doublets – the Scandian was, without question, the best fighter and wrestler in the Silver Eagle.

Both men, despite their choice of unit, had a good name for honorable behavior.

"Not brave enough to take him on one at a time?" Fredrik went on. "At least Red Dirk had the balls to try it."

"Red Dirk maybe not got balls anymore," Sascha muttered thunderously, hunching his massive shoulders.

"Fighting among ourselves is against the Orders," one of Dirk's friends, a short, dark-haired boulder of a man, said piously. "The Elf's tent fell down, was all, and we were going to help him dust off his clothes. I guess Dirk tripped on a rock or something."

"Sure he did. Piss off, I don't want to look at you anymore. Better take Dirk to a chirurgeon. I think that rock caught him in a painful place."

The three men heaved their fallen comrade up and slouched off. Wolfram turned gratefully to his rescuers. "Thank you. I was afraid that was about to get ugly."

Fredrik smiled and shook his head, his long waves of dark gold hair rippling brightly in the lowering sunset. "My friend, it got ugly the moment you were sentenced here. But we do what we can to keep things clean, because if there's one thing I hate, it's bullies. You might want to watch out for Dirk in future, though. He's a grudge-holder."

Wolfram sighed. Surviving five battles would be hard enough if only the other side wanted to kill him. In Forlorn Hope - who would look too closely into where a death-wound had come from?

"Get your tent back up, then we go eat," rumbled Sascha. "We got better food than swill they give other ones. Benefit of being volunteers."

While they ate, Fredrik, with occasional mutters from Sascha, filled Wolfram in on his fellow condemned. Wolfram had thought that his years in the Landsknechts had accustomed him to hard and hopeless men, but most of his former comrades looked like knights from the romances of chivalry compared to those who had chosen Forlorn Hope over execution. Sascha and Fredrik were not the only volunteers; simply the only ones who had managed to survive for any length of time.

"Usually men volunteer for Forlorn Hope when they can't get up the courage to stick their own swords in themselves," Fredrik said. "Sascha and me, we're different. I like a challenge, and there aren't many fighters who can give me a chance to show my stuff. As for Sascha - " Fredrik clapped his huge comrade on the shoulder - "he just likes breaking heads. He needs a place in the line with lots of targets to keep him happy."

Sascha nodded. His massive hand went to the haft of the long-handled mace resting against the tree at his back, its gleaming steel butt spike digging into the earth. In camp, a leather hood encased the weapon's spiked head, but Wolfram had seen it in action. Backed by the immense power of the big man's body, those spikes could punch straight through a proofed breastplate.

Even without the spikes, the weight of the ball – nearly the size of two closed fists – was enough to cave in helm and skull, it was a horseman's weapon, not a foot-soldier's, but Sascha was strong enough to flick it about as another man might flick a willow switch. Of all the Company, the only man who could match the giant Kievian for weight and strength was Marcus, Hauptmann of the Sleeping Wolf Fähnlein. But where Marcus was genial and unfailingly as kind and easygoing as his office permitted, Sascha's huge muscles seemed to seethe with a constant simmering fury, little blue eyes glowing like angry sparks in his round sunburned face.

Wolfram had met few men who made him physically nervous. He was very glad; however, that Fredrik had taken him under their wing as a friend. When they had finished eating, Fredrik filled a large pipe with tobacco and lit it with an ember from their fire, leaning back in his camp stool and stretching out his long legs.

"We could move your tent over here, if you want," he offered. "Make sure there aren't any more accidents with those shit brains."

Wolfram considered the offer. It would be more sensible, he knew. He slept lightly, but he had to sleep. Sooner or later, if his attackers kept trying, they would succeed in making him the badger in the bag or worse, if their initial defeat had made them angry enough.

It's not a matter of maintaining authority. Here, I have none to worry about. I only have to make it through five battles, and I'm free again. But some spark of stubbornness, or stupidity, flared up in him, and he said,

"No, I can manage where I am. I appreciate the offer, though."

Perhaps because word of his protectors had gotten around, or perhaps because even the men of Forlorn Hope knew better than to try jumping the Elf-blooded in the dark, Wolfram made it back unaccompanied to his tent without worse than a crawling sensation between his shoulder-blades. Nor, though he looked carefully, was there any sign of damage to the tent or his possessions. Still, Wolfram slept very lightly that night. He had heard that true Elves could enter a state between sleep and waking, where they rested as if in the deepest sleep, yet were aware of all that passed around them and could spring into full combat in less than a heartbeat.

Perhaps it was something in the blood that he had not inherited; perhaps it was a skill that had to be learned in the Elven homes. Whichever, Wolfram could not do it, but if he were not too exhausted, he could stop himself just below the surface of sleep and start awake with none of the usual yawning and eye-rubbing. Before crawling into his bedroll, as well, he had carefully unfastened his tent-pegs in several places. Unless an unlikely windstorm blew up, it would not weaken the structure too much; and if the bullies did try something again, they would still be looking for him to come out the door.

CHAPTER 6

What awoke Wolfram was not a sound, but a smell - the heavy smell of tallow and an acrid hint of smoke. His eyes snapped open to see the flames crawling inside his tent-flap. He gathered himself, creeping silently out the back where he had left two pegs free and peering carefully around the corner. Two of the men he had fought earlier, the lanky one and the medium one, were waiting by the opening.

"I thought I heard him move," the lanky one whispered. "Should I."

Before he could finish his sentence, Wolfram was on them, flinging the middle-sized man headfirst into the fire licking its way up to the top of his tent. His short hair caught at once, flaring up around his head as if it had been soaked in pine sap, and he screamed as the tent collapsed under his weight. The other man backed up, almost falling over his own feet as he gibbered, "I'm sorry, Michael tripped with the lantern, we didn't mean to."

The burning man flailed and rolled in the folds of canvas - folds that were, fortunately, already smothering the flames.

Wolfram stooped to jerk the side of the tent free from the ground, throwing it over him and beating out the fire with fierce, wild swings of rage. They must have poured oil on the canvas for it to catch so quickly, he thought.

"Help your friend," Wolfram said coldly. His Elvish sight showed him the tall man's fear-pale face, blue eyes glittering wide in the faint starlight. "He will probably need to see a chirurgeon."

Still the other man only stood there until Wolfram stepped back from the moaning body. Then, unsteady in the darkness, he stepped forward to unroll his companion.

"Michael?" He said uncertainly.

Michael only groaned. When the taller man pulled the folds of blackened canvas off him, Wolfram saw that Michael's head was a hood of oozing skin over a mask of blood, his nose flattened and askew and his eyes puffing up already. His breath came hard and wheezing. Wolfram suspected that he had cracked a couple of the other man's ribs in beating out the fire.

They walked to the guard-post together, the injured man's friend supporting him.

"What is it?" One of the sentries asked roughly.

"Sir," Michael's companion said. "We were walking back to our tents when Michael tripped. He and the lantern fell into this man's tent and caught both of them - the tent and Michael, that is - on fire. Permission to take him to a chirurgeon?"

The guard held his own lantern closer. In the pale yellow light shining through the translucent panels of split horn, Michael's face no longer looked like anything human; more like a half-charred, half-bloody lump of meat that had been kicked across a dirt floor.

"Is this true?" He asked Wolfram.

"Yes," Wolfram said. Fredrik had warned him that, whatever quarrels he might find in Forlorn Hope, there was one overriding rule: not to betray his fellows to a quicker and more certain death than they were condemned to in battle. "We need every one of these evil bastards with us in the charge," Fredrik had said. "We can lump each other up, as long as we do it where the guards don't see but no telling tales: there is no reprieve for the twice-condemned."

"Stupid piece of shit," the guard said, and spat to the side. "Jürg, escort the roast to a chirurgeon. You two, get back to bed. Dream about the latrines you'll be digging tomorrow."

The tall man walked with Wolfram, though safely out of range, until they were well out of hearing-distance. Then he stopped, clearing his throat and coughing softly.

"I got no grudge," he said. "I was just sticking by my mates, but I guess they've had enough out of you. Is it over?"

Wolfram's immediate impulse was to take the offered truce and be glad of it, but some instinct made him pause, then say, "You would do best to make sure they let it be.

More trouble out of one. I'll hold all responsible. Do you understand?"

The other man shivered. "Michael and Jürg and I won't bother you no more. I can say that. Dirk - I don't got much to do with him. He's crazy, don't listen to no one. If he does give you trouble, he's all on his own, understand?"

"We'll see," Wolfram replied. "If that's so, then I'd better see you helping me and not him if you get a chance."

"Will that make it right between us?"

"Yes."

"My name's Erich." The lanky man started to stick out his hand, then seemed to think better of it.

Of course, Wolfram thought, he saw what happened to the last man that offered me a handshake. "All right, then."

He turned and was about to walk away when Wolfram said, "Why did you start it in the first place?"

The other laughed softly. "This is Forlorn Hope. If you don't have the balls to stand against us, you sure as Chaos and Dark don't have the balls to stand with us - and we don't want your wet arse in a fight, because Fredrik and Sascha won't have time to save your butt when we charge out to die. But you can always go back and take your sentence if you can't stand it here."

"Ah. Well, if anyone else gets ideas about testing me."

"Won't happen. It's over."

Wolfram stood in the dark for a little while after the other man was gone, glad of the cloaking night that hid his faint tremble of reaction. His knuckles stung where the harsh canvas had rasped the skin from them, and a couple of small blisters on his palms bit into him like brands. He thought of the burning flames engulfing Michael's head, of the fury that had filled him as he beat the body writhing beneath the folds of canvas, he wanted to be sick, remembering the surge of satisfaction he had felt.

Is it the taint of my blood, coming out at last? Wolfram asked himself. The Dark Elves joy in the pain of others. They burned all the babes at Wellenheim, just as I threw that man into the fire without thinking. Other memories stirred in him. The fierce hot joy of battle as his sword cut into a foe's shoulder, bright blood fountaining out to spatter into his helm's eye slots. The solid ease of his blade's tip driving deep into a man's guts, the sucking flesh clinging to the metal as he pulled it out of the falling body, leaving the screams behind as he turned to seek a second target, the flare of anger urging him to rowel his horse's flanks till they bled as the exhausted steed stumbled, leaving him to fall further and further behind his retreating unit.

More afraid of himself than of being caught among the stragglers, Wolfram had held himself back then, but what of all the times when, like tonight, he had acted without conscious thought, going for his targets with instinctive brutal ferocity?

Trained brutal ferocity, like that of any skilled swordsman, he told himself. Michael would have done worse to me than I did to him. I could have burned alive in my tent. I have never knowingly harmed the innocent, not woman nor child and many Landsknechts can't say the same. I could have dealt with Michael without throwing him into the fire. Would it have ended this test as thoroughly if I had not shown them I am someone worthy of fearing? But, I do not want to be feared. The Dark Elves.

The men here don't know the difference between fear and respect. Civilized means for civilized men, for Forlorn Hope, doomed and crazy madness to make walking dead men wary.

Wolfram went back to the wreckage of his tent, digging out his bedroll and the bag of plain clothes that were all he had brought with him. His armor and weapons, save one small eating-knife, had been confiscated, to be returned only for drill or battle. Most of the men in Forlorn Hope wore their stained finery defiantly as they mucked stalls and dug latrines. Wolfram; however, had packed his good clothes carefully, leaving them with his hire-wife Gretel along with the promise of a substantial payment if they were all there when he had won his freedom again. The assurance - witnessed by the other men for whom she cooked and washed - that if he died first, she might sell them as she pleased.

The tent itself stank of smoke, with a long black charred patch from the flap to the peak where Wolfram's two assailants had tossed the lamp oil, and the flap itself was burned to rags. Other than that, and a couple of broken support-poles, it was in surprisingly good shape.

Still, he could not bring himself to sleep in it again that night. Sitting down on his bag of clothes, and wrapping his bedroll about himself, Wolfram leaned his back against a broad oak tree and dozed in the clean starlight, his senses still wary lest anyone should come too close to him. As the guard had promised, Wolfram was one of those set to latrine duty the next day. He shoveled endless piles of dirt into stinking holes, then moved over to dig clean ones for befouling.

Though his hands were thickly calloused from a lifetime of weapons-work, he found within an hour or two that digging rubbed on different places. His blisters from the previous night had broken almost at the start and every shift of the shovel's handle seemed to scrape the raw skin deeper.

He gritted his teeth and dug, determined not to wince or complain. If proving himself tough enough for Forlorn Hope had been worth injuring two men, it was certainly worth suffering the burning pain in his hands and the slow knotting ache in his lower back without showing how he hurt. Once he paused to look around. Pike-heads glittered against the blue sky as their wielders marched back and forth in the square, turning, setting their weapons, and raising them again.

The Doppelsöldner, so called because they received double pay for skill and risk, the two-handed swordsmen and halberdiers who came forward in the line to cut through pike-shafts even as the foe's great weapons stabbed and hacked, drilled with each other, a sergeant calling cadence. From further off, Wolfram heard the rattling boom of arabesques shooting almost together only broken by a rough rasp too distant to break into words. From the uneven sound of the volleys, Wolfram knew that the officer was likely swearing to scorch his shooters' ears.

He caught his breath at the glimpse of a long burgundy robe shot through with threads of silk in all the colors of stars and planets. His head turned involuntarily, hoping to see auburn braids shining in the sunlight but the wearer's hair was dishwater-pale, the scuffling walk far from Gudrun's confident stride.

Wolfram bit his lip and turned to his digging again before their guard's whip could fall on his slackened shoulders. Although he was kept at hard physical work throughout the hours of daylight - the Forlorn Hope men alternated punishment labor with drilling under guard.Wolfram found that he had far too much time to think. He kept his eyes and ears open, as best he could, for any hint of trouble in the regiment.

Fredrik and Sascha, who could come and go as they pleased, were Wolfram's main sources of information. He had not told them any of his suspicions, for that would have meant reiterating his innocence, and complaining after a verdict with so much apparent proof of his guilt somehow seemed like an insult to his pride.

Certainly the other fighters of Forlorn Hope had nothing but contempt for those men who whined about their sentences being unjust. Sascha would hardly care. Fredrik, Wolfram suspected, would understand and perhaps even believe him but he could not bring himself to speak of it.

Instead, he ate dinner with them every night, talking of all manner of things, but always bringing the conversation around to what was happening in the greater camp outside.

"We're going to have to get a move on soon," Fredrik commented at one point. "Money's running low, and the townsfolk aren't any too happy to see us still here. A few of our men went in on their leave-day and got into a scuffle with some locals over cards and the Obrist had to go buy them out. Some of the inns are starting to close their doors to us too not that it's any loss, the brew's better here in camp and the whores are cleaner and less likely to rob us. It's a sign we've worn out our welcome."

"Any word of a new contract coming up?" Wolfram asked.

"I know Obrist Helmuth's put word out that we're available. I heard someone saying that we might be going to swing down south for a while, on account of the city-states down there always having work for Landsknechts. That's a long way to go with nothing guaranteed at the end of it."

"Getting soft in camp," Sascha grumbled. "Leave a weapon unbloodied too long, it forgets its edge." His huge hand closed on the steel shaft of the mace swinging from his belt, as volunteers, he and Fredrik were allowed to keep their weapons on them.

"A rest is fine but enough's enough," Fredrik agreed. "Anyway, if we don't get a new contract soon the Company's going to have to start selling its share of the plunder from the last one at quarter-price to keep us all paid. I heard Dirk the Proviant Meister bitching about costs from the locals going up yesterday too."

"Wouldn't mind going east again, or north," said Sascha. "Fighting's better. Might even get hired against Orcs, if we went east."

"The pay is better in the south, and Orcs don't have anything worth plundering," Fredrik answered mildly.

"Too fucking hot down there," muttered Sascha. "Knives and poison and little men that aren't worth wasting a good mace-swing on."

"They do make some of the best armor," pointed out Fredrik.

Wolfram listened absently to the two of them wrangling. He had heard the same discussion in most of its variants before, every time the Silver Eagle was between contracts. It was all a waste of breath. Obrist Helmuth went where the pay was best. The only exceptions were when the Empire called its Landsknechts to service or those rare occasions when Helmuth doubted, for whatever reason, that their employer would choose to or be able to keep the contract.

Once that Wolfram knew of, the Obrist had turned down one of the southern city-states because its ruler had a bad name for welching on his mercenaries. There had probably been other times as well but it was the Obrist's policy to keep details of prospective employment away from his troops until the contract was signed. Wolfram had only heard by chance the one time. Still, one thing was absolutely certain. The Silver Eagle would have to sign a contract soon, or go where well-paid work was likeliest.

Since the Empire was at peace with Broceliande in the west now, that probably did mean the south. Wolfram was content enough with that, since it kept him far away from anyone who might have ever met him in his former life. For if my father, Graf Hildebrand ever found that I was in Forlorn Hope, let alone hearing the reason why - no matter that I can no longer call myself his son; I would still die of shame.

CHAPTER 7

In the week following Wolfram's trial, Marshal Gudrun did her best to put the half-Elf out of her mind. The odds were astronomically low that Alberich could have fouled something as simple as a truth spell, for both the Zauberobrist and Wilhelm to have made the same mistake was impossible. Wolfram was an exceptional actor, who had fooled her so well he could have gone on the stage. He had endangered the whole regiment by his self-destructive carelessness. It was no wonder most regular military troops refused to take Elves, who had no real concept of the discipline of Men. After a while, she managed to work herself into a high temper of rage at him.

Drunk on duty, persistently lying in the face of the evidence, making her, after all her efforts to be accepted as a professional and an officer among the men of the troop, look like a soft-headed female who could be swayed by turquoise eyes and a broad pair of shoulders tapering down to a narrow waist. If Alberich noticed his Marshal's ill humor, he gave no sign of it. When Gudrun and Wilhelm were completing a scrying spell designed to find out if the Company would do better to purchase more firearms for their next contract, or if an attempt to enlist another squadron of pikes would be more useful, she withdrew from the finished enchantment with a slam of power that left Wilhelm rocking, holding his head in pain.

"Arioris and all their Chaos, Gudrun, what did you do that for?" Her fellow mage said plaintively when he could talk again.

Gudrun was about to snap at him, but bit her lip. She knew why she had cut off so hard, it was because an image of Wolfram, his sword sheened with turquoise fire as if to reflect the glowing brilliance of his eyes had flashed in her mind at the last, and she had not wanted Wilhelm to see it. Forcing the storm of confusion and anger back down inside herself, she replied, "I'm sorry. I thought you were already withdrawing, and my vision was starting to break down. I wanted to get out before I picked up any unwanted energies or visitants from the flux."

Wilhelm blinked, scrubbing the back of his hand across his watering eyes. "I had a hard time linking with you too. Are you sure it's not, erm, coming on for your time of month?"

"Where were you schooled? You should know that's no more than superstition, at least where spells like this are concerned." Gudrun's voice had gone dangerously harsh, but she welcomed the chance to be legitimately angry with someone.

"Well, but you can't say your physical state doesn't affect your control at least a little," Wilhelm pointed out reasonably. "I know when the spring flowers bloom, I have to work twice as hard to keep my focus through the itching and sneezing."

"I am NOT coming on for my Chaos-damned time of month," Gudrun squeezed out through gritted teeth, spacing each word very slowly. "It is none of your business anyway. Understand me?"

"All right! All right!" Wilhelm said, waving his hands in surrender. "Donmar's sake, I didn't mean anything by it. But?" He fell silent, glancing around the tent as if hoping that the gleaming brass curves of the astrolabe, or the silver brightness of the engraved scrying mirror, even the rune-carven wood of the warded chests where the components for the simpler spells were kept might offer him some escape from what he wanted to say.

"But what?" Gudrun said impatiently. She knew a mage was trained to be honest with herself, for self-deception could kill faster than almost anything in magic that she was hoping for Wilhelm to say something offensive so that she would have a chance to shout at him again.

"You haven't been yourself since that Lieutenant went to Forlorn Hope. It's getting so I don't dare breathe around you without you biting my head off. Now it's affecting your magic and you can't look me in the eye and tell me it's not."

Gudrun stared straight into the other mage's watery blue eyes and opened her mouth to tell him just that. No sound came out. She closed her mouth, opened it again, and realized that she must look like a fish out of water.

"So, Herr Grand Inquisitor," Gudrun said sarcastically. "What do you advise?"

"I don't know. But I do know that you'll have to work it out and pull yourself together. You never paid him any attention before he was arrested. Why are you so obsessed with him now?"

"Because." Gudrun snapped her lips together. Because I still don't believe he's guilty, she had been about to say. She did didn't she? She had spent the whole week in a fury at Wolfram for deceiving her, of course she believed he was guilty.

"Look," Wilhelm said gently, "he has nothing to lose by telling the truth now. He's already in Forlorn Hope. Unless he does something else to breach the Orders, he can't be executed, and he's been tried in a full court. There's no chance of an appeal. Maybe you should talk to him, get things sorted out in your mind. For certain you should do something, or I'll have to tell the Zauberobrist what your problem is."

While there was no rule against a mage in the Company being affected by emotion, Alberich did have the power to expel Gudrun if he judged that she was no longer competent to fulfill her duties or worse, if he judged that she had deliberately allowed the regiment to be put at risk by hiding her unfitness.

Then where would she go, disgraced in polite society and with the stigma of being thrown out of her position to keep her from being hired on by any other regiment? At best, she might end up as a village spell weaver or city fortuneteller, with the ever-present specter of suspected whoredom to keep her from bettering herself.

Certainly she would never have the chance to go on with her studies, let alone to use her magics to their fullest as she did here.

"All right," she said. "I'll do something, but I'd take it as a favor if you could do your best to keep out of my sight for a little while, unless our duties require it."

Gudrun dithered for another week, waiting for an excuse to see Wolfram that wouldn't seem overly transparent and to get up her courage to do it. Her appointed work helped her there, the Obrist and the Zauberobrist were embarking on a series of complex contract negotiations which required the almost constant attendance of the two junior mages for communications. An ongoing series of divinations as parameters changed, astrological analyses, gathering background information on the potential principals as their bids rose.

Gudrun went to bed every night, when she got to bed exhausted, but relieved beyond measure that the tricky process of negotiation took so much of her time and thought that she no longer had the chance to think about Wolfram.

As the final stages of decision approached, Alberich's need for his assistants waned and Gudrun realized that she would have to move soon, if at all. In the end, she remembered that when Wolfram had joined the Landsknechts he had, as the Orders required, declared his sword to bear enchantment. It must have been Wilhelm, rather than herself, who secured the weapon after the Lieutenant's arrest. But considering that he had been sentenced to Forlorn Hope, she was perfectly within her rights to ensure that it did not, for instance, hold a charm that protected the wielder against bodily injury, which would negate the whole point of Forlorn Hope.

While legally she did not need permission to examine a condemned man's blade, to interfere with anyone's enchanted weapon without their knowledge was bad for morale, and encouraged soldiers to conceal such items or refuse to give them over for storage when required. Her next problem was choosing a time and place to speak to Wolfram.

She might have simply pulled him out of the line during the Forlorn Hope labor detail but in the warm summer weather, the men normally worked stripped to the waist, their hose- and trouser- lacing simply looped around a belt rather than attached to a doublet. Not only were their naked chests on display, but their lower garments frequently slipped to reveal their upper thighs and small clothes - if they wore any.

It was not that she feared to see Wolfram's body thus revealed she could not have missed seeing him now and again as he dug or shoveled manure, the muscles of his shoulders and back rippling beneath Elven-pale skin. But if she took him, dressed thus, away to speak to alone, even if they never took a single step out of view of every man and woman in the camp.No, it would have to be at nighttime. She had a legitimate excuse; she had the authority, if their conversation went a little farther than the subject of examining Wolfram's blade, who else would know?

CHAPTER 8

udrun passed through the guard-post to the Forlorn Hope encampment without difficulty, although one of the sentries said, "Marshal, would you like to have a guard with you? These men, they're not as well-disciplined as the regular soldiers, and some of them haven't been near a woman in a long time."

Gudrun looked coldly up at him. "I can take care of myself, sergeant," she said, tapping the wand in its leather sheath at her belt.

"I'm sure you can, Marshal," he answered hastily. "I meant no offense, ma'am. If you like, I can send in and bring the man you want to talk to out for you."

For a moment Gudrun was tempted, but then it occurred to her that the guards were hardly going to leave a condemned man alone with her, especially a night-sighted Elf. It would have been too easy for Wolfram to stick a knife into her unexpectedly and run. Though she was certain he would do no such thing, for her to be alone with him outside the guarded camp would still be the first step in eroding the regiment's security measures.

"I will go in to him," she said.

As Gudrun began to walk away, the sergeant said hastily, "Marshal would you like me to call Fredrik or Sascha to show you where your man is? You don't want to waste time looking for him, do you?"

Gudrun touched her wand again. "I expect I can find him easily enough," she said dryly. "Be assured, if I need help, I will ask for it."

The Forlorn Hope camp looked little different than any of the Company's other encampment areas. Loose rings of tents surrounded campfires, with the occasional one off on its own, more, perhaps, than in the regular Landsknecht camps, where the practice of several men hiring a woman to cook and wash for them encouraged more grouping together, and where even married couples preferred to gather with others to share the work of gathering firewood and heating water and other such chores.

Still, something nagged at Gudrun's awareness. It was only until she had walked past two campfires, the men dicing beside them falling silent to stare until she had passed, that she realized what seemed strange, the complete absence of women and children. There were not so many female fighters among the Landsknechts, most of those were among the artillery, where a keen eye and deft hands were as important as strong shoulders and arms.

Most men had wives, hire-wives, or companions, many of the wives and whores had children, of all ages from suckling babes to twelve year-olds eager to be taken up as pages to the officers or arrow-runners to the archers or similar tasks. Here, it almost seemed to Gudrun that she could feel the unrelieved masculinity beating against her like windswept waves pounding a cliff, except that the looks on some of the hard bearded faces were more like the expression of hungry mongrels watching a piece of meat slowly passing by their noses.

Gudrun's hand went to her wand, and it was an effort not to draw it. In camp, her mage's robe was enough to dim that look on the soldiers' faces, there were plenty of whores attached to the regiment, Hurenweibel Peter to make sure that their prices stayed reasonable and they saw the chirurgeon regularly. If she did not want to sit down with all those starved gazes on her and go into the light trance she would need to seek out Wolfram for herself, she was going to have to walk up to one of those campfires and ask where he was. For a moment, she seriously thought about going back to the guard-post and requesting the sergeant to have him brought out, after all. Have him see that a Marshal of the Silver Eagle is afraid of the soldiers? I don't think so.

The thought strengthened Gudrun enough to walk up to the nearest campfire. Drawing herself up ramrod-straight, she said, "Soldiers, attend! I am looking for Leu... For Wolfram called Longsword or Half-Elven. Take me to him."

The nearest man to her came slowly to his feet, though slouching rather than standing to attention. He was a full head taller than Gudrun, broad-shouldered and with a thick sag of belly. The shiny twisted track of a badly-stitched scar cut through his bushy dark beard from right ear to chin, pulling his mouth into a sneer.

"Are you now Marshal?" He rumbled casually. "Well, I believe we can help you find him - can't we, boys?"

The other men, seven in all, got up from the campfire, moving in around her. A tremble of fear twisted Gudrun's stomach like the first cramp from bad meat. Still she restrained herself from pulling her wand. They had not, after all, done anything wrong, they were obeying her order. The big man offered her his arm. Gudrun was not sure whether the gesture was a parody of courtly gallantry, or some last remnant of it.

"The ground's bad here, Marshal. You don't want to trip in the dark now."

With an inner sigh of relief at the excuse, Gudrun drew her wand at last, whispering the word that brought a star of light to its tip. The white glow was bright enough for her to see her guide clearly, and the sight did not reassure her. His lips were thick and wet, his tongue oozing out to touch them as he looked down at her. Smaller scars seamed his face, most of them the thin white lines of knife-flicks, but a large chunk of his left ear was missing.

There were men in the Company who were less well-favored such as Little Kai, whose face proclaimed his Orcish blood like a badly-made banner. The flat hot light in his eyes made Gudrun want, not only to look away, but to run as swiftly as she could. Still, she had her wand out now, and it would be a very great fool who tried to molest her.

"I can walk well enough," she said.

The encampment was bigger than Gudrun had thought, set up on rocky ground broken by small groves of trees. They made their way carefully through boulders and over cracked slabs of stone until they reached one of the larger groves.

"He's in here, Marshal," the big man said. "I guess Elves just naturally go to the trees."

"Thank you. You may go."

As the last words came out of her mouth, a flare of pain burst in Gudrun's wrist. The light of her wand went out as it fell, and suddenly she was crushed so tight that she could hardly breathe, gasping in the choking stink of long-unwashed male clothes.

"Now that would be unfriendly of me to leave you all alone here, when you came in looking for a man," her guide said mildly. The other men laughed at his words.

Gudrun's heart fluttered in desperate terror. She tried to pull herself free but he was too strong, far too strong. No man had ever laid hands on her in her adult life. Nothing had ever prepared her for the strength years of wielding a pike could give a man's arms, especially compared to a woman who had never lifted anything weightier than a heavy grimoire.

"You'll be executed if you harm me," she managed to gasp, then cried out as his big hard hand forced its way down the neckline of her robe. Callused fingers pinched her nipple, and she could not keep from yelping.

"Oh, we don't mean to harm you," he said, deep amusement rumbling through his chest. "We'll give you a better time than that scrawny Elf does, just see if we don't. Even if you managed to identify any of us afterwards. Well, we've heard that the Obrist's about to sign a new contract, a big one. Might as well die for getting some as die without it."

The other men closed in. Hands grasped Gudrun's rump, twisting her buttocks about. She heard the fast panting as another hand snaked about her to close on her free breast. The night air was suddenly cold on her legs, and she knew they were pulling her robe up. *Magic is not in the wand, nor in the circle*, she remembered her old teacher at University saying. *Magic is in the mage.* Gudrun clamped her thighs together against the probing fingers, letting the indignities stoke the rage within her to the point of explosion.

When she could hold it no longer, she spoke one word. Without a wand to aim it, the power exploded out from her body in all directions, a single thunderclap of light. Suddenly no one was touching her, all the aching places where they had gripped lost in the tingle of discharged magic over her skin. Gudrun stooped to sweep up her wand in a single motion, calling its light again. The men blinked up at her from their backs, lying half-stunned in a rough circle around her. Undirected, divided among so many targets, her magic had done no real damage, but now she was free and had her wand in her hand.

Before any of them could think to leap up and grab her from behind, she darted over to a huge oak tree, setting her back against its broad trunk. One by one, her assailants stood, watching her warily. Two were backing away, shaking their heads and stumbling, but the big man hardly seemed dazed.

"I will kill you if you come within two arm-lengths of me." Gudrun told him.

"If I don't? Are you going to try to get me executed?"

"You attacked an officer," Gudrun said. Too late, it dawned on her that she had just told the man he had no reason not to try for her. She lifted her wand, ready to let fly the moment he moved. She would never even go to trial for killing him.

The Provost could pass judgment straight away when it was warranted, the Freimann accompanying him with beheading sword and executioner's noose was no mere symbol of his power and Alberich took a dim view of soldiers assaulting his Marshals. But her assailant hesitated a moment, and in that moment, a pale figure flashed out from between the trees. Gudrun thought the new attacker might have grabbed the bigger man by the waistband of his trousers. Perhaps there had been a kick to the back of his knee as well, but in any case, he was spinning away to measure his full length in the dirt.

"Get out of here!" Wolfram's musical voice shouted to the men who were still standing about. "Move, now, or you're all for the gauntlet and the wheel tomorrow - by Donmar, I'll report you myself if I have to. Get out, leave her alone, don't come back."

The men melted into the darkness. Wolfram's victim had time for one fierce look back, then he too, got to his feet and limped away as quickly as he could.

"What are you doing in here, Marshal?" The half-Elf asked Gudrun. "This is no place for..." She thought he was about to say, a woman, but then changed it with a sigh to, "anyone civilized."

"I came looking for you," Gudrun said. That sounded too personal, she coughed and straightened her disarrayed robe as best she could with the wand still in her left hand and her fingers trembling like aspen leaves in the storm.

"An examination of your sword is required. As is our custom, I came to inform you in person in case you had any questions or information beyond what you declared upon entry to the Company with the weapon, as well, any grounds to raise a challenge to the examination."

"Oh," Wolfram said, rather bleakly. He had, Gudrun thought distractedly, lost some weight since being sentenced or perhaps it was only that the white glow of her mage light brought out the slant of his high cheekbones more starkly. His clothes had changed too, from the conservatively-slashed doublets and close-fitting hose of fine fabric that she remembered to simple tunic and trews such as any peasant might wear.

The Orders mandated that soldiers wash twice a week, but unlike the man who had grabbed Gudrun,

Wolfram smelled as though he had been washing his clothes as well. "Why do you need to look at my blade?"

"To ensure that it is not carrying any charms which will protect you from harm in battle. There would hardly be any point to your being here if that were the case."

One side of Wolfram's mouth twisted up in something like a smile. "Hardly. Perhaps I can save you the trouble." He pulled back a loose sleeve, baring his arm for her. A pink scar snaked up the sharp-marked cords of muscle from the back of his narrow wrist to the bulge over his elbow where it ended in a disk about the size of a silver shilling.

Gudrun guessed that a sword-tip or arrow had plowed its way up the arm, sinking in and perhaps twisting at the end. He was lucky not to have lost the use of his elbow, given how close it had come to the tendon. "I got that in our last contract. You can ask Feldarzt Falkenstein if you like; he was the one who took the arrow out and sewed me up."

"I will still need to look at the sword. It could protect you only from crippling or fatal wounds."

"So it could. Though it doesn't. Then, I suppose you would hardly take my word for it."

Gudrun could taste the bitterness now, a scorching draught of self-hatred? It would fit with his guilt, if he were guilty. "It is not a question of your word, but of following the procedures of the regiment," she said, trying to sound dispassionate, or at least like an officer.

"Those procedures require that I treat you just as I would treat someone like that man from whom you, the man who assaulted me, in the same circumstances." Why, she thought, surprised at herself, can I not admit that Wolfram rescued me? Perhaps because I did not truly need him. I would have blasted the fellow if he had charged me, just as I would destroy a soldier attacking our position in a battle.

To her surprise, Wolfram's taut stance eased a little, his expression more like a real smile this time. "I understand. I should not have forgotten so quickly what it is to be an officer. Well you have seen what most of the men in Forlorn Hope are like. At least, the ones who don't simply want to die."

"And you?" Gudrun asked, watching him carefully. *How he answers will tell me a great deal, I should think.*

"Oh, I want very much to live," Wolfram said, his turquoise eyes intent on hers. "I have no name to clear, no name but my own," he added hastily. "But I owe the Silver Eagle in a way I cannot describe, and if I die, so does the evidence that someone means it harm. I owe a great revenge of my own to that person as well."

Gudrun drew in a deep breath, stunned by his intensity. She would have wagered every ounce of her power that the half-Elf meant what he said *but if he lied, and would not admit it out of pride, then what else would he say, and how else should he try to behave than to convince me?*

"There has been no sign of trouble since," she said slowly. "No disturbances to our wards, no reports of suspicious occurrences by our sentries."

"That puzzles me," Wolfram admitted. His tone, Gudrun thought, was more like that of someone who, on hearing one suspicion denied, has another confirmed, the one he least wanted to hear. *What does he know that he is not telling?*

Instead of continuing on that subject, the half-Elf said suddenly, "I hear that we may be about to take a new contract. The details are slow to get through here, but is there anything you can tell me yet?"

Gudrun blinked. Some aspects of contract negotiations, by custom, were kept secret. The amounts bid, and likewise any secondary considerations regarding accommodations, chances of plunder, and so forth, were never told to the troops until a final agreement had been signed, nor did they ever learn such details about offers that had been turned down, lest differing personal goals should lead to dissension. But some things were free to become general knowledge, and there was no reason Gudrun should not tell Wolfram those. She had seen his image as part of a scrying about the upcoming contract, even if it was only a flicker at the end when the spell began to give way.

"It is a bidding war between Graf Sigfrid von Helmberg and Graf Berthold von Hellenwald, at the western edge of the Empire near the border with Broceliande. The two of them are at feud, and each is looking to hire a Company against the other."

Wolfram raised a sharp-arched blond eyebrow. "Do they know they are bidding against each other for us?"

"Yes. The General decided that we would get better offers from both of them that way."

"Ah." Wolfram paused. "I have heard good things about Graf Berthold von Hellenwald."

Something about the way he said it made Gudrun look sharply at him. The Silver Eagle had mostly operated on the eastern and southern borders of the Empire. Until she had undertaken the background research the General requested about the two feuding neighbors, Gudrun had never heard of either of them. "Can you tell me more?"

"Only that he is one of the staunchest supporters of the Emperor's policies, and devoted particularly to Saint Hildebrand, for whose sake he built a small cathedral early in his reign. The sculpture was almost all done by the artist Tilman Lindenschneider. I believe that Graf Berthold is commonly given the credit for recognizing Lindenschneider's greatness and employing him so that he could pursue it."

"Lindenschneider, the name sounds familiar," Gudrun mused. She had never paid much attention to any art save her own.

"The creator of monochrome woodcarving. Instead of the detail work being done in gesso on a rough wooden frame and then painted, everything is done in the wood itself, brought out only by a brown stain. It is quite a stark and haunting effect, but very beautiful."

There was something in the way Wolfram was talking, Gudrun thought, that reminded her of the nobles she had met at the College, discussing art for hours over their wine. What had annoyed her as an affectation in them, however, seemed quite genuine in Wolfram. There was a wistfulness to his voice as he spoke of Lindenschneider's sculptures which made her think that he truly loved the woodcarver's art, truly missed being separated from it. Yet, I have never heard an Elf speak of the art of Men that way.

They pat us on the head as if we were children who showed a little promise at whittling, and have little love for innovations, unless those should chance to match their own.

"I had never thought of you as a connoisseur of sculpture," she said.

"I'm not," Wolfram answered, his face closing as she watched. "I happened to see some of Lindenschneider's work once. Anyway, that's what I know about Graf Berthold. I don't know anything about Graf Sigfrid, except I've heard that his neighbors have always been wary of him. If he's managed to provoke a man like Graf Berthold into feud, they probably have good reason. Do you have any idea which side we might be on?"

"There is no telling yet," Gudrun temporized. In truth, Alberich had been arguing for Sigfrid out of a variety of reasons, not least that their prospects of a longer-term contract were better with him.

They stood there for a moment, and Gudrun realized that she had nothing else suitable to say to Wolfram. She was trying to think of a way to end their discussion when Wolfram said, "If you have no further need of me, Marshal, I would be pleased to accompany you back to the guard post to make sure there are no more untoward incidents."

"Do you know the name of the man responsible for that one?" She demanded.

"His first name is Gottschalk. I don't know his last name, if he has one."

"The first name should suffice. I should be returning to my tent now."

Wolfram walked along beside her, careful not to touch her uninvited, but close enough that, if she were to stumble on the bad ground, he would be able to catch her. It struck Gudrun that she had never known an Elf who kept so carefully to human manners, and for a moment she wondered where he was really from. But that was none of her business.

Although the night was warm, when Gudrun was back in her own tent, she found that she was shivering uncontrollably, on the verge of tears. She remembered her first battle, when she had looked at the charred and twitching shape of a soldier she had blasted and vomited until there was nothing left in her stomach, then retched again and again.

Even that had been better than the lingering memory of her utter helplessness in the big man's grasp, that one moment of feeling that he could do anything to her, that she was no better than any common girl caught in a camp overrun by its enemies.

She crossed her arms over her chest as if hugging herself tightly, feeling the faint prickle of her power as she rubbed her hands up and down the chilly silk of her upper sleeves. The rush of magic, and the distraction of talking with Wolfram, had kept her from feeling how deep the bruises on her breasts and buttocks were; now they ached horribly, as if those men, those animals, still had their filthy hands on her.

I protected myself, she reminded herself. Even without my wand, they learned that it does not do to maul a mage. Tomorrow I shall make my report and have Gottschalk brought up for execution. Except that it will mean a public statement about what I was doing in the Forlorn Hope camp. Wilhelm already knows why I was there. Will Alberich guess? If he does, if there is the least chance that Wolfram is right and there is a danger to the regiment, would I not discredit any possibility I might have of being able to help? That, in turn, led to the question, Do I believe him? Yes, I'm beginning to think I do. Can I do anything about it?

She knew the answer to that as well. Wolfram had been tried and condemned.

Whatever had gone wrong with her fellow mages' spells, trying to convince Wilhelm, let alone the Provost, of it would be like banging her head against a stone wall. The wall would not break, but her skull might very well. All she could do was watch, and wait.

The truth was distasteful, another fit of shivering took Gudrun again as she choked it down. She felt violated, was deeply bruised in several tender places, and more than that, she was still seething with impotent fury at how easily her rank and power had been brushed aside by brute male lust. Still, she had been in the Company long enough to know that Wolfram would have a better chance of survival if there were more targets in Forlorn Hope when he went into battle.

Although Gottschalk was scum, although he deserved the brutal death of the gauntlet or the wheel, she did not doubt that he was a good fighter. So I should let him think he could get away with what he did to me? Vied in her mind with, Is my pride worth making Wolfram's risk worse? In truth, if she had listened to the sergeant at the guard post, the incident would never have happened. Should a man die for my stupidity? It was likely enough that Gottschalk would die in the next battle, or the one after that.

Even if he did survive however many he had left and make it back into the regular regiment, a man like that was sure to fall foul of the Landsknecht Orders again quickly enough. One way or another, he was a walking dead man. If he had not known it too, he would never have attacked her in the first place.

I will let him live, she decided. If Donmar ever dealt out justice from His heaven, that man will take the ball or blade that might have been meant for Wolfram. Gudrun was not certain why, but the thought soothed her, as though, in making the decision, she had somehow countered the attack on herself. She made herself a cup of chamomile, knit bone, and wound wort to finish calming her nerves and help against the bruises, then went to bed and rather to her drowsy surprise as she felt herself dropping off straight to sleep.

CHAPTER 9

Gudrun watched in fascination as Alberich dipped the tip of the virgin quill into the ink. The white of the feather's stripped spine in his hand glowed bright enough for her to see the faint blueness, like the blue-white glow of the finest diamonds. The ink's shiny surface was black as a tiny pool of the Void, so black that the same blue light shone off it, as though utter black and utter white became one in their full intensity. The quill-tip touched the smooth parchment, slowly shaping the spiky letters of the Empire's most formal style of hand. The Provost's lean face was knotted in utter concentration, the pale witch light shimmering about him scarring the lines of forehead, eyes, and mouth dark as the marks of his quill on the page. His two Marshals stood, barely daring to breathe, trying to absorb every nuance of Alberich's movements, of the soft words trembling on his breath, on the delicate shifting balance of the power writhing about him.

Gudrun could feel the shivering rope flung out from their tent, across more than half the Empire to a chamber where a Graf waited, watching his own mage - perhaps in awe, perhaps in well-concealed fear or perhaps, as Obrist Helmuth waited beside them, with the careless acceptance of a man who knew nothing of wonders except as they worked for him. The mage to whom Alberich wrote would be looking at a pool of ink lying upon the surface of his own parchment, a pool that rested without sinking in, separated from the fine white hide by a layer of air so thin no man's eye could see it.

This was magic at its most delicate and controlled. The million minute droplets of ink each touched by the Chaos-flux of improbability that kept all of them hovering above the parchment until Alberich's quill stroked through, letting only so many through, only in the exact shape of those same droplets which the Provost selected on his pen now. The result would be a letter before the Graf which read just as the one Alberich wrote now did. If the court mage had poured the right amount of ink. Otherwise, the letter would cut off short, or its recipient would have a puddle on his rug when the excess rivulets suddenly to the side. Though perhaps, in the course of the previous negotiations, he had learned to put a tray underneath.

Gudrun mentally slapped herself back to attention, moving her lips silently in the form of the words Alberich whispered, though she was careful not to give them any breath, or allow the least trickle of the tingling power that crawled over her skin seep into them. At last Alberich nodded. Obrist Helmuth heaved himself from his chair, stepping carefully forward to take the quill into his hand and set his name to the document. The contract was signed now. At dawn - less than six hours from now - fife and drum would sound the command that the Company's heralds would echo in words. Pack up and prepare to march! From Obrist to whore's brat, they would load all they owned onto the wagons. Weapons and light armor would be issued for the road; and in less than two days, the Silver Eagle would fly.

Wolfram awoke to the familiar sound of the fife's skirling and the heavy beat of the drums booming the orders out over the camp. Pack up and prepare to march. His breath caught in his chest, his heart beating a little faster. Camp life between contracts was an odd sort of limbo, the daily round of duties and drilling floating in a state seemingly unconnected to the memories of battle and the knowledge that battle would come again. The Landsknecht's dream of drinking and dicing and whoring at night, of bright-bladed weapons and flamboyant clothing stained with nothing worse than sweat and beer, and swaggering and bragging with no fear that dawn would bring the need to prove brave words at the wrong end of sharp blades, arquebus balls, and mage fire.

Now it was over again: every fighter and fighting mage in the Silver Eagle knew, once more, that this might be their last march down the road to death. Wolfram reported to the gate for duty as usual. Quartiermeister Helmbrecht looked over the assembled Forlorn Hopers, giving a short nod of his close-cropped blond cannonball head. He pointed with his baton, separating the men into groups and giving them their orders, until only Wolfram was left.

"You, Longsword. Come here." Wolfram stood before him, bracing at attention. Helmbrecht went up on his toes. He was a short man, though built like a mound of low boulders, to sniff at his breath. Wolfram's face reddened with humiliation and anger, but he held his tongue. For a man who had been condemned for drinking on duty, he might have done the same himself.

"Come with me. Armor and weapons inspection and packing."

Wolfram accompanied him to the wagons without a word. His cheeks still burned, but he reminded himself that he should feel complimented. This was one of the most vital duties in the regiment, calling for sharp eyes, a thorough knowledge of armor, and integrity. Each soldier was responsible for his or her own kit after battle or drill: this was the point when everything had to be either in good repair or in the hands of the smiths.

Wolfram would report carelessness, if he found any and he would also be responsible for making sure the armor was properly greased and carefully packed in straw in the wagons, for skimping on work there would mean deformed plates, broken rivets and straps, and gnawing layers of brown rust on iron and mildew on leather where-ever a patch had gone without grease. He looked down at the back of Helmbrecht's head, the pink skin shining through short blond stubble, and wondered what the Quartiermeister thought about him now - if Helmbrecht's memory of his former fellow officer's reliability and competence was stronger than his doubts about one who had been convicted of drunkenness on duty.

Not altogether, or the Quartiermeister would not have sniffed Wolfram's breath. Yet, if Helmbrecht's confidence had not been substantial, he would not have put Wolfram in a position where the condemned man could harm the regiment by taking a bribe. Say, a bottle of spirit, in order to overlook an armor fault that could earn the careless soldier twenty lashes. There were two men set to inspect and pack at each armor-wagon, most pairs consisting of a Weibel or Feldweibel and an ordinary soldier. Wolfram did not know his partner's name, though he had seen him around once or twice, a big black-bearded sergeant who favored huge puffy brown Plederhosen with gold slashes showing through, gartered in at his knees above striped stockings of virulent green and yellow.

Even in the morning cool, he wore only a sleeveless leather doublet that was too small for him, lashed across the wide gap of hairy chest and belly with a cross-weave of leather thongs.

"Wolfram Longsword," Helmbrecht said to the big Feldweibel. "Forlorn Hope, so don't let him wander off. You're responsible for him. He won't give you any trouble."

The man only grunted, tapping the hilt of his long Katzbalger and giving Wolfram a cold look. "Better not."

The first soldiers were already coming towards them, bent low beneath the heavy sacks over their shoulders.

"I'll see you inspect one first," the Feldweibel said to Wolfram.

Going through the fighting gear was oddly comforting to Wolfram: the familiar smells of metal and leather, sweat and old grease; the movement of articulated plates sliding across each other, the motion of his own hands sliding swiftly over straps to check their integrity, tapping on dented helms to make sure they rang smooth, tugging where he thought a rivet might look loose. This knowledge had been part of his life since he was seven, together with the art of the sword, was one of the few things he had not lost when his mother's death betrayed him. Now he found that even his last loss had not diminished it.

Whatever happened, until his own death, Wolfram would still have a home in the warrior's trade and all its accouterments, armor and weapons and horses.

"Do we know yet who the contract's been signed with?" Wolfram asked his partner in one of their rare moments of rest. The sun was high now. Wolfram sweat relatively little, a legacy of his Elvish blood, but the other man's leather doublet was dark-stained under his armpits and across his back and the curly hair over his forehead dripped in tendrils.

The sergeant tipped his head back, squirting a stream of water into his mouth from a leather skin, and sighed.

"Makes no matter to me. Either way, we got to go most of the way across the Empire before we get there. For what it's worth, the name I heard was Sigfrid."

The cold chill in Wolfram's belly had nothing to do with the cool water he had just drunk. He had told Gudrun some of the truth, but by no means all of it. He was no longer a Graf's son, no longer even an officer. His duty was to follow his orders and fight where-ever the Obrist decided the Silver Eagle should go. To question or criticize an employer meant weakening his comrades, as great a danger to the Company as being drunk on duty ever could have been. Still.

The Silver Eagle was an honorable regiment, it fought for pay, but it would not willingly fight for Darkness, or the Empire's foes. If Wolfram, even shamed as he was, had known anything worth bringing to the Obrist, their commander might have listened. All he knew were a few rumors, a few mutters from visiting nobility.

Those he had heard only because visitors to his father's chapel often remarked on Lindenschneider's carvings. To speak of Lindenschneider was, almost inevitably, to speak of his first great patron. Once in a while, to speak of Berthold von Hellenwald was to drop a few words about his rival. By all accounts, Sigfrid was a hard man, brutal in his justice and implacable in his hatred, who paid his taxes grudgingly and disliked Berthold for his piety and steadfast, vocal support of the Emperor's efforts to bring the outlying regions of his realm under more control.

Yet a ruler could be harsh and somewhat independent-minded without serving the Dark; nor had Sigfrid ever been accused of treason to the Empire. The Obrist would have judged upon more knowledge than Wolfram had and if Berthold were the better man, the fee Sigfrid offered must have been enough to make up for that. All the same, Wolfram would rather have been fighting for Lindenschneider's patron. If it came to it. He wondered if, should the Silver Eagle be victorious, the cathedral Graf Berthold had built to St. Hildebrand would be sacked?

That would be a little thing to most of the men in the company - a crime against the ages. *The ages have survived many such crimes*, Wolfram reminded himself. *Even if we are victorious, I may not live to see it.* By noon of the second day, the Silver Eagle was ready to move out.

Obrist Helmuth rode at the head, his white harness and the fluted metal barding of his great bay horse glittering in the sunlight. Beside him rode Provost Alberich, his split robes flowing down over his gray horse's saddle in twin rivulets of black silk sheened with bright glimmers of silken embroidery like lines of tiny gems in dark metal. The drummers swung into a marching beat, fifes piping high above them; the pikes flashed high, the brilliant ribbon, slash finery of the Doppelsöldner with their great two-handed swords fluttering in the breeze like an hundred tattered banners. Then the wains began to roll, their wheels grumbling a deep drone along the paved road. Gudrun would be in the Black Wagon with her fellow Marshal Wilhelm, guarding the mages' supplies and belongings.

Involuntarily Wolfram looked as it passed, the deep sable hangings rippling along its sides, but the head of the driver was pale blond, not dark auburn. *I am as glad that she cannot look to see me like this*, Wolfram thought. The condemned men of Forlorn Hope marched beneath a plain black banner, each man manacled to a partner, right hand to left.

The iron cuff on his right wrist was light, the chain long enough to allow both men to eat and move easily. It was the symbolic humiliation that gnawed at Wolfram, not the digging of metal into his flesh. He knew that when they passed through towns, the folk who turned out to watch the regiment pass - eyes wide at the glittering helms and breastplates and pike-heads, staring in fascination at the mercenaries' wild finery in its bright colors and exaggerated styles - would reach for rotten vegetables and clots of dung, gleefully pelting the men who marched in disgrace as they would pelt any condemned criminal on the way to the gallows.

He had never yet seen Forlorn Hope's guards lift a finger to stop the mocking shower of muck: after all, every man who walked in manacles had endangered the Silver Eagle, potentially if not actually. Only Fredrik and Sascha, marching free beneath the black banner, would act, and they, too, were bound to follow the Obrist's orders - no killing civilians except in self-defense or sack - so their protection was limited. Who did this to me? Why?

"Hey, cheer up," said the little man to whom Wolfram was chained by the wrist. "You can go brave to your death, what a bit of shame along the way, heh?"

Wolfram bit back the answer, worse than death, that sprang to his lips. That was an answer of his old life, one he had thought slain long ago.

"Come on, you ever see Forlorn Hope march sullen? Go ahead, laugh. Show them all, don't care what they think anymore! Dead don't care about manacles, don't care what flag they march under, don't care what thrown at them or said to them. Dead, my friend, is free. That the great thing about dead."

Unwillingly, drawn by his companion's grotesque humor, Wolfram laughed.

"There you go! It get easier as you practice, just see. Look at me, I smile all the time, and it's no trouble at all."

That was true a wicked slash across the small man's left cheek had drawn his wide mouth up into a grotesque grin. The scar was old, very white against his olive-tan skin and tufted little dark beard. His coloring, as well as his rough Imperial, suggested an origin in one of the Southern city-states, like most Southerners, he was shorter and more wiry than Men of the Empire tended to be. Wolfram had hoped that, if he must spend the next three weeks in another man's close company, it would at least be someone who would leave him be.

He did not want to encourage the Southerner to talk, but the old habit of politeness was too deeply ingrained in him to let him turn away without at least asking, "What is your name?"

"I'm Mishni...Mishni the Rat. This my third time in Forlorn Hope."

Wolfram stared at him incredulously. It was a wonder that Fredrik and Sascha had survived as long as they had but Sascha the Mace was inhumanly strong and half a berserk in battle, and Fredrik was quite simply the best fighter Wolfram had ever seen. Granted, Mishni had the sort of wiry quickness which would have kept the half-Elf well away from him in an alley or tavern, the tricky speed and movement of a skilled knife man.

Wolfram had seen plenty of street-fighters who thought that the reflexes that kept them alive in the gutter would serve as well in battle, and died in minutes under the disciplined lines of pike, halberd, and greats-word, or been splattered by cannon and mage fire. Such a tale will be easy enough to check, Wolfram thought. Then he shook his head, laughing bitterly at himself. He was still thinking like an officer. What did it matter to him if Mishni had never been in Forlorn Hope before, or had spent half his life there?

"Hard to believe, huh?" Mishni said, laughing himself. "Don't bother saying not, I can see it on your face. You think, how little Southern gutter rat survive when big strong Empire men getting killed all around him?"

Reluctantly, Wolfram nodded.

Mishni tapped his head with his left hand, the chain that linked them jingling. "Smart enough to know when duck, when lie flat.

Lucky, nothing hit me just wrong. Remember, my friend, you not knight no more. Not knight, not noble - don't try fight like you are, or you die fast, unless you crazy-arse like Sascha or Fredrik."

Wolfram stared at him, the sudden flash of cold anger from his heart freezing his tongue. Mishni only nodded in satisfaction.

"I right, or I right? No worry, know Landsknecht man has no past." His voice softened, suddenly serious and tinged with sadness. "But some things. Some things, we got to remember to forget."

Wolfram bit his lip, letting the sharp pain force the tears back from his eyes. "Why are you in Forlorn Hope now?" He asked harshly, hoping that the question, the question not to be asked, nor answered would shut the other up.

Instead Mishni grinned. "Stole something. Again. Got caught this time. Not worry, my friend. Your stuff safe from me, now you look my pockets if it disappears. Anyway, I not stupid enough steal from someone might save my butt in a fight, he weren't pissed with me." He cocked his head, very like a rat indeed. "March out in few minutes. Come on, help dress line, laugh at these fuckers here to guard us."

Forlorn Hope swung out to a plain drumbeat, but when they were out on the road, they heard the song rising before them, joined in lustily.

> *"Death comes on a black stallion riding,*
> *In his cloak of darkness hiding,*
>
> *When Landsknechts march along to war,*
> *He lets his steed gallop on before.*
> *Peril at hand.*
>
> *Death rides to Berthold's lands,*
> *Death rides to Berthold's lands.*
>
> *Death rides on a palfrey shimmer-white,*
> *Fair as a sunrise-beam of light,*
>
> *When the maids dance in their ring,*
> *He glides to join their dance and sing.*
> *Peril at hand.*
>
> *Death also knows the drummer's art,*
> *You feel his drum-beats deep in your heart,*
>
> *He drums long, and loud beside,*
> *He drums on a dead man's hide.*
> *Peril at hand."*

CHAPTER 10

"At his first drum-roll's sharp sound,
The blood spurts out from heart to ground,

The second drum-roll that he plays,
Then the Landsknecht is borne to grave.
Peril at hand,

Death rides to Berthold's land."

The Company was still singing three and a half weeks later, as they marched along the winding road that led between the pine-grown mountains to Burg Helmberg. Gudrun raised her own voice in high harmony above the men's deep chanting, following the sparse golden strands of the female fighters' singing. The first time she had heard that song, it had frightened her: it had seemed to dare what should not be dared. But now she had been in battle herself. She had frozen the first time a soldier, charging the mages with a berserk snarl, had driven a two-handed sword towards her heart. Gudrun had stood with her wand upraised, unable to believe he meant to kill her.

She still did not know what had unlocked her voice, but she had blasted his chest to ruin at the last fraction of a second, the tip of the blade, driven by his last desperate lunge forward, had jabbed her left breast, leaving a small puckered scar.

She had never hesitated again when she heard the Landsknecht songs again, she understood why the soldiers sang them. They were friends and colleagues of Death, clasping his hand with their sword-hilts or pike-hafts even as Gudrun did when she drew her wand in battle. That realization was often what saved their lives in battle. To shrink from Death in a fight was to die, and so they welcomed him cheerfully as they marched.

Forlorn Hope

Graf Sigfrid's castle was about two-thirds of the way up one of the mountains, presumably the Helmberg from which he took his name. At the mountain's foot was a large sloping meadow with a spring running down one side, a perfect place for the Company to make camp.

The castle itself, Gudrun thought, was an old one, at least partially. A central tower rose high above two sprawling wings, inside a wall that rose and fell with the mountain's contours like a drunken snake. From the driver's seat of the Black Wagon, she could see the polished gleam of sentry helmets, and when she half-closed her eyes, a dark rainbow corona shone about the irregular protrusions of the castle's turrets, magical protection undoubtedly, but there was something about it that disturbed her on a deep, half-sensed level.

The long train of the Silver Eagle spilled into the meadow like a river into a dry lake bed, filling it up slowly. Hauptmann Heinrich directed the layout of the camp. The wagons that bore armor and weapons in the middle, the cooks' wagons by the water, the latrines at the far side from the spring.

Waiting her turn for a place, Gudrun saw Hurenweibel Peter stomp up to Heinrich, stopping with his toes almost on top of the smaller man's and shouting. She smiled to herself: the two of them had the same argument every time the regiment made camp. Peter would argue that it was stupid to put the whores and drink too far from the main camp.

The enemy could easily capture them and set an ambush. Heinrich would reply that if enough men to capture the whores' camp got that far into friendly territory, the regiment was already screwed.

Though he would put it more politely and there was only so much space in the central area to allot. The whores would have to set up in the clearing they had passed twenty minutes ago.

Neither man would bring up his real issues. Peter got his share from all the flesh and drink sold in the whores' camp and the farther the soldiers had to walk, the fewer would feel the need to go.

Heinrich felt that the Silver Eagle was in no need of pleasant distractions while they were on a contract. While he knew the Landsknechts would whore, gamble, and drink even if they had to walk ten miles in a night, at least pushing temptation right in their faces could be avoided, in accordance with the statement in the Orders that, "The sins of gambling and drinking are to be kept within reasonable limits."

Gudrun smiled, wondering if the men who had written the Orders had been partial to more than a reasonable limit of whoring themselves. There are times, she thought, when I am so glad I'm a woman! Even Wilhelm sometimes crept out of the mages' pavilion or the Black Wagon at night, stumbling back in with a whiff of aqua-vitae and cheap perfume on him.

Once Gudrun had mentioned it and he had gone beet-red, then had a fit of sneezing and coughing so severe she feared she had killed him. Out of pity, she had taken good care after that to pretend to be deeply asleep when he made his visits.

Of all the single men in the Company, only Alberich seemed to be immune to the rule of his scepter. Alberich, perhaps Wolfram. Does he sleep with whores? She could not imagine it, but then, to be honest, she hadn't thought Wilhelm would have the nerve to if she hadn't smelled him herself. At last Peter stomped off and Heinrich beckoned to Gudrun.

"Marshal, I have a temporary place for the mages, but don't start unloading yet. The Zauberobrist has gone up to the castle with the Obrist to consult with our employer, and he says that it may be more prudent for you and your equipment to be billeted there, if Graf Sigfrid is willing."

Gudrun shaded her eyes and looked up at the castle again. Maybe Wolfram's remark about Graf Sigfrid's neighbors being wary of him had affected her nerves more than she realized. Certainly, from all she had heard, she would have preferred to fight for his rival if she had a choice. Still, if they could make use of the castle's own wardings, that would save valuable power and time. Graf Berthold would undoubtedly have his own court mages, there was no telling whom he might have hired when the Silver Eagle turned him down.

Sometimes a ruler under threat would spend his gold marks

on a few high-powered mages rather than a company of fighting men. Gudrun had heard some of the stories of those battles, and sometimes prayed afterwards that she would never be in one herself.

Not least, because the junior mages were usually the most certain to die under the foe's spells. Gudrun clucked to the horses, driving the wain carefully over to the spot Hauptmann Heinrich had indicated.

She had an easier time of it in the milling press than most of the drivers. Even the bare-legged children running about kept their distance from the Black Wagon.

Once in a while, a brave child would dare to touch the hangings; the scorching it got would keep others from trying the game for a long time. Wilhelm came out of the wagon, rubbing his back.

"Whew, I'm glad we're here at last," he said. "As are my kidneys. Did I ever tell you how much I hate traveling in wagons?"

"Frequently," Gudrun said dryly. "It's a pity you ride like a sack of mangelwurzels."

His watery blue eyes drooped, Gudrun felt as though she'd kicked a dog. To apologize, she said, "Could you have a look at the castle? Tell me if you see anything unusual."

Wilhelm squinted up, his face relaxing into a half-trance. Since he was slightly nearsighted, his other sight was generally better than hers, especially at middle and long distances. "Magic, yes," he murmured. "Fairly strong, and active, might be a life wreaking. Not a standard spell. I can't quite tell from here, and I'll wager that there's a layered series of protections. Particularly around the upper story of the middle tower, one of the best I've seen.

Not really unreasonable for a Graf, but unusual, unless he has a lot of enemies. Though it sounded in negotiation more as though he doesn't have any friends."

Wilhelm shook his head as though he were rising out of the water, blond hair flying in dirty strands about his face. "That's all."

"Thank you. It'll be interesting to talk with the mage who set those, if we get a chance."

"It certainly will," Wilhelm agreed enthusiastically.

Gudrun glanced back up at the castle again. It still seemed a trifle disturbing. But at the moment, noticing how long it had been since Wilhelm's last proper bath made her all too aware of how long it had been since the last time she had managed a full soak. She pushed her own hair back, grimacing at the touch of the road-dirtied mass. If Graf Sigfrid let the mages stay in the castle, he might also let his servants give them hot baths.

Gudrun guessed that she and Wilhelm had been waiting almost two hours before the Zauberobrist came back, his black figure on the high winding road from the castle growing from beetle to crow to raven to man. Seeing the changes of perspective as Alberich walked downward, Gudrun realized that Graf Sigfrid's stronghold was larger than she had thought, the old-fashioned central tower an immense war-keep.

It was built in disputed border-territory in those days, if I'm right about its age, she reminded herself. It must have been one of our central bases. Even a command center for the Emperor during part of the wars. History had always been one of her weaker subjects. She was more interested in what magical research could bring for the future.

Still, enough age and greatness could even stir her heart a little. She found that she was almost looking forward to seeing the castle.

"Up to the castle," Alberich said, climbing into the wain. Gudrun took the reins and clucked to the horses again, turning the Black Wagon around again. As she drove, the Provost spoke.

"Graf Sigfrid has kindly granted us lodgings with him. You can undoubtedly see the advantages. While in the Graf's castle, you will behave with the utmost courtesy. You will ask no questions that are not necessary, and if you have questions relevant to our work, you should ask me. Go nowhere unless directed to. Especially, you shall stay out of the central tower, for that is where Magister Klaus von Ludo has his study. He has agreed to work with us as is necessary but he is also involved with certain experiments of his own, which could be dangerously disrupted by intrusion. Also, do not even think about doing any unsupervised magic of your own inside the castle's walls." Alberich paused, taking a deep breath and considering his two juniors.

"Neither of you is accustomed to court protocol. Whenever you meet Graf Sigfrid or Gräfin Katerina, you will bow and curtsy, speaking only when spoken to. You are permitted to sit at table beside me, but at meals, you may not take your seat until the Graf and Gräfin are seated, nor is it appropriate for you to depart until one of them does, unless I order you to.

If you are in any doubt about your rank in regards to any of the castle's staff, you should show deference, though you should also remember your dignity as mages. Is that clear?"

"Yes, sir," Gudrun said firmly. Wilhelm echoed her, his voice wavering.

"When we reach the castle, you will unload and carry our equipment to the room that is prepared and secured for it. As soon as that is done, you will clean the filth of the road off yourselves and do your best to make yourselves presentable. Graf Sigfrid dislikes untidiness in any form. Fortunately, your mage-robes are acceptable as uniform dress. You will have to move quickly, since the Graf and Gräfin prefer to dine early."

As she drove in beneath the great barred portcullis of the outer gates, Gudrun felt the power tingling in the roots of her hair. For a moment she almost had trouble breathing when the feeling ceased and they were inside. It was not terribly unusual to feel reaction when magic touched a magical ward, even when passage was permitted, but that had been unusually strong.

She breathed deeply, shaking it off, looked around. Graf Sigfrid's castle was very well-kept, the cobblestones almost gleaming and the sentries standing straight in neat-tailored uniforms of gold and blue. Gudrun almost smiled, thinking of the ragged flamboyance of the Landsknechts below. She wondered if all castles were like this, or if Graf Sigfrid was simply unusually orderly.

Several smaller areas inside were fenced by wooden screens. She could see glimmers of green inside, guessed that they were gardens of some manner - herbers, gardens of pleasaunce, or kitchen gardens, perhaps. There was no way to tell from outside. Not so much as a single tendril of vine crept through the thin gaps between the fence posts, no trees rose above them. The wave of reaction was stronger as she drove into the inner bailey, almost nauseating. Gudrun swallowed hard, trying to keep her hands steady on the reins.

The two sturdy geldings who pulled the Black Wagon swished

their tails and stamped, but they had been trained at expense and effort at least as great as that of training a warhorse to stand firm with magic crackling over their heads and backs. Gudrun was grateful for that. She was no rider herself, but she had seen how most steeds reacted to even a tingle of magic. Untrained horses would most likely have bolted, perhaps had the wagon over on the slope of the cobbled courtyard. A liveried servant - blue, with a gold griffon on the chest - was waiting in the courtyard, standing straight and silent.

He gestured the wagon to a stop, Alberich climbed down. "Remember what I told you," the Provost said quietly to the two junior mages. "I shall see you again at dinner."

As Alberich walked away, the servant strode up to Gudrun and Wilhelm, staring down a long nose at them. Gudrun suddenly felt every crumb of journey-dirt on her face and hair.

Certainly Sigfrid's man was looking at the two young mages as though he would have liked to sweep them up and cart them out with the rubbish.

"Get your things and follow me," he ordered.

Gudrun and Wilhelm glanced at each other.

They had strict orders never to leave the Black Wagon wholly unattended when it was loaded, orders that could not be countermanded by anyone save the Obrist or Alberich himself. "You stay. I'll carry our things," Wilhelm said.

"Both of you," the liveried man ordered.

Wilhelm licked his lips nervously, glancing at the great doors which had just closed behind Alberich. Gudrun cleared her throat.

"Sir," she said politely. "Pray do not take it as insult, but we are under orders not to leave our equipment unwatched in the wagon. One of us must stay with it. Nor are we permitted to allow others to touch it. If there is a difficulty with this, sir, you must speak to Zauberobrist Alberich. We can only follow our own orders."

The servant frowned, narrowing his eyes. At last he said, "Very well."

Gudrun and Wilhelm brought in the last load together. Gudrun had to carry the bulk of it, since Wilhelm was wheezing and pale from the exhaustion of the earlier loads. By the time they reached the secure room, her arms had gone past soreness and well into numbness, she could not keep from sighing and rubbing her back as she straightened up over the heap of bags.

"Your chambers are this way," Sigfrid's man said sharply. "Follow me."

He walked at a very brisk pace, allowing the two mages no time to linger. In truth, there was not much to see. All her life, Gudrun had imagined castles to be full of great works of art and exotic treasures.

Perhaps the Graf and Gräfin kept such things in their own chambers, or the chapel or great hall. But in the passageways, there was nothing but scrubbed stone, polished wood, and gleaming whitewashed walls broken by the occasional iron bound door. It must take an army of servants to keep this place so clean, Gudrun thought. I wonder where they all are?

"Marshal Wilhelm, this is your chamber," the servant said, taking a ring of keys from his belt and unlocking a door that seemed identical to all the others. He moved a little along the hallway. "Marshal Gudrun, this is yours. The door at the end of the passage is the privy. Unless you need to go there, you shall stay in your own rooms until called for. Dinner will be served in an hour and a half. You will be summoned shortly after you hear the clock strike six."

He waited, staring pointedly at them. At last Wilhelm turned and went into his chamber, and Gudrun could do nothing but go to hers, though she badly wanted to talk to her fellow mage. When she saw the steaming tub of hot water in the center of her chamber, however, Gudrun forgot a great deal of her annoyance.

The Graf's servants had also provided good soap, thick fluff-napped linen towels, and a muslin bag of sweet-scented herbs for her bath. Gudrun might have stayed in the tub much longer than she did, but the sound of the clock striking the half-hour reminded her that she did not have too long to dress for dinner. Even if Alberich had not warned her about the Graf's penchant for tidiness, she would have been sufficiently alerted by what she had seen of his castle.

She had just finished braiding her hair into a neat knot when she heard the knock at her door.

"Marshal Gudrun, your presence is required," a woman's voice said sharply.

Gudrun was only halfway across the chamber when the door opened and a stout woman in a blue and gold livery dress strode in. She looked the Marshal up and down, finally giving her a grudging nod.

"That will do. Come with me."

Gudrun followed her through the passage to a spiral staircase, downstairs and along another passage, to a huge pair of iron-bound doors of old oak.

From their stoutness, Gudrun guessed that this had once been an outer door of the central tower. Here, too, was the first adornment she had seen here, the hinges and ironwork twisted into elaborate shapes in the oldest style of the Empire. The wood in the middle of the door was slightly paler, smoothly-sanded, as though something had been taken off it recently.

An ornament that had not suited the current Graf's ascetic style, perhaps? Already tired of staring at blank walls, Gudrun suddenly felt a fierce wish to know what it had been but Alberich's order not to ask questions was still fresh in her mind. The Graf's great hall was big enough to hold close to three hundred people, though there was only one table in it at the moment.

The hall's ornaments consisted of a large black-faced clock with gold hands and numerals, a huge banner showing the gold griffon on its azure field. Otherwise, the hall was as scrubbed and sterile as the rest of the castle.

Alberich and Wilhelm stood behind their chairs, as did another man in mage's robes and a few others in clothing which, to Gudrun, looked appallingly plain for a Graf's court. Yet they could not be servants, or they would not be at Sigfrid's own table - would they? Obrist Helmuth and three of the captains were also there, though their wives were not. Gudrun wondered if the General did not entirely trust the Company's new employer, or at least not enough to put potential hostages in his hands.

She also noticed that even the mercenaries' court clothes, the good silk and velvet they wore only for dealing with their most important clients, seemed out of place in the bare echoing emptiness of Graf Sigfrid's great hall, bright and gaudy as a whore in a cathedral. At precisely fifteen minutes past six, the Graf strode in, his wife trailing behind. Even without the pearl-pointed coronet on his ruddy head and ermine cape about his broad shoulders, Gudrun would have recognized Graf Sigfrid as the ruler here. His very footsteps echoed through the hall with the certainty of a command, his blue eyes took the measure of the three mages in a glance that almost made Gudrun gasp at its brief intensity.

The woman who followed him hunched her shoulders a little,

scuttling in his wake like a servant. Though her coronet was pinned perfectly even on her two coils of braid, the nervous tilt of her head made it look as though it were sliding forward. *No wonder she seems frightened, married to such a man!* Gudrun thought.

Sometime between entering the castle and seeing the Graf, her niggling wariness of Sigfrid had turned into an intense dislike. Graf Sigfrid seated himself, and everyone else at the table followed him. As they sat, liveried servants marched in with pitchers of wine and began to pour. *Like clockwork,* thought Gudrun. *One of those clocks like the great one at the College, where little knights and monsters come out at the first stroke of twelve and fight until St. Hildebrand slays the Great Wyrm on the last stroke.* She reached for her goblet - fine silver; at least the table setting could not be criticized - then realized that no one else was drinking yet, and her hand dropped back.

Only when the Graf took a sip, a small wintry smile on his broad face, did the others dare to drink. The wine was fine-quality, as well as Gudrun could taste it, but it had been watered down to barely quarter-strength. While Gudrun usually watered her wine herself, and often took no more than the quarter-part that was needed to keep plain water from giving her the flux, it seemed a shame to treat this vintage so roughly.

Nor had she ever heard of a noble host not simply providing his guests with their own pitchers of water, that they might mix their draught to their own taste. *But, of course, the Graf has no patience with drunkenness.* The thought almost made Gudrun want to hasten down to camp and buy a bottle of aqua-vitae.

Sigfrid's conversation over the meal, as Gudrun might have expected, was entirely about military matters. He briefed his guests on what he knew and suspected Berthold had done since their bidding war for the Silver Eagle, then he and the General turned to discussing possible tactics.

As far as Gudrun could tell, certainly in those parts of their plans, that involved magic. Sigfrid sounded fearsomely competent. By the thoughtful look on Obrist Helmuth's face and the number of times he nodded in agreement, the Silver Eagle's commander thought so too. *Perhaps,* Gudrun said to herself and by this point, she was quite certain that her own conversation was the only kind she was going to get tonight, *the Graf is one of those men who thinks of nothing but war.*

There are plenty of them in the regiment, and they are not bad

men, if rather boring. She thought of a story that had been making
the rounds in her last year at the College. A young knight at one of
the Emperor's balls, when one of the court ladies had asked him to
dance, had explained stiffly that he did not dance, nor engage in any
fripperies that might distract him from the arts of battle.

She had replied, "Well, then, I think you should make sure you are
well-greased to keep yourself from growing any rustier, and hang
yourself up in the closet with your armor until you are needed." And
the Graf might be better-off if someone had suggested that to him
when he was younger! Gudrun told herself, forcing herself not to
smile.

After dinner, Gudrun was escorted back to her chamber by the
same middle-aged woman, who lit the single candle by the bed and
bade her goodnight. The mage sat by herself, listening to the utter
stillness. To her surprise, for the noise of camp, especially at night,
was usually an irritation that she had to work to deafen her mind to,
she felt oppressed by the quiet. No men's voices singing or talking,
no women calling for their husbands, no children's high shrieks or
giggles, not even the gentle crackling of campfires or rattling dice.
How long has it been since I was truly alone? Gudrun wondered.

Before she joined the Landsknechts, there had been the rooms she
shared with two other young women at the College, and before that,
though she had a chamber of her own at home, there had always
been the sounds of voices and footsteps through the walls. Now
that she had the quiet she had always wanted for her workings, of
course, she had no books to study, and was not allowed to do magic.

Gudrun's mouth twisted in a nervous smile. The Chaos and all
their demons take it, I do not like this place! Maybe part of it was
the mage's natural bent towards Chaos, the ability to sense and
touch the flux of change and chance and probability, that also
seemed to lead to personal chambers resembling magpies' nests, as
the offices of most of her professors had been. This castle seemed
like nothing so much as a shrine to pure Order, the one Force in the
world without personification or worship, save as Men honored it in
the unimaginably diluted form of the law.

Then Gudrun realized what had been particularly odd about the gathering of the Graf's court, beside the absence of women other than the Gräfin and herself. The Graf had been attended by his mage, by several of his senior knights, and by his chamberlain. There had been no priest there. While Alberich had been largely correct in his remark on her ignorance of courtly protocol, she had read enough, and heard enough from those higher-born than herself when she lived in Mannerheim, to know that the court priest should have been at the table with his Graf.

So perhaps he was busy, or indisposed. Or Sigfrid wanted to make sure that it would be exclusively a military conference. Some priests have power on the battlefield too. Even if Sigfrid's only prays for protection and healing, he would still be a factor to consider. They were talking about Graf Berthold's priests, weren't they? So maybe Sigfrid's priest disapproves of the feud. After all, Berthold is best-known for his piety. A good priest will uphold the gods above the whim of his employer. Sigfried could have quarreled with him, maybe even sent him away, at least until it's over.

The candle was burning down, and the weariness of the long weeks' travel was beginning to grumble in Gudrun's bones and lower back. She had to admit it to herself, a mage could not lie about such things, she wanted to be very sure that if she were frightened in the night, there would still be some of the candle left to light her silent room. She blew it out, undressing and climbing into bed in darkness - and lay very still in the dark for quite a long time, her ears straining to hear any trace of sound, other than her own heartbeat, through the thrumming stillness.

CHAPTER 11

When Quartiermeister Helmbrecht unchained Wolfram, he directed him to the armor wagons again without, Wolfram noted gratefully, bothering to smell his breath again.

"Issue everything," Helmbrecht directed him. "No telling when we may be going out, and I'm told our new employer is a demon for efficiency." He paused, frowning, and spat thoughtfully onto the trampled grass.

"Don't pass this around, but he isn't real excited about the Landsknechts. Doesn't like the way we dress, doesn't like the way we act - too untidy for him."

"So why did he hire us?"

"Because he felt he had to. The point is, we're being well-paid and we don't want to screw things up by pissing off our employer. If you have any influence on the men in, ah, your division, try to keep them from making too much of a show, if you know what I mean."

Wolfram knew exactly what he meant. For the last three weeks, Wolfram had heard his companions in Forlorn Hope jeering harshly at town folk and Company members alike, sometimes cursing and spitting at anyone who got near enough and sometimes shouting bitter mockery. Often, it had been like marching in a chain of the damned on their way to the Hells of Darkness, heavy with the soul-stink of brutal lust, nameless rage, and pride curdled and tainted to an empty howl of despair.

There were a few like Wolfram himself, hoping to redeem their crimes and names, who stood silent. But among all of them, only Fredrik's laughter had rung wholly clean. Sascha might have volunteered, but he had volunteered to die. Fredrik had come only to prove himself the best, as he did, not only at every battle, but through every day that – when another man might be dragged into the Chaos-Void by the mocking despair of those around him. He managed to hold his heart and put new hope into those like Wolfram who had not wholly surrendered.

"I'll do my best," Wolfram said, though he doubted that there was much he could do. What could sway men who were already condemned to near-certain death? Still, Heinrich's request glowed warmly in his chest as he turned to his work. He had no doubt that only the officers had been told of Graf Sigfrid's dislike. That the lieutenant had passed the information on to him reassured him immensely.

If I survive my battles here, I will truly be redeemed. As always at the end of a long march, Wolfram marveled at how much damage travel could do to even the most carefully-packed armor. The smiths had set up their forges by the bottom of the field, plumes of gray smoke rising high as the charcoal caught fire, and soon the sounds of steel striking steel rang out over the noises of the camp.

After a while, Wolfram's back began to prickle uncomfortably. He turned, and saw two hard-faced men in blue livery with gold griffins on their chests staring at him: Graf Sigfrid's men, come to inspect, no doubt. He turned back to his work, but the hairs on his neck kept prickling up. There is something wrong with them. The thought came out of nowhere, disturbing him as much as the cold stares did. He shook his head, and the Doppelsöldner in front of him glared, his droopy brown mustaches twitching.

"My breastplate was perfect when it went into that cart," the man said angrily. "If you've gotten it dented, even scratched."

Wolfram looked down at the piece of armor in his hands, finely fluted and polished mirror-bright under its thin coating of grease. Raised to fight as a noble in full white harness, it had never ceased to amaze him how many Landsknechts went without armor or with only a steel cap and breastplate but most of the good armor was found among the high officers and the elite troop of halberdiers and two-handed swordsmen.

This man's harness was particularly fine.

"No, there is nothing wrong with it," he said calmly, handing it over. "It's a nice piece, and you take fine care of your gear. I wish everyone did as well as you."

"Hmph," the Doppelsöldner grunted, but he seemed pleased enough as Wolfram looked over the rest of his armor, returned it, and scratched Wolfram kept hoping that there would be at least a brief lull in the stream of men coming up to him to retrieve their gear, but he had no luck there.

The best he could do was snatch the odd glance back, until Graf Sigfrid's men decided they had seen enough and moved on, leaving him to try to figure out what had disturbed him. *I wonder if the Graf also dislikes, or distrusts, Elves,* Wolfram wondered. *Certainly that was the most obvious reason why they should have stared at him so long. If it were so,* his eyes flickered down the wagon-list of names, *he might be able to confirm it soon.* Sure enough, Piriel made his way over to Wolfram's wain eventually.

Although the full-blooded Elf was an archer rather than a fighter in the square, he owned a breastplate which would have done for an Imperial parade, dark-blued metal adorned with complicated twining silver inlay. Unlike most parade armor, its quality in a fight matched its beauty.

Wolfram had heard that the Elf's breastplate had shed longbow arrows at less than fifty paces, and crossbow bolts at thirty; even applying the usual camp-tale discount, it was still impressive protection. He got it out of the cart with the care due such a precious item, unwrapping it carefully before Piriel's eyes. The Elf moved his fingertips carefully over it, testing every inch of the surface, every strap and rivet, and finally smiled.

"Well-done, as always."

"Thank you," Wolfram said. He dropped his voice so low that he knew no one but the two of them could hear it.

"Piriel do you notice anything strange about the Graf's men?"

The Elf's fine brows drew together, his expression shifting like pale water beneath a breeze.

"I had meant to ask you the same," he murmured. "Two of them stared at me for a very long time as I put up my tent, and when I finally stared back. You know how Men are, how everything they do seems to scar itself on their skins? The darker-haired one, I looked at the lines of his face, and it seemed to me that this was a man who had looked more closely into Darkness than he should have. I also noticed though it may be no more than coincidence that he kept his left hand cupped, as though to hide something in his palm. But I could not guess what."

"Will you speak to Arkoniel about this?" Wolfram asked.

"For this, yes. I do not know if it will do any good, or even if it matters. The man is not the master, after all, should Sigfrid be able to seek into his servants' souls? And, for certain, the Obrist will not break a contract because we do not like the face of one of our employer's men. There are worse in this very Company, after all." Piriel looked straight into Wolfram's eyes.

Wolfram held himself from jerking back from the full-blooded Elf's gaze. Does he know? Wolfram wondered. Can he sense the taint of his dark cousins? Wolfram avoided the Company's Elves when he could, for just that reason.

But he replied calmly, "I believe I have met some of them in Forlorn Hope."

"No doubt. Come, get my helm out, the line is building up behind me."

When Wolfram came back from the wagon with the helmet, he saw the two cold-faced men staring straight at himself and Piriel, and another shiver went down his spine. Graf Sigfrid himself came down the next morning, walking side by side with the Obrist to inspect the camp. Obedient to Helmbrecht's quiet order, Wolfram, together with Fredrik and Sascha, had spoken to several of the worst of the Forlorn Hope men, who might not care about the Company, but had no wish to anger the best fighters in their unit on the eve of battle.

Still, Wolfram could not help, just for a moment, looking at his companions with a gaze no longer hardened to Landsknecht regiments. Several of them had ripped one leg of their puffed and slashed hose off at the knee or thigh, sometimes almost up to the buttocks, an odd, but common, fashion among the Landsknechts.

Mustaches drooping past their chins, hair long and disheveled or shaved brutally close to their skulls; garments of ripped and stained silk or velvet thrown over rough wool and linen, mixes of colors that were enough to make Wolfram's eyes wince. Beribboned codpieces big enough to hold spare gloves, spirit-flasks, and purses of money and mismatched pieces of armor spotted bright where welds had been made or dents beaten out, pieces that might as well have had Battlefield Spoil stamped on them in glowing letters. The Landsknecht companies, alone in the Empire, were not obliged to obey sumptuary laws. Emperor Maximilian I had so decreed it, saying,

"Their lives are miserable enough let them have what pleasure they can get."

A coal of shame glowing deep in Wolfram's belly, he looked over at the Graf. An inch or so shorter than Obrist Helmuth, who was not a tall man, Sigfrid was broad-shouldered and stocky, but moved lightly as a dancer in his full armor, helm held easily beneath his plated arm.

At his right side hung a hand-and-a-half sword with golden hilt and scabbard-fittings. At his left dangled the spiked head and short steel haft of a one-handed morgen stern. His ruddy hair was cropped closely about his ears and the back of his neck. His face was wide and flat, hard to read as the blank face of a closed door.

At least, though Wolfram had no doubt of the man's contempt as he looked over the camp at the soldiers' wives laboring at cook fires and washing their men's clothes at the streams, he had the sense not to show it. *After all, he needs us as badly as we need him and he is no fool*, Wolfram thought. By evening, word had filtered down the ranks that Graf Berthold had hired the Sun Azure to fight against them. Wolfram nodded thoughtfully when Fredrik told him over their shared meal.

"I've heard of them," Wolfram said. "After the Lion Rampant, they would have been my next choice if this regiment had turned me down."

"They're tough fighters, and very choosy about the contracts they take," Fredrik agreed. "Truth be told, I hadn't expected to ever face off against them. Their Obrist is much of the same mind as Helmuth: a hard bargainer, yes, but loyal to the Empire first, hmm, they're not exactly knights from a romance, but they pick their men more carefully than most troops, even including us. It'll be good fighting, though they're heavier on cannon and magic than I'd like."

Wolfram's entrails knotted, the bite of juicy roast capon in his mouth suddenly dry and hard to swallow. It would be Forlorn Hope that charged through the sulfur-clouds and mage-flame, and the odds were that most of them would die before they had a chance to close with the foe. Fredrik clapped him on the shoulder.

"The thing is not to be afraid. Drop when you see the experienced men drop – especially Mishni. He's got a real sense for it. Don't hesitate when you get up, and above all, don't pause for even half a heartbeat when you charge the mages. If you falter at all, they'll fry you while you're still out of range but if you're fast and determined enough, you can run them down like rats if you're lucky, or at least make them retreat into the formation where they can't get as clear a shot out."

A different pang shot through Wolfram, he could see Gudrun's slim figure as if through a cloud of powder-smoke, see an armored man lunging to slam his sword into her with all his weight and strength. Mages almost never wore harness; they could not afford the weight to slow their hands, or the exhaustion of bearing armor to slow their minds. But she has been through battle herself. She is as much a veteran as I, Wolfram reminded himself.

Chapter 12

Whatever one might think of Graf Sigfrid, he was efficient. The Silver Eagle received their orders that day. They would march out at dawn the next morning. It was two days' march to the border of Sigfrid's lands, they would go in and see whether their foes would come out to meet them, or whether the Silver Eagle would have to draw the opposing Company and their support out by attacking the small villages. A troop of Sigfrid's heavy cavalry would ride with them, since that style of fighting, the prerogative of those trained to it from childhood, was the one thing Landsknecht companies generally lacked.Wolfram received Treuherz back with more relief than he had imagined. He had blocked the shame of losing it from his heart. Now he felt that a black veil had been drawn away from his mind, leaving the colors of all his thoughts brightened and their shapes sharpened. His blood sang in his ears as he drew the blade, looking at the glimmer of green brightness flaring along the mirror-polished metal beneath the sun's brilliance.

Perfectly balanced, although it weighed nearly three pounds, both heavy and long for a bastard sword, it seemed light as a rapier in his hand, sharpened to a shaving-edge along both sides above the six inches of ricasso where he could grasp the blade beneath the hilt to thrust through chain mail or strengthen a direct block against a heavier weapon. Graf Ulric had given Wolfram all he could of what should have been his second son's, and this sword was the most precious of all. In the battle itself, of course, Wolfram would be fighting with the five and a half-foot long Zweihänder for chopping through pikes and smashing heads and shoulders, or the short heavy Katzbalger if he survived to get in close enough to use it.

There was no place for the graceful footwork and whirling maneuvers of bastard sword fighting in the crush of Free Company warfare, it was all chop and punch-stab but nevertheless, he felt better to have it back. None of the lightness had left Wolfram's heart as the Silver Eagle swung out the next day, though the summer weather had finally broken, clouds blowing up during the night to shade the pine-grown mountains to a dark purple-black and cast a scatter of cold droplets into the mercenaries' faces. He sang lustily with the others, his voice full through the brittle mirth of his companions under the black banner.

Forlorn Hope

"You real cheerful today," Mishni said to Wolfram. "Ready to fight, hey?"

"I am," Wolfram answered.

"Good, good. Just you remember what I said. I hear rumor we charging into bad-nasty shit when the battle starts. Stick by me, duck when I duck, hey?"

It was not until the Landsknechts settled down for the evening that Wolfram began to feel the difference between his old post and the Forlorn Hope. As a lieutenant, it had been his duty to see to the Fähnlein's men, encouraging their spirits, making sure they went easy on the drink, and, often enough, writing a last letter for someone who had never learned the art of the quill.

No one asked him to do that in Forlorn Hope. The dregs of the regiment and former prisoners, these men had no one waiting at home to hear if they lived or died. Nor, though Wolfram had won their respect by force, did anyone save his few friends seem to wish to talk.

It struck him that Fredrik and Sascha were being ignored likewise, perhaps because they had made it through so many battles.

Did his fellow condemned not see him as likely to die with them in the next few days? Or was it only that they, like dogs, could smell that he had not truly given up hope? The weather was worse the next day, cold drops soaking through Wolfram's hood to run chilly down his neck and under his backplate.

He had greased his armor and helm well, but even so, it seemed to him that he could see the first bloom of rust on the metal like a brush of ruddy dust. The drums' beats sounded low and slack, as though the wetness in the air were loosening their heads, and the fifes shrilled slightly off-key, setting Wolfram's teeth on edge.

The archers were too far from Forlorn Hope for Wolfram to hear what they were saying, but he could fill the words in from memory, an endless grumble of curses. The gunners would be no happier, trying to keep the damp out of their powder but since Wolfram would be charging towards cannon on the other side, he found it suddenly hard to sympathize.

Still, I hate marching in the rain, he thought. I want to be back in my own Fähnlein, marching proudly under Hauptmann Heinrich's Golden Bear, with the men of my Rotte at my sides. Little Kai, Georg, Franz, Ruprecht, and Maximilian, the six of us are worth ten ordinary soldiers. He smiled grimly to himself. Our pay rates prove it. Proved it. Three Gods of Darkness. If Wolfram had still been Heinrich's Lieutenant, he, together with his captain and Fändrich Kai, would likely be discussing the reports on the lay of the land where Helmuth hoped to do battle, whether the Company would attack in echelon formation, or pull into the tight defensive square called the gevierte Ordnung.

How the wet weather would affect the firearms and hence the disposition of the mages. Where the four hundred men of the Golden Bear would be placed, being one of the more experienced Fähnlein, the Bear was most often placed in the very front to protect the artillery, but occasionally at the very rear of the gevierte Ordnung in order to discourage the new or fearful soldiers from hopes of retreat. And sometimes they served as the concealed reserve described by Fronsberger, perhaps Wolfram's favorite position, sweeping in to hit an advancing enemy in the flank and crush their forward momentum. There is only one place for Forlorn Hope.

Towards the middle of the afternoon, the word came back, "We're crossing the border into enemy territory." Wolfram knew that it would make little difference: the forces would fight where they met, on Berthold's land or Sigfrid's. Nevertheless, it seemed to him that he could feel the air growing heavier, as if the wretched drizzle were gathering its strength to explode into a thunderstorm. The thick leafy boughs of the oak groves that dotted the rolling hills were no longer a welcome distraction for the eye, but a subtle, intricate camouflage for danger. Yet, even as the hairs on the back of his neck prickled with suspicious alertness, Wolfram also felt a peculiar lightening of his heart.

Perhaps the clouds really were thinning, but it seemed to him that leaves and grass were just a little brighter green here, that the red-and-white cattle grazing on one of the further hills moved a little more placidly than the cows on Graf Sigfrid's land. *It is only that I know good of Graf Berthold, and none of his foe,* Wolfram thought. *Or, my own blood is tainted. If I feel easier here, does that speak well or ill of Berthold?*

Or maybe it's just that the prospect of a fight, if anything, is better than slogging through the mud with nothing to think about except how much I hate marching in the rain! At least the widened toes of his cow-mouth shoes were good for walking in mud. They looked more like duck's feet than anything having to do with a cow, to Wolfram and the hobnailed bottoms kept him from slipping as he walked.

The leather was long since sodden through, his hose squishing inside the shoes with every step he took, sending muddy water oozing out through the decorative slits in the tops which also let mud and water in when he stepped in one of the frequent puddles. *At least I'm not an arquebusier who has to worry about his powder, or an archer with a wet string. Or a mage who will suddenly become the very favorite target on the field if the guns are too wet to fire!*

Few mages could match the four hundred-yard maximum range of an arquebus, but within fifty to an hundred yards, they were far more devastating; and in foul weather, they became the primary distance weapons on the field. Driving rain could make an arquebus volley useless, no matter how well the powder was kept dry. Magic worked in every weather, but actually gained power from the Chaos-field of a storm. *I wonder where Gudrun is now?*

With the Black Wagon, no doubt but the Obrist liked to change its place in the order of march on a daily basis in case of being taken by surprise. There was no point in letting a foe know beforehand just where one of the most valuable elements of the Company would be placed. Wolfram's Rotte had served as bodyguards to one of the Marshals or the Zauberobrist before. Not Forlorn Hope. The Silver Eagle was into a more heavily wooded area, not actually a forest, but fairly well-grown with trees by the time the drums and pipes signaled the company to halt and make camp.

Presumably the out riding scouts had come back and reported it safe, but Wolfram, carving the wet bark and outer layers from a stick to get at the dry interior for lighting a fire, knew he would sleep lightly that night. *If I weren't in Forlorn Hope, I might be either sent to scout or kept on watch much of tonight. At least I'll get more sleep.* It was both the advantage and disadvantage of his blood that Wolfram could be pulled away from his normal duties when dark-sighted eyes and ears keener than a Man's were needed.

Without that distinction to draw the attention of his superiors, he doubted he would have been promoted so quickly. On the other hand, it had been a nuisance at times. *It got me here, for instance. But why?* The constant question, *who would have framed him, who could have crept up on him unnoticed? By the Gods of Darkness and Light, why not just kill me if someone wanted me out of the way? It would have been as easy. Easier, and safer.* Wolfram had gone over those thoughts hundreds, thousands of times, and still come up with no answers. *Within the Company, Alberich could have, and perhaps his two assistants: they were both fine mages, if not in the Zauberobrist's class.*

Why would they? Except and his mind had flinched from this thought before, but now he made himself follow it through. *If Gudrun did it, and then felt guilty enough to try to change what she had done. She seemed nearly convinced of my innocence, despite what seemed watertight proof to the contrary. Of course she couldn't confess, not without being executed herself. Why would she? A Mage could tell the difference between Dark Elf and Light Elf blood. Maybe she thought she had reason to hate me, and found out differently only afterwards* Wolfram shook his head. The stick was damp through, useless. He snapped it angrily between his hands and picked up another one.

Fredrik and Sascha came back to the Forlorn Hope later that evening with news.

"Our scouts say the Sun Azure is out and moving, so it looks like we won't be starting with Berthold's villages after all," Fredrik said. "In fact, we might be fighting as early as tomorrow, all going well."

"No more marching in fuck-your-mother mud," Sascha rumbled grimly. He patted his mace. "Smash heads instead. Lots more fun." A grin like a snarl twisted his wide scarred face for a moment, his little blue eyes gleaming.

"Keep raining, fuck the guns, everyone fights in close. Going to be good battle, I think."

"Ah, yes," Wolfram said uncomfortably. *Donmar and Alagrith, I'm glad he's on our side!* "Any ideas on what formation we'll use?"

"Hmm," Fredrik answered. He tamped the wide bowl of his pipe full, reached down to pick up a long twig and set its end alight in the fire.

Carefully he moved the little flame around and around the pipe-bowl as he puffed until at last the tobacco was glowing to his satisfaction.

"I guess it all depends on where we meet them, and maybe who catches whom by surprise. There was some talk of lurking up ahead where the wood's thicker, but then they might not even come this way.

Or, if they did, it'd be because they scouted us. I heard what the Obrist is hoping for is to catch them with their hose half-up, but I don't think it's all too likely. I'm expecting a straight-out hammering match, where he who hammers hardest wins. What the fuck do I know? I'm a madman, no one ever tells me anything."

He sucked on his pipe thoughtfully, blew out a fragrant cloud of smoke.

"The only thing I do know is that whatever happens, we'll be charging up in front. So there's no point to worrying about it. Shit, my friend, you've been fighting a good long while. You'll sleep fine tonight. It just sucks that we can't rent whores from here."

I'm not sure I want to, Wolfram thought. The whores were back with the main baggage train. They would be prospering tonight, but not through the convicted men of Forlorn Hope. But I would like – maybe – to speak to Gudrun. At least to look in her face, see if he could find any trace or twitch of guilt, or if it was just that swirling the endless questions around in his mind had worn his sanity down like stones grinding each other to sand under the ceaseless swell and ebb of the waves.

If she were guilty, what would I do? Could I turn her in to die? I would need to know why she did it. The fear that had driven Wolfram from his home, that his dark blood would lead him, even unwilling or unknowing, to do evil, could a mage have foreseen something in his future that made his death now necessary?

Why, then, would she have changed her mind? A woman's soft heart? It was one thing to kill in the heat of battle, charged by armed men, another altogether to watch, or perform an execution. Or the Freimann would have more friends.

"Cheer up," Fredrik said. "With any luck, you'll get your five battles in quickly enough on this contract, and there'll still be plenty of women about for you. I've seen you training, and you have better armor than most of the men – Chaos, most of the officers – in this company. If you're not just shit-unlucky, you'll live out your thousand years and more. If you haven't already – never mind."

He waved his speculation aside, the trailing smoke of his pipe pale against the firelight, fading quickly into darkness. It was rude enough to ask an Elf his age in the normal way, in a Landsknecht regiment, it was too close to a question about Wolfram's past. The Silver Eagle began to spread out early the next day, Hauptmann Marcus' Fähnlein pulling off behind a long, low ridge of hills that would shield them from the enemy's sight, but be quick to cross, and give them the advantage of coming down from a height.

Four hundred men was a good reserve, and the big Hauptmann had one of the better units. *On the other hand, it will be all too easy for our foe to come over a hill at us, and then the Forlorn Hope will be charging up,* Wolfram thought.

The weather had cleared, as well, though the road was still muddy. The only question for the firearms on both sides would be how much damp had leaked into their powder over the last days. *If I were still Heinrich's Lieutenant, I'd be taking stock of our arquebusiers now,* he thought gloomily.

The clear weather was better to march in but Wolfram knew that it meant his chances of surviving the first charge had dropped dramatically. It was still two hours to noon when Wolfram's keen ears heard the sound of a single arquebus firing behind the ridge where Marcus' Fähnlein was shadowing the main body of troops. *Accidental discharge? Surely not from one of the Sleeping Wolf. I wonder if they shot a scout. Both forces would have a few light horse as outriders, certainly. I hate not knowing!* Wolfram thought. It had been bad enough as a soldier before his promotion. He had been raised to think and lead, not simply to fight where he was told to.

After a while, Fredrik, the closest thing to an officer that Forlorn Hope boasted by virtue of his volunteer status and experience, was called out of line. When he came back, there was a wild smile on his face. "We've found them," he said.

"They're sitting on a hill like a bunch of cows, waiting for us to surround them. We need to attack in a wide frontage, to make their arquebusiers retire. Stay spread out, far enough to give the firearms trouble and make sure their mages can't blast more than one of you at a time. When we get in real close, tighten up three by three to chop gaps straight through their front lines.

That's all we have to worry about, although I hear there's a cute plan in mind for everyone else. But we'll have the Golden Bear and Three Bezants behind us, so we're well-supported. Oh, and watch out for their falkonets, everyone. The mages are going to try to make them blow up, and you don't want to be too close when that happens."

"No shit!" Jürg muttered.

"Wolfram, you go between Mishni and Erich. You go high, Mishni goes low, Erich guards and pushes forward. When we head up the hill, drop when Mishni drops. Good luck." He turned away, arranging a few other trios to his liking.

On their high ground, the Sun Azure were visible from a long way away, the pikes of their central gevierte Ordnung standing up like the spines of a giant hedgehog. Wolfram's long sight could already make out the banners. The blue sun of the Company itself in the middle of the square, flanked by the three central Fähnlein, another two towards the front, white field and gold.

He looked for the plain blood-red banner, like the one fluttering above Sascha's head and the white beret-feathers like those he wore himself.

Those would mark out the men of the Sun Azure's Forlorn Hope, but he couldn't see either banner or feathers. What do they have in mind? Wolfram wondered instinctively. He couldn't see the faintly blurred green and brown of the Sun Azure's mages, either. Granted, both mages and artillerymen wore the same dull colors in order to fade into the background as best as possible and not make things too easy for the foe's sharpshooters, and mages often had spells of concealment or partial concealment on themselves.

Still, Wolfram had never failed to pick out those most dangerous members of an enemy's force before. What he did see was the neat rectangles of arquebusiers curving around the sides of the hill, making the whole upward slope into a field of crossing fire, and the four long black cylinders with blood-red fittings that were the falconets Fredrik had warned them about, set to fire down and slantingly across.

This might be the worst setting for a frontal assault I've ever seen. Or is it just that I'm in the Forlorn Hope this time?

It looks like they're trying to discourage our frontal charge. Which means they have something nasty waiting for us on the other side of the hill. But our scouts should have told us that and it's not my problem now. Donmar and St. Hildebrand be with me.

Let the Gods of Light know that I was sent here in innocence, and forgive me for the birth I could not help!

On the left wing of the company, Gudrun looked at the falconets, her mouth dry. *Cold iron and Men had praised Donmar for that* since the first smith dug it from the earth, it was the hardest of all metals to touch with Chaos, and hence with magic. There were only certain circumstances that made it possible at all: under the fires and hammers that transformed it into shaped steel and when gunpowder, almost as much a substance of Chaos as fire or storm, was burning in it.

Here, Wilhelm's short sight gave him the advantage being unable to see, it would be easier for him to sense the moment to loose his spell, whereas she would have to watch for the match and guess. Wolfram will be in their path. She took a quick swig of heavily watered wine from her field canteen. The last thing she needed was her voice failing her at the key moment. She was too short to look over the heads of the Doppelsöldner in front of her and see where Wolfram stood in the front line, but she could see the blood-red banner of the Forlorn Hope stirring in the cool breeze.

At least the Sun Azure's upslope position made it possible for her to stay back in the protection of the lines, rather than out on the edges with the artillery, judging the moment when she would have to retreat from the charging foe and trust in the four guards of her Trabanten to get her safely into the middle of the regiment.

The drums kept up their steady boom, fifes skirling above them: the Silver Eagle marched on, three paces to every five beats of the drum. First falconet to her own left. Gudrun breathed deeply, the faint glimmer of the Chaos-flux sparkling before her eyes as she murmured the first words of power, her skin beginning to tingle with the strength she was raising. Still too far, but she could see the master gunner in his green and brown more clearly now as the thin thread of her awareness stretched out, skimming away from the cold iron surface of the artillery piece, focusing on the man behind it.

The beat quickened, carrying her forward. The front line was only five hundred yards away from the closest of the enemy arquebuses now, the first long barrels raising up...four hundred fifty. The fifes shrieked out the first note of the Forlorn Hope's charge. Wolfram broke into a run as the first shots exploded in his ears, the scent of sulfur harsh on the air. It took all his will not to outdistance the line, although Mishni and Erich seemed to be plodding in half-time beside him, gruesomely exposed to the balls whizzing past.

At this range, granted, being hit was a matter of sheer bad luck, but they were coming closer every second as the arquebusiers reloaded. A man screamed, the high agonized sound a horrible counterpart to the fifes, and then another and another.

A sparkling halo hazed the master gunner's face in Gudrun's sight, but she could still see the grizzled features set in concentration, mouth frowning thoughtfully beneath the long droop of badger-grayed black mustaches. He nodded to something she could not hear, lifted the match, touched it to the fuse, and stepped back. The flare of Chaos-potential almost blinded Gudrun to the fire eating its way to the powder. Somewhere far off, in the back of her mind, she could hear herself counting. One...two...now!

The power burst through her as though she had become a cannon herself, firing directly into the falconet's mouth with incredible speed as the other flame slowly blossomed into the powder, her own ball striking just as the other began to move with a jolt of recoil that flung her down. Pain exploded in her back and head, flaring to blackness.

Suddenly Mishni plunged forward. Only luck saved Wolfram, tripping over the small man's halberd as the world exploded deafeningly. He felt himself lifted up and slammed down on the hillside again. Dazed and gasping, screams ringing tinnily in his ears, he scrambled to his feet, running again through the bursts of arquebus fire, and the thickening tendrils of stinking smoke drifting across the hill. He could not see what had become of the falconets. The arquebusiers were only silhouettes in the smoke on either side, dropping back from the charge that was almost upon the last of them.

Wolfram glanced to his side, were Erich and Mishni still with him? Mishni, yes. Erich? Wolfram was just in time to see the blue fire flaring up around the other man as if he were an oil-doused torch, feel the wave of heat beating through his eye slits. He closed his mind to the dark human shadow writhing within the flame, the wail of agony lost among the other screams, and ran on. Mishni was closing tight on his right side. This time, Wolfram saw the Rat's movement: he followed it, hurling himself down and sideways, rolling frantically as the blast of fire passed over the two of them with a great whoof.

In one of those strange still-flashes of vision that struck men's mind in combat, Wolfram saw the long green grass in front of his eye-slits crackling suddenly black, a sharp lightning-scent filled his nostrils, and he rolled forward and up, dashing onwards.

Mishni was still with him, though the white feather in the Rat's red cap was a blackened quill now, and the huge shape of Sascha was lumbering in towards them, crossing Wolfram to take the middle position. The sunlight glittered off pike-heads and the long blades of two-handed swords ahead, like a wall of sharp steel facing them. Wolfram slanted his own wavy-bladed two-hander in front of him, ready to chop or parry as needed, careful of the ferociously spinning menace of Sascha's mace as they closed.

Pick one man. Sascha was in the middle now. It was Wolfram's job to defend, to make his long sword into a steel shield to deflect pike and sword and halberd as the three of them plowed through. Wrist-numbing shocks landing on his blade again and again, the sharp crack of his sword biting into wooden pike shafts and its duller crunch into bone.

Bloody faces twisting with screams or battle cries, the shriek of a steel point skidding from the dome of his breastplate, the crunch of Sascha's mace almost lost in the sounds of shouting and screaming and gunfire, but the spraying gushes of blood and gray brains unmistakable, the low boom of a cannon, the higher voices of arquebuses barking again, stumbling over the uneven footing of maimed soldiers squirming beneath his feet but the survivors of Forlorn Hope were cutting in deeply, driven by the yells of *"The Eagle! The Eagle!"*

Behind them and the pressure of bodies to both front and rear packing them more and more tightly together, too tightly to fight freely. Tall as he was, Sascha was wielding his mace over Wolfram's head now. He grasped his sword one-handed by the ricasso, using quillons and hilt to deflect the occasional overhand pike-thrust to the side, and drew his Katzbalger for the short punching stabs of the brutal close-in fighting, thrust in, angled up under ribs or breastplate for heart and lungs, or dragged down for the disemboweling stroke, scuffling his feet forwards to keep from tripping on entwining nests of intestines, feeling his way over thrashing bodies.

Now he saw how Mishni had survived so many battles in Forlorn Hope, ducking down below shoulder-height where taller men's overhead blows couldn't reach him and stabbing up beneath armpits and under breastplates, waterfall after waterfall of blood soaking him red and shiny as a flayed man. Soaked with sweat, breathing like a bellows as he struggled against the equally exhausted men packed in front of him, Wolfram hardly noticed when his feet began to stumble downhill. His mouth was full of salty sweat and blood. His left hand was numb on the ricasso of his sword, left shoulder bruised to the bone through the pauldron.

He barely had the strength to keep stabbing with his long dagger, his parries were minimal deflections slanting slashing blows to the side, twisting hips or shoulders to make thrusts skid from his armor, ducking or turning his head so that high thrusts would glance from his helm. Time and again now, all that saved him was that his foes were as worn as he was, with blunted weapons, arms too tired to swing a blow that could hurt Wolfram through his armor, aim trembling so that a thrust that should have pierced eye slot, armpit, or groin skipped harmlessly away. Wolfram had almost reached the bottom of the downslope on the other side when he heard the drums and fifes behind him singing out the command for halt, hold position.

The Sun Azure was still withdrawing. Wolfram sheathed his Katzbalger, taking his two-handed sword by the hilt again. He had no more strength to strike with it was all he could do to keep deflecting and swaying away from blows until his enemies were out of reach.

The Sun Azure seemed to be pulling out in fairly good order, their arquebusiers coming forward again to cover their retreat. Wolfram wondered through his exhaustion how many of them still had powder and shot, but no command came to renew fighting, in any case. The only sounds he could hear were the cries of the wounded behind him and to the side, pierced by a few pitiful high horses' shrieks a little further away.

Someone quite nearby was making a hideous gurgling sound. Strangling on blood from a wound to throat or lungs, Wolfram knew. No point to pursuit, he thought. I suppose we've won, but they must have mauled us a bit. Enough to make it not worth trying to catch them at this stage. I don't care what Fredrik thinks. I hate slugging matches between evenly matched regiments. The battlefield was a dream of demons.

The green hill had become a mound of churned muck bleeding over what had been a meadow beside it, strewn with the battered bodies of the dead and writhing with the muddy, bloody bodies of the wounded as though the earth had half-chewed a host of great misshapen worms and spat them out again.

Wolfram's keen Elvish vision was no blessing, he could see each figure twisting in the blood-muck like damned souls in the mire of Dark Hell, the glistening shapes of pale organs and purple organs spilled out on the ground, heads lolling back over red-gaping necks. He could even make out the agony-twisted faces, or ruins where faces had been. Some, Wolfram recognized. When he saw Georg from his old Rotte curled with his hands clenched in around the broken pike-shaft sticking up beneath his breastplate, lips moving in desperate prayer or supplication, Wolfram turned his gaze back to the front. He could do nothing to help anyone until the order was given to break ranks: it would have been no different even if Gudrun, or his own father, Graf Ulric, rather were lying there.

When the Sun Azure was not only out of arquebus range, but bow shot as well, Wolfram opened his visor, though the command to break had not yet been given. His breath had evened out, but the air outside his helmet, even laden with the stinks of the battlefield, tasted like clean water in his mouth. He spat a mouthful of blood, he'd bitten his tongue when a pike shaft glanced off his helm, he thought and reached for his canteen, only to find a flattened mess of metal and blood-soaked leather. The flies were already gathering thickly around him, drawn to his sweat, bloody armor, and the spatters around his eyes.

He wiped some of them into black smears as they gorged, but the rest settled back the moment his hand dropped.

"Have some of mine," Mishni said. Wolfram took the little man's flask between shaking gauntlets and swigged gratefully. The tart hint of sour wine in the water cut through the thick gumminess of his throat, and he had to concentrate with all his strength on not downing half the canteen's contents at once. He gave it back, stood leaning on the hilt of the two-hander to support his quivering legs.

"So long they not try get cute, you made through first battle now," Mishni said, tilting the rim of his kettle-helm back to look up at Wolfram. A mask of darkening blood furred with crawling black flies turned the little man's grin into the grotesque sneer of a kobold. "Congratulations! Only four more to go!"

CHAPTER 13

The Silver Eagle's mages had managed to blow up one falconet completely. The resulting destruction among the arquebusiers explaining how a fair number of the Forlorn Hope men had made it up the hill. Wreck one beyond repair, leave one broken but reparable, and capture one in good condition. Quartiermeister Helmbrecht was supervising stripping the bodies of fallen foe-men, the wives and hire-wives who had followed with the baggage-train were tending to their injured men, or weeping over the bodies of the Silver Eagle's dead. Dietrich Falkenstein, the company's chief field doctor, had efficiently commandeered some of the men to help with the wounded.

The worst-hurt of the Silver Eagle were marked out with small red flags for the attention of Feldscher Ruprecht, the Obrist's own healer. The Sun Azure men who might last until the Feldscher had recovered his own strength were marked with blue flags, and those who were too grievously injured to survive until he could aid them were given mercy. The company's chaplain, Vater Franz, walked among them. Despite the ankle-deep churn of bloody mud, his white robes gleamed spotless.

No stain would cling to the mark of the gods' grace. Here and there, he turned aside to lay his hands on a fallen man, murmuring a blessing. Some sat up healed beneath his touch, some slumped back, gone beyond the worlds in peace, it was the gods' will that Vater Franz did, not his own. When Wolfram looked out of the corner of his eye, he could almost see the golden radiance like a reflection of sunlight from the chaplain's robes. Isn't he fortunate? Wolfram thought.

He had quenched his thirst, cleaned his weapons, and poured water over his head, but it would be a little while yet before the big water barrels were dragged up. He would be a long time cleaning his armor, drenched in blood and matter as it was. His gambeson would have to be soaked for hours to get the blood-stink out of the padding before it began to rot. Some of the Forlorn Hope men didn't bother, and Wolfram thought their stench by itself was a weapon, though once battle was joined, to be sure, it was hardly noticeable.

He would also have to get the worst of the dents beaten out. His left pauldron was badly caved in, the dent grating against his bruised shoulder with every movement. Praise St. Hildebrand, the blow had struck the pauldron's cup well above the lame, if the articulation had been crushed, it would have frozen his arm in place and he would certainly have died.

Wolfram had to give Vater Franz credit for this at least, he did not flinch at even the worst injuries. Beneath the clean sleeves of his robe, the priest's hands were red to the elbow, streaked with darker matter. Wolfram saw him kneeling to gather up a man's trampled entrails and set them gently back into his body, replace a dangling eyeball on a shattered cheekbone, and ease a woman's near-severed breast into its proper place.

Wolfram swallowed at the last, glancing away. He knew he had killed or maimed women himself. Very few females had the muscle to wield a pike or two-handed sword, or shoot a heavy bow at distance but a sturdy woman could kill him with arquebus or halberd as well as a man could, and there was no time to mark the sex of a foe in battle.

Still, he found something instinctively distressing about seeing hacked female bodies afterwards. He had gotten used to everything else even after his first fight, for instance, he hadn't been able to look at a string of sausages for a month, whereas now he could enjoy them on the same evening without ever thinking about the pale lumpy coils falling out over his hand as he withdrew his Katzbalger. Only that one thing still sickened him a little. *From my upbringing, I suppose.* Once in a long while, a noblewoman trains to fight and jousts in tourneys, but they almost never go to war – certainly not in the lines.

"You!" Feldarzt Dietrich shouted at Wolfram. "You can tie a bandage, get over here."

Wolfram shrugged and followed the chirurgeon's gesture. The man Dietrich indicated had a hand-sized piece of jagged iron sticking out of his right thigh, but it was on the outside, and the blood flowed rather than spurting when Wolfram drew it out, he would probably live. Wolfram washed his hands and the wound with a little wine-tinged water from his patient's own canteen, wiping away the flies that were gathering to the blood on the the patient's leg, and shook his head to get rid of the ones feeding on the sweat around his eyes.

He drew his Katzbalger to cut a strip of blue slashing from the injured man's short left breech. The other had been ripped off altogether by someone already and then shook his head in disgust when he looked at the blade. Some Landsknechts' gaudy doublets concealed breastplates or steel-reinforced brigandines: grating an edge against metal and occasionally bone, and shoving it through heavy leather over and over again, did its sharpness no good.

"Use mine," the wounded man said in a strained voice. "Didn't make it into the close fighting, so it should still be sharp."

Wolfram nodded, taking out the other man's blade and cutting the strip of cloth free at both ends. That was one advantage to the layers of slashed clothing favored by the Companies, he thought. There were always bandages available.

No one would even notice one's been cut off. At least if he hadn't chosen that vile yellow as an under color. Now that he looked closer, the absence of a right leg to the knee-length breeches was deliberate too. Some said it made it easier to kneel under heavy fire, Wolfram suspected it was just one of those things people did.

"Thanks," his patient said. "I guess I should give you my parole now. I'm Lieutenant Ludwig of Hauptmann Umberto's Fähnlein, and I swear not to try to escape or fight against you until my ransom is paid."

"I am..." Wolfram bit his sore tongue again before he could give his old title. "Wolfram of Forlorn Hope. I accept your parole."

Ludwig nodded, and they clasped wrists. The Lieutenant was close to Wolfram's own age, he guessed, with close-cropped hair pale as sun-bleached wheat stubble, a pleasantly round face, and a pale mustache drooping down on either side of his mouth. With the bandage around one bare leg, cropped head, and long mustache, all he needed was a plumed and slashed hat to look like the model for one of the popular woodcuts mocking Landsknecht fashions. Wolfram bandaged a number of other men, though no others tried to give him their parole. By the time he had done all he could, the camp-wagons were just starting to roll up.

Hürenmeister Peter was always very reliable about making sure that the whores, sutlers, and other such folk who lived off the Company stayed away from the battlefield until the plunder had been taken in and accounted for, but getting them into a nearby campsite quickly enough to tend to the needs of tired and hungry soldiers in good time. Wolfram was relieved to see that the decision had been made to camp here.

The thought of marching made him want to lie down and sleep for a week. Other men were already on the ground. The small group of Suome who fought in Marcus' Sleeping Wolf Fähnlein had half-stripped and collapsed into a pile, wet heads resting companionably on each other's bare shoulders or stomachs as they passed a bottle about and Fredrik, likewise half-stripped and half-washed with his long hair dripping pale pink stains over his muscular chest, was lying in the grass and staring at the smoke rising from his pipe.

Something tapped Wolfram's shoulder. He turned to see the Provost's bailiff glaring at him. "Why aren't you with the rest of Forlorn Hope?" The man asked, his dark eyes fixing coldly on Wolfram's.

"The Feldarzt ordered me to help bandage the wounded."

"You seem to be done, so I'll take you over now."

Wolfram followed him without argument, until he thought of something. "One of their injured gave me his parole. Should I stay with him, or give his oath over to someone else?"

The bailiff's deep-creased brow furrowed more heavily. "I'll ask the Schultheiss. Come on."

Schultheiss Otto looked dubiously through his little spectacles at Wolfram when the half-Elf explained his question, stroking his gray beard. "The oath of parole should be good to any member of the regiment," he said. "As for your responsibility. How badly wounded is he?"

"A deep cut in the thigh."

"And he is an officer, and hence entitled to courtesy. Hermann, get me one of the Marshals, if either of them is still awake. If I can get an oath I can trust from you, I don't see any reason not to detail you to assist him."

Wolfram pressed his sore tongue against his teeth, letting the small pain distract him from his flare of fury. Running up that hill had been bad enough, but he'd charged in the front line with arquebus balls whizzing and mage-fire flaring around him before and never at odds quite so bad, but death only came one to a customer.

What truly gnawed at him. Nobody ever doubted my honor before. Now, nobody believes in it. Except Gudrun, maybe. She must be all right; if we'd lost a mage, it would be all over the Company by now.

Wolfram waited, watching for the ruddy gleam of deep auburn braids in the late afternoon sunshine.

Instead, he saw the watery-pale glimmer of ash-blond hair above a dark robe, the other Marshal, Wilhelm. He pronounced me guilty, where Gudrun could recognize an honest oath. If Wilhelm said he lied again, Wolfram decided, he would stand firm and insist that Gudrun examine him. She would agree, he was certain of it.

The young mage looked as though he had come close to bleeding out, face gray under a blistering sunburn and hands shaking. Wolfram wondered if he had been wounded. There were no bandages visible, nor did he limp, but the Feldscher's arts could have taken care of that. Nor was it surprising that he didn't show the glow of health usual after a healing and when dealing with the battle-wounded, when there were so many who needed aid, most Feldschern did only the least they could to keep each man from dying. As Wilhelm came closer, Wolfram saw that his pale eyebrows were singed as though he had been too near to a muzzle-blast, the ends of the hair around his face frizzing dark. Muzzle-burn, not sunburn, Wolfram thought. I wonder how that happened?

"Donmar and Alagrith, man, what happened to you?" Otto exclaimed.

Wilhelm curved his lips into a painful smile. "Backlash from trying to wreck the falconet," he said hoarsely. "I stayed in the link a moment too long, and the potentials, never mind. What is it you need me for?"

The Schultheiss looked at Wilhelm a long minute, then at Wolfram. Wolfram met the older man's dark blue eyes without flinching.

"Never mind," he said. "It's a minor enough matter. You get something to eat and lie down. How are the other mages?"

"The Zauberobrist is fine. Nothing fazes him, you know that Gudrun is still unconscious, but Feldscher Ruprecht says she'll be all right by tomorrow. Hers was the one that blew up completely."

Then I owe her my life, Wolfram thought. He was about to speak, but a sudden fear seeped into his mind. Wilhelm might have lied knowingly or his magic might have been deceived; the Schultheiss might have kept him from truth-reading Wolfram again for a reason. If Wolfram, during the spell, had blurted out his innocence. Does Otto trust me because he knows I told the truth the first time? Can I stay in this Company after I win free of Forlorn Hope?

Not unless I find out who did this to me, and why.

"Go see to the captive," the Schultheiss ordered Wolfram abruptly. "You've dealt with captured officers before, you know what courtesies he should expect."

"Yes, sir."

Slowly as Marshal Wilhelm was walking, it was only moments before Wolfram caught up with him. In spite of the crusted blood flaking off Wolfram's armor, the young mage gratefully accepted his offer of an arm to lean on. Tired and bruised as the half-Elf was, that was nothing to Wilhelm's exhaustion.

"You mages did well," Wolfram said. "I was surprised at the decision to blow up the cannon, though. We don't usually try that."

It was difficult, it knocked most mages out for the course of the battle and in a field battle like the one they had fought, artillery reloaded so slowly that it was less valuable than hand-guns or magic.

"The word is, if we get through, we'll have to besiege. Graf Berthold is expected to fight to the last man. This is a grudge-feud. There won't be anything left of the loser."

We'll be recruiting again afterwards, Wolfram thought. At least we'll be in good funds, between our usual payment and the sack. For a moment he wondered if he had made it out of Forlorn Hope by the end of the campaign, would there be any chance of getting one of the wood carvings from Graf Berthold's chapel? No. A brief flush of shame heated his cheeks. If I see the chapel Tilman Lindenschneider decorated, the woodcarvings will most likely be flame and ash by then.

"I hear it was a Darkness-demon of a fight today," Wilhelm went on. Some men were silent after a battle, some babbled. The Marshal seemed to be one of the latter.

"It's a good thing we had Graf Sigfrid's heavy cavalry with us. Hauptmann Konrad's Fähnlein faked a rout, they tried to pursue, and Sigfrid's cavalry came over the hill and smashed into them as soon as their formation opened. They'll be turning a couple of flags into shrouds tonight."

It was the custom throughout the Companies for the "little flag" from which the Fähnlein divisions took their name, and which bore the personal heraldry or chosen insignia of the Hauptmann, to become his shroud when he was killed in battle.

"This is good country for tactics like that. I wish I'd seen it," Wolfram said. *I wouldn't have anyway,* he consoled himself. *The Golden Bear was right behind us.*

"So do I. We all do our part, I guess."

Wolfram walked the exhausted mage to the Black Wagon. *Gudrun is probably still unconscious, I won't see her here,* he thought. *I'm not sure I want her to see me like this. Though I suppose she's seen worse. Darkness, she's done worse, if not as messy for her.* He paused a few moments anyway, until he caught sight of Alberich's lanky figure sweeping through the crowd, the gold brocade on the stiff black pleats of his Waffenrock's skirt glittering in the sunlight.

He made his way in the other direction as quickly as he could. Graf Sigfrid's heavy cavalry, Wolfram noticed, were setting up their own camp a little way from the Company's.

At that distance, a Man might not have been able to tell but Wolfram could see that, though there were servants in brown homespun raising tents, carrying firewood, and stirring pots, none of them were women. *He must pay well, we know he does. He outbid Graf Berthold for us, and the Sun Azure is an expensive regiment.* Wolfram paused by the water barrels long enough to clean himself off as well as he could without armoring down and stripping to the skin, then stopped by the sutlers to buy bread, cheese, and wine for himself and Ludwig. *When he had a chance to get his pack out of one of the Forlorn Hope wagons, he could come back for stew,* he thought. After a moment's thought, he also bought a small flask of aqua-vitae.

The men in Forlorn Hope only received two guilders a month, half an ordinary pike man's pay and barely enough to cover the swill that was sold in their encampment, but Wolfram's former salary of twenty guilders a month had left him with a fair bit still. Lastly, he made his way to Fat Georg's wagon. The broad-bellied smith was already hammering on a dented breastplate, sweat shining through the thin strands of black hair drifting over his balding pate and dripping down his round red face.

A banner showing Kunig's crossed Hammer and Tongs, iron-black on flame-orange, floated over the smith's wain, though the sound of clanging alone would have been more than enough to advertise his trade. Still, Georg was more pious than most who accompanied the Landsknechts, and never failed to acknowledge the god of his calling.

"Take it off and put it on that stump there," Fat Georg said, never pausing in his rhythmic blows for a moment. "I won't have time to try refluting it for a while. I'll have a Darkness-damned time trying to match that kind of fine work, more so with the abuse it's taken already but I can get it patched up to serve you tonight or tomorrow. It'll look like crap, but it'll do its job."

"That will be fine," Wolfram said. "Thank you."

Fat Georg was the most expensive of the smiths traveling with the Silver Eagle, but he had repaired Wolfram's armor before, flutings and all. Despite his self-deprecating warnings, he had never cracked a piece of it in the reforging, nor failed to restore its original beauty except in the short term at times like this, when everyone who wore metal harness just wanted their damaged parts made functional again. The captive Lieutenant was sitting propped up where Wolfram had left him, puffing on a long-stemmed clay pipe.

He must have been in considerable pain from his wound, but gave little sign of it aside from the paleness and tiny lines about his eyes.

"Excellent," Ludwig sighed, taking a long pull at the aqua-vitae. He passed it back to Wolfram, who sipped lightly for the sake of politeness. "Now, if you could just fetch me a woman. No, I'm joking I don't think I'd get much good from one until I'm patched up. That was a demon of a charge your lot made, you know, even for a Forlorn Hope."

"Thank you. I think," Wolfram added. How many of his erstwhile comrades, wretches though many of them were, had died on that hill?

As many as half? And what would that do for his odds of surviving another battle, or four? Although there were always new men in Forlorn Hope after a hard fight. Green soldiers who had panicked, tried to desert, and not been killed straight out for running. That was why an experienced Fähnlein was generally placed in back. Not to mention the inevitable few who tried to sneak plunder from the dead into their own pockets before it was counted, or creep off with a fallen man's helm or breastplate without waiting for the general distribution

"Our Fähnlein was right in front, and we thought your commander was just throwing you away as a distraction. If that falconet hadn't exploded. It took out quite a few of us when it did. I don't think you'd have made it."

"Likely not," Wolfram said. The flatness of his own voice, and the numbness in his heart at the thought, surprised him.

Well, you can only clasp wrists with Death in person so many times before you stop fearing his shadow.

Ludwig had seen even less of the battle than Wolfram. He asked a number of questions, but was disappointed by the answers. Another young officer with ambitions, Wolfram thought. He felt half-drawn to the man, so much like I was and half-disgusted by him, so much like I was! And why would anyone bother framing someone like that? The answer had to be something to do with Wolfram's Dark Elvish blood: seeing his near-mirror as a Landsknecht officer convinced his heart of that.

After a time talking and drinking, Ludwig eventually commented, "Graf Sigfrid must be paying very well to have hired the Silver Eagle away from Graf Berthold. We heard you'd been approached as well, and we were surprised at which side you'd chosen. Especially given how much Berthold offered us."

"How much were you offered?" Wolfram asked reflexively.

"Twenty-eight thousand a month, for a six-month contract," Ludwig grinned.

The Sun Azure was about the same size as the Silver Eagle, around two thousand me, the six-months hire was standard, but twenty thousand guilders would have been on the high side of normal for such a regiment.

Berthold must have learned from being outbid – but we would have done better if the Sun Azure had been hired first. Six thousand guilders a month better!

"Good pay," Wolfram said noncommittally.

"Yes. No offense, but we were thanking the gods we answered the bid before you did. Graf Berthold's a good man to fight for."

Still thirsty from fighting, and determined to live down his fouled reputation, Wolfram had hardly touched the spirits and accompanied each small swig of wine with three large ones of water. The remark might have passed unnoticed if he had drunk as much as his wounded companion. Instead, it made the tiny hairs on the back of his neck suddenly prickle alert as if he had just heard the crunch of a strange footfall in the woods, not knowing if it were foe, friend, or bear. They lost the higher bid by being too slow, was the word in camp.

No matter how the Obrist tried to keep the details of contract negotiations quiet, something always leaked out. Obrist Helmuth had announced, high contracts like these were good for morale, that the Silver Eagle was receiving twenty-two thousand a month on this contract, enough over the odds to be pleasing all around, especially with the hope of a particularly rich castle to be sacked at the end of it. Maybe Berthold had decided for some reason that he really wanted the Sun Azure, and raised his bid for them but not the Silver Eagle?

Maybe Graf Sigfrid had feigned a bid to the second company to drive the price up for his foe. That additional six thousand guilders a month for six months would be a noticeable drain even on a rich Graf's purse. Maybe Ludwig is lying to me in order to lower our morale. The Silver Eagle had used words against its foes before, spies in the enemy camp spreading rumors, men ordered to give certain answers if they were captured and questioned. How can I find out? Even if Wolfram had the heart to torture a man he had bandaged, then sat eating, drinking, and talking with, the Lieutenant had given his parole and Wolfram had taken it. There could be no interrogation, only the courteous care due an officer until Ludwig was ransomed. Then it struck Wolfram that he was free of the Forlorn Hope guards, for now.

He might, if he were very careful, be able to approach one of the mages to cast a surreptitious truth-reading on Ludwig. Gudrun is the only one I know can cast the spell accurately. If I can trust her.

CHAPTER 14

Gudrun awoke to dim light and the cool damp air of morning filtering in through the dry scents of incense and herbs. Every inch of her body ached as if she had been beaten with rods on the wheel, and each breath hissing in and out of her lungs was a dry scorched pain. Clothes and blankets hurt against her tender skin, the soreness of a bad sunburn. Nevertheless, she smiled, even though the slight movement made everything hurt worse. I did it. I blew up the falkonet. Cold iron, hair-fine timing but I made it explode well and truly. The Silver Eagle had either won or retreated in good enough order for her Trabanten to carry her off. The scents around her could be those of the other Company's Black Wagon, but there were no manacles on her hands, no cold iron collar about her throat to damp the vibrations of any words of power she might speak, and no iron half-band fastened over her eyes to thwart any remaining force of will that might linger in her frustrated gaze.

"Ah," Alberich said. "Awake already. Here, you will want this." He came over to her, assisting her to sit and pushing a glass phial into her hand. Gudrun managed to keep her grimace down to the barest flicker, it would not do for the Zauberobrist to see her yielding to a bodily distaste for what she needed and swallowed the draught in a single gulp.

It was ferociously bitter wormwood, yarrow, comfrey, and willow bark, together with dill and hyssop, could only yield a tongue-puckering nastiness. Nevertheless, she was already starting to feel a little better. It took half an hour for the brew's herbal components to take full effect, but the easing they, and the enchantments they bore, brought worked very quickly.

"Congratulations," her commander went on. "You destroyed the cannon very thoroughly, and made a nice hole in their front lines. While it might have been better if you could have held back slightly to leave it reparable for further use, your achievement is not to be denied." There was a surprising warmth in his sharp Magdeburg accent.

"Thank you, sir," Gudrun replied.

"When you are recovered enough, you will take the rear patrol from Wilhelm and send him up to the front. Until then, you are responsible for the Wagon. I believe you know your duty."

"Yes, sir," Gudrun answered. Normally Alberich rode in the Black Wagon to guard it, while his two magical subordinates went to front and rear on horseback to search for sorceress traps, attacks, or concealed forces.

If the Wagon were assaulted while she was in it and the efforts of herself and the soldiers around it were insufficient to keep it from capture all three of the mages knew how to activate the final defense which would destroy the wagon and spread death for an hundred feet around.

I won't be able to find out if Wolfram survived, she thought. Forlorn Hope is usually near the front, and I can't ask Wilhelm to look for him.

Would Alberich change our assignments? No. The front is the likelier to run into magical traps, and Wilhelm is in better shape than I. I would have to have another reason, anyway. But, Donmar and Alagrith, I wish I knew!

"Excellent. Do not strain yourself: your services will be needed soon, and in two to four days, you will have to be at your best."

"Are we expecting another battle, sir?"

"We are under specific orders to enter the village of Bad Oberstein if at all possible. It is expected that we will have to fight for it, though whether we will meet the Sun Azure there or not is an open question."

"Yes, sir." The command seemed odd to Gudrun. Why should one particular village be so important?

She had expected a straight march in towards Graf Sigfrid's castle, or at least a certain amount of maneuvering around to cut down as many of his forces as possible before having to besiege. But tactics were hardly her business: maybe the village occupied an important position?

The Zauberobrist paused. A look of faint abstraction softened his gaze, like a wisp of cloud dimming the hard blue brightness of the Southern sky. His narrow brows drew inward, his high forehead furrowing. Gudrun waited patiently.

At last Alberich said, "You are not particularly religious."

"No, sir." Except for the Church's Sorcerer, very few workers of magic were.

The worship of Alagrith's Earth-Wives encompassed their intuitive magics of herb, healing, and prophecy but that was very different from the true mage's work with Chaos direct. The enchantments of Elves might be different as well, but Men's magic was a matter of human will and control of the ever-shifting force at the root of all things was, as the pious saw it, a matter of Men striving to gain that power that only the gods should hold. When one had once touched the Chaos-void and shaped it to one's own choice, it was hard to revere a Church that taught acceptance of the gods' wills above all.

The more so, in Gudrun's mind, when one had seen Vater Franz after a battle, moving among the wounded with no power of his own to decide who should be healed and who should just die, even if it were his best friend who lay there. Not for me, thank you.

"You may not be aware that Graf Berthold is. He taxes his folk and squanders the wealth on fantastic chapels. He supports a herd of priests in luxury, but gives not a penny to magical research in his land." Alberich's thin lips curved into a brief smile. "I know you resented not being able to find out more about what Magister Klaus von Ludo is doing now. I would have, too, were I in your position. Regrettably, I cannot tell you now, but it is my hope that I may be able to do so in the future."

For the first time Gudrun had ever seen, the Zauberobrist's smile widened to a grin, his blue eyes brightening like smoldering tinder suddenly flaring up into a full blaze.

"Not to torment you with frustrated curiosity, but it is truly quite remarkable work."

Alberich's jaw clenched, pulling his mouth into a tight-closed frown again. The radiance of his blue gaze was gone as suddenly as if heavy iron shutters had clanged down behind his eyes. This look was familiar to Gudrun. It was the previous one that had surprised, like seeing a house that was normally shut and barred suddenly open and blazing with light for just a moment.

"Whereas Berthold's fanaticism has led him into all manner of follies, not the least being that he is far more willing to spend money on his churches than on the men to protect them, as a result of which we are fighting against him, rather than for him, right now.

"And I must say that I am not displeased with that. In any case, Bad Oberstein is notable for being one of the major shrines in Berthold's land. Though less luxurious than most, it is one of the three main sources from which his priests draw their strength, and must therefore be dealt with. That will largely be our task. We can necessarily expect no help from Franz."

Alberich's voice softened. "I know this will be difficult for the pair of you at first. It is one thing to pay little reverence to the Church. It is another thing to act directly against it.

Nevertheless, I have great confidence in you, Gudrun. You have shown me your courage, your power, and strength of will, you have also proved to me that, regardless of your sex, you have the incisive and logical mind and the firm self-control required for progress to the higher levels of magic. I do not doubt for a moment your ability to use those characteristics to aid me in doing what needs to be done when we reach Bad Oberstein."

Gudrun swallowed hard, the wave of pride rising from her heart nearly choking her. Alberich seldom gave compliments. The best she could say about working with him was that he had always upbraided her in exactly the same terms as he used for Wilhelm. He criticized them both for being fuzzy thinkers, swayed by emotion and appearance, subject to trivial physical distractions, lazy memorizers, and so forth. Indeed, until this moment, she had always thought the Zauberobrist put up with his two Marshals only because he could get no better. *He really thinks I am good! Or, could be, at least.*

The oath of loyalty a student of magic swore to her primary teacher, if enforced only by the ranks of mages rather than by the awesome arm of law, was yet as strong as a knight's oath of fealty. Gudrun had kept her vow in word and deed since swearing to Alberich. Now, for the first time, she felt its strength in her heart, and swore to herself that she would redouble her efforts for him. Alberich did not exactly smile, but his frown loosened.

"I know that I am a harsh teacher, but perfection in result requires intolerance of even the slightest flaws in process. I am telling you now, as I have told Wilhelm, because I also know your limits, and this is not a matter which should be sprung upon a young mage by surprise. Believe me now, when I tell you that making the shrine at Bad Oberstein unusable by our foes is an important, perhaps a vital, part of our Company's strategy. If we did not know that Berthold's priests will be opposing us in battle when we are nearer his castle, we would not have to do it. But they who forsake the neutrality of the Church forsake likewise its sanctuary."

"I understand, sir," Gudrun said, pressing her palms flat against her thighs to keep herself from shaking. It was a frightening thing Alberich was asking her but how, now that she knew how highly he really thought of her, could she disappoint her teacher? "You can depend on me."

"I am sure of it. Well, I must not linger. If Berthold stints his mages, the Sun Azure does not, and there is no telling whether they have any traps in mind along our way."

Gudrun lay silently for a little time, overwhelmed by what Alberich had told her. *Would he think so well of me, if he knew that I cannot control my mind well enough to keep from thinking of Wolfram? As stupid and emotional a distraction as ever got a peasant girl in trouble? He got drunk on duty, who can say that he wouldn't do something equally as insane or dangerous to any woman who. Oh, never mind!* As the draught she had swallowed did its work, Gudrun was able to get up and move about.

The greenish-brown robes she had worn in the battle were singed a bit about the edges from the force of the backlash that had knocked her out, but otherwise clean enough. Still, riding mages' patrol was not a good time to wear them.

The dull colors might be harder to target in pitched battle, but if their foes had sharpshooters in the wood, they would mark her out for special attention, either a mage or a master gunner, and a choice kill in either case.

Instead she put on a loose blouse of deep gold linen with a russet bodice and matching large slashed sleeves. Breeches underneath for riding, then a long russet over skirt, the extra length hoisted up to hang over her gold-mounted belt, low riding boots, and a hat of dark green velvet with a spray of russet feathers held on by a large gold brooch. Her wand went into its silk-lined case at her belt, hanging opposite her belt pouch and the long silver-pommeled dagger behind it. Now she might pass easily for a non-combatant staff member such as the Obrist's scribe or interpreter, an officer's wife, one of the lesser members of the artillery, or a well-off camp follower.

While Gudrun dressed, she tried very hard to keep blocking the thought. Did Wolfram survive? Things had looked very bad for the Forlorn Hope yesterday, what little of the battle she had been able to see.

He had one of the best sets of armor in the Company, but that might have made him a target: good armor could be as much danger as protection in these days of firearms and battle-mages, for a man who had to charge his enemy from a distance. The Forlorn Hope would be close to the front of the column. Alberich would be there, and Gudrun might as well cut her tongue out as send a query to him.

I do not want to draw his attention to Wolfram. She remembered the look on the Zauberobrist's face when he had remarked about Wolfram's un-Elvish behavior. Alberich did not like mysteries.

At least, she added dryly to herself, he didn't like other people's mysteries. He certainly enjoyed keeping secrets of his own. The light in his eyes when he mentioned Magister Konrad's private work. Though, to be fair, he might well have liked to tell her more of that, if he could have. *I would lay odds it's some sort of battle-magic,* Gudrun thought, remembering how utterly martial Graf Sigfrid had seemed. *I can't see Sigfrid spending money on research otherwise. Unless it were, say, a spell to immediately whisk away any trace of untidiness or dirt in his castle and lands. Any trace up to the size of a Landsknecht! Donmar, how it must grate him to have to rely on scum like us.*

He won't even let his men camp with us for fear we might pollute them. Although the basic camp warning, warding was normally set by Gudrun and Wilhelm, Alberich went over himself every night to put one about Sigfrid's heavy cavalry, explaining to his juniors that he had been requested to do so by the Graf, who did not wish his men distracted on campaign. Wilhelm knew better than to ask more questions of the Zauberobrist, but when Alberich had left to do his task, he had said plaintively to Gudrun, "How would I distract them?"

To which she had replied, "Maybe they've been deprived so long they won't care?"

The two of them had muffled their guilty giggles, a brief quiet revenge for the frustrating evening at Graf Sigfrid's castle.

"I feel sorry for their horses, then," Wilhelm had whispered back, and that had seemed even funnier.

Being among the Landsknechts has coarsened me, Gudrun thought now. The daughter my parents raised would have been far too shocked to laugh at such things. But so what? The daughter my parents raised would be married to some boring burgher by now, breeding his fat babies and maybe casting the odd horoscope and dying slowly inside. To be praised by a great mage like Alberich why should I care what anyone else thinks? I can make my own way.

Gudrun was still shaky enough from yesterday's backlash to ask one of the eight-man Trabanten that ringed the Black Wagon to help her up into the saddle, though. The big man grinned nervously, garlic and a whiff of last night's stale wine breathing out between his broken and stained teeth.

"Of course, Marshal," he said. She couldn't remember his name, the duty of guarding the Black Wagon rotated between the Doppelsöldner but he had been one of her four in the battle, as well.

He squatted down in the road like a boulder covered in brilliant folds and streamers of particolored red, yellow, and blue fungus. His huge hands enclosed her foot to the ankle.

He boosted her up as though she weighed nothing. Gudrun wondered, for a moment, what it would be like to be so strong: she must seem like a child's toy to him. But he averted his eyes respectfully as he bowed to her and hurried to call the pair who marched just ahead of the Wagon's guard. One Dwarf with a halberd and one Man with a two-handed sword, Gudrun's own Trabanten for the march. *He is more wary of me than I of him.* She would never be at the mercy of the soldier's physical strength, no more than she had been at that of the Forlorn Hope ruffians who had tried to assault her. *It's too bad all women can't work magic! Or, perhaps, that arquebuses are so heavy and slow to reload, and wheel-lock pistols so rare and expensive .*

Gudrun turned the palfrey and started towards the rear, careful not to outdistance her Trabanten. Even in the middle of the Company, she could never hope to be entirely safe. One of the principles of Landsknecht strategy as laid down by Fronsberger was the advice to infiltrate the enemy's camp in disguise, and that was an easy thing to do.

Sometimes for information; sometimes to affect morale by spreading distressing rumors and sometimes to quietly assassinate an important officer.

In some ways, humans were very like particles in the Chaos-flux, you never really knew what they were going to do, and the very act of watching and guessing could bump them off what had seemed to be their course. She nudged the horse on a little faster. The Dwarf had to break into a trot to keep up, but that was nothing to worry about.

He or she, as the case might be, humans never could tell with Dwarves could keep that pace for forty-eight hours at a time without stopping for a rest. I have to admit, though, that Dwarves really do look silly in Landsknecht clothes. The huge puffed shoulders that made slender Men impressive and big Men gigantic made Dwarves look like bright toadstools, an impression emphasized by the yellow hat nearly half as wide as the guard was tall. His wide Pluderhosen bagged immensely over his knees, and the pink and yellow of his outfit added the final ludicrous touch.

Still, his halberd gleamed wickedly sharp, and Gudrun had no doubt that he could wield it well enough to shave the mustaches off a man's face in two strokes from five feet away. Dwarves could be a touchy race, and they had done such things in the Company before. She rode along the column of men.

Some had halberds over their shoulder or two-handers sheathed across their backs, some carried their arquebuses, but most had long pikes trailing behind them. Normally the sixteen-foot weapons were carried on the baggage carts, being unwieldy to march with, but not in hostile territory. After Gudrun had ridden a little while, she began to feel Wilhelm's power pushing against hers. He was coming up to meet her. She dropped the spell. It would become actively uncomfortable for both of them as he got closer. The day was bright and clear with a strong breeze, she could see the gold and black of the Sleeping Wolf Fähnlein fluttering at its full length in the wind.

"'Little flags', indeed," she muttered to herself, the Fähnlein was ten feet long and wider by half a foot than Gudrun was tall.

On the march, some of the best archers were spread out along the sides of the column. An arquebus ball might hit harder than a bow, and the art of using it be easier to teach, but it was more difficult to shoot accurately and slower to reload; and if an enemy scout were spotted, for instance, the archers would have the best chance of taking him down.

The sun gleamed magnificently off the deep blue and silver of Piriel's breastplate as she passed him. He ignored her completely. Elves generally had little use for human mages.

For just a moment Gudrun wondered what he, or the other full-blooded Elf Arkoniel, were doing among the Landsknechts but that was none of her business, and she had work to do.

"Heyla," Wilhelm called as he rode closer. "Good to see you up again. That was a fine job you did on the cannon!"

"Alberich said I should have held back a little so we could repair it for ourselves," Gudrun said ruefully. "I think the honors go to you. Anyway, Alberich wants you up front. You'd best move as fast as you can, the Wagon's been left alone too long already."

"True, if you're here and he's not there. I'll try not to fall off." Wilhelm kicked his horse into a slow canter, bouncing uncertainly on its back.

Gudrun reminded herself that she had no room to laugh at his riding. She had been far worse when she joined the Landsknechts, and still wouldn't like to ride a horse over fields at a full gallop. Gudrun murmured the incantation again that allowed her to stretch her senses through air and earth. The drums and fifes that kept the soldiers' time faded in her hearing: the tramping of the Landsknechts' feet was like heavy raindrops pattering on the skin of a mile-wide drum, the wagons' wheels rumbling like the bass drone of a bagpipe the size of a mountain. She reached further.

The late summer air breathed clean and fresh over the land. The low hills and fields were hazed faintly golden.

The healthy earth glowing like a woman new with child, scarred only on yesterday's battlefield, where the marks of war-magic still burned black and painful. The earth's strength was brighter around them, as blood and corpses began to digest back into the soil. Alagrith was called mother and a goddess of Light, but it was not well to forget that she also received strength from the bodies of the dead.

Gudrun gazed lightly afar, looking for the faint ripples in the air that would hint at concealed troops or scouts, near, she scanned more closely, searching for traps set to go off after a certain time had passed, pursuant curses winging in towards the Company, or signs of untoward magic even among their own troops.

Her course took her around the length of the baggage train. Harm could be concealed among the disorderly civilian wagons more easily than among the Landsknechts themselves. She looked especially closely at the enemy prisoners. They might have given their parole, mostly, a few were chained up, but most were not but it wouldn't be too hard for something to be hidden even upon an unknowing person. Or a knowing one who might just decide to break his oath.

The damage, say, a mage-pomegranate could cause if it exploded in a man's pouch while the Company's Felscher or Feldarzt were bending over him. So caught up in her work, Gudrun's natural eyes almost missed the blood-red beret with its white feather walking beside one of the open sick-carts. She blinked, the spell breaking, and looked again. A Forlorn Hope cap, and shining blond hair below it, the broad-shouldered, narrow-waisted figure in full fluted armor, the hilt of a two-handed sword jutting up above one shoulder.

"What in all the hells of Darkness are you doing here?" Gudrun said aloud before she could stop herself. Her guards looked up at her enquiringly. Furious at herself, she glared back at them. After all Alberich had said earlier, for her to let uncontrolled words burst out like that – as stupid, in a mage, as dancing with one finger on the trigger of a loaded arquebus.

"Marshal?" The Man said, puzzled. She looked for his name, the long scar that split his face, a shiny track of pink running through left eyebrow and right mustache, should remind her.

"Tobias, fetch me that man. He shouldn't be here."

The guard followed the direction of her gaze – no uncontrolled gestures! Gave a low whistle as he took in the sign of Forlorn Hope.

"Right away, Marshal. Valin, you stay with her."

The Dwarf grunted, but shifted his grip on his halberd, deep-socketed dark eyes glancing about like a wild boar's from the thicket of his tangled brown eyebrows, hair, and cheekbone-high beard.

Tobias trotted over to the cart. They were too far away for Gudrun to hear anything without magic, but Wolfram drew the wavy-bladed great sword from its back sheath and handed it over to the guard. Then Tobias pointed at the slim bastard sword at Wolfram's waist. The half-Elf shook his head vehemently. Tobias reversed his grip on the two-hander, bringing its point up from the ground.

Gudrun sighed. It only took a little power to extend the range of her voice: she called sharply, "Tobias, let him keep the weapon. He's not under arrest, I just need to ask him a question."

Reluctantly, Tobias gave the great sword back to Wolfram, who sheathed it in a single smooth movement, and led him back to the Marshal's palfrey.

"What are you doing here?" Gudrun repeated as soon as he was close enough. "Have you been cleared?" Her heart fluttered for a moment like a sparrow trapped inside her ribs, but she clamped down on it ruthlessly, the red beret and white feather had answered that question already. The sparrow gave a broken-winged beat and died.

Wolfram's face went lifeless too, the gleam fading from his blue-green eyes. "No," he said flatly. "I received the parole of Lieutenant Ludwig yesterday. Our Schultheiss kindly granted me permission to act as his servant and guard until he is ransomed."

Normal courtesy to a wounded officer, but still, Gudrun thought, a shame to Wolfram, that he should be an orderly to a man of his own rank. Former rank.

He is alive!

"It is, I'm glad to see you survived," Gudrun offered stiffly.

A little more light gleamed in Wolfram's eyes, as though polished turquoise were emerging from beneath a film of mud.

"Thank you. I believe..." He stopped, cleared his throat. "I believe I owe it all to you."

There was something strange in his voice, almost hostile. I wasn't the one who fouled the truth-reading spell, Gudrun thought. Maybe he was at the edge of the falconet's blast when it went?

"For blowing up the falconet? I hope you weren't too close?"

Half of Wolfram's mouth twitched up into a smile. "If I had been, I'd be dead or in a sick-cart now. That was what happened to my prisoner. He got a shard of iron in the leg. No, you took out enough of their arquebus-men with that blast to give us a chance of making it up the hill."

Gudrun smiled wholeheartedly. "I am glad."

They both stood without anything to say for a moment. Get control of yourself, woman, Gudrun thought. Would you like Alberich to see you standing dumb as a stump for no good reason? "Well, I must continue with my duty. I only wanted to see why you were back here."

"Of course." Wolfram stood a moment, then took a step closer to her.

An arc of light flashed. Tobias' two-handed sword was suddenly slanted between them. "No closer to the Marshal," the guard growled.

"Is there something else you wanted to say?" Gudrun asked softly. Out here? In front of my guards?

"There is Marshal, may I speak privately with you?"

Gudrun looked from one guard to the other. Tobias was scowling. It was hard to read Valin's expression beneath all the hair, but his beard seemed to bristle more fiercely.

"I don't think so. Wait. May I enter your mind?" As soon as Gudrun had spoken, she realized what she had said. "No offense meant," she added hurriedly.

"I apologize...I didn't mean..." Elves consider mind-contact from human mages the height of personal invasion. I might as well have casually asked if I could rape him.

"Apologize for what?" Wolfram said, staring at her with a bewildered look on his fine-boned face. Gudrun stared back, confused and completely wrong-footed. "Of course you may, wait, this won't let you see everything in my mind or something, will it?"

"Of course not. A few surface thoughts, perhaps, no deep memories, unless I were to deliberately probe. I would never do that without permission, unless it were part of an authorized interrogation." Still, her heart sank as she spoke. *He doesn't want me to see that he was guilty as charged, and lied about it.*

"All right."

Gudrun breathed deeply to settle herself, staring into his eyes. It was like sinking into the water of the Middle Sea in summer. The same clear blue-green, rising about her like a warm bath and for a second her memory flashed an image from the Southern campaign two summers ago, the pale gold walls of Duke Federico's mansion above the beach, just outside Pompeio, the gritty sand beneath her feet and the line of goats trundling along the rock-scarred hill high over her head.

The mind-picture sank down and she could feel the clear line of resonance between Wolfram's skull and her own, the little flickers of Chaos through their brains harnessed to shape each one's thoughts to match the others, like a lesser version of Alberich's message-spell. *What is it you have to say?* She thought, feeling the echo in Wolfram's mind. *"My prisoner he claimed that Graf Berthold is paying them twenty-eight thousand guilders a month, on a six-month contract, and that the Sun Azure accepted first, rather than being left with the low bidder. I need to know whether he's telling the truth, or just trying to interfere with our morale."*

"Have you mentioned this to anyone else?"

"No. I need a mage who can cast a truth-reading spell correctly, and you're the only one who's proven you can. I don't want to mention the matter until it's proven and I don't want Ludwig to know I'm doing it. He spoke freely last night, but if we start questioning him under magic, that's perilously close to breaking the terms of his parole. I don't want to interrogate him. I just want to know if he's deliberately trying to foul us up, which is also close to breaking parole, in spirit if not letter."

"I see. How am I supposed to do this without him noticing?"

"How close do you have to be to cast the spell?"

"Within ten feet. Unless if you let me in a little deeper, so that I could look out through your eyes."

"All right, Wolfram agreed at once." Gudrun knew he could sense her surprise, but the link wasn't close enough for him to know why. She could just barely hear him thinking, I suppose most people are too frightened of mages to let them do this afraid they'll be made into puppets.

"I wish I'd thought to demand that my mind be read at my trial. Unless."

He's not guilty! Gudrun thought, too startled to hold the thought back out of reach of her spell.

"No. I'd hoped you believed me."

Now she could feel his sadness, sharp and crystalline as shattered glass between his ribs. *"If you will, I'll let you look at my memory of that night, if you promise to only read that, and no others"*. He paused, she could sense something going on in the back of his mind. A Man with no training couldn't have hidden his thoughts in the link like that, but the Elf-blooded? Who knew what Wolfram could do?

"Nothing after I woke up. Will you promise?"

"I don't know if I can do that, Gudrun answered regretfully. *I'm sorry but, you wouldn't have offered if you hadn't meant it. Alberich might be able to."*

"Could you ask him?"

"I'll try". Alberich had to be ordered to let Wilhelm check his work on the truth-reading. The chance that he would undertake a delicate, difficult working for the same purpose now.

"You don't think he will."

"No."

"But please ask him anyway. I want, I need to be cleared. Not forgiven, but cleared. Can you understand why? "

"Yes." She paused again – but Wolfram had given her truth, and a bit of his feelings, he deserved the same from her. I, too, know what it's like to be suspected of something shameful.

'As a woman among Landsknechts.

Of course.

Now, we have this to see to.

Carefully, deeper."

Gudrun had only done this a few times before. It would have been easier if she could simply close her eyes and lie down, letting all her awareness go with Wolfram. She had to stay on her horse and perform the spell. The double vision was the first thing that let her know it was working. At one and the same time, she was looking down from her horse at Wolfram's blue-green eyes, the silky fall of golden hair about the sharp clean lines of his face and she was looking up at her own green-gray eyes and dainty features, dark auburn hair gleaming beneath the dark green velvet folds of her wide floppy hat.

The large puffed and ribbon-slashed sleeves and the abundance of her skirt overwhelmed her small tight bodice. She looked like a finely-made doll in fashionable clothes of russet and gold. When Gudrun reached for her wand, her arm and hand felt like tongs of flesh being moved by something further back. Her guards had come in closer, fingering their weapons and looking suspiciously from Wolfram to her. Gudrun drew in a breath, this was one of the hardest parts, breathing without letting it bring her back to the center of her body and made her mouth and throat move, saying, "It's all right. Valin, take him back. I will need to concentrate for a while. Tobias, hold my horse's reins, and both stay close in case I begin to slip."

"Yes, Marshal," the Dwarf said. He took Wolfram by the arm, marching him back. Gudrun could feel the churning of the half-Elf's indignation and shame, the strength with which he resisted his own anger.

It was peculiar, almost dizzying, looking around from a man's height. Everyone seemed so much shorter, the wagons so much lower. She stayed with Wolfram as he returned to his captive. A handsome young man in, Gudrun guessed, his early twenties and about the same age Wolfram appeared to be, though of course the half-Elf could be centuries old. Ludwig's eyes were bright and his dark-tanned face slightly flushed with fever, but that was only to be expected.

With a relatively minor wound like his, he would be one of the last to be healed, unless his slight fever reached a dangerous level.

"What was that about?" The prisoner asked.

Slowly, carefully, Gudrun began her spell. It was easier transmitting it through Wolfram than it would have been through either an ordinary Man or another mage. It was as though he had a wider channel than a human, and no resistance at all.

"...Have expected that," Wolfram finished. For all the welling bitterness within him, he spoke lightly, showing no sign of his feelings.

"Well, if you survived yesterday, you must be hard to kill," his captive answered.

They talked casually for a little while. Lieutenant Ludwig was obviously in some pain, wincing at every sway and bump of the cart, but he seemed happy to talk, as though it were taking his mind from his wound. Wolfram poured out a cup of wine for him, some of it spilled with the cart's jolting, leaving blood-dark stains on the peacock-blue and brilliant yellow of Ludwig's slashed doublet, but he seemed to get a good amount inside him. Come on, Wolfram. I can't keep this up forever, Gudrun thought in the back of her mind.

She suppressed the thought ruthlessly, she could hold the two spells as long as she needed to.

"Have you seen the chapel to St. Hildebrand yet?" Wolfram was asking. "I've heard it's a marvel."

"Oh, yes. The officers got to attend a blessing there before we marched out. I'd never seen such carvings. It seems dull at first glance with no colors but the wood, mind. If we hadn't been in there so long, I'd hardly have noticed it. The carving itself is something impressive, but I'm not sure I like the idea of just plain wood hanging there. If the Graf had it painted, now, or slapped some gilding on, then it would really be impressive." Ludwig drained his cup and held it out for more.

"Don't know why he doesn't, really. It looks funny to have gold candlesticks lighting up the kind of bare woodwork you'd get in a peasant church where they can't afford gilding and don't know how to use that plaster stuff for covering real statues under the paint. He's got the money, and he's sure as shit not cheap with it."

"Sounds like. How much did you say he was paying you?"

"Twenty-eight thousand guilders a month, normal six-month contract," Ludwig said proudly and the truth-reading spell was still ringing clear in Gudrun's head. Had the Sun Azure Lieutenant lied, his voice would have degraded into a sort of squawking buzz, the sound of Chaos undirected.

At the very least, Ludwig believed everything he was saying. "I'm glad we were the ones to get in first. No offense to you, of course but every regiment has to look out for itself in cases like this."

All true, Gudrun thought, the words resonating in Wolfram's head. I don't know what it means but either he's been lied to himself, or he believes what he's saying, anyway. The threads of the spells were raveling thin, now, the tiny particles breaking away into the Chaos-void.

She could have gone deeper to strengthen them but, dimly, she could feel her own body shaking. If she tried to hold much longer, she would lose the strength she needed to finish her patrol. With a quick snap, she broke the lines, pulling deep into herself with several low, centered breaths. Tobias and Valin were staring up at her. Tobias' scarred face was tight with concern. Valin was, well hairy. "All is well," Gudrun told her Trabanten.

Though she wasn't sure it was, at all.

CHAPTER 15

Towards evening, word came back to the wagons at the end of the line that arrangements for the ransoming of the Silver Eagle's captives the next day had been made. Ludwig seemed pleased by the news, and was likewise in good spirits thanks to an herbal concoction which the Feldarzt had sent to him, which had lowered his fever and dulled the pain in his leg. Wolfram had checked the wound himself and, though it was a bit swollen and red about the edges, showed no sign of going seriously bad. Even without holy or magical aid, Wolfram thought it would probably heal cleanly enough.

Wolfram himself, however, was not finding it easy to keep up the pleasant chat with his captive. While Ludwig was an undemanding involuntary guest, his good cheer was helping to wear down Wolfram's nerves. Who can I tell? Who would listen to me? As Lieutenant in the Golden Bear, he would have gone to his captain. Hauptmann Heinrich, for all his efforts on Wolfram's behalf, had only looked through him coldly when they passed afterwards.

He was, Wolfram thought, convinced that his Lieutenant had not only gotten drunk on duty, but lied about it afterwards but lied well enough to fool Heinrich himself. Even if Wolfram survived four more battles in Forlorn Hope and was reinstated to his position, he was certain that he would not be holding it beneath the Golden Bear flag. One of the other Hauptmänner? Marcus, good-tempered and genial as he was, might let him speak. He would undoubtedly ask why Wolfram had not gone to Heinrich, and he might not see it as his affair in any case. The Obrist decided, the regiment obeyed. None of the other captains, Wolfram was quite certain, would listen to a wild story from a man in Forlorn Hope.

Would they listen to it from a Marshal? He wondered. That seemed like a much better idea to him. There was no stain on Gudrun's name, and Wolfram was certain that she had been as much distressed by the strangeness of the information as he had. Maybe, just maybe, she will speak to Heinrich about the possibility of getting Alberich to read my memory. If only she could do it without discovering the taint I bear. When the Silver Eagle halted for the day, Wolfram made his way to the Black Wagon under the pretext of going to fetch Lieutenant Ludwig's evening meal.

He was halted by the scar-faced human guard who had been accompanying Gudrun on her patrol around the column. Tobias, that was his name.

"What do you want?" Tobias asked roughly. "I need to speak with Marshal Gudrun."

Tobias shook his head. "The Zauberobrist gave us strict orders not to let anyone disturb the Black Wagon tonight for anything less than a major emergency. Is it?"

Maybe. It seemed to Wolfram almost as though he stood on the edge of a road that forked off in all directions, and he could see darkness and foul-colored flames burning down most of the pathways. He blinked to drive the fancy from his mind.

"I suppose not. At least, not in any way I want to explain to you."

"Then be off with you."

Wolfram made the rounds of the sutlers. The camp sounded and smelled less like a village market now, it had been a while since there was a chance for anyone to buy more livestock. Only a few geese and chickens still cackled from their crates, and nearly all of the pigs and sheep had been slaughtered, though some enterprising forager had collected a calf out of one of the fields on the way.

Frau Anna's boys had managed to slip away from the road and pot several fat hares, which Anna had roasting on spits now, basting them with a savory mixture of ver-juice and herbs. Wolfram paid for one to share between himself and Ludwig, though it would be a little time before it was done through. Together with the bread Anna let rise in her wagon and baked in big lidded pots set in the coals, it would make a good meal.

What will I do? Wolfram wondered. He had to get his information to someone who knew what to do with it before the captives were ransomed back, or there would be no way to confirm it. Even with Gudrun backing him up, if he waited until the primary proof were out of reach, his whole story would look that much more like another lie from a proven liar. His fists clenched. He forced them to unclench, trying to still the shaking in his hands.

I have to tell Heinrich. If he doesn't believe me, I'll talk to Marcus and if, well, if Marcus wouldn't believe him either, he would think of something else to do. He would follow this until it was explained, one way or another. It would have been almost impossible for a Man to pick out Hauptmann Heinrich's small black hat and somber clothes among the crowd at the sutlers' cook fires in the darkening twilight. Wolfram could still see as well as if it were bright day, a little recompense for all his tainted blood had brought him. No one spoke to him as he made his way through to the Hauptmann, though a few stared curiously at him, wondering, perhaps, what he was doing loose.

"Herr Hauptmann?" Wolfram said when he was too close for Heinrich to easily avoid him.

Heinrich looked up at him, then ostentatiously turned his back. Wolfram felt as though he had been punched in the belly with a Katzbalger. First the numbing blow that knocked his wind out, then the feeling of abdominal muscles clenching hard on the blade and the cold of steel inside and last the huge rending pain and sense of hopelessness that left most men writhing and screaming underfoot. But he could neither writhe nor scream. He had a duty to do. Wolfram leaned close to Heinrich's ear.

"Herr Hauptmann, if ever I served well under you, if ever I chopped through a pike that was pointed at you, or cut down the man whose Katzbalger was seeking your eye slot. Whatever you believe I've done or haven't done, for the sake of the regiment, will you listen to me now? If you doubt what I say, you can ask Marshal Gudrun of it tomorrow morning, or the man who told me tonight."

The close cut of Heinrich's burgundy doublet showed the angry set of his shoulders. His head moved, Wolfram heard the tiny sound of his spittle hitting the ground, and despaired for a moment. Then the Hauptmann turned, so tight-muscled with tension he seemed to jerk like a jointed wooden puppet, and spat out, "Tell me, then."

"Herr Hauptmann, this is best not said in public." I'm pushing him, Wolfram thought. But what else can I do?

If this is nothing after all, then it will do immense damage to start the rumor for all ears and if it is something, who knows what it will do?

Heinrich paused, his winged dark mustaches twitching jerkily as if to show by signs whatever invective his tight lips were holding back.

But at last he said, "Come on."

Heinrich stalked off, not looking back to see whether Wolfram was following him. The half-Elf trailed the Hauptmann to where the Golden Bear Fähnlein was camped beneath its ensign. Wolfram felt the Forlorn Hope cap burning like a torch of shame on his head, walking through his former men, his former friends. Little Kai, sitting by a campfire, glanced up from the piece of wood he was whittling, shook his misshapen head, and looked away. Maximilian spat on the ground; Ruprecht only stared, his thin pockmarked face sad and wondering.

Conversations hushed as Heinrich and Wolfram walked by, to rise again in a wave of curious and angry muttering. *I will never be free of this, unless I am cleared.* But that Wolfram had known. *This matter might be more important.* He had Gudrun behind him, both in his truth and his judgment of it and she knew him innocent. That cheered him more than he could have hoped. Heinrich stepped into his tent, gesturing Wolfram in with a single terse wave. It was really more a small pavilion than a tent, in truth: bell-shaped, large enough for a writing table and two chairs, with several lanterns hanging off the overhead spokes radiating out from the central pillar. He sat down, not offering Wolfram a chair.

"Say your say."

"One of the prisoners for ransom is an officer. He told me that they were getting twenty-eight thousand guilders a month from Graf Berthold, and said that they had made the choice of bids to accept first. Marshal Gudrun performed a truth-reading spell on him and confirmed it."

Heinrich leaned forward, his sharp face suddenly intent. "Is it a short contract?"

"Six months."

"Why didn't you bring Marshal Gudrun with you?"

"Because the Trabanten around the Black Wagon said that their orders were to allow disturbance tonight only in a major emergency. But you can ask Gudrun tomorrow. Or ask Lieutenant Ludwig yourself. He was quite happy to boast about it. I asked Gudrun to do the truth-reading to make sure he wasn't trying to spread trouble among us."

"Sit down."

Wolfram sat. Heinrich stared at him for quite a long time. The lantern-light darkened the creases on the Hauptmann's forehead and at the corners of his eyes to deep furrows: he looked suddenly old, tired, and troubled.

"If this is true," Heinrich said, "then something is very wrong. Either we have been lied to about our pay, in which case someone high up must be pocketing the difference, or the bidding was interfered with in some manner. Maybe Graf Berthold, outbid and outnumbered, decided to open his purse-strings wider for surety but though the Sun Azure is not a cheap company, twenty thousand a month would certainly have bought them.

Berthold has a name for wealth and generosity. I was, to be honest, surprised that Graf Sigfrid outbid him, though Sigfrid has never been the particular kind of fool who stints military expenses." He sighed deeply.

"Those were my thoughts as well, sir," Wolfram said.

Heinrich regarded him for a little longer. "It took nerve for you to approach me with this, after having been proven a liar." He paused. Wolfram was about to speak when the Hauptmann continued. "Then, you have never lacked for courage."

"Besmirched as my name has been, I could hardly have gone to anyone without the knowledge of Gudrun's witness to support me. But I had to do it tonight, while the prisoners were still with us, in case you wanted to speak to Ludwig yourself." Wolfram added, "it may be that my name will yet be cleared. Spells can fail, but I have asked Gudrun to request the Zauberobrist to read my memories of that night." And I would not have done that if I were guilty.

Heinrich coughed. "Either you are a better liar than I thought even after your performance in prison and court, or you are telling the truth. I wish I could give you the benefit of the doubt, but how?"

"Add your voice to Gudrun's in speaking to the Zauberobrist," Wolfram said at once. "Or ask Schultheiss Otto if he will order it."

The Hauptmann shook his head sadly. "I fear that once a case is closed, it is closed, unless some startling new evidence is unearthed. Though usually it is too late for that, which is why we have no provisions for a retrial.

I am not Gemeinweibel this month, and even if I were, I could hardly see our Provost consenting. He is a man of great and rigid rectitude, who was not unimpressed, say, rather, counter-impressed with your performance at the trial. If you survive to come out of Forlorn Hope, I will help to arrange a mage's further investigation.

If you have told the truth, I will owe you a very large apology and you will be welcome beneath the Golden Bear again. If you have lied to me as I thought, and once more about the same." He shook his head.

"Regretfully, the Orders have no provisions for punishing personal lies. Be assured, I shall find some way to make you regret it."

"If the mage can find the truth, you will discover that I have told the truth," Wolfram said stiffly.

Heinrich waited a moment to see if he would say any more, then nodded.

"We shall see. In the meantime, say nothing to anyone else about this other matter. Remember that, except when the Empire calls us up, we do not crusade for Light against Darkness, or any such cause. It is not our duty to enforce anything save the Emperor's will and our own Orders, and to fight for our employers as we are paid to do.

If someone within this regiment has offended so greatly against our rule and custom, I trust it will be found out. Now, go, and remember to keep silent."

Wolfram bowed and departed. All through the Golden Bear's camp, he had to breathe deeply to keep his muscles from tightening up. He could feel the looks falling on him like stave-blows. He felt as if he were scouting in hostile territory, every sound coming more keenly to his ears, every flicker of movement registering more sharply at the corner of his eyes, as he waited for the attack to strike him. No one struck him, no one even spoke to him as he walked out, back to collect his hare and bread from Frau Anna, buy another bottle of wine, and bring Lieutenant Ludwig his dinner. His ears still rang with Hauptmann Heinrich's last speech.

What did he mean about not crusading? Wolfram wondered. What does that have to do with a question about the details of the campaign's bidding and hire? What does he know that I might know, were I still his Lieutenant? Wolfram shook his head as if to rid himself of a swarm of flies buzzing into his ears and nose. He had done his duty. Hauptmann Heinrich would be able to deal with the problem from here.

CHAPTER 16

udrun waited in the Black Wagon until Wilhelm had left on his first patrol around the column. Alberich was reading one of the heavy leather-bound books from the sealed chest that was forbidden to the younger mages. A few minutes passed before he seemed to notice that she was still there.

"Are you delaying for a reason, Marshal?" He asked, dry voice ominous.

"Sir. I have a request to make of you, sir."

"Out with it, you're late for your duty."

Gudrun breathed deeply to calm herself. Alberich's gaze bore down on her like a pressing-board with more stones being added every moment. She wanted to quail and flee to her duty. But a man's life and honor are at stake.

"Sir, it has occurred to me that, since former Lieutenant Wolfram challenged our truth spells twice, after demanding them himself, that it might be worthwhile to seek out his actual memory of the night of his arrest. That would clarify matters beyond."

Gudrun's voice ran down. Alberich was looking coldly down his narrow aquiline nose at her, thin lips drawn up into a disapproving frown.

She had been used to that expression from him, but knowing that he could smile with pride made it much worse.

"I am disappointed in you, Gudrun," he said coldly. "Do you respond to praise by abandoning your effort?"

"No, sir!" Gudrun answered, deep auburn braids flying with the vehemence of her head-shake. "My concern was for proving the accuracy of our spells beyond supposition, or identifying their inaccuracy for correction and for the overall sake of the regiment. Wolfram was a very competent officer," she added quickly.

Alberich's voice was very quiet, almost gentle, and yet it chilled Gudrun in a way that even the Zauberobrist's sharpest rages or most biting sarcasms had never managed. "I trust," he said, "that you have not been thinking continuously about the incident, or about the Elf-blood, since it occurred?"

"No, sir!" Gudrun repeated. That was true enough, if word-splitting. She had thought about other things as well.

"If you must know, both Wilhelm and I have privately tested our performance of the truth-reading spell, separately and in each other's presence. Privately, of course, because it would not do at all." Alberich put no more emphasis on those words than any others, but they sank piercingly into Gudrun's ears like drops of ice-cold wintergreen oil, filling her skull with their keen chill intensity. "To have our Company thinking that its Zauberobrist and Marshals doubted their own abilities at that most crucial judicial enchantment. Are you satisfied, Marshal?"

No. "Sir," Gudrun said, feeling like a swimmer in a dark underground stream who had gone too far to turn back before drowning, and now could only press on in desperate hope that she would find air ahead, "I spoke with Wolfram when I established that his enchanted sword carried no charm of invulnerability, and have had occasion to observe him briefly on patrol. He seems to still believe himself innocent. Further, I find it entirely possible that a spell might fail twice on one of the Elf-blooded and yet work perfectly on a Man. Sir, I still think it would be best if you read his memory."

Alberich looked at her for a very long time. At first it seemed to Gudrun that she could feel her heart curling up and shriveling like a spider in a flame, but after a while, she realized to her great surprise that the look on his face was one of contemplation, not glacier-cold rage.

"His blood would create a difficulty in the process," the Zauberobrist said. "With a Man, I might pluck out a memory whole. With an Elf, even half an Elf, I would have to search through the entirety of his mind, not so much to find it as to make sure it was real and not a memory-dream such as they construct for themselves in their long contemplations.

"You see," Alberich went on, "Elves, among their many abilities, are not only capable of reliving events from the past within their minds. They are actually capable of changing them."

Gudrun's eyebrows shot up. Surely no one could change the past? There would be no history, no reality.

"Not in actuality, understand. But an Elf could, oh, for instance, go back to the night when he chose to bring a flask of spirits on duty and, reliving it, choose not to experience a long and boring watch, relieved in the morning. To continue in his post, and so forth. Intellectually he would still know what had happened, but emotionally the shame, self-disgust, whatever you will, would be gone, the true memory faded into a page from a history book with no emotional content. He could even, deliberately, have lived a memory when he stayed sober that night, but was struck down by surprise, awakening to find himself in a cell, framed by someone who had knocked him out, poured spirits over him and left his head on a rock to account for the blow to it.

In my opinion, that may have been why Wolfram thought he could beat the spell of truth-reading. A full-blooded Elf might have been able to, at that."

Gudrun realized that her mouth was hanging open like a dimwitted peasant's. She shut it hastily. But I was in his mind. I am quite certain he did no such thing. It is theorized that this ability is one of the things allowing Elves their length of life. They do not have to bear a Man's burden of sorrows and shames. To them, the dead live in memories in a way we can never know. An Elf who has lost loved ones need only return to the time of loss and recreate it differently to experience their continuing lives.

"And, in addition to the innate difficulties regarding working mind-magic on this Wolfram, well, to begin with, we know him only by a false name. A Man's name, at that. No hint or key to his nature. We have no way of knowing his true age, his history, or his magical training. My guess, if his style of fighting is related to his origins in any way, that he might be from Broceliande, but that is only a guess. Therefore, such a work could present a grievous danger to me. More, it would require at least a full day and night to undertake. Then I would spend as long or longer recovering." Alberich paused. "However, if he is willing to consent to open his entire mind to me to the degree necessary, then I will consent to perform the deed as soon as our duties permit."

Gudrun forced her face to a mask of stillness, but she could not keep her heart from leaping, its thudding echoing out to its fingertips.

"I think that would be well, sir. Do you wish me to inform him, or would you prefer for the choice to come from the Schultheiss?"

Alberich's gray eyebrows drew together. "I do not intend to suggest reopening the case unless there is real evidence it is necessary. Marshal Wilhelm shall inform him. You are forbidden to speak with him, or otherwise contact him, unless military need requires it or he is cleared, and ordered to use your mental skills to your best ability to erase him from your mind. Is that clear?"

"Yes, sir," Gudrun replied neutrally.

The Zauberobrist's gaze sharpened, a thin cold line of blue steel piercing into Gudrun's skull.

"That is not merely an order, but a battle-order. Those who fight with powder and blade, engage only when the enemy is within range of their weapons. We must be constantly vigilant of mind. For a mage, to allow yourself distraction on a campaign, whether you are moved by considerations of justice or something more personal." He paused, giving her a long searching stare.

Gudrun's heart thudded more quickly again, quick as the beating of the regiment's drums when they drove the soldiers forward into battle, but she stood up under her superior's glare. "I trust, for your sake, it is not," Alberich said.

The deadly mildness in his voice sent a chill shivering through Gudrun's nerves. She hoped with all her heart that Alberich, great mage that he was not so great as to be able to read her mind without her sensing it. "In any case, to allow yourself distraction in the middle of a campaign, in circumstances where it interferes with your duty, is the equivalent of turning away in the middle of battle. The punishment is the same, immediate death on the field, execution afterwards, or consignment to Forlorn Hope. We have had two women in the last ten years who chose Forlorn Hope. One killed herself, and the other was killed fighting her fellow malefactors before their first battles.

And your wand would certainly be confiscated before you were put into camp."

Now Gudrun was certain that Alberich had guessed at her attraction, be honest with yourself to Wolfram. For all her self-control, she could not keep herself from shivering at the thought of being thrown, defenseless, in with Gottschalk. Or, if the man who had assaulted her was dead now, men like him. Nor would a mage have even a forlorn hope of surviving such a charge as the one Wolfram had endured the day before.

"I understand, sir," Gudrun said stiffly. "By my oath as your student, and my oath to the Silver Eagle, I shall obey."

"Good. It would displease me greatly to lose you, whether to a misplaced sense of justice or a common wench's folly. As a mage, you must be above both. I believe that you are, do not disappoint me. Consider the very great risk I am willing to undertake for you in dealing with the mind of this Elf, whatever your motivation for speaking to me on his behalf is, and be content with that."

"Yes, sir," Gudrun whispered. Shattered as she was by the Zauberobrist's order, his words still fanned that kernel of warmth in her heart that yesterday's praise had kindled. Alberich was, indeed, showing her more than a matching loyalty in making his offer. Which she had been certain he would not do even when she had no idea of the risk and effort to him: how could she not obey him willingly now?

"Go do your duty, Marshal."

Wolfram stayed with Lieutenant Ludwig until they had reached the place appointed for ransoming the prisoners, a wide-open meadow with a few cows grazing on it, too far from hills or woods for an ambush to be possible, and split by a broad, slow-flowing stream. The captives were gathered under guard by the single bridge crossing the stream, a log bridge just wide enough for a small cart to rumble slowly across. A little table was set up near the middle of the bridge where the Obrist's scribe would tally names and receive prices.

Alberich stood on the bridge as well, flanked by the bailiff in his gray cloak and the Freimann in his red. He would guard against any magical trickery.

"You!" The Provost called to Wolfram. "What are you doing here?"

"Tending to Lieutenant Ludwig, at our Schultheiss' behest, sir."

"That duty has ended. Return to Forlorn Hope at once."

Wolfram did not even sigh. He had hoped that Gudrun would speak to Alberich, no, he had been certain of that. He had hoped that Alberich would listen to her. A forlorn hope, indeed, he said grimly to himself.

"Farewell, then," Ludwig said, clasping Wolfram's arm. The Sun Azure Lieutenant was already hobbling a little with the help of a stick. He could not walk far, but should be able to make it across the bridge on his own.

"Donmar and St. Hildebrand see you alive through your next battles. Though, I hope you don't kill many of us in the process. When this is over, Gods of Light willing, I'll meet you in a tavern somewhere and buy you a beer."

"May it be so," Wolfram answered. "It's been an honor to know you. I hope we're fighting on the same side next time."

"So do I. Gods go with you, my friend."

The Forlorn Hope was stationed off to the side, perhaps an hundred and fifty yards from the bridge, fully armed.

If any treachery occurred, they would be responsible for the first charge in to blunt its teeth and buy time for the rest of the Company to respond. Fredrik and Sascha were standing over Wolfram's armor, casting ominous glances at anyone coming too close.

"Want help?" Fredrik asked.

"Thank you." Between them, they got Wolfram quickly into harness.

His gambeson was still chilly and damp. It took a long time for soaked padding to dry completely but as warm as the day was, that would do him no harm. If I even can catch chill, Wolfram thought. He had as a child, disguised by enchantment. Now that he thought of it, he could not remember being sick since his transformation. Revelation. Whichever. One more penny of gain against the guilders of loss.

The Sun Azure was just coming into view past the most distant line of hills now, a column of toy soldiers armed with a long forest of sparkling needles and bannered with tiny scraps of cloth, so far away even Wolfram could barely make out the devices. He glanced back down at the captives. He had left Ludwig with a half-flask of wine and some bread and hard sausage: the Lieutenant was sitting comfortably with his back propped against a chocked cartwheel, eating and talking to several of his fellow-prisoners as the wine passed around. If Hauptmann Heinrich wants to talk to him, he had better do it soon, Wolfram thought.

Hopefully Heinrich had already spoken to Gudrun. Wolfram had no doubt that the dapper captain would not have taken his word alone. It would seem odd, for a Hauptmann to break ranks to ask such a question of a man about to be ransomed. Thank Donmar and Alagrith that Gudrun had the rear patrol yesterday! The sound of the Landsknecht drums and fifes carried a long way: far off as they were, Wolfram could already hear the faint whistle of the pipes. The drums, he felt rather than heard, the slightest rhythmic shivering in the warm summer air. He wondered idly if Arkoniel and Piriel could make out the Sun Azure's marching tune. In the four years of his exile, he had not dared to inquire about Elves of any sort, lest he betray the depths of his strangeness by the depths of his ignorance and hence raise suspicion.

Had his birth never been revealed, he would still have died to defend his home, his father, Graf Ulric and his brother. Since his disappearance was the best defense they would allow him, he was as resolved now as when he had left to make sure that no one would ever be able to link Wolfram the Landsknecht to Wolfram, the vanished second son of Graf Ulrich. The unnatural clarity of memory rose up to whelm him unbidden, the day he had joined the Silver Eagle. The town of Eckendorf was set in the angle where a small river flowed into a greater, far to the south of sea-guarding Löwenstein.

Down here, the sharp dark angles of wood set against whitewashed house fronts, the Fachwerk of the north, were seldom seen, instead, tiled roofs rose to sharp peaks to shed the heavy inland snows. Low mountains rose on either side of the rivers, their coats of summer-green trees slashed with outcroppings of jagged gray rock. The towers of a small fortress-castle stood dark against the sky on the western height a little south of the town: Wolfram had seen an hundred like it on the way down the river. It was no match for Löwenstein. If Graf Ulric's son had come to it, he, well above the lord's station, would have been a greatly honored guest but Wolfram had shunned castles and manors on his way as if the Plague raged in each one. Eckendorf's marketplace was full that day, bustling with the rich trade the rivers brought.

Vinters haggled over wine barrels or offered sips of wine to
wealthy-looking passers-by, fishers displayed pike and blue trout
and catfish. One of the odd whiskered fish was bigger than any river-
fish Wolfram had ever seen, a good six feet long, though no match
for some of the mighty finned creatures some of his father's men
brought in from the deep sea. There were booths with round cheeses
from the size of Wolfram's hand to the size of his outstretched
arms. Chickens, ducks, and geese cackling from their crates, bolts of
cloth, rough hemp and wool, smooth linen, with a few pieces of silk,
velvet, and brocade displayed beside them to tempt buyers to closer
inquiry.

Salt herring and cod brought upriver from the sea, beeswax
and tallow candles, ironwork and leather word, eating-knives and
fighting-knives. Wolfram thought wistfully of his shrinking hoard of
money, and remembered, too, why he had come to this market on
this day. Although Wolfram wore a green homespun hood to hide
the distinctive points of his ears, he could not hide his face, nor the
sound of his voice. He had learned to speak as little as possible, but
people still stared at him, marking the Elvish lines of his features.
At least Men could not tell one breed of Elf from another without
magic. The first weeks of Wolfram's flight had been spent in dread
that, revealed as kin to the cruel raiders from the sea, he would be
taken and burnt without hope of recourse.

Still, for one whose hope was to pass unnoticed, the near-
reverence that most men showed for Elves and Elf-blooded was
almost as bad. Even were it not for the marks of his birth, his
armor would draw nervous glances where-ever he went. To avoid
questioning by local watchmen and small lords, Wolfram had
carried it in a bag for almost his whole journey, but he knew better
than to leave it unguarded in the inn, and he wanted to make his
value clear to the recruiters. Wolfram set himself to ignore the way
everyone seemed to stare at him. Soon he could do his business and
be done. The Sun stood overhead now. The notes of the midday
hour rang out from the great clock in Eckendorf's chapel tower.

At first the sound of the drum seemed like a lingering echo underneath the clock's chimes, but it grew louder and louder, cutting through the sound of the crowd. Wolfram made his way towards the middle of the square as most other folk moved backwards, until he was at the edge of an empty space. At the eastern side, a cannon was set up with two men sitting beside it. One, a little scribe in a plain long robe with a quill in his hand and ink pot on a little table before him, was unremarkable. The other more than made up for him. Not just massive, but immense, Wolfram guessed that the Landsknecht recruiting officer was twice his own weight, plus fifty pounds or so.

The puffed and slashed sleeves of his brilliant red doublet made his great arms into an ogre's. The slashing over his huge chest and belly showed white linen through the red wool like wounds in reverse. The width of his chest displayed a number of thick gold chains: clearly he had done well among the Landsknechts.

One of his tree-trunk legs was covered by a puffed and gartered half-breech of yellow wool slashed in ribbons to display bright blue hose; gigantic thigh and calf muscles bulged against the tight red and black-striped hose on the other leg. The two-handed sword over his broad back looked like a toy against his size. Despite his fearsome looks, however, the round face beneath the brim of the Landsknecht's wide red hat was remarkably pleasant, snub-nosed, clean-shaven, and smiling.

The drums fell silent with a final flourish, the big man lumbered to his feet, flourishing a gold-ribboned parchment with a shimmering golden seal upon it. He was only an inch or two taller than Wolfram, to the latter's surprise, but his breadth more than made up for it.

"Hear ye, hear ye," he called out, his voice carrying strongly over the muttering of the crowd and the occasional calls of, "Fresh fish!" "Buy my chickens, fattest chickens in Eckendorf!"

"Hear the patent of Freiherr Helmuth von Wesenburg, Obrist of the Silver Eagle. 'Let it be known that We, Emperor Maximilian the Younger, do grant unto Freiherr Helmuth von Wesenburg a further continuance of his right to raise and maintain a regiment of Landsknechts as their Obrist for a term of ten years or until released by Imperial decree. Let it be known that Obrist Helmuth von Wesenburg owes his first duties to the Empire, which shall override all other contracts, though compensation shall be offered if a contract is interrupted. Let it be known that, so he fights not against the Empire, and comes when the Empire calls him, Obrist Helmuth von Wesenburg shall have the right to take other contracts at will and to recruit whensoever he has need. Let it be known that Obrist Helmuth von Wesenburg shall have the duty and right to enforce the common Orders of the Landsknechts upon those soldiers sworn to him, and to employ such officers and means of justice as are required to enforce those Orders.

This do We, Emperor Maximilian the Younger, state and seal upon this twelfth day of February, in the seventeen hundred and fifty-first year of the Era of St. Hildebrand, patron of the Empire."

The recruiting officer grinned at the crowd, flinging his big arms wide.

"Step up, step up! Who'll be a Landsknecht, the glory of the Empire and the terror of our foes! Feared by all men, loved by all women or the other way around for our fighting ladies and starting at four guilders a month. That's twice what you can earn laboring in town, and it goes up to eight if you're skilled with halberd, two-hander, or arquebus! Your birth doesn't matter, a peasant lad can shake the cow dung from his shoes and rise to Hauptmann at forty guilders a month, or even higher. Come up, give your name, and take your coin from the gun barrel. We'll tell you where to muster, and then you'll be a Landsknecht!"

The line was already forming when the recruiting officer sat down, quite a number of young men and a couple of sturdy farm girls making their way around the edges of the disintegrating clearing. Wolfram had to nudge backs a couple of times, but generally walked in a space of his own. When he reached the cannon, the recruiting officer looked at him closely, genial smile fading. "You really want to join the Landsknechts?"

"Yes, sir."

"Hmm. You swear that you're not a fugitive from any law?"

"I swear it," Wolfram said at once.

"You know that there are no privileges for race in the Company? You'll be expected to do as any other soldier does, follow the commands you're given, and obey the Orders just as a Man must?" He looked pointedly at Wolfram's armor – good fluted work, too expensive for any but a nobleman or very successful mercenary. "The same is true regarding whatever rank you might have among your own folk. Or anywhere."

"I understand that, sir."

The big officer's face grew thoughtful. "We have a couple of Elves, but that's all. Do you think you might want to talk to them before making your decision?"

"No, sir."

The Landsknecht sighed, nodding to the scribe. "Your name?"

"Wolfram Longsword."

The big man folded his immense arms across his chest. "That's your name?"

"The only name I have, sir," Wolfram told him. He could feel his legs beginning to tremble, just a little bit.

If the Silver Eagle wouldn't take him, it was hard to imagine any legitimate regiment that would, and he had made no other plans. Please, dear gods. If you'll hear me at all. I've come so far already; please let them take me!

"Write it down," the officer ordered. "Age?"

Wolfram stared at him. Little as he knew about Elves, he did know that they considered questions about their age, at least from Men, to be rude beyond belief. After a moment, the Landsknecht sighed. "If you were human, I'd say you were about twenty. Put down twenty. Occupation?"

"Soldier."

"Fine. I'll give you your coin and muster point, but understand that the Obrist will have to make the final decision about you. We don't take criminals except for the Forlorn Hope, and if Obrist Helmuth thinks there's too much risk in taking you, we won't take you even for that. If you were stupid enough to volunteer. Nothing personal. If you can work in with us, I think you'll be a fine one to have. I'm Hauptmann Marcus of the Sleeping Wolf Fähnlein. Welcome, I hope." He laid a penny on the gun barrel; Wolfram reached to pick it up.

"Wolfram?" An uncertain, snuffly voice was saying in his ear. Wolfram jerked back to the present, blinking the gleam of copper against blackened metal from his eyes.

"Yes?"

It was Marshal Wilhelm addressing him. Wolfram looked at the weedy mage, wondering for just a moment what Wilhelm could want with him. Then his heart fluttered, had Alberich sent the boy to read his mind now? To free him, end the constant, gut-gnawing rage and shame?

"I have a message for you from the Zauberobrist," Wilhelm said uncertainly. Every nerve in his body suddenly pulled twanging-tight between a sudden exaltation of hope and bowel-knotting fear, Wolfram wanted to grab him and shake it out of him.

"Tell me!" Wolfram tried to keep his voice even, but some of his savage desperation must have shown in his face. Wilhelm's pale cheeks blanched even further, and he took half a step backwards.

"The Zauberobrist says that he will examine your memory."

Wolfram felt the grin aching at the corners of his mouth, but Wilhelm was still talking. "Through the entire contents of your memory, to be sure he has separated true events from the Elvish memory-dreams. That will require at least two days of Company inactivity. But at least,"

Wolfram felt as though a bucket of melting snow had been sloshed through his body, freezing his heart and lungs, pooling cold in his entrails. It was not the unlikely chance that the Zauberobrist would have two days without duties in the middle of a campaign, deep in hostile territory. He could have borne the thought of gambling his life on the bad odds of four more battles with Forlorn Hope.

Wolfram could not, could not allow anyone to go through the whole of his memory. To discover, not only his taint, but his secret. Not even my secret to give away.

It belongs to the Graf von Löwenstein, the hidden sapper's mine that could bring Löwenstein down.

"Please tell the Zauberobrist that I appreciate his offer. I would gladly have that one memory read, that my name be cleared. I cannot open the contents of my mind beyond that to any man. I am sorry."

Wilhelm nodded, too rapidly, several times. "Yes, yes. I'll tell him. Thank you." The Marshal hastened away, the hem of his deep burgundy robe fluttering behind him like the tail of a sunken flag.

Wolfram wanted to weep, to scream, to draw his sword and throw himself against the whole regiment in a fit of blood-soaked fury. Since he could do none of those things, he bit deeply into his lip until the sharp pain brought him to himself, the familiar salt-copper taste of his blood trickling down his tongue and throat. He could bear it, he would have to.

Now, whether he died or lived in shame, Wolfram had something other than outraged innocence to stiffen him to his fate. No one but himself and the gods would ever know what he had done in rejecting Alberich's offer. What he suffered was part of the defense of Löwenstein, paying his endless debt to Graf Ulric and making real his love for his brother. Rudiger would have kept me in spite of the danger to himself. I can do no less than make sure he is spared that threat, regardless of the danger to me.

Wolfram turned his gaze back to the captives, looking for Ludwig, but couldn't see him. Probably, Wolfram thought, the Lieutenant was lying down in one of the carts to rest, gathering his strength so that he could walk back to his Company on his own two feet instead of being carried. Wolfram truly did wish him well, Ludwig seemed a strong man, and a good one, reminding Wolfram of several of the youths which whom he had done squire service. It was only a shame that they had met as captor and captive, at a time when Wolfram was in no state to enjoy the other's cheery company.

The Sun Azure drew up two hundred yards from the stream. Several men walked out. A scribe followed by a soldier loaded down with a little table, a stool, and a small but apparently heavy chest, a mage, a man in full armor with his visor up, probably their Obrist Arnolf von Lichtenfels, and the eight soldiers of his Trabanten surrounding him. Obrist Helmuth and his own eight-man Trabanten came out from the Silver Eagle ranks at about the same time. Odd, how suspicious both sides are this time, Wolfram thought. Ransoms and prisoner exchanges were normally times of truce between Landsknecht units. To attack during such a peace would be the act of a renegade band, probably leading to disallow by the Emperor. Yet we are both taking the kind of care we did when dealing with the troops of Ravennia down South.

On the other hand, Sigfrid's heavy cavalry is with us, I, at least, don't know where the rest of his troops are, and I don't think I would trust their Graf if he were my foe, no matter what oath was sworn. Perhaps, in a war so bitter, our Obrist feels the same way about Graf Berthold. Or, doesn't trust Sigfrid's troops either?

The two leaders met in the middle of the bridge. Helmuth handed Arnolf a lengthy parchment, the list of all the captives, those still alive and those who had died since being recorded, and the agreed-on prices of their individual ransoms. It would be signed by himself and witnessed by Vater Franz and Alberich. Arnolf looked closely at it, nodded, and they clasped wrists, gauntlets to greaves. Helmuth and Arnolf crossed back to their own sides of the bridge, the Sun Azure scribe set up his own table opposite his counterpart's and the exchange began.

Each man gave his name to the Silver Eagle scribe, took the few steps across the bridge's width, and identified himself to the Sun Azure scribe, who marked his tally, gave him his ransom, and let him cross again to pass it to the Silver Eagle scribe. The mages stood staring into nothingness: Wolfram felt a faint tingle in the air, and guessed that the Sun Azure mage was ensuring that no enemy trooper crossed in the guise of one of his own men. As for Alberich, who knew? Making sure that the ransom coin was no illusion, perhaps, or looking for other forms of treachery beyond a non-mage's imagining.

There were nearly sixty surviving prisoners. The slow crossing took a while, especially since a number of the men had to be helped across. Wolfram thought resentfully that Alberich might at least have let him stay to assist Ludwig. He did offer me an aid which he didn't have to, at some possible cost to himself. Wolfram wondered if his efforts to discover what was behind Lieutenant Ludwig's boast had at least partially redeemed him in the Provost's eyes. If the matter had come to Alberich yet, but what else could have moved him to a change of heart, when before he had grudged Wolfram a second Truth-Reading? Wolfram had expected Ludwig to cross by himself but perhaps, after all, the Lieutenant had found the effort of walking on his wounded leg too great.

It was only when the last of the injured had been carried across, and the two scribes' assistants come to pick up their burdens and return to the ranks, that Wolfram could believe that his captive had utterly disappeared sometime between when Wolfram had said farewell to him and when the exchange had begun. How? Why? When was simple enough. There had been plenty of time when Wolfram wasn't watching the prisoners. Putting his armor on, lost in the unexpected rise of overwhelming memory, talking to Wilhelm. But why? He was registered as being captured and having given parole. How could he have disappeared from the list?

Not by magic, surely, with a Zauberobrist from each side keeping a close watch on everything involved with the ransom process.

Could Hauptmann Heinrich have taken him away to talk to? Or, could he have disappeared for, not interrogation as such, but verification? It was a comforting thought: Wolfram didn't know how likely it might be. It depended, he thought, on how far up the chain of command his information had gone. Perhaps, on where the corruption had crept in? If the deception originated within the Silver Eagle, rather than, say, with Graf Sigfrid himself, or as a collusion of the two? Despite the fact that his clammy padded under-armor had warmed up and was making him sweat a little as the summer sun beat down on the metal of his full harness, Wolfram felt suddenly cold.

If something has happened to Ludwig, am I to blame?
Almost certainly.
Wolfram resolved himself to speak to Hauptmann Heinrich again that night, however he had to do it. He no longer had the freedom of the camp, but Fredrik and Sascha did. However many people thought the Forlorn Hope's two volunteers mad, there was no one who did not respect them. Or at least Fredrik. Sascha was just a little too crazy, even for a Landsknecht.

CHAPTER 17

"Can you tell me why you want to talk to Hauptmann Heinrich?" Fredrik asked Wolfram that evening, cocking his head and looking curiously at the half-Elf.

"I think it would be better not to. But I have to talk to him. Please."

"All right, my friend. If you don't want to tell me, then I won't ask you any more questions. I'll see if he's willing to come in here."

Wolfram waited patiently by their campfire. The flames leaped and twined, a pattern of yellow and orange and red slashed against the dark logs. A seductively enchanting pattern: several times Wolfram found his eyes trying to follow it, his mind fading into a strange clearness where there was nothing but the shifting of the flames, and had to force himself back into full awareness with a twitch like that of a tired sentry jerking his drooping head back up from his chest before he could slip entirely into sleep. At last Wolfram turned away from the fire, looking out into the camp. He could see, quite clearly, the other Forlorn Hope men gathered about their own fires, in small knots or sitting and brooding by themselves.

Drunken, angry songs rose from some of the fires from others, there was only sullen muttering. He was glad that he had missed the first two nights after the battle, when the survivors gave in to relief and hate, and the newly condemned tried to drink or fight out their resentment and fear. The unit was smaller than it had been: more than half their number had been killed in the charge up the hill. *That means that the rest of us are more likely to die next time,* Wolfram thought dispassionately. He looked to see who he could recognize among the survivors. Gottschalk, *Alagrith shrink his balls!* Was still alive, and Jürg. Michael, whom Wolfram had thrown into his burning tent, was gone, as was Erich.

Wolfram would never need to worry about Red Dirk's grudges again, he, too, lay stripped and bloating in the pit where the bodies had been shoveled. Of the other faces Wolfram had grown to recognize, if not know, on the march to Graf Sigfrid's lands, perhaps two dozen were still alive. The man with the big wen on the side of his nose was gone. Was the fat fellow who had been condemned to Forlorn Hope for slitting his comrades' purses, and the tall gaunt one whose forehead bore the brand of a black boar's head beneath the letter G. The emblem marking a rapist's face with the stamp of Gurvethor as the Dark Ravager had marked his soul.

Of the three criminals who had chosen the probable doom of the Landsknechts' battles to the certainty of Freihafn's executioner, only the lanky blond one was left, staring at a small fire by himself with a brooding, coiled intensity that made Wolfram think of an iron throwing-pomegranate, its fuse smoldering slowly down towards the half-pound of gunpowder within. At the edge of the guarded area, heads were turning, human eyes blinking against the darkness. Fredrik was coming back in, and Wolfram could tell he was unhappy.

What went wrong? Did Gudrun? Surely she wouldn't have denied what she found? Unless she was afraid to speak, afraid to admit she had worked magic without permission on an officer who had given parole.

"I'm sorry," Fredrik said gently when he reached Wolfram. "He wouldn't see you."

Wolfram swallowed hard. "When things seem worst is when you need most to keep your head," Graf Ulric had told him once. "To hold your wits about you in the middle of disaster: that is the mark of a man."

"Did he say why?" Wolfram asked. "Can you tell me what exactly he said?"

Fredrik sighed. "He said, 'Tell Wolfram not to speak to me again. Tell him whatever the labor schedule for camp is, he is on latrine duty for the next week.' Then he turned his back and walked away. That's all. I'm really sorry I couldn't do better for you."

"That's, thank you, in any case. At least you tried."

"Is there anyone else you could talk to about whatever it is?"

Gudrun. Or, would Alberich help? No, until Wolfram knew more, he couldn't try to trust in any of the regiment's senior officers. He might not be able to trust Gudrun as he had thought.

"Not now. Thank you for trying," Wolfram said again.

For a moment he wondered if he might do well to explain the situation to Fredrik. But he had already seen his friend's explosive temper in the face of wrongdoing, and he knew how little Fredrik was cowed by rank. Not a fault, necessarily. Indeed, Wolfram respected him the more for it. But if Fredrik knew what Wolfram had heard, he would go shouting straight to the Obrist, demanding that something be done. Wolfram might already have brought ill to one man today by sending his news up the ranks. There was no reason to make it two.

It was possible that Heinrich was making his own quiet investigations, and being seen speaking to Wolfram, when he had undoubtedly voiced his opinion of the half-Elf widely after Wolfram's trial, would compromise them. Given a choice between that theory, and the other options, that Gudrun had betrayed him from cowardice, or that Hauptmann Heinrich had been sucked into whatever corruption might be going on. He would choose it in a moment. *Heinrich is making his own investigations, and Ludwig was kept back as part of it. Gudrun is true.*

The memory of her gray-green eyes staring at him, soft as a misted lake, rose up to blur Fredrik's face into nothingness. Wolfram pushed it back down, forcing himself to focus on his friend's night-grayed blue eyes and dark gold hair, the little tilt of the nose that lent a merry look to his fierce features. *All I can do is be patient, and see.*

"Well," Fredrik said, "if I can help with anything else, let me know. Come have a mug of wine with us, anyway. It'll do you good."

A sharp boot-toe in the ribs roused Wolfram well before dawn the next morning. He rolled out of his blankets and to his feet, ready to fight. Then he saw that the man standing in front of him, his face grotesquely half-illuminated by his lantern like a Agwar's Feastnight mask, was one of the guards set on Forlorn Hope.

"You're on latrine duty this morning. Pack your shit fast, you've got a lot more shit to deal with," he laughed roughly, "and get up to our post. If you're not there in half an hour, I'll come get you and you won't like it."

"I'll be there," Wolfram said tightly. He crammed his eating gear into his pack, rolled his blanket to tie to the top of it, and dragged his armor bag and pack outside. Long practice had taught him to take his tent down swiftly: he had everything stowed in his usual wagon and was standing by the guards before any of the other men on the morning latrine detail.

"Forward, march!" The guards commanded, prodding the Forlorn Hope men into line with sticks.

Wolfram caught a sharp poke in the ribs and turned to look at the man who had hit him, as though he were storing the face for future revenge. To his surprise, the guard stepped hastily backwards with a look of fear flinching across his face, making a warding sign and spitting between himself and Wolfram. Then he straightened his back angrily, jabbing at Wolfram with his stick again.

"Try your Elvish tricks on me, and I'll see you're for the gauntlet," he blustered.

Wolfram looked away, sick at heart. He had heard that Dark Elves could cast terror with their eyes: he could not doubt that his black heritage had risen for a moment. Rage, hate, the lust for violence. I need to get free of Forlorn Hope. I have seen what it does to true-born Men. What will it do to me, if I stay too long? But four more battles will free me, one way or the other. The latrine trenches were illuminated with widely spaced hanging lanterns, smeary golden light flickering through their translucent horn panels.

The trenches themselves seemed like nothing but cracks of blackness that might go down to the depths of the earth, the stink of shit rising from them made Wolfram think of the battlefield, and of Darkness' hells.

He took a shovel and began to heave back the earth that had been dug out the night before. He had almost gotten into a mind-stilling rhythm when the unmistakable broken accent of Mishni the Rat chirped in his ear, "Nice breakfast they give us here, yes?"

"Good morning, Mishni," Wolfram said wearily. What he wanted to say was, Shut up, Mishni. The little Southerner had saved his life at least once, maybe twice. Four years as a Landsknecht was not enough to choke out eighteen years of training to courtesy.

"Good to talk, shoveling over shit," Mishni said. "Talk through mouth, can't smell a thing."

Wolfram puzzled over that a moment and decided to ignore it. But Mishni seemed happy enough to have a listener, and after a little time, as the sky slowly grayed in the east, it began to occur to Wolfram that the scarred Southerner's prattle did seem to be making the unpleasant work go faster.

"Shit here, shit there, shit all round," Mishni said. "Hey, got real Landsknecht song for you." He began to chant softly, 'Shit, he ride a stallion brown and squishy. Shit, he ride a palfrey yellow-pissy. He fart so loud, he fart so well – Shit, shit, shit must you all! Shit is at hand, We're shitting in Berthold's land."

Mishni cackled soundlessly; Wolfram pressed his lips tight together to keep his laughter from drawing the guards, snorting through his nose.

"Never hear you laugh before," the Rat said, well-pleased. "Got to laugh. Even if you not do what you here for, you got to laugh."

Wolfram started, all his amusement wiped away.

"I plead innocent at my trial too," Mishni said, leaning a little closer and dropping his voice to a whisper. "Might have stolen sometime, but never stole what they said. That mage Wilhelm – skinny one with face like boiled parsnip – he say I take pouch full of money. Never did. Found old pouch, all scuffed up, nothing in but few skaggy pieces parchment. Not bank notes or nothing, all written over."

Wolfram drew in his breath, heedless of the sharp stink biting his nostrils. "Mishni," he murmured, "what did they say? Do you still have them?"

"'Course not. What I do with parchment, wipe my butt? Parchment all slippy, dry grass much better."

"Did you read them?"

"You think flea-bitten gutter rat can read? You think I stupid enough hang onto stuff pointing finger at me, say thief? Even if I just found it? Why I keep worthless rags?"

The Southerner's dark eyes glinted at Wolfram, the scarred half of his mouth tucked up in its perpetual twisted smile. Wolfram thought about it a moment, looking straight into Mishni's eyes. The broken Cimbrian is deceptive, he thought.

He could almost see something behind the defiant cheer of the Rat's glittering gaze, something like, an intricate maze of tunnels and string, was the best way he could describe it, a maze cunningly littered with rubbish to hide the shining danger of trip-wires and glittering promise of gems. Treasure disguised as trash.

"As a matter of fact," Wolfram whispered carefully, "I think you can read. I don't know what you think is worthless."

Mishni laughed his soundless laugh again.

"You think too much. Don't be tripping self, now. Get on with what you got to do, 'cause all you got to do now is stay alive through next battles. The Rat not big or strong, not got fancy learning, but maybe he know something even Elf don't about staying alive."

Wolfram nodded slowly. "I saw that at our last fight. I'll stick by you in the next one too, if you don't mind."

"Good thing to do. I got luck, me." Mishni glanced about at the guards, then, very quickly, hooked something out of the ragged neck of his padded jerkin.

Wolfram blinked. It was a rat's skeleton held together by dried sinews and dessicated skin with a little patchy hair left on it, hanging by the tail from a leather thong. Morbidly fascinated, Wolfram stared until the Southerner dropped it back under his dirty shirt.

"Nothing stay alive like rat. Big proud lion roar and die, rat run and slither and stay alive, breed lots of little rats. Speaking of run and slither, the Rat hear we going to village next, village very important to Berthold. If it held by full troops, that be bad. Guns in place everywhere, maybe fences or ditches. Then you see what Rat best at because who got to run and slither through ditches, through fences, under fire, and take those guns? Forlorn Hope, that who."

"Yes. But we'll make it through," Wolfram said firmly.

Mishni grinned. "Now you talking sense. Even Forlorn Hope better than no hope, when your back up to wall. Maybe, talk right place and time later, I find you better hope than Forlorn Hope." He turned his back to Wolfram, humming loudly as he shoveled.

He said nothing more while they worked that morning, nor did Wolfram dare to speak to him again. Instead, the half-Elf contemplated the irony of the situation: natives of the Empire were supposed to be bluffly honest men of their word, while the Men of the Southern city-states were known for lies and treachery. Yet it was Mishni the Rat in whom Wolfram was beginning to feel an inexplicable, but certain, faith. While, at this point, he wasn't certain whether he could even trust Hauptmann Heinrich.

Or, for that matter, himself. Dark Elves were supposed to be as violently treacherous among their own as they were towards Men and their bright cousins, lacking even the concept of trust. His misgivings about the Silver Eagle's officers.

Heinrich and Gudrun in particular, were they another sign of inborn nature, his thoughts slowly twisting until the whole world was smirched by the darkness in his own eyes? Wolfram did not know; could not know. But whatever might be wrong with Wolfram or his superiors, the best thing he could think of at the moment was to take Mishni's advice: Get on with what you got to do.

CHAPTER 18

According to the maps in the Black Wagon, Bad Oberstein lay close to the river snaking through Graf Berthold's land, nestled amid low, heavily-forested mountains. The shrine itself was a little above the town, surrounded by the natural defenses of crags and thick-growing woods, and further protected by stone walls, as well as whatever strengths the spring of power granted to the priests and priestesses who served there. It was a good thing, Gudrun thought as she mounted up in the chilly morning fog, that she had some idea of what the land ought to look like, because the mist was so thick that the marching column of Landsknechts faded into shadows at ten paces before and behind her, the trees that lined the road no more than a low dark cloud melting into the general grayness. A tall shape detached itself from the shadowy mass of men ahead of her. About to turn, she waited until she could see more clearly.

Kettle-helm pushed back on dark hair like an inconvenient hat, red and yellow slashed clothes hanging on the lanky body like ribbons and banners festooning a festival pole for the Feast of Glory. This was Götz, Obrist Helmuth's adjutant.

"Marshal Gudrun," Götz said, his deep voice resonating scratchily in his chest as though he were about to hawk up a thick gob of phlegm. "The Obrist wishes you to ride with the scouts until the mist clears." He unfastened the pistol belt around his narrow waist, handing it up to her. "Take this. If you run into trouble, use magic only to preserve your life. The Obrist doesn't want the enemy to know that one of our mages is running loose, if possible but your talents of observation are needed in this fog."

"Thank you," Gudrun said. The wheel-lock pistol, encased in its leather sheath, seemed very heavy in her hands. Three brass vials of powder and a weighty bag of lead shot pulled the belt down on the other side.

The loading-rod hung through a small brass loop, like a wand or sword readied for quick drawing, and there was a little bag with patches in it as well. She had learned, as part of her early training with the Silver Eagle, how to load and shoot a pistol. It was uncomfortable and not very accurate, compared to mage-fire, but she understood why Obrist Helmuth wanted her to carry it.

"I've already loaded it for you," Götz told her. "You're riding with Arkoniel. He should, ah, here he comes."

The Elf's horse was a nondescript dapple gray, Arkoniel himself dressed in a simple tunic and breeches of mottled grayish-green, with a hood of the same color hiding his golden hair. Its close fit emphasized the long, narrow shape of his skull and the slant of his cheekbones and clear green eyes. Nerves prickled down Gudrun's back, it was hard to believe that the Elf was flesh and blood, not a spirit shaping itself out of woodland and fog. He gave her a contemptuous glance, but said nothing. Nor would he. The regiment's discipline had to override all feelings, which was one reason Elves were so few among the Landsknechts.

So what brought. Never mind. Gudrun suppressed the thought, as she had a great deal of practice in doing now. She belted the pistol around her waist. Even pulled to the last hole, the belt was a little loose for her. Standing, it would have sunk halfway down her hips but it would do for riding. A bit of shuffling brought pistol and wand to where she could draw either quickly at need, and she was ready. Arkoniel nodded, then, with a slight shift of his waist, guided his horse between the trees. Gudrun followed him more clumsily, ducking branches and kneeing her horse away from bushes and boulders.

"If we have to flee," the Elf said softly, his chiming voice blending with the sound of fog dripping on leaves so that it seemed more like a whisper of wind through the woods than speech, "come you up behind me, if you can. You ride too clumsily to escape on your own, most like."

"I understand," Gudrun murmured. Thank you very much too, you arrogant tree-screwer.

Again, she wondered briefly what. What Arkoniel is doing among us, she told herself firmly. Of the Elves in the Silver Eagle, he was most like the common view of that blood. Secretive, arrogant, contemptuous of Men's lack of the graces that he had learned over hundreds of years of more. Piriel was better, but even in Gudrun's few interactions with him, she had not been able to shake the feeling that he was deliberately trying to make her feel inferior.

Of course, they also resent the strength of Men's swift breeding and urgent deeds, and see human mages as an insult to their own power, she reminded herself. So she had been taught at the College, in any case, and nothing she had seen from the full-blooded Elves of the Silver Eagle had suggested differently to her. The enchantment allowing Gudrun to sense through mist and hills and trees was, fortunately, a diffuse one, or she would never have been able to follow Arkoniel despite his obvious efforts to ride slowly and easily for her.

Still, it was difficult for her to maintain both her seat and her concentration, the more so since fog made spells of concealment terribly easy. The seething of tiny water-droplets in the air lent itself to magic. It was almost a reflection of the seething of Chaos-particles in the Void and nothing was easier than making something do what it was naturally inclined to, in the case of fog, obscuring vision. She also could not help wondering if this heavy mist was Bad Oberstein's first defense against the approaching Landsknechts. What simpler to do from a holy spring than to raise water into the air? True, she could feel no charge of additional magic thickening the air, as she would if the fog were mage-raised.

The workings of holiness were another matter. If a priest had called the fog, Gudrun might or might not have been able to sense it. If the shrine itself had raised it would seem would be, save for its appearance at a time of need a working of nature. She shivered, and could not tell herself that it was only from the clammy cold seeping in through the thick green wool of her gown. The gods give us shrines, but it is Men who direct their power, Gudrun told herself. Alagrith and Froni have no love for seeing fields of grain destroyed, either. How often do they avenge themselves when an army tramples or burns its foe's resources? This is much the same and while a mage must recognize the strength of what she fights, she must not yield to a peasant's superstitions, either.

Arkoniel led Gudrun on a long, looping path around the column. Twice they startled roe-deer, the graceful little beasts glancing up with limpid frightened eyes before leaping high over bushes and vanishing into the woods. A far-off fox barked three times, then three again, Arkoniel answered it so perfectly that Gudrun found herself glancing around for a ruddy brush whisking into the undergrowth before she realized that the call came from her companion.

A signal? The Elf did not bother to vouchsafe to her what it meant but her wide-spread senses had already located another of their scouts, and no one else near him. Then she felt the second man riding quietly, just at the edge of her range. After years of fighting and marching with the Silver Eagle, Gudrun had at least glimpsed the faces of every man in the troop. She knew the drumbeats that spoke to their bones and limbs before the commands ever reached their minds, the names and shapes of every Hauptmann and Fändrich to whom they looked. This was a stranger, still a Landsknecht, but not one of their own.

"Arkoniel," Gudrun murmured, knowing that the Elf's keen ears would pick up her bare whisper. "Enemy scout..." She pointed. "About five hundred yards from our man, coming towards him."

The Elf acknowledged her with a slight nod. Gudrun, a city-dweller until she joined the Landsknechts, could not have said what bird made the cheeping whistle issuing from the Elf's lips, though she knew she had heard it often enough riding through the woods. Arkoniel whistled twice, once, and twice more. Gudrun felt their scout stop, slide off his horse. Leading the beast away from the trail, he crouched down in the undergrowth, waiting with bowstring nocked. The other man was still moving towards him. Gudrun sensed the horse shying, the arrow going wide and thumping into a tree; the brief struggle, blood spurting, life and mind fading together.

"Our man is dead," Gudrun whispered. "Should we go back to report?"

The Elf looked down his nose at her, as if she had said something appallingly foolish, and shook his head. His dapple-gray horse turned, moving in the direction she had gestured, and she followed him. For once on this hot summer campaign, Wolfram was grateful for the warmth of the padded gambeson beneath his armor. The fog was thick enough to bead on the polished surfaces of the metal plates, turning his "white harness" to cloudy gray. Soon enough, the gray would brighten into a bloom of rust. He would have to ask Fredrik to see if any of the sutlers had goose fat: there was nothing better for protecting freshly cleaned armor.

Wolfram remembered the smell of the armory at Schloss Löwenstein. Leather and metal and sweat, overlaid with the tang of old grease. His mother had always wrinkled her nose at it, but to Wolfram, as a boy, it was the smell of all the stories of heroes and knights his father had told him, the smell of the big men in their glistening armor who swept their swords through the air as lightly as he and Rudiger could wield reeds at play, of all the Grafs and champions of Löwenstein who had fought against Scandian raiders and Dark Elves sweeping in from the sea or Orcs marching east from Perkunan and Mirkheim.

Graf Ulric sitting with a strong warm arm wrapped around each of his young sons' shoulders to keep them from getting too chilled in the cold stone room after the hard training that had all three dripping with rapidly cooling sweat, saying, "This is the true chapel of St. Hildebrand. Scribes and peasants and tradesmen pray to him for help amidst stained glass and candles but here is where he speaks to the warriors that will fight beside him when need comes to the world. Rudiger, Wolfram, don't ever forget this.

Whatever the priests say, warriors know that the smell of fresh-raised sweat and armor is better to St. Hildebrand than sweet incense. Every blow you strike the pell is more to his liking than telling a prayer-bead, and if he ever wants you to fast, it's only to harden yourself to march and fight on short rations.

Now, make a quick prayer to him, and then go wash off and get dressed before you take a chill."

Wolfram sighed silently, forcing the memory down before it could grow clear enough to suck his mind in altogether. For a time, he had entertained dreams, fantasies as bright in his mind as waking reality of the Silver Eagle coming to Löwenstein's aid, of dying heroically in battle, perhaps even while slaying the Dark Elf who had set him as a cuckoo's egg in his mother's womb, of Graf Ulric holding his body as the life ebbed from it, saying, "You are truly my son, Wolfram."

The strength of those hopeful daydreams had grown in his mind until he turned from them, fearing that they would suck him down into madness and then he had seen how unlikely it was that any such thing would ever happen. Nor had he truly prayed to St. Hildebrand or Donmar since, though he could not break the habit of using their names when troubled. Neither the Defender nor the Creator of Men would listen to one such as him and there was little space for religion in a Landsknecht's life.

"Fucking shit-ass fog," Jürg was grumbling next to Wolfram. "There could be ten thousand of the enemy in charging distance right now and we'd never know it. I hate marching through fucking woods, too. It's like asking to be ambushed."

"You're asking to be ambushed, you keep whining," Bad-Eye told him.

A burly, dark-haired man whose left eye wandered randomly away from the right, Bad-Eye had ended up in Forlorn Hope as a result of beating the every-man's-wife who washed, cooked, and occasionally whored for himself and three other men, then chewing one of her nipples off when she asked for more money to compensate her. Wolfram remembered Gretel, who had done the same duties, absent the whoring, for himself, Maximilian, Little Kai, and poor dead Georg, shuddering when she told him about it.

"Even if I were willing to lie down for money, I wouldn't go near him for an hundred guilders," Gretel had said, chapped fingers clasping her blue shawl tightly about her bony shoulders as if winter had breathed a sudden sigh of ice over her through the warm spring air.

"Fuck you, too," Jürg replied sullenly. "You're on the outside, they'll get you first."

"I'll get you first if you don't shut up, you gaping asshole," Bad-Eye growled.

"You and how many others, shithead?"

Bad-Eye clenched his fist. In his much-dented iron gauntlet, it looked like a misshapen club-claw, as though Chaos had left its mark on his body. "Smash your fucking head in."

"Yah, yah, save it for battle," Jürg muttered. "You can't tell me you like all this shit around us, though."

"If you can't blow the fog away by flapping your lips, just shut the fuck up."

Jürg made a few more defiant mutters, but eventually quieted down, to Wolfram's relief. Although he knew that the combination of fog and thick woods could be dangerous, he had to admit that he was almost enjoying it. Even through the sounds of drum and marching feet and clinking armor and gear, he could hear the soft dripping of mist-beads rolling off leaves and the faint twittering of unseen birds.

The dampness brought out the forest's scents, rich earth and leaf-mold, the sharp green smell of plants trodden underfoot, an occasional whiff of sweetness from late summer flowers, the pungent smell marking where a sounder of wild swine had passed. I wonder what it would be like to hunt now? Wolfram thought.

He had not hunted, had not even roamed the woods alone since the day of his mother's death. It was only at times like this that he caught a glimmer of what it might be like, to wander in the wild with Elven senses, tracking game by the scent of its passing, the distant whisper of hooves touching grass, the sight that could mark where a deer had brushed past by the least traces. Far in the distance, a fox barked. Another answered it. There was something just slightly wrong about the sound, a roughness to the first, a belling music to the second that caught Wolfram's attention.

Our scouts signaling each other. He had not been used often as a scout, but sometimes there were patrols on moonless nights which required dark sight. Just as, he was certain, one of the junior mages would be out with the scouts today, trying to pierce the blinding-thick fog. Because if it's a danger to us, it's also an opportunity.

If the Sun Azure, or Graf Berthold's own army, or both were out here, the Silver Eagle had as good a chance of taking them by surprise as of being taken. Much depended on the mages, though Wolfram had been told that fog aided magical concealment and made piercing it harder. More depended on prior intelligence and luck. If, for instance, their enemies had some idea of where they were going or what their plans were. Wolfram wished desperately that he knew more than Mishni had told him.

Going towards a village, yes, but how far? He had not managed to see so much as a map of Graf Berthold's lands. In any case, Obrist Helmuth frowned severely on information leaking from his officers to the ranks, it was too easy for an enemy to disguise himself, slip into camp, and start up a conversation.

Forlorn Hope was especially cut off from any knowledge which might make it easier for its men to plan an escape. For instance, if there were a sanctuary-shrine in these woods and I knew roughly where it was, I might think trying to give our guards the slip in this fog was worthwhile I wonder how Mishni found out what he knows?

Among the faint whistling and twittering of the birds too far out in the forest to be frightened quiet by the marching Company, Wolfram almost failed to notice the slight strangeness to one cheeping whistle. Twice, once, and twice, one of their men was warning another of an enemy scout. Surreptitiously he let his hand creep back to his two-handed sword, tugging slightly to make sure that the heavy dampness in the air hadn't swollen leather or wood.

That had happened to him once, marching to fight in a driving rainstorm. If he hadn't abandoned the effort to draw the stuck two-hander, pulling his bastard sword from its waist-scabbard just in time to slightly deflect the foe's stroke instead, he would have certainly been killed.

Instead he had collected a lump in his left collar-bone where it had been broken and mended, but better that than his helm smashed and skull shattered. Wolfram listened carefully, but heard nothing else that sounded like a signal. As they marched, he began to notice the first signs of men. Trodden undergrowth, a tree cut not too long past, the pale wood still showing beneath trails of crusted brown sap, brush cleared away around the dark sodden remains of a fire. They passed more places where trees had been felled. Some had been chopped on the spot, splinters and curls of bark scattered about. A charcoal-burner's work, perhaps. Wolfram was sure he could smell the faintest hint of smoldering wood.

Others had been limb-lopped and dragged onto the road almost entire, leaving crushed trails behind them like the tracks of giant worms. The earthen roadway was already churned to mud by the Landsknechts' trampling feet ahead of Wolfram, but he thought he could still see, once in a while, the deep tracks left by wagons carrying a very heavy load. To fortify the village? Do they know we're coming? Or for other purposes? How far are we from Graf Berthold's castle? Is he preparing for a siege, or has he other plans?

Arkoniel stopped suddenly, pulling back his hood and cocking his head to listen. He dismounted in an easy, graceful leap and whispered something in his horse's ear before gesturing Gudrun off her own mount. She got down as quietly as she could, though the Elf still frowned at the sound of her shoes crunching on fallen twigs. He came over and murmured something to her horse as well, then took the reins from her hand and let them fall. One long-fingered hand folded into a fist. The other covered it, palm-down. One of the few scouts' signals that Gudrun knew, since it was also a mage's gesture: Conceal us. She drew her wand, carefully weaving the spell into the air around the two of them. In the thick fog, it was almost absurdly easy.

Had anyone else been watching, the Elf and the woman would simply have faded into the mist, shapes becoming gray shadows melting to silent fog. Neither sight nor sound nor scent would give them away, another mage, looking, might have noticed the slightly greater concentration of Chaos-flecks among the million droplets of water hanging in the air. Gudrun followed Arkoniel through the trees, envying the Elf his water-smooth passage. Brambles snagged at her skirt, the wide toes of her shoes caught on roots and stones, and every step she took sounded as loud and clumsy to her as if she were stomping through the woods with a knight's long-pointed metal sabatons on her feet.

Arkoniel's fair narrow brows drew in. He gave her one contemptuous look, then shook his head and kept going. She could tell that the Elf was slowing to a fraction of his normal pace to accommodate her, and at that, she was already beginning to sweat and breathe a little heavily. Would, never mind. Take it that Elves are like that and go on, she told herself. A bit more practice, and surely she wouldn't even have to suppress the thoughts from which her teacher had ordered her to turn her mind. Awareness outstripping her stumbling feet and fog-blinded eyes, Gudrun sensed the end of the wood ahead.

The left side stretched on as far as she could feel, up to the
mountains ahead. Its edge swept down over a long slope, into a
deep curve and up into a sharp horn on the right before sloping
back again. The road the Silver Eagle was following came out in the
center of the inward curve. As little as Gudrun knew about tactics,
she could see that it was almost an ideal place for an ambush. *If we
believe Bad Oberstein is a vital point to take, surely Graf Berthold
doesn't think any less of it? Especially since he is known for his
piety?* Gudrun tapped Arkoniel on the shoulder. The Elf whirled,
his sword half out of the sheath and green eyes cutting into her like
whetted spears of emerald ice.

"Never touch me," he whispered.

"Fine,"Gudrun hissed. "Let me tell you what's ahead." She quickly
described what she had perceived, as best she could."

Arkoniel nodded slowly. "Are they there?"

"I can't tell from here. Concealment works both ways."

"Could you, were you closer?"

"Probably. It's much harder."

He cut her off with a swift gesture. "Come."

Gudrun ground her teeth a moment in resentment. *He might have
wanted to know whether I meant that it was harder to hide many
than two, or to keep a spell of concealment going at close range! If I
hadn't meant the first, we'd be risking both our lives, putting them
even more at risk, by going much nearer.* She put it out of her mind,
anger and thought both sinking away. Ahead of her, the image
formed with a strange double clarity.

The dark trees rising along the ridge to the left, spreading in
the distance ahead to fur the low mountains, the green sweep of
meadow sunken between the ridge and the other long spur of trees
hiding the river to the right, stands of tall golden flowers above
the thick drifts of grass, the green broken by scatterings of red
poppies, blue flax blossoms, white daisies, brilliant dandelions,
the dark trodden earth of the road cutting through it like a scar,
leading on to meet the river where it swept in and around the foot
of the mountain at the same time, the woods as the faintest shadow
through the gray blanket of fog that hid road and flowers and grass,
glimmering almost like the Chaos-void itself, though the sparkling
power simply hung in the air instead of whirling, joining, and
dispersing in Arioris' endless dance with itself-themselves. Arkoniel
led Gudrun closer and closer to the edge, halting beside a huge
gnarled oak.

He looked at her, raising one golden eyebrow. Gudrun slowly drew in a breath of cool damp air through her nose, letting it seep through her body and leak slowly out her mouth. She could feel the glittering power whirling at the edges of her mind, her thoughts fraying, disintegrating, merging with it. Too even, too thick, too neatly spread in a pair of long columns along the sides of the meadow, and one spot in the center, a great triangle. Her sight wavered, for just a moment, she saw through fog and magic and that one blinking glimpse was enough.

"It's a trap," she whispered. "There, there, and a wedge in the center. They're waiting for us to come out, hit us from both sides and down the middle while we're partially out and trying to form up."

Arkoniel glanced at the thick mist lying over the meadow, then back at the woods and calculating time and distance? He whirled and leapt over a great mossy fallen tree as lightly as a wildcat, vanishing into fog and forest without a trace, or a word to her. Gudrun kilted up her skirts and ran, stumbling and cursing under her breath. Branches slashed across her face. She raised one arm to protect her eyes and ran even faster. A root snagged her foot, and she slammed into the earth, a rock catching her low in the ribs. Wheezing, she pushed herself to her feet and kept going, though a little more carefully.

Where did we leave the Darkness-damned horses? She thought. Three gods of Darkness eat Arkoniel, what did he think he was doing, leaving me here by myself? Even in her frustrated rage, she knew that the Elf had done the best thing. Unless their foes, too, had a mage out scouting, no one was going to find her. She might miss some of the battle, but better that than letting the regiment be taken by surprise. Wait. I've been reacting, not thinking. I can just go down to the road where it joins the meadow and head towards the Company.

Even if the Obrist decides to try getting everyone off the road and through the woods, Alberich's spell against magical detection won't hide them from me, since I was inside it when he cast it. Now that her mind was clear, Gudrun had little trouble finding the horses.

Somewhat uncertain, she spread her spell to cover them, then walked up to Arkoniel's dapple-gray, hoping that the Elf hadn't told his steed to attack anyone approaching it until he came back. It let her take the reins, leading it over beside her own mount, and waited patiently while she heaved herself up and into the saddle.

Actually riding while leading a second horse by the reins was more of a problem, though. Gudrun vaguely remembered seeing men with strings of horses, but it seemed to her that they had been using some sort of rope to connect them. Or something. On the other hand, some horses just seemed to walk along with everyone else as though they knew where they were going.

"Come on, horse," she muttered, dropping the extra reins. "Just follow me." To her surprise, the dapple-gray fell in behind her brown as if they were soldiers on the march. Without Arkoniel to lead, she didn't dare to take them any faster than a slow rack, but they had outpaced the column by a noticeable amount. She thought she should make it back to the Silver Eagle in time to help fight. Although, Donmar and Alagrith know, I feel like I've already been through the battle.

CHAPTER 19

The regular boom of the marching drums broke into three sharp blows and stopped. The signal for a halt. Wolfram reached back to loosen his two-hander in its scabbard again, listening carefully, but heard only the sounds of curious muttering, armor and gear shifting, and a man's voice further down the line shouting, "Halt! Didn't you hear the drum, shithead?" At the front of Forlorn Hope, Fredrik detached himself from the line, walking back down the column. Wolfram watched him go, trying to suppress the hot black spark of envy scorching his heart.

"We in for it now, you bet," Mishni's accented voice said beside Wolfram. The Rat looked up and giggled, as though he could read Wolfram's thought. Where in Darkness and Chaos did he suddenly come from? "Scout must found the enemy. Pretty good trick, weather like this."

"Yes," Wolfram agreed absently. The fog had thinned in the last hour, but he could still hardly see more than twenty yards ahead.

"Not to worry," Mishni said. "Even if trap, always way to get cheese out and not break neck."

He touched the lump of his dead rat luck-piece under the neck of his padded jerkin.

"We find it."

"I hope so."

"Silence down the line!" Someone called.

Wolfram waited quietly, listening. Dripping dew, hoarse breathing, the soft squishy sound of feet shuffling in mud as men shifted their weight from one foot to the next, a horse's lip-fluttering sigh. Are they in the forest with us? Is it the Sun Azure, or Berthold's own forces? Landsknechts were usually at an advantage over a local ruler's troops in the open, but fighting in the woods, where the sixteen-foot pikes were a hindrance rather than a help and it was impossible to form the close-set blocks of men that proved so deadly on the field.

Of course, this is no terrain for knights either. Not outside of the stupidly romantic one-on-one challenges so loved by the chivalry of Broceliande, anyway. A halfway decent infantry troop, backed up by bow and arquebus, could do a good deal of damage to the Landsknechts in a situation like this, with the Silver Eagle caught on the road and the woods and fog to keep them from falling easily into any sort of formation.

Wolfram breathed deeply, forcing himself to relax as he remembered his father's advice.

"If you let yourself tense up before a fight, you'll wear yourself out before you ever draw sword," Graf Ulric had said. "Make your decisions firm, trust in Donmar and St. Hildebrand, and do your best. Every speck of worry about something you can't help is another bit of strength lost needlessly."

Eventually Fredrik came back, grinning. He stood beneath the blood-red banner of Forlorn Hope, waving the men to fall out and gather around him.

"All right!" He said. "The Sun Azure thought they had a trap set for us, but we're going to turn it into a trap for them. The situation is like this." He quickly outlined the lay of the land, with the two-wings-and-wedge formation waiting for the Silver Eagle to emerge.

"Our job is to make them think we're all charging out, and blunt the wedge. We come out at a run. The Blue Chevron and Sleeping Wolf will be right behind us. We bunch up to hit the point of the wedge and hopefully break their momentum. The wings should start closing on the boys behind us; at that point the other Fähnlein come out of the woods and pound them flat, continuing on to hit the wedge from three sides at once. Basically, all we have to do is run in and hit them like mad bastards. Stay quiet, now, but, can we do that?"

Fists thrashed the air, halberd-blades gleamed dull as they clove the fog. Wolfram found himself grinning, his gauntlet's straps tight on his clenched hand as he gestured his assent. *I may never be certain why Fredrik is here, but by St. Hildebrand, I'm glad he is.* The half-Elf thought. He found it hard to imagine another man who could raise any enthusiasm from the hard-cases and scum of Forlorn Hope. *Or even from me, as things are with me here.*

Three sharp drumbeats to signal move on, no more. This was no time to announce their progress, or the way the Fähnlein behind Forlorn Hope and the two units supporting its semi-decoy charge were spreading out to either side. Wolfram could hear the sounds of the Company fanning out, but he wondered if anyone else would be able to for very long. Except Arkoniel and Piriel, of course.

They kept going until one of the scouts ghosted suddenly out of the mist in front of them, holding up a hand palm-outward to signal a halt. He moved forward, whispering, "About fifteen yards to the edge of the wood," to Fredrik. The Scandian nodded, gesturing the Forlorn Hope men up into a rough block. Wolfram was in the front, between Sascha, who carried the red banner under one arm, and Mishni. The most dangerous place; but he could not have dropped back, even if the other men would have let him.

"Forward," Fredrik mouthed silently, waving them on slowly. "Forward, forward...Draw weapons,"

He pulled his own two-hander free, Wolfram did the same, holding it at a slant in front of him, ready to deflect blows or chop downward. "Charge!"

The Forlorn Hope pounded out into the fog. Arquebuses cracked, brief bursts of flame lighting the grayness as the screaming began, the dark layer of cloud before them began to resolve into the specter-faint figures of individual men. A terrible blue light burned through the mist, one of Wolfram's comrades going up in a gout of mage-fire. Sascha slanted towards the left, Wolfram following him. Now he could see the one robed shape among all the others, wand outstretched towards him, still almost thirty yards away, plenty of time for the mage to burn them both down and flee.

The lightning cracked out from the mage's wand. Time seemed to slow. Wolfram saw Sascha swinging in front of him, the snake of blue flame leaping to the spiked head of Sascha's mace, twining down the oaken shaft and over the big Kievian's arm to spiderweb all over his body, spreading and joining into a single fire as he bellowed in awful agony.

He was still on his feet, still running even as the soiled ribbons of his slashed sleeves and breeches flared and shriveled into blackness, the wide brim of his kettle-helm beginning to run and shed white-hot droplets of molten metal, and his breastplate burned through the doublet, red incandescence glowing through slashings of black charcoal. Wolfram could hear Sascha's flesh sizzling, smell the awful savory scent of roasting pork and the Kievian was still on his feet, still charging the mage. Blue lightning crackled again, and Wolfram knew that the wand was aimed at him, and that he would never be able to drop or dodge fast enough.

Sascha's course wavered just enough, the sky-bright fire struck him a second time, burning up around him as though he had become the wick of an immense candle flame glowing azure through the mist. The giant Kievian plunged forward in one final desperate surge. The mage had stepped back, two halberdiers in front of him. Burning, heedless of the blades chopping into his face and shoulder, Sascha struck them like a fiery ram, plowing through them to fall burning on top of the mage who had killed him.

Wolfram charged after him, dispatching the mage's stunned and singed protectors with two swift chops and then he was into the enemy lines, caught up in the whirlwind of sharp-edged weapons and struggling bodies. His sword tip sank into a bearded face, grating through gristle and bone. The point of a halberd stuck for a second in the rim of his eye slot, a finger's width from his left eye, dragging his head brutally to the side as its wielder shook it loose.

Something struck Wolfram hard in the side, sending a flash of pain through his body with every panting breath. He sliced through a pike shaft to his left, knocked another away from his face as he wheeled his sword up again, and chopped through a third on the right.

He never felt the blow on the top of his helmet, only his knees collapsing underneath him, the blood-spray and mist in his eyes darkening to blackness as he tried to curl defensively on his side beneath the trampling feet.

CHAPTER 20

Gudrun stood in the middle of her four-man Trabanten as the sounds of battle died into the screaming and whimpering of the wounded. Her hair lay wet across her forehead and her legs were trembling, but tired as she was, she felt the warm inner glow that always came when she had raised her power to its fullest and then released it explosively, a pleasure only another mage could understand. She looked up at her bodyguards. No Dwarves this time, a magician's guards in battle were always tall and broad enough to shield her body from arrow and ball.

"Well done, Marshal," Johann said, looking down at her in turn. "None of them got within thirty feet of you. I don't know why you need us." He grinned, and Gudrun laughed back. Of all the men who rotated through her Trabanten, Johann was the only one who never seemed frightened of her. Perhaps a man who was six foot five and muscled like an oak would never have had a reason to learn to fear.

Perhaps he would have been just as self-confident even if he had been her size.

Larger men had treated her warily before.

"I'll always need you," she replied giddily. Johann, thoroughly married as he was safe enough to flirt with. He only smiled and took her arm, leading her off the field to the Black Wagon.

Wilhelm was already there, gobbling bread and cheese like a starving man. He handed her some, trying to say something as he chewed. Gudrun was about to rebuke him, but the food just smelled too good for her to waste time waiting for him to clear his mouth. Wilhelm swallowed hastily, coughed, and drank from his canteen.

"I said," he articulated more clearly, "aren't you supposed to be keeping track of their retreat?"

"Not that I know of. Perhaps Alberich is doing it himself?"

"Have you seen him?"

"Not since before the battle." Despite Arkoniel's sudden departure, Gudrun had made it back to the Black Wagon in plenty of time for Alberich to give her instructions and set her in place among the left wing in the woods. "Give me more of that." She snagged half of the roll in Wilhelm's hand, cramming it into her mouth.

"Hey! Find someone to send for your own. This is mine."

"Nmph urph mrgle." She chewed a bit more, swallowing the bread down in lumps. "Not any more."

The argument was stalled when Greta came back with another platter of rolls, cheese, and smoked ham, passing it to Gudrun and Wilhelm without a word. Like the mages' Trabanten, the women who cooked and washed for them were not allowed to stay on that duty very long.

Gudrun knew she had little in common with them, mostly wives of dead men, who had chosen to stay with the Company rather than make their way home to be dependent on relatives. Very few of them were particularly educated or intelligent. Nevertheless, sometimes she thought it would be nice to be able to get to know another woman in the Company.

She had not really had any female companionship since she joined the Landsknechts: the fighters had little to do with the mages, she was too far above the various types of camp follower, and the officers' wives who petted Wilhelm at dinners and dances treated her like some sort of dangerous and unpredictable creature. *If I had another woman to talk to, I might not have been so silly about.*

"Have you heard anything of what happened during the battle?" Gudrun asked. "I couldn't see past thirty yards or so. I mean, obviously we managed to run them off, but do you know how many we killed, or lost, or anything?"

"I didn't see any more than you did," Wilhelm answered regretfully. "Probably less. I did hear that one of the Forlorn Hope men got hit by mage-fire twice and still kept going to kill the mage, though." He shivered. "I hope it's just a rumor. I've never seen anyone get more than a couple of steps without falling down. If there are men out there who can't be stopped by blasting."

"People can do odd things in battle. Still fighting with arquebus balls in their hearts, even standing and swinging a sword with their heads chopped off, like a beheaded chicken still running around. If that's possible, why shouldn't one be able to keep going for a time while he burns?" Gudrun spoke absently around the skein of cold slowly winding in her stomach.

An Elf, or half-Elf, might be able to resist a Man's magic well enough to survive for a few moments with mage-fire consuming his flesh. Magic is a matter of will, of learned and conscious direction of Chaos. I did not cause Wolfram's death by blotting him out of my thoughts!

"Scares you too, huh?" Wilhelm said.

Gudrun nodded. Her stomach seemed to be cramping around the lumps of bread she had forced down so hastily. For a moment, she thought she might be about to spew. She breathed deeply, fixing her gaze on a nearby ash tree. Smooth gray bark, long fronds of oval green leaves. Turning to blue-green in her dazed sight, like slanting turquoise eyes.

No. She reached for another piece of bread, chewing it very slowly and deliberately. This was only after-battle reaction, such as she had felt many times before. After-battle reaction and magical strain. Not nearly as bad as the backlash from blowing up the falconet, but quite sufficient to leave her hands trembling and bowels feeling knotted where they weren't liquid.

"Excuse me." Gudrun walked into the woods as hastily as she could while maintaining some dignity, two of the mages' Trabanten following at a seemly distance.

She scooped out a little pit with her hands and drew up her skirt. She was lucky, she thought as she winced at the liquid stink, that she hadn't soiled her under-braes. She had done that before, too, in those seconds of terror when it looked as though she wouldn't be able to get back into the protection of the lines in time. From the rough jokes she had overheard here and there, she doubted that there were many soldiers in her regiment or any other who hadn't had the same experience. At least there was plenty of soft damp moss here.

Greta, or whoever did the next load of washing for the Black Wagon, wouldn't be able to laugh with her friends over the fact that mages, too, left the stains of battle in their small clothes. By the time Gudrun had composed herself to go back to the Wagon, Alberich had returned. He, too, had strained himself close to the limit, she thought.

His face was yellowed like old parchment, forehead and eyes scored deeply with the runes of age, and the gray of his beard and hair seemed lifeless as damp ashes.

"They are retreating to Bad Oberstein," he said quietly. "Rest and prepare yourselves. It will be a siege of some note for those who fight with steel, and for us, a challenge." Alberich smiled like a dry lich.

"At least one of the scum in Forlorn Hope made things easier for us. Herr Doktor Manfred von Niedersheim is dead, and he was an excellent mage, as most of those among the Landsknechts go. Well above either of you, for instance. He was a couple of years behind me in the College." For a moment, it seemed to Gudrun that she saw a dark gleam of sorrow in Alberich's blue eyes, like a black fish flicking its tail just at the surface of a sky-glimmering pool.

"Let his death teach you something," the Zauberobrist went on quietly.

"He struck his target twice, the second time within a few steps of the man's reach. If he had believed the evidence of his eyes, realized that a soldier could briefly go on through a spell that had hitherto destroyed all its targets straight away, he could have retreated into the lines in good time, and lived.

Instead he stood and tried to repeat what clearly was not fully successful. Perhaps Manfred's target had some portion of blood from a race other than Men, perhaps he sneaked some magical protection past the restrictions on the Forlorn Hope.

Maybe he was in a berserk frenzy, or just had the strength of body and will to keep going. Or was, for reasons unknown, particularly blessed by a god."

Alberich looked deeply into Wilhelm's eyes, then Gudrun's. Fine sweat dewed Gudrun's palms and her legs began to tremble again. If she had not emptied her bowels moments ago, she thought they might have spilled now. But she kept her gaze steady, her mind concentrated on her teacher's lesson and if some tiny part of her was whimpering with anguish, it was locked away like a mouse inside a steel cage inside the deepest stone dungeon of the Queen of Mirkheimr's hollow mountain keep.

"If you know yourself, and know your enemy, your victory is assured. But you can never truly know your enemy. Arioris laughs at those who think they have provided for every circumstance. A mage who clings to belief at the expense of reality will certainly die of it, one way or another. Wilhelm, tell that woman to fetch some more food." Alberich walked slowly into the back of the Black Wagon. Gudrun did not watch him, but when he came out, he was carrying a green glass bottle and three silver goblets.

Hands shaking, the Zauberobrist carefully pulled the goblets full, the wheat-gold wine turning the silver inner bowls to worn gilt. Alberich lifted his goblet.

"Let us remember Herr Doktor Manfred von Niedersheim.

Much of his life was dedicated to the study of mage craft; in his death, he has taught the most important lesson of all. See that you learn it!"

The three mages drank. The wine was rich and sweet, but with its honeyed flavor countered by the clean citron-taste of the grapes, so that it was neither cloying nor sharp, but perfectly balanced. Still, Gudrun could not help thinking, deep in that minute imprisoned part of her mind where even she could barely hear it: Is this not an argument for the hope of Wolfram's innocence? If he still lives! And if it was he who died, how will I cast mage-fire again without seeing it burn his eyes white, his skin black, the entrails in his bursting belly to a heap of steaming cinders? I know the death I deal too well: what if Wolfram received it?

CHAPTER 21

Darkness, and pain, radiating out from the top of his head and his left side with every heartbeat, striking bright and hard with every struggling breath to leave flowers of light bursting inside his eyelids. He tried to move, could not. Something was crushing his chest painfully, keeping him from getting a full breath. Am I buried? He thought, frightened? Cast into a mass grave under corpses and earth, pinned, dying slowly as his air gave out or the weight on his body crushed him to death. He tried to move. The pain-flowers brightened, and faded back into darkness. Dark, still, but the pain was less. Now Wolfram could hear something, a scratchy voice humming under its breath.

"And in the field my grave is laid, Now do not weep or sorrow, In grass all green, you'll sleep serene, 'Neath cloud and wall and harrow. Tra di ra la la la, la la..." A familiar voice

"Mishni?" He said. The name came out as an unintelligible croak. His cough shattered through his chest, he swallowed, gasping against the pain, and tried again.

This time, weak as it was, his voice was clear. "Mishni?"

"Yes, that me," the Southerner murmured. "You awake? Know who you are, who Emperor is, all that shit?"

Wolfram thought a moment. Even to half-Elven eyes, there was barely enough light for him to see that they were indoors, in a large windowless building. He could just make out the gabled peak of the roof above. Beneath the hospital stinks of blood and shit and wounds, the building smelled of straw and old dung, a barn that had been cleared out, perhaps: there was no lingering scent of smoke to suggest that fires had ever been lit in here. No wonder, he thought, that his first half-waking awareness had been the fear of burial alive in a mass grave.

A tight bandage wrapped his chest, holding his broken ribs in place: the compression his dazed mind had interpreted as the crushing weight of bodies and earth on his chest. His hands and feet were tied firmly, but not too tightly: he could still feel fingertips and toe-tips. Wolfram's memories all seemed clear – too clear, as they had been since his transformation. Sascha's insanely heroic immolation, the fighting; he must have taken a blow right on top of the helm. Amazing that his helm and skull hadn't caved in together. He had seen that before, often enough.

"Yes. I'm lucky to be here."

Mishni gave a soft scrabbling laugh. "Not luck, my friend. Me."

Wolfram blinked. "You? You hit me?"

"Not at all. Rat not hit friends from behind, only enemies! No, Jürg. Saw him behind you, halberd blade coming down square on head. No time grab arm, run into him back, so shaft hit you instead. Otherwise you head in two pieces now."

Wolfram drew in a deep breath, very slowly. He could feel the broken ribs grating in his chest. Fortunate as well, he thought, that one of them hadn't pierced a lung. That could happen easily enough when a man was down and being trampled in the thick of hand-to-hand fighting.

"Thank you," he breathed. "From the depths of my heart."

"Very welcome. Jürg might just have made accident, might not. Not sure, didn't think so then. Can't ask him, though. Him dead and looking for own head on field now."

"What happened after that? Where are we?"

"Sun Azure realize trap fail, pick up and withdraw pretty damn quick. We stuck out by ourselves in middle of them, I surrender for both of us, make them take you too. Thought if someone in Silver Eagle try to kill you then, someone else maybe try to kill you later. Safer here, I think. We in Bad Oberstein now, with few other prisoners. Hope Obrist ransom Forlorn Hope men." The Rat giggled.

"But got to have someone stick stupid necks out. Now we know town, might be worth something."

Mishni paused. In the darkness, Wolfram saw the little man's head jerk, as though he were glancing nervously about out of habit.

"You got better hear, better see, than Man," Mishni breathed, barely even whispering. "You tell from breath if anyone else still awake?"

Wolfram listened. Someone was wheezing painfully, the slow hitching breaths of a man nearing death. A few were breathing even and comfortable. Others seemed labored, but still quiet. He was about to speak when a low moan sounded from the corner, then another.

"Shit," Mishni hissed. "He have all awake again. How good you hear? This quiet?"

A Man could not have made out the Southerner's words from a foot away. Wolfram, in the next bed, could hear them clearly.

"Yes."

"Sssh." Mishni's small claw like hand closed on Wolfram's shoulder. "One twitch yes, two twitches no. Understand?"

How did he get his hands free? Wolfram wondered. He twitched his shoulder once.

"Good. Jürg have personal reason to kill you?"

Two twitches.

"If no personal reason, must be other reason, yes?"

One.

"Jürg not think of reason by self. Not sharpest knife in box. Maybe person want kill you same person got you in trouble? Make sense?"

Wolfram thought about it a moment. Slowly he shrugged his shoulder once. It made good sense. At least, it fit with the mill wheel of thought that had ground round and round in his head for months. Almost since he first awoke in prison with his skull aching much as it did now, Wolfram had been certain he had an enemy in the Silver Eagle. The question was still: who? With his, perhaps would be assassin dead, there were no more hints now than before. The moaner's voice rose to a low scream. Another moan joined him, like the drone on a bagpipe for the damned, and a deep female voice grunted, "Shut the fuck up or I'll come over and put you out of your misery myself."

Mishni breathed a soft little snort. "Sound like Big Katy captured too. Maybe they be sorry for that!"

Despite Katy's threat, the screaming went on and on. Two men were moaning now, someone else whimpering softly, as the noise awoke the wounded to their own pain. Beneath the gruesome harmonies, Mishni whispered, "What change between last two battles? Why anyone need kill you now, more than before?"

Wolfram's head was hurting worse now, each scream jolting a sharp spike of pain from the aching lump on top of his skull. Even so, he knew the answer at once. He had been right in thinking that something was amiss when he heard what Ludwig had told him about the Sun Azure's pay, right enough for the matter to be worth a murder.

"Who it scare that bad? Answer that, then you know."

Qui bono? Wolfram thought, a maxim from the old Remulan Empire. Who benefited from interfering with the Company's contract? If the money had been pocketed, then whoever had gotten it: the only two likely candidates for that were the Obrist and the Zauberobrist. If not, Graf Sigfrid, perhaps, the Sun Azure was good, but the Silver Eagle was larger and better. Could Sigfrid have planted an agent, or several agents, within the regiment? Possible but this smelled to Wolfram of something involving the upper ranks, and all those men had been in the Silver Eagle for years.

A conspiracy between the higher officers, sharing out the money that should have gone to ensuring the Landsknechts' pay for a time after this contract was done? That made more sense, even to the removal of a sharp-eared Lieutenant from a race, supposedly from a race, notoriously immune to corruption. If only they knew, Wolfram thought bitterly. But no one outside himself, the lord and heir of Löwenstein, and Graf Ulric's court mage would ever know what manner of Elf had sired Wolfram.

He forced himself back to the road of his thoughts. Confronted directly, as Wolfram had confronted him, a guilty Hauptmann Heinrich would have had no choice but to feign ignorance and shock. To refuse Wolfram speech thereafter and to arrange his murder in the bloody Chaos of a pitched battle. Who would ever have guessed that the blow cleaving a Forlorn Hope man's head had been struck from behind, rather than in front? Or, if the direction were noted, who would think anything but that he had penetrated too far ahead, so that an enemy soldier might close ranks behind him and turn to strike? Gudrun, perhaps?

The mages seldom walked the battlefield when their duty was done. By the time she realized he was dead, he would be long since under the ground. A particularly shrill cry of agony lanced through Wolfram's head, and he let out a breathy moan himself. If only the man would shut up! He was almost ready to go over and grant the screamer mercy himself, if he could have moved. From the rising wave of grumbles and snarls, most of the other patients in the room felt the same way.

Big Katy was cursing in a steady stream of imaginative profanity, thickly larded with threats and garnished with a scattering of ripe multilingual oaths suggesting travels from Kievia to the Red Land. Still, no one came to silence the cries with either healing or potions. This was the first time Wolfram had been in a hospital for captives, and he was fast beginning to suspect they would be treated like howling dogs: cursed at occasionally, but left to their own devices within their prison until their captors were ready to tend to them. From the screamer's particular keen cry of despair, Wolfram was guessing that he was permanently maimed in some way.

Careful tending might restore his mind and health, but even the gods' healing very rarely extended to rejoining a lopped limb, and almost never to restoring one destroyed. One of the moans had a bubbling quality that suggested a lung wound, perhaps the broken rib piercing through that Wolfram himself had avoided by luck or by Mishni's efforts to stand firm over his downed body. Wolfram tried to roll over in order to blur at least one ear's hearing in the straw tick on which he lay. Another small sound escaped his mouth. It was frightening how good and natural it felt, at least in comparison with the stabbing in his ribs and the pain trying to dig its way out of his skull.

He bit his lip, trying to block out the urge to join the hellish chorus of agony and cursing. At least I am human enough not to enjoy the sound of others in pain. The thought brought him a measure of relief, almost as good as a cup of willow-bark tea. Wolfram had heard rumors that the Dark Elves made music with choirs of torturers and tortured, tuning the pitches of human screams to suit their inhuman harmonies. Perhaps that was only a tale, but when the black ships glided out of the winter night's stormy waters, those who could not resist with weapons were advised to take their own lives rather than let themselves be captured. Orcs would eat Man's meat when it was left on the battlefield, just as they scavenged the flesh of their own slain, but they generally butchered Men for food only when they could get nothing else.

Whereas it was certain that villages had been found where Dark Elf raiders had slaughtered the livestock for fun, but prepared banquets of human flesh by long torture before cooking alive. Wolfram shook his head slightly, jarring red spikes of pain down from the top of his skull. He would slay himself before he gave in to that heritage. The vow he had made that first sleepless night on the road from Löwenstein, frightened, bewildered, and desperate, still held true.

Though when he had first met the Elves of the Silver Eagle, he had wondered if they would do it for him. Memory arose, and for once Wolfram was glad to give himself to it, letting it blot out the pain shooting through his head and ribs, and the sounds and stinks of the wounded around him. Wolfram had arrived at the Silver Eagle's muster point a couple of days early, hoping that if the Obrist had doubts about admitting him, he might have a chance to prove his worth.

This was the first of the Landsknecht companies Wolfram had ever seen, and he had been amazed. Some fifteen hundred soldiers, and perhaps two thousand camp followers or more, made the Silver Eagle a town in its own right, as large as the village outside which they had arrayed themselves, or larger. The sheer mass of sutlers, families, and so forth was also a surprise to Wolfram. He had been trained in the logistics of raising and maintaining the considerable forces that Löwenstein could muster, but the needs of soldiers off the field in a summer-long campaign or a battle of defense were very different from those of the men for whom the Landsknechts were a lifelong career.

For instance, the Graf von Löwenstein provided his army's food and fodder, whereas, if Wolfram had heard correctly, Landsknechts were responsible for buying their own. Certainly the crowd of sutlers' wagons supported the rumor. The Silver Eagle was obviously a permanent, if mobile, livelihood for quite a number of cooks. In fact, at first glance, looking at the camp's bustling market with its own crafters and merchants, thronged as much with women and children as with men and a fair number of the women respectably dressed as any burgher's ladies or prosperous farmers' wives, the Silver Eagle struck Wolfram as less an army than a mobile town.

Even granted that the occasional booth would belong to a local merchant taking advantage of soldiers' open pockets, the complexity of organizing such a thing in tandem with a fighting company struck him as vaguely insane. The village itself was already overflowing with hopeful prospects from the recruiting parade. The Silver Eagle had taken fairly heavy casualties on their last campaign, and were looking for some five hundred fighters to bring them back up to their usual strength, five Fähnlein of four hundred men each.

They would have no trouble making up the numbers here. Wolfram had only gotten a room to himself in the inn by the simple expedient of paying the four men who were sharing it to go away. Whether it was the money, the quality of his armor and weapons, or the marks of Elven blood on his face that convinced him, they had not argued with his offer. *Now, how do I get to see the Obrist?* He asked himself, standing on the edge of the Landsknechts' marketplace. Freiherr Helmuth von Wesenburg, a nobleman, and, by virtue of his position, the equivalent in the Company of a Graf in his own lands, *surely a recruit couldn't just walk up and demand to speak with him?*

A soldier would go up through his chain of command. An outsider. What would the equivalent of a steward, or a seneschal, be? Or perhaps I should try to find Hauptmann Marcus: he recruited me, and he was the one who said that the Obrist would have to make the final decision. Wolfram had just made up his mind to ask someone where Hauptmann Marcus might be found when a deep, raspy voice grunted, "Excuse me, but are you one of the new recruits?" Wolfram turned to look in disbelief at the man talking to him.

He was one of the ugliest men the young noble had ever seen. About Wolfram's height, but half again as wide through the shoulders, walking in a shambling, almost hunchbacked stoop with his arms dangling.

The narrow slashed puffs, yellow over black, that ridged all the way down his long sleeves only emphasized the look of slight deformity, as did the big slashed puffs over his thick stumpy thighs, one black over white, the other white over black and the hideous green that showed through the slashing of the black doublet displaying the muscle-gnarled breadth of his chest and shoulders. The wide-brimmed black velvet hat with its spray of golden ostrich feathers did nothing to disguise the massive brow-ridges over tiny black eyes, nor the odd forward jut of the Landsknecht's wide jaw.

His skin was very sallow, and when he grinned, Wolfram saw that two of his lower teeth were thickened almost into vestigial tusks. Orc! Wolfram thought. Or, part-Orc. Wolfram's first blooding had been against true Orcs, a tribe that had raided deeply enough into the lands of Men for his father's cavalry to catch up with them before they could withdraw.

He remembered the odd shambling gait, noticeable even in the deepening twilight; he had gotten his first wound, a long shallow cut along his left thigh, from underestimating the inhuman reach of those arms. Am I making a mistake in joining this regiment? Still, the man, or whatever he was, had spoken politely. Wolfram bowed slightly and said, "I am, indeed. You would be?"

"I'm Kai, from the Golden Bear Fähnlein. Are you just here to see what you're getting into, or is there something in particular I might help you with?"

Wolfram frowned, considering. Surely Kai was no officer but with his dubious ancestry as clear on his face as Wolfram's Elvish blood, he might have been examined in the same way.

And I hardly have the right to despise a half-Orc for the taint of Darkness, he thought, his self-loathing oozing up again like matter seeping from an abscess.

"I was told that the Obrist would have to make the final decision regarding my acceptance into the company," Wolfram said stiffly.

Kai's ugly face cleared, and he nodded. "Of course. We don't get many Elves here. Anyway, Obrist Helmuth likes to know about any special talents his soldiers have. For instance, all of us who can see in the dark are likely to be called for night watches or reconnaissance, and Arkoniel and Piriel usually get tapped for woodland scouting, and so forth.

Hmm, Hauptmann Heinrich and our Feldarzt are looking over the new lads in the village market right now, just to make sure they're all healthy enough to fight and march before signing them up. I'd say if you go there, Heinrich will see to you. He's a good man, and I should know, he's my Fähnlein's captain. All right?"

"Thank you."

"In fact, trusting you get in – and I can't see why you wouldn't – I'd advise you to ask for the Golden Bear if you get a chance."

Wolfram realized, then, what seemed odd about Kai aside from the discrepancy of his face and his friendly courtesy.

The Orcish Landsknecht was the first person Wolfram had seen since leaving home, with the possible exception of Hauptmann Marcus, who hadn't met him with fear, awe, suspicion, or all three.

He smiled, the stiff muscles of his face stretching with the unaccustomed expression, and said, "I will. Thank you for the advice."

"I'll buy you a beer to celebrate if you get in with us," Kai said. "Good luck, now."

Wolfram walked down the dusty road to the village, avoiding the deep wagon-ruts and piles of horse and ox droppings without thought. Although he had been carrying his helm all along, he felt strangely as though he had just taken it off after a long day's training, light-headed and suddenly aware of the breeze ruffling through his golden hair and the gentle warmth of the Sun on his face.

It took him a moment to recognize the unexpected feeling of hope. The scene in the market square was similar to what Wolfram had seen in Eckendorf. A line of young men and a few young women, mostly farmers or workers by their clothes, although there were three red-bearded Dwarves together, probably cousins or siblings from the Drachenberg colony, stood in front of a table where a scribe looked through papers and marked off names.

Instead of the huge Hauptmann Marcus in his gaudy Landsknecht fashion, the officer sitting there was a small, dapper man wearing a restrained doublet of dark blue brocade.

Beside him was a black-robed man with grayish-white hair, probably the field doctor. Nor could Wolfram see either cannon or drum.

The need to lure recruits with show and glory was over. Now it was time to see who was worth keeping. He also noticed that this time, all the potential recruits bore some manner of weapon: mostly pikes, leaning or dragging about at every angle and occasionally tangling with each other to the sound of muttered curses and apologies, but there were two human halberdiers and two boys with arquebuses, while the Dwarves all carried halberds. No other swordsmen, though. The Landsknechts required each soldier to equip himself, Wolfram remembered. Looking at the awkward way most of the candidates held their pikes, he wondered how many of them had been bought in the last three weeks.

Wolfram caught himself on the way to cut in at the front of the line. He was no longer a nobleman, he reminded himself, thinking of Hauptmann Marcus' words. His chances of acceptance might be slim enough; best not to thin them any further by acting like someone who thought himself entitled to special treatment. The physical examination seemed simple enough.

The Feldarzt looked at teeth and felt muscles, made candidates walk to prove the lack of a limp, and sent the occasional one for a brief run. In a couple of cases he insisted that shoes be taken off, presumably to examine some slight deformity or suspected deformity of feet. Wolfram suspected that the recruiters had already weeded out anyone with obvious defects, to travel, say, here from Eckendorf would be a long and costly endeavor for a farmhand or tradesman's assistant. Certainly Hauptmann Marcus had made it clear to Wolfram that his acceptance was by no means guaranteed. The line moved on slowly. One pike wavered off-balance and fell towards Wolfram. He slipped out of the way in one of those unnaturally fast and smooth movements that happened when his mind was distracted, catching the shaft before it could hit the ground and gently helping its red-faced owner right it.

"Thank you," the boy muttered, looking down and scuffling a shoe in the dirt.

Peasant farmhand, Wolfram thought: broad-shouldered, the bowl-cut brown hair around his round tanned face streaked blond from a warm summer's work outside. For a moment the farm boy's mouth worked, as though he were trying to think of something to say. Then he blurted out, "You're an Elf, aren't you? I never seen an Elf before."

Wolfram found himself sorely tempted to say something like, And if you keep dropping pikes on them, you aren't going to see too many more but restrained himself. Courtesy to all men, his father, Graf Ulric had taught him. Besides, if all went well, this raw peasant would be one of his comrades-in-arms.

"Never saw anyone move so quick like you did there, either," the inept pike man went on. "Is all Elves that quick?"

How in the names of the Three Gods of Darkness should I know? Wolfram thought. In truth, his unexpected flashes of Elven speed and grace frightened him. Not only as a sign of his tainted heritage, as certain as the points of his ears and the sharp upward arch of his eyebrows, but because he had no chance to practice weapons-work since his transformation. Suppose he did something like that in a fight, and it resulted in a fatal miscalculation of range or timing, as if the weapon in his hand had changed unexpectedly from the weight and length of a two-hander to a swifter, shorter one-handed sword?

"Perhaps you'll have the chance to see for yourself later," Wolfram said, forcing himself to smile gently so that the boy young man, really, perhaps even a year or two older than Wolfram himself, wouldn't take the statement as a threat. "There are two in the Silver Eagle, I'm told."

"Are they kin to you? Is that why you're here?"

Wolfram sighed soundlessly. "I mean no offense," he told the boy courteously. "I know it is different among Men, but among the Elves, it is considered very rude to ask personal questions, especially of a stranger."

"Oh. I'm Axel Michael's-son." He looked expectantly at Wolfram.

"Wolfram Longsword."

"That's not an Elvish name!" The farm boy blurted out. "Aren't Elves supposed to have names like I don't know, Galimurifaethiel or something like that?"

The flash of black anger at Axel's persistence clenched Wolfram's heart like a fist, as unexpected and frightening as his moments of Elven movement. He regained control of his temper with an effort, but the peasant lad had already paled beneath his tan, edging away with his knuckles standing out white as knobs of bone where he gripped his pike.

"I'm sorry, m'lord!" He muttered. Axel's hazel eyes darted to either side. Wolfram thought he might have broken line and run if he could have managed it with the pike.

"I'm not going to hurt you," Wolfram said gently, ashamed and unnerved. "Just don't ask me any more questions. All right?"

Axel swallowed, nodding convulsively. He tried to turn and look towards the front of the line, but kept sneaking glances back over his shoulder at Wolfram even as he edged away.

"That was ill-done," a soft, singingly musical voice said at Wolfram's shoulder. He turned, glancing up into slanted, incandescent green eyes.

Wolfram knew at once that he was looking at a full-blooded Elf. Three inches taller than himself, but much slimmer, without the muscle that a young lifetime of training in full armor with double-weighted weapons and shields, not to mention the additional exercises for strength his mother had urged on him; she always knew, had packed onto Wolfram's body. The Elf's face was more clearly alien than the one in Wolfram's mirror, a long triangle tapering down to a very pointed chin, ears and eyebrows more sharply up-swept and eyes more slanted. In the sunlight, his long golden hair glistened with a faint sheen of shimmering rainbow colors, like the polished surface of a pale topaz. It took all Wolfram's strength to keep from looking away from the full-blood's glare, and yet he found himself half-enchanted by the other's beauty. Is this what Axel felt, looking at me? With no more than a farmer's training in courtesy and self-restraint. No wonder he couldn't shut up.

"Come with me," the Elf ordered, turning and walking away without looking to see if Wolfram was following him.

With a regretful glance at the line of recruit-candidates that had formed up behind him in the meantime, at least another hour's wait in the sun already, Wolfram trotted after him, doing his best to ignore the stares.

The Elf led Wolfram out of the village, to a meadow where a great linden tree stood. A few ribbons still fluttered shreds of bright color through the tree's thick green leaves. On Froni's Day and the Day of Glory, the villagers would tie ribbons and offerings on the branches and dance about the thick trunk, no doubt. The Elf settled himself on the ground in a single movement more graceful than the slimmest maiden's dancing.

Wolfram sat down as well, feeling awkward, yet strangely comfortable, as though he had regained some of his humanity by contrast.

"I am Arkoniel va-Israen, born of Malerai va-Israen and Thaaleran va-Alemaie," he said. "Will you grant me the courtesy of your name in return?"

Caught in the beauty of his speech, it took Wolfram a long moment before the horror sank in. Arkoniel was not speaking the Cimbrian tongue, nor Remulan. Nor any language that Wolfram had ever heard.

Yet he understood, though there seemed something strange about the Elf's accent. More, he knew that it would be easy for him to answer in the same language, and he could almost hear in his mind that he would not sound quite the same. Harder, slightly more guttural, and some differences in the words.

Perhaps I would betray myself thereby.

For if he knew the tongue in his blood, it was the blood of a Dark Elf. It made perfect sense that the speech of the Noble-Born. The Dark Elves, o Donmar, that is what they call themselves in their own language! Would be some what changed from that of the Light Elves, and recognizable thereby.

"I am a half-breed, and a bastard," Wolfram said carefully in Cimbrian. "I don't speak Elvish."

Arkoniel raised his sharp golden eyebrows. "How may that be so? It is born in our bones."

After a second's pause to make sure the Elf had spoken in Cimbrian, Wolfram replied, "As I said, I am a half-breed. I was raised among Men, knowing nothing of my heritage. I am a bastard of a noble house among Men. I was trained as if I were a son of that house." Since learning that there were true Elves in the Silver Eagle, Wolfram had worked very carefully on his story. He did not know if it were true that Elves could recognize a lie by clues no Man could detect, heartbeat and breath and the tiniest changes of voice and face, but he was unwilling to take the chance. Certainly Arkoniel was watching him as closely as if the tale were true.

"So," the Elf breathed. "True enough, and yet. What is your name?"

"Wolfram Longsword. The first was given to me; the second I chose for lack of a better."

"Lack, or unwillingness to use it?"

Wolfram stared back unflinchingly. "A bastard is not entitled to his stepfather's name, and my mother died before she could say who sired me. If she knew herself." *She was raped. She must have been, the other choice was, no, she would never have betrayed Löwenstein, in any way.*

He thought of her gentle fingers stroking his hair, her soft voice praising him, how she had clapped her hands and cheered when he made a particularly good stroke in the practice yard, and his anger at the nameless Dark Elf who had condemned her, almost certainly through pain and fear, to a lifetime of worry for the sake of her only son's concealed bastardry, rose up in him like rotten food trying to spew out of his belly. *Surely she meant to tell me someday. How could she die and abandon me so soon?*

"I begin to see," Arkoniel said. "So you carry your burden of anger against both mother and father. Well, there are many Men who have joined the Landsknechts to discharge just such burdens. Since I will not tell you why I am with the Silver Eagle, I have little right to ask you. Yet I must also tell you that, without some good answer to that question, it is unlikely that Obrist Helmuth will take you on. He felt that you might prefer to explain it to one of our own kind, as well as expecting my counsel on the matter."

Wolfram mastered himself, unclenching his fists and breathing deeply. When he felt he could speak evenly again, he said, "That is easily told. A human bastard of a noble house might have stayed on where he was born, as steward or Hauptmann of the guard or any of a number of other posts. The more so if he were sired by the lord. But for a half-Elvish bastard planted as a cuckoo's seed where the lord's should have fallen, there was no good place.

If I had a talent for magic or scholarship, I might have sought out a career at a university. My only true skill is fighting, as I have been trained to do all my life. I had heard that the Landsknecht regiments take little account of race or birth, if a man is a good fighter who obeys orders and follows the company's laws. I had also heard that the Silver Eagle was a regiment worthy of respect, and an honorable one."

Arkoniel considered Wolfram for a long moment.

"Why do you not think of seeking out your Elvish kin? Children do not come to us so often that we will turn one away, not even one who bears some blood of Men, not even one who has been so uneducated that he refuses to hear our language with his heart. Your father may have been slain, or sent on a mission he could not delay by his Queen. I can think of no other reason why he would have abandoned you to the care of Men, but you assuredly have other kinfolk who would be glad to take you in."

"I want nothing of that heritage!" Wolfram said violently, hands trembling with the truth of it. "If I could have, I would have stayed where I was born and raised. My place is with those who cared for me and taught me, not." He stopped before his tongue could betray him, trying hard to get himself under control again.

Arkoniel only stared at him, the lambent green whirlpool of his gaze drawing Wolfram's sight in deeper and deeper. Wolfram felt uncomfortably as though the Elf's glowing emerald eyes were stripping his skin away layer by layer, uncovering the dark locked rooms of his mind. Even those which he had not opened himself yet, the dungeons of thought where, he hoped, the taint of his heritage would stay locked forever.

"True, but incomplete," Arkoniel said at last. "I do not know what has been done to you. Grievous harm, I fear. Do you pray to the gods of Men?"

"To Donmar and St. Hildebrand, yes," Wolfram answered. At least I used to. "And Alagrith and Froni on their feast-days, for love and good harvests. We always kept Agwar's Feast-Night, and I have fasted on the Fast of Dread and St. Hildebrand's Vigil since I was fourteen."

"Have you ever given worship to Darkness, or the Chaos?"

"Never," Wolfram said firmly.

The Elf mused on that, long enough that, though Wolfram had noticed, since his transformation, that it was hard for him to raise a sweat. He could feel the thin gloves inside his gauntlets growing damp at the palms. Reading an Elf's face against his will was said to be impossible. But there was something about Arkoniel's hawk-keen stare that made Wolfram want to leap to his feet and draw his sword to defend himself. The Elf's emerald-hard eyes held a killing cold, like water locked beneath thick ice. Wolfram had seen the eyes of a fighter intent on taking his life twice. During the Orc-raid, and once when Graf Ulric took his sons as well as his knights out to wipe out a band of brigands that had been preying upon his roads.

Both times, that had been in hot blood: he had never seen the icy gaze of an executioner turned upon him before. Yet, he is thinking about slaying me now, Wolfram thought. Might it be better so? A hound that is half-wolf will turn on its owner, however kindly it is raised. What of a Man who is half-Dark Elf? Will my tainted soul surprise me as my body does, so that I do evil without thought or recognition?

"You seem to speak truly," Arkoniel stated. "Yet, well, as you were raised by men, and have suppressed so much of your true being, it may be that the darkness I sense in you is only that of a man's soul. Were you fully of Elvish birth, or did you even have a half-blood's usual portion of our nature, I should think differently. You have so little control of your power, that you cannot keep from showing it to frighten a poor human child, and so little use of it that you could hardly do more. You cannot even speak our tongue, and have repudiated your inheritance before me." The contempt sounded clearly in his musical voice, like the high sharp note of a fife cutting through the melodious thrumming of a harp's strings.

"Be a man, then, and good riddance to you, so long as you choose to do no better. I shall tell the Obrist that there is no reason to keep you out of the Silver Eagle, though I expect that you and I shall not meet in the course of our duties without some remarkably good reason. You seem to have no desire to speak with me, and I certainly have no further wish to speak with you until you have discharged your man's folly."

"Thank you," Wolfram said.

The Elf sniffed and waved him away with an irritated gesture. Wolfram decided to take the hint, getting up and leaving Arkoniel to sit beneath the linden in whatever meditations might cross his Elven mind.

He was almost back to the village square when the reaction hit him, shivering hard through his legs so that he wanted nothing more than to sink down on one of the houses' stone thresholds and collapse. He was about to kill me, Wolfram thought again. If I had tried to speak Elvish with him, if he had recognized my blood as Dark Elvish, that blood would be staining the grass under that tree like ale at Alagrith's Wedding right now!

Wolfram went back to the end of the line. At least there would be time enough for him to compose himself before his examination, he thought. Eventually the trembling passed off, the palms of his gauntlet-gloves drying out. But he could not help looking quickly around himself every now and then to make sure that Arkoniel wasn't creeping up on him again. Do I really want to be in the same regiment as he is? Wolfram wondered. Elves might be uncommon among the Landsknechts, but there was no guarantee he could find a regiment with none.

Particularly if he held to his intention of joining a regiment with a reputation for honor and skill: those were the very ones most likely to attract Elves or the Elf-blooded. He did not want to have another such conversation as he had held with Arkoniel. For a number of reasons. When Wolfram finally reached the head of the line, the officer in charge. Hauptmann Heinrich, if Kai had been right, looked up at him and nodded.

"Wolfram Longsword?"

"Yes, sir."

"Marcus told me to expect you. We'll look you over, then send you to the Obrist for his final decision." The Hauptmann's voice was that of a highly educated man, sharp and clear with no hint of a regional dialect, and his eyes were bright with intelligence. Wolfram thought of Kai's advice, and decided straight away to take it, if he were allowed to join.

The Feldarzt gave Wolfram's teeth a perfunctory glance and asked, "Have you any sickness? Ever been treated for the Southern disease?"

"No."

"Any sign of worms? Do you ever produce tarry black stools?"

"No."

"Walk about a bit for me. More used to riding a horse than to marching, I dare say?"

"Yes," Wolfram admitted.

"You might want to lose the sabatons when we're on the march. They'll eat your shoes pretty quickly, then start tearing up your feet. You seem healthy enough. Mark him down as fit," the Feldarzt said aside to his scribe. "Now, the Obrist is billeted over there, the big house next to the Rathaus with all the white fretwork around the windows, you see it? Good, go on."

Wolfram walked across the square to the building the doctor had pointed out. He guessed that it would usually be either the mayor's house or belong to the wealthiest merchant in town, and wondered what the Landsknecht commander was doing there.

Well, fifteen hundred trained soldiers, and another five hundred eager to join, probably seem quite convincing. The boy who opened the door was about twelve years old, thin and dark-haired, dressed in a red tabard with a silver eagle embroidered on the front. A page or servant, rather than a son, Wolfram guessed.

"Wolfram Longsword, to see Obrist Helmuth von Wesenburg," Wolfram announced.

The boy bobbed his head. "I'll ask if he can see you now, sir," he said. Almost certainly a servant, with that rapid nasal Bärenstadt drawl, Wolfram thought. Perhaps a runaway apprentice boy, or just a street child with a sharp eye for his chances and a quick enough wit to catch the Obrist's attention.

The youth was back in a few moments. "This way, sir."

Wolfram followed him through the house and up the staircase. The building was a little shabbier inside than outside, its braided rugs worn and the smooth split planking of the floor not polished for some time. Down the main corridor, he saw a flash of cerulean skirts and rich brown hair braided up under a net, ducking quickly into a door.

The lady of the house? Hired entertainment? Or did the Obrist take his wife on campaign – assuming he had a wife?

Obrist Helmuth had taken over a very nice room as his office. The windows were real glass, set in frames that would swing out to allow the summer breeze in, with finely painted shutters to keep the cold out in wintertime. The green-enameled stove was unlit at the moment, a vase of red and yellow roses sitting on top of it, but it would make the chamber very cozy in winter. Two large paintings hung on the wall. One was a well-executed version of St. Hildebrand's Vigil, in which the light of the altar candles reflected from the saint's armor gave him a subtle halo, pressing back the dark.

There was something vaguely frightening about it, more of a sense of menace and struggling defense than the image itself seemed to warrant. When Wolfram looked closer, he saw that the texture of the thick oil paints had been used to create, black on black, the faintest shadows of half-formed monstrosities with grasping claws and twisted faces in the darkness outside the warrior-saint's own light.

The other painting was simpler, a middle-aged man and woman in burghers' finery sitting at a table laid with meat and cheese, fruit and wine.

Probably a portrait commissioned by the owners of the house, many artists these days made a good living by painting the moderately well-off.

The Obrist himself sat at a table by the window, a low stack of parchment and a higher one of cotton-paper in front of him.

Freiherr Helmuth von Wesenburg was a short, heavily built man in, Wolfram guessed, his middle fifties, his hair and square-cut beard more than half-faded from golden brown to gray. He wore a conservative Waffenrock of deep gold velvet trimmed with bands of brocaded gold-on-brown silk. The garment's close cut over his upper torso and lack of excessive pleating in the skirt showed him to be in fairly good condition despite the large-boned man's natural tendency to put on weight at his age, muscular chest and shoulders drawing the eye away from the beginnings of a solid paunch not unlike Graf Ulric, in fact. Obrist Helmuth blotted his quill on a much-blotched cloth, looking at Wolfram.

"Sit down, Wolfram Longsword," he said, his voice resonant with the confidence of long command. Wolfram sat at once, long training pulling his spine straight and his feet together as though he were still at attention. The Silver Eagle's commander took his time looking the half-Elf over, his blunt-featured face giving no hint of whether he liked what he saw or not.

"Arkoniel tells me," he began abruptly, "that you were raised by humans, and think of yourself as a Man rather than an Elf."

"Yes, sir."

"Have you the Elvish hearing and ability to see in the dark?"

"Yes, sir."

"Will you resent it if I order you onto night watch or reconnaissance missions for that reason?"

"I will do as I am ordered, sir."

"That wasn't what I asked," Obrist Helmuth said, his voice a little gentler.

"A good commander uses the resources to hand, sir, I won't resent it."

Helmuth nodded. "You are hardly the first soldier to find the Landsknechts a welcome escape from a difficult situation. There are a fair number of well-born younger sons, and bastards, among us. Nor will you find that any man looks down on you for your blood."

He smiled ruefully. "Except perhaps Arkoniel and Piriel, but I suspect that they look down on all of us. In any case, you seem to have been sent out well-equipped. Have you fought in a real battle before?"

"Twice, sir. Once against Orcish raiders, and once clearing out a band of brigands."

"Hmm. Hardly battle in our terms, but at least you're blooded. Heavy cavalry, I assume?"

"Yes, sir."

"But you are trained to fight on foot, as well?"

"Yes, sir."

"You will find our style of fighting very different from what you are accustomed to," the Obrist warned him. "If you have the basic skill with a two-handed sword, you can learn it quickly. Can you read and write?"

"Yes, sir."

"What languages?"

"The Cimbrian tongue and Remulan, quite well. I can speak the tongue of Broceliande well enough to be understood, and puzzle my way through a book in that language, though I write it only very clumsily. I speak Scandian well enough to talk to their traders, but don't read it at all."

"Very few do," Obrist Helmuth remarked. "Well, then. I think we shall start you as a Doppelsöldner at eight guilders a month and see how you do. Should you prove out well, you seem to me just the sort who might make a good officer in the course of time. You still have three days to change your mind before you pass the portal, of course, but I think you will make a worthy addition to the Silver Eagle. Perhaps," he added more softly, "you may find yourself happier here than you have been hitherto." He stood, and Wolfram got to his feet as well.

The Obrist clasped wrists with Wolfram, his grip firm on the sun-warmed metal of the half-Elf's fluted vambrace. A strange feeling welled up in Wolfram's heart, prickling at the back of his eyes. I am truly welcome here, as I had not thought I could be anywhere again.

CHAPTER 22

Tired as she was, Gudrun slept badly that night. It seemed to her that whenever she closed her eyes, she saw all the men she had killed in battle burning before her, writhing on the ground as hat-plumes became momentary flames, armor glowed and melted, agonized faces blackened and split to show white bone for a heartbeat before that, too, charred and some of them rose up again, coming for her as they burned. Twice she awoke whimpering, grinding her fist into her mouth to keep her screams from awakening Wilhelm. At least Alberich slept in his own pavilion, leaving the two younger mages to guard the Black Wagon. He would have known at once what troubled her, and been so disappointed. Perhaps, Gudrun thought bitterly when she started awake at dawn, her shift drenched in sweat and her clammy blankets entangling her like a pair of huge eels, all the men who have said that women are too soft to be Landsknechts are right. Maybe I can't really deal with the brutality of battle.

I was fine as long as the men I killed were just creatures trying to kill me, with no more humanity than a mad dog, but when it comes to someone I know, receiving the same death and I would have killed him, just like the others, if I had joined the Sun Azure instead of the Silver Eagle. Though hopefully I would have had the sense to get back when I saw him keep coming. At least he avenged himself. Gudrun pushed her mass of sweat-soaked hair out of her face, lifting it for a moment to get the cool morning air on the back of her damp neck.

She felt as though she wanted to cry hard hot lump in her throat, eyes squeezing shut and face contorting into a silent wail but no tears would come. Gradually she got control of herself again, remembering all her training in self-mastery. I cannot bring Wolfram back to life. If he is dead! Alberich only said that Elvish blood was one possibility for Doktor Manfred's slayer surviving long enough to avenge himself. Orcish blood would answer as well. They have strong resistance to magic. As do Dwarves, though we haven't any in Forlorn Hope but also some Men. There is no telling what a man in battle-frenzy is capable of, when it comes to withstanding pain or damage. Wolfram may be alive and well, and all this anguish nothing more than a girl's stupid vapors. Wilhelm was still asleep, a lump between blankets and pallet.

Gudrun decided to take the rare opportunity of privacy to wash herself thoroughly. She might not have been in the clash of combat, but after her night of bad dreams, she was as sore-muscled and sweaty as though she had fought in the line.

The cold touch of the wet rag on her bare skin calmed her further, as though she were wiping off all the poisons of fear and worry and guilt. Even the strongest have weak moments, she reminded herself. Better that I should stumble after a battle than before or during. By the time she had put a clean shift on and begun to dress herself, Gudrun was quite certain that her bad night and attack of self-doubt were nothing more than after-battle shock. She had seen large and powerful men, soldiers for many years, collapse shivering and whimpering in the evening after a hard fight, when their spirits crashed down from the exalted heights of battle.

The usual treatment seemed to be a comradely pat on the back and a mug of wine or spirits. Gudrun was on her own, but there was nothing keeping her from drawing a half-mug of plain sharp red from the cask the mages shared. She filled the mug the rest of the way with water, lest the drink go to her head too quickly, despite the way she had eaten the afternoon before, her stomach was growlingly empty but the gentle diluted warmth helped, nevertheless. A short, muffled shriek sounded behind Gudrun.

Bodice still unlaced, she whipped about to see Wilhelm staring wild-eyed at the ceiling, breathing hard and fast.

"Wilhelm?" She said carefully. "Are you all right?"

The other mage started, flinching as though she had kicked him. The anguished look on his pale face was something Gudrun had never thought to see. He looked as though he were staring at the remains of some terrible crime, she thought, and realizing that his hands are covered in blood. Wilhelm's breathing slowed, Gudrun could see him using the same techniques of self-mastery she had used herself, and waited for him to speak.

"Just a bad dream," he said. Beneath the blankets, she could see his body relaxing out of its frozen rigidity. He pushed himself up, shivering in his long linen shirt. "A dream about something very bad that happened a few years ago."

"Hmm." The first shoots of a suspicion were beginning to poke into the light of Gudrun's mind. A suspicion, she realized, that had already started spreading its roots beneath her awareness yesterday.

The fog had been unduly convenient for their foes: if the Obrist had not been willing to take the risk of sending one of his precious mages out on a scouting mission, the Sun Azure's trap would have smashed his Company.

"I had nightmares too," Gudrun said carefully.

A little furrow appeared between Wilhelm's ash-pale brows as he looked at her. Neither of them wanted to say it, but Gudrun knew he was thinking the same thing she was.

"I have heard," she said at last, "that holy shrines have their own defenses, both in the physical world and of the soul. The best mage could hardly detect such a thing, whether it were guided by priests or not."

"That is true," Wilhelm agreed. The shudder rippled over his body, like a horse shivering off flies. "I hope we're done with this soon." He glanced nervously at the entrance to the wagon and leaned towards Gudrun, speaking more softly. "It's a bad business, setting out to destroy a shrine like this. I see the tactical need for it, but I guess Alberich would shout at me for giving in to superstition. Still, even if we don't depend on the gods, how can it be a good idea to offend them? The gods do send dreams as a warning, sometimes."

Gudrun sighed ruefully. It was hard not to agree with Wilhelm, to think that their dreams were part of the shrine's defenses or a warning. Personally, she had little time for either Alagrith's Earth-Witches, with their insistence that women's magic was a matter of mystic intuition rather than control, or the priests of Donmar, who largely seemed to feel that a woman's place was at home as wife or mother; and the traditional celebrations of the lesser gods, Agwar and Froni and Waldriga and so forth, ranged, in Gudrun's mind, from peasant superstition to the grotesque.

Still, it was one thing not to be pious, and another thing to deliberately offend, even if the offense were incidental on the way to another goal. Nevertheless, Alberich had been quite certain that destroying this shrine was necessary, and she was no peasant to spit over her shoulder in fear of bad luck.

"It's no worse than things the Company has done in the past," Gudrun said. "We've both been in sacks before, for instance. Some things have to be done, and this is one, if we want to fulfill our contract. The Orders say that priests and their holy places shall be protected, so long as they remain neutral. If you have any more doubts on the subject, talk to Alberich about it. He seems to have it on good authority that Graf Berthold's priests will act against us."

Wilhelm shook his head. "I don't need to. I just Three Gods of Darkness, that dream just upset me, was all. I'm all right." In truth, his color was coming back, and the drawn muscles of his face were relaxing slowly.

"Since you're just about dressed, why don't you see if Greta's made our breakfast yet?"

Gudrun and Wilhelm had almost finished eating when Alberich arrived. A dark frown tightened the Zauberobrist's ascetic face, his heavy black velvet robe swishing about his ankles like the tail of an angry panther.

Gudrun swallowed hastily, the bite of sausage and bread thickening into a choking lump in her constricting throat and her heartbeat thudding in her ears.

She did not know if she was more afraid that Alberich might know that Wolfram's fate was still in her mind, or that he might have guessed her misgivings, and Wilhelm's, about assaulting the Bad Oberheim shrine. I said all the right things, she reminded herself. But she knew how hollow her words to Wilhelm had rung in her own ears.

"We are to be delayed for a day while prisoners are exchanged," Alberich snarled. "Even though we drove the Sun Azure off, they managed to take enough of our men that the Obrist thinks the effort worthwhile. Despite my advice," His lips pressed tightly together. Gudrun thought that she had never seen the Zauberobrist so openly angry. Normally Alberich prided himself greatly on his self-control.

Indeed, now she could see him bottling his fury back down, as though he were forcing the cork back into an overheated beer barrel in despite of its spurting fountain of foam.

"Well, be that as it may. At least that gives us an additional day to plan and prepare for our portion of the endeavor."

Wilhelm glanced nervously at Gudrun, his watery blue eyes blinking quickly. Hoping, she suspected, that it would be she and not he who brought up their dreams and misgivings.

But if Wilhelm wanted to risk Alberich's angry disappointment, especially when their teacher was in such an ill humor, he would do it by himself. Wolfram blinked at the light streaming through the open door of the barn, broken by the silhouettes of several men. The one in the forefront, a slender man with threads of silver through his long dark hair and close-cropped beard, wore a white robe with a flaming sword embroidered on it in glittering gold thread: a priest of Donmar.

He passed among the wounded captives, stopping here and there to look more closely at one and nodding to the armored Landsknechts behind him. At last he reached Wolfram. Wolfram felt the gaze of his clear blue eyes like a breath of wind passing through him, as though the man were looking through his flesh and considering his bones. After a moment, the priest stretched out his hand, holding it just above the lump on Wolfram's head. His faint frown hardened his gaunt face to a mask of hard-hewn bone.

"By his injuries, this one should come up to our shrine as well," he said to the gaudily dressed men behind him. "But I am loath to risk it."

Wolfram held his breath. He could feel each beat of his racing heart through his broken ribs and the lump on his head. Was he about to be exposed now, after all he had been through and done? And if so, would they kill him here?

The Sun Azure might protect him, as a fellow Landsknecht, but he could hardly depend on that, when he didn't even know if his own Company would ransom him yet.

"Do your fellows know that they have one of the Shadow-Kin among them?" The priest asked Wolfram mildly.

Wolfram stared up at him, mouth open. At last he said, as quietly as he could, "I have not lied. If I have not told all the truth about what drove me from my home, how many Landsknechts have?"

"A sad question, but not to the point," the priest replied. "A lie told by silence is still a lie."

The barn seemed to be whirling around in Wolfram's vision. Only the priest's face was still. The tight mouth, the stark promontories of his cheeks, the dark straight slashes of brows above his infinitely clear blue eyes. It seemed to him that he was caught in a trap, that he could not move, nor speak, except that he told the truth.

"The full truth was not mine to give away. Before Donmar and St. Hildebrand, I have stayed as true to the man who raised me as I could and he was a good man. I repudiated the other inheritance, wanting no part of it."

"An interesting point. A Man's soul is shaped by the choices he makes, and his worth is shown not by his thoughts or plans, but by his deeds. Nor may virtue be inherited, a good man may have an evil son, or vice versa.

Yet for the Elves, I hear it is otherwise. Indeed, were it not, I could hardly have recognized the shadow upon your soul." He paused, considering Wolfram deeply. "Let the risk be on your head, then. Will you be taken to the shrine, and see there if Donmar will heal you, or smite you?"

Wolfram paused, his tongue limp as a dead dove on the floor of his mouth. It was a temptation. *If I go, and the god heals me, I will know that I have hope of cleansing myself someday.* Divine assurance, to answer all his self-doubts, how could he not leap for it at once? Yet Donmar's priest had seen the Dark Elvish taint at a glance. Even St. Hildebrand had wavered once, come near to failing his Vigil. The saint knew that all mortal hearts were flawed, that mortal arms must tire, mortal souls falter on their path. But Donmar's sigil was the Sword of Light, and that only the emblem through which Men could guess at a sense of his perfection.

Can I bear the judgment of the god?

Do I want the judgment of the god?

I do. A sword to cut through the tangled knot of his birth, his nature. A final answer to the question of whether his long effort to be a Man, and a reasonably good man, had succeeded or failed. A chance to put himself to the proof at last, and know whether he were better to live or die. How could he refuse, and not know himself a coward? Wolfram drew breath to say that yes, he would go. Then, just as he opened his mouth to speak, he remembered what Mishni had told him.

Bad Oberstein, the village of the shrine, was the Silver Eagle's next point of attack. If Wolfram were ransomed, he would be bound by honor and oath to fight here and while the Silver Eagle might leave the shrine itself alone, the village was its support and presumably under its protection.

The priests would undoubtedly do their best to protect it. *Even if I were healed instead of slain, how should I accept that gift from a holy stead when I am about to raise my hand in battle against its people?* A soldier must honor his oath and obey his orders, thus even the blessed St. Hildebrand had taught.

There were a few orders which a soldier was morally bound to refuse. Rape, torture for pleasure's sake, deliberate murder of the innocent but, though Wolfram disliked the thought of attacking a shrine's village, it was in no way something he had a right to protest. Knowing that, he would not ask the holy spring for healing.

"No," Wolfram said.

The priest nodded, as though he had expected nothing different, and moved on. Eventually, with the help of the Sun Azure men accompanying him, those who were too hurt to walk were carried out, presumably to be put in carts, and the walking wounded were marched out behind them, until Wolfram and the uninjured Mishni were the only captives left in the barn.

One of the Sun Azure Landsknechts, a burly fellow with an unfashionable tangle of ruddy-brown beard, stayed back a moment.

"They have to be fasting to visit the spring," he explained, jerking a thumb towards the door. "I'll see to it that you two get some breakfast, and the doctor will come to take a look at you when he gets the chance. Why the Dark aren't you going to the shrine, anyway? Some Elvish thing?"

Wolfram nodded reluctantly, though the question relieved him. The priest had spoken very softly, now that he thought back on it but the difference between what he could hear and what a Man could hear was still sometimes a surprise to him.

"Well, your hard luck," the Sun Azure man said. "There is a guard on the door, by the way, so don't even be thinking of trying to escape." He looked sharply at Mishni, who gave him a quick toothy smile back. "Especially you. I doubt your friend's going anywhere for a while. I'll be back."

As soon as the door closed, Mishni leaned over to Wolfram, his dark pupils huge in the gloom.

"Now ask what I couldn't last night," he whispered in the same near-silent breath he had used before. "It Alberich, who hate you?"

Wolfram blinked. He had never spoken to the Provost before his arrest. Granted, Alberich had seemed unfriendly but how else should the man responsible for enforcing the Company's laws behave, when dealing with what appeared to be an open-and-shut case of drunkenness on duty?

Yet, he had been wondering since then how a mage of Alberich's skill could have fouled a simple Truth-Reading. Granted that Wolfram knew little of magic, it even seemed reasonable that the Zauberobrist might have interfered with Wilhelm's spell. Alberich had advised him to choose death rather than Forlorn Hope.

He said he was willing to read my mind, to try to clear me if he could. He could as easily, more easily have rejected the request out of hand.

Unless he knew I would refuse? How could he know?

"Why?" Wolfram breathed. "How would you know, Mishni?"

The Rat showed his teeth for a moment. "Wilhelm not have balls to lie outright. But swore, in court, saw me take money pouch. Never did, only pouch of letters he thought dropped in fire. Who fool mage like that, but better mage? Pouch hold letters from and to Alberich. To Sigfrid's mage, from Sigfrid's mage. So certain Silver Eagle fight for him, before bids made. Working together on own plan."

Wolfram grunted as though someone had rammed a halberd-spike into his belly. The Zauberobrist was the one person who could falsify communications, or even send letters swiftly over a great distance. Even the Obrist was in no position to carry out secret negotiations from a month's march away without a mage's help. It made sense.

"Why me?" He asked. "Why would he want me out of the way?"

Mishni shrugged. "Who know? Maybe afraid Elf see something, hear something Man don't? Maybe you overhear something shouldn't, or Alberich think so?"

That would make sense, Wolfram thought, except that he had never been in a position to overhear anything the Zauberobrist said.

As Lieutenant in the Golden Bear, he was exempt from taking a turn in the mages' Trabanten, so he had never guarded the Black Wagon, nor the house where Alberich had been billeted.

There was just a chance that he might have seen or heard something the night he was framed, and that the blow on the head had jarred it out of his memory, but he doubted that. Except for the two Elves, who other than a mage could have crept up on me unseen? And if Arkoniel or Piriel had, say, discovered my birth and decided I needed to die, they could have knocked my skull in as easily as they knocked me unconscious. More easily.

That kind of cruel subterfuge just isn't like an Elf. At least not a Light Elf. Ludwig disappeared, completely, between the time I left him and the time the Sun Azure prisoners crossed the bridge. He was sitting there with his companions, and then he was gone. His name must have vanished from the register, too. Who except a mage could have done it?

"Do you still have the letters?" Wolfram murmured.

Mishni showed his teeth again. "You don't know, you can't tell anything. I tell you. Alberich look, his wand point straight at me but never find letters. Ever see what rat do with parchment?"

Wolfram felt the blood draining from his face, leaving his skin chill and lifeless. "You ate them?"

"Not prove anything. Not enough there. Else would have shown them in trial. Not safe, piss off Provost and Zauberobrist unless really nail him. Just suspicions."

And that's all I have, really, Wolfram thought bleakly. Mishni was crazy enough that he might really have eaten the letters. Ludwig had disappeared completely, leaving Gudrun as the only witness to what he had told Wolfram about the Sun Azure's contract and Wolfram still wasn't completely certain about how far he could trust Alberich's student. Certainly he wasn't sure about it if it came to a question of her betraying her master. It all makes sense, he thought. But how can I prove it, really prove it?

"But maybe we have same enemy," Mishni went on. "Maybe four eyes open better than two. Especially if two Elf eyes." He glanced sideways at Wolfram, the swift frightened eye-flick of a rodent about to disappear down a hole. The Rat had been close enough to hear what the priest said, Wolfram realized. He must know.

No one scorns Little Kai for his Orcish blood. Orcs were brutes, but not, by that, necessarily tainted. They would keep an oath sworn with blood and steel. Although they would torture to test a captive's courage unto death, and sometimes for sport, they did not do it with the delicate, obsessive enjoyment of the Dark Elves. An Orc, even from one of the tribes that did serve Darkness directly, would lack the wit and self-control, say, to serve in a Landsknecht company for years, either undermining it in subtle ways all along, or waiting for one final betrayal. Wolfram was certain that the priest of Bad Oberstein's shrine would not have paused in taking Kai for healing.

"You have no reason to be nervous about me," Wolfram said, his voice catching. "You've saved my life at least twice now. If I can ever do anything to help you, I will, and I certainly wouldn't harm you."

Mishni looked away, and it seemed to Wolfram that he could guess exactly what the Southerner was thinking. Wondering if Wolfram's seeming humanity was a cunning pose, most like.

It would take tremendous skill for an Elf to act so like a Man, if Wolfram was other than the immense improbability he tried to seem, nothing he said or did could be trusted. Knowing that his Elvish blood came from the Shadow-kin.

Wolfram closed his eyes, the unexpected sharpness of the pain in his heart drowning out the throbbing of his ribs and head. Mishni would talk, when they were ransomed, and then there would be no choice for Wolfram, if he survived Forlorn Hope, but to leave the Silver Eagle for good, and avoid any other Landsknecht companies whose men might have a chance to speak with his erstwhile comrades. Which meant all of them, in the course of time.

He might be able to get work in one of the Southern city-states, which often hired mercenaries, fighting with no scrap of honor and always alert for the faintest whiff of poison in his food. I might give up altogether, and make my way north to Myrkheimr where the Dark Elves rule. If there is no place for me among men.

The temptation was a sudden, unexpected pulse of pleasure through Wolfram's body, as keen and shameful as a youth's first involuntary night-seeding. He felt the flush spreading through his cheeks, and turned his own face away, though Mishni was no longer looking at him. Even if they took me in, I could never endure watching what they do. Getting used to an honest battlefield's slaughter was bad enough.

The twinge of excitement still echoed through him, and for the first time, Wolfram wondered if he truly lacked the ability to take pleasure in his dark kin's cruelty, or was simply unwilling to admit it, still struggling to deny the truth that had exiled him.

It doesn't matter. Whatever taint the creature that sired me bequeathed to me, I also inherited some part of my mother's soul. I can choose. Men say that a horse can't be taught to hunt, nor a dog to pull a cart, but in the wilds of Kievia, there are tribes of men whose sledges are hauled over the snow by teams of dogs, trained to their work as puppies, just as Graf Ulric trained me as a boy to seek the right and do it as best my understanding allows. Telling over the long-polished words of his determination in his mind again and again.

Wolfram slipped into an uneasy half-doze, wakening fully only when the barn door opened to let a long rectangle of silhouette-broken sunlight in. The man who entered was tall and stout, with a neat gray-blond beard, dressed in green silk brocaded with gold.

A thick gold chain glittered around his neck, and gems sparkled a bright rainbow of color from his fingers. His face was heavy-featured and craggy, with deep pouches beneath sharp blue eyes.

"Johannes Eberhart, Provost of the Sun Azure," he introduced himself briefly. "You are the two from Helmuth's Forlorn Hope?"

"Yes, sir," Wolfram answered.

Eberhart considered them minutely. One thick eyebrow twitched, he gave no other sign that Wolfram's race surprised him.

"I understand that you wore full armor when you were taken, along with a personal sword of the very highest quality. Did you hold rank before your conviction?"

"I was Lieutenant to Hauptmann Heinrich of the Golden Bear, sir."

"Do you think Obrist Helmuth will pay to get you back?"

"I don't know, sir."

"Your ransoms will be set according to your former ranks and equipment. With, I think, an additional surcharge. Men who can survive in the Forlorn Hope are dangerous. If Helmuth wants you back, the price will have to compensate for your danger to us. Nevertheless, we will make the attempt.

If Helmuth refuses to pay for you will be allowed the opportunity to buy yourselves free. If that proves impossible, you will be executed quickly and cleanly. That is all."

The Provost turned on his heels and marched out. Beyond the door, Wolfram could just see the flash of his Freimann's red cloak and a corner of his bailiff's black garb as the two men turned to follow him.

Mishni shifted uncomfortably. "How much you think he charge?"

"I don't know." Wolfram thought of the last lot of guilders stored safely in the Silver Eagle's strongboxes, along with the bank-book that gave him the right to draw, on signature, on regimental funds to the level of his account.

Many Landsknechts carried their wealth in the form of heavy gold chains around their necks, but the more prudent especially the officers, with their higher pay, kept their savings with the regiment until they passed through one of the large cities, where it could be safely deposited with the bankers. Wolfram had done that, and could have retired with enough money to set himself up in business, if he had left before his arrest. He thought of the healthy sum he had saved but he also thought of the cost of full armor, and an enchanted sword of the finest workmanship. *Even if it costs every penny I have even if I have to go without armor, I won't leave the sword Graf Ulric gave me behind.*

"It shouldn't be too much for you," he added, hoping to comfort the Southerner. "You don't have much armor, and you weren't an officer. Three months' pay, and whatever he wants for Forlorn Hope on top of that."

Mishni was a Doppelsöldner, hard as it was to associate that proud title with the Rat: eight guilders a month. Twenty-four guilders, plus whatever Eberhart meant by a surcharge. A lot of money, more than a laborer could make in a year or more but reasonable, as Landknechts' pay went. Mishni shook his head.

"Not so good at cards," he said mournfully. "No ransom, the Rat screwed."

"Could you escape?" Wolfram whispered.

The Southerner shook his head again. "Tried last night. Barn is mage-warded. Even rat not get out, until ward down."

Guards brought the prisoners stew, bread, and water; the day moved slowly on. It was mid-afternoon, Wolfram estimated, when the Sun Azure Provost came back. He was flanked by his Freimann, a thin man in the red cloak of his calling, who fingered the hangman's noose at his side with an unpleasant look of satisfaction, and the stocky-muscled figure of his bailiff, like a moving black boulder.

"Obrist Helmuth has refused your ransom," the Provost said quietly. "Can you ransom yourselves?"

"How much?" Wolfram asked, hoping he had calculated correctly.

"One hundred and thirty guilders for yourself with all your equipment. Seventy with nothing except the clothes you stand up in. Ninety for your life, armor, and weapons excluding your enchanted sword. For your companion, thirty-five."

"I can pay it, if you give me leave to send to our Pfenningmeister," Wolfram said confidently. It would take every penny he had saved up in the course of his service, but he could do it.

If Neidhart isn't in on the conspiracy! The cold thought bit into his belly like a frost-rimed dagger. But if the rot had spread so far in the Silver Eagle. He grimaced, put it aside.

No point in worrying now, he would get his savings back, or not.

"And you?" Eberhart said, looking down at Mishni. The small man's olive complexion had gone to pale, dirty gray, his eyes flicking here and there in search of escape. His right hand held tight to the lump under the neck of his jerkin, as if hoping that his patron vermin might gift him with some escape at the last moment. Beneath the skittering glance, Wolfram saw something in the Rat's eyes that he might have recognized in a mirror, if he had been able to look at himself in the first days of his exile. The realization, down in his guts, that the impossible, appalling thing was truly happening to him.

"No," Mishni whispered at last.

Wolfram felt his heart turning over. He had hoped desperately that they would be ransomed, or, beyond that Mishni had some means of escape. Johannes Eberhart looked at his bailiff, nodded. The black-clad man picked Mishni up without any sign of effort. The Rat hung limp in his grip, as though his heart had failed him at the last, but one eyelid shivered at Wolfram in the barest trace of a wink.

He will try to get away as soon as they are out of here, Wolfram thought. Most likely, Mishni would die, too. No matter how quick and agile he was, there would be too many armed men watching for him to make a successful escape.

"Stop," Wolfram said quietly. "I will ransom him."

Eberhart raised a heavy gray-blond eyebrow. His craggy face showed no other sign of his surprise, he merely said, "Put the prisoner back. How do you wish to go about this?"

"Please ask our Company's clerk to send all the money I have, up to the total of what is written in my bankbook. If you can give me quill and parchment, I will write a note confirming my transfer of the account to regimental funds in return. The Schreiber may want that in advance. I will sort the rest out with you when the money is here."

"Very well."

The Provost signed to his bailiff, the man dropped Mishni back on his pallet. The three of them left without another word.

"You suppose Provosts always pricks?" Mishni asked, with a shadow of his usual grin. "Requirement for job, maybe?"

"He could have been worse," said Wolfram absently.

No matter how he ran the numbers around in his mind, there was only one possible outcome. Either he would have to give up the sword that had been Graf Ulric's last gift to him, or Mishni would have to die.

Even if Wolfram abandoned his armor instead and he would never survive his next battle if he did. Its price had only been set at twenty guilders. The last of my home, the proof that Graf Ulric loved me, even if he didn't sire me.

Except for his sojourn in Forlorn Hope, Wolfram had only been parted from Treuherz when the blade was taken from his unconscious body. Perhaps he had only used it once or twice a year at most, it being unsuited to Landsknechts' fighting and Wolfram not being inclined to brawl outside the battlefield. Nevertheless, it had been a sort of anchor to his soul. His armor was certainly fine, but anyone could have good armor, whereas that particular sword was the only thing he owned that was truly part of Löwenstein. Wolfram had spoken up in desperation to save Mishni's life, now he wondered if he could really go through with it.

Wolfram cursed himself now for not putting more aside. He was frugal as Landsknechts went, but he enjoyed good food and fine wine, staying in the better inns when the troops were turned loose to find their own billets in town; and the shape of his body, longer-legged and slimmer at the waist than a Man's of his size was likely to be, meant that, if he were to wear the close-fitting garments he preferred, they had to be carefully shaped and cut to him. He had never had any reason not to dress like a noble's son. Amid the flamboyance of a Landsknecht company, his silks and velvets were everyday wear, standing out only in their restrained color and design.

All the times he had bought the drink for the other men of his Rotte, or covered Gretel's pay when the others she cooked and washed for were low on funds, but how could I guess I would have to ransom myself? He thought plaintively. I conducted myself as an officer because I also had an officer's privileges, and value. There was no way for me to guess at this insanity.

"If you'd known it was going to happen, it wouldn't have happened," Graf Ulric's voice scolded in his memory. "You have to think about what could happen, too. Or something you don't know about is going to leap up and bash your fool head in someday."

For a moment Wolfram couldn't even remember what the Graf had been talking about some boyish silliness or other. Then the memory came back. The flash of terror as the tree-limb cracked beneath him, the flailing fall and the earth hammering him breathless. His father arriving just in time to find Wolfram picking himself up, staring down at the boy with the face of a thundercloud reddened by the sunset. Ulric had lifted him off the ground and shouted at him, and finally Wolfram had stammered, "The branch just broke. I didn't know that was going to happen."

On the other hand, there was a difference between reasonable probabilities and unreasonable ones. While a few Landsknechts lived to grow old and retire, it wasn't the sort of profession where squirreling away money for long-term plans instead of spending it to make oneself more comfortable and keep armor and weapons in top condition could be considered a good risk.

To the Three Gods of Darkness with it: I'm here now. Bent over with Black Nikki's cock about to ram up my arse, he added to himself: the rough peasant phrase had never seemed so appropriate. If only I hadn't taken the damned sword into battle! That was stupid, really stupid. I don't use it in our fighting, too short and light for hacking pikes through and too long for close quarters. So why did I take it?

Wolfram knew the answer to that: he wore Treuherz into battle because he wore it everywhere. Because it was his father's, Graf Ulric's gift. It was the last part of his old life to which he could still cling. Because it proves that I am still Graf Ulric's son. In heart, if not in body. He looked over at Mishni again. Small, greasy-haired, scar-faced, with a dead rodent around his neck. What was he, compared to steel bright as sky and sun mirrored in a stilled pond, light breaking silver off fine-whetted edges, and the comfortable warmth of fluted ivory against Wolfram's palm, its flutings lined with twining strands of twisted gold to keep his grip from slipping in blood?

The faint greenish storm-glimmer shining from the depths of the blade in battle, sign of the enchantment that kept the sword's razor-keen edges from chipping on bone or wood or metal, as such thin sharpness would do without magic to aid and all of that was nothing against Graf Ulric's roaring lion set into the hexagonal pommel. Wolfram had gotten a fine smith to conceal the arms beneath a thin facing of silver, lest the heraldry be recognized and questions asked but he bore it still, because Ulric had thought him worthy. *All I have of home.* No one would even know that Wolfram had made the offer and changed his mind, except the Provost of another Company, and Mishni himself and the latter, not for long.

If he could win his honor in the eyes of the Silver Eagle back at all, leaving Mishni to his death would be no hindrance to it. *No one would know. But I would.* Wolfram's hand stole down to his side where his sword no longer hung, as if to touch the hilt like a talisman. *Could he bear to look at himself in a mirror, if he betrayed the man who had saved his life? I can hardly bear it anyway.* Four years later, and the face he saw when he could not look aside was still a stranger's. *At least the soul behind it is familiar. Would it still be, if I abandoned Mishni?* Wolfram lay there, his thoughts going around and around. After a little while, a priest, not the tender of the shrine; probably the regimental chaplain, came in, putting his hands on Wolfram's head and ribs.

A sharp pain shocked through both points; Wolfram bit back a startled yelp. But the bolts of pain faded quickly, the deeper aches draining away behind them, and when Wolfram lifted his head to see the priest's white robes retreating again, he realized that both dizziness and soreness were gone. Eventually the Sun Azure Provost came back, Freimann and bailiff trailing him like the black and red shadows of a sunset battlefield. The bailiff set a small chest down by Wolfram's bed and cut the ties binding his hands.

"An hundred and thirty-six guilders," Eberhart said briefly. "You know the prices: what do you want to do?"

Wolfram slowly counted out the seventy for his life, twenty for his armor, two-handed sword, and Katzbalger, and paused a moment. He could not look at Mishni. *How much do I owe him for my life? Is the sword of Löwenstein's second son worth more than that? And if I do betray Mishni now, after what he did for me, and I look in a mirror afterwards, will I see Graf Ulric's beloved son, or the spawn of the Dark Elf who raped his wife?*

"And thirty-five for Mishni, with such armor and weapons as he had," Wolfram said firmly, counting out the last of the money and slipping the eleven remaining coins into his pocket. Now he could meet the Rat's eyes, wide with wonder. Wolfram realized that his companion had expected to be betrayed at the last moment.

"Done. Cut their bonds and escort them back to their Company. They can claim their equipment on the way."

The Provost was turning to go when Wolfram said, "Will, would there be any chance that I could buy my sword back later?"

Eberhart looked coolly at him. "If you can raise the money and get it to us before the end of this campaign, I suppose there might be. Otherwise, it will be sold with the other booty and the price divided accordingly, unless someone, one of our officers, for something of that value, chooses to keep it as his share or a part thereof. In that case, you would have to negotiate directly with the man who claimed it. If it is sold on, you would be dealing with whoever bought it, probably one of the arms dealers in Bärenstadt or Schönburg, depending on where we go after this."

"Thank you," Wolfram said bleakly.

At his rate of pay as a Lieutenant, it would take him at least two months to save up the ransom price. For which, of course, he would have to be free from Forlorn Hope.

The campaign would long be over. Only the gods knew how much an eventual owner might ask, if he could track down whoever bought or claimed it and that person were willing to sell. Still, and the thought was like a sunburst inside Wolfram's head. He could wait until a young man of twenty died in his nineties, to purchase the weapon from his heirs.

Unless he fell in battle, he would still be as young and strong in an hundred years as he was now: the urgency of a Man's short life need not drive him any longer.

"I trust that, if I send to your company clerk later, he will be able to tell me the fate of the item?"

"Most certainly," the Sun Azure Provost replied. "Martin keeps very close accounts, and you would hardly be the first to seek the late reclamation of a treasured weapon." He glanced at Mishni again, the faint twitch of one fleshy nostril suggesting how little worthwhile he would have thought Wolfram's bargain.

The bailiff bent to cut the bonds on the two prisoners' feet. "Come along, now. There is no time to waste."

CHAPTER 23

To Wolfram's shame, it was Little Kai who took charge of the two Forlorn Hope men when the Sun Azure bailiff marched them back to their own lines. The black Orcish eyes met Wolfram's for a second, then squeezed tight-closed, as if a sword had struck Kai across his overhanging brows. *It wasn't as you think!* Wolfram shouted silently. Of course Kai had taken his disgrace personally: he had welcomed Wolfram to the Silver Eagle, he had been Wolfram's Fähndrich, and as much of a friend as Wolfram would allow any of the Landknechts to be. *I wronged you in that, too,* Wolfram thought.

I held back, thinking myself your better not only because I was born in a castle and you in a peasant's hut, but because Men look up to Elves and down at Orcs. For the first time, he wondered if Kai felt that contempt as his due, as something to be overcome only by his endless faith and unrelenting competence, or if the coal of resentment burned as deep in his guts as in Wolfram's own.

In either case, how could he have failed to hate the noble of half-Elven blood, given by birth all the antitheses to the things that caused his pain? Yet Kai had tried to be Wolfram's friend, and if he had failed, it was Wolfram's fault, not his. *If I come out of this whole, I will try to make amends to you.* Kai said nothing to Wolfram as he walked the half-Elf and Mishni back to the Forlorn Hope compound. Only nodded to the guards and said briefly, "Ransomed themselves." He turned his back and walked away without a glance or word, knobby fingers tapping at the slashed yellow puffs just above the knees of his hose.

"Keep fire going late," Mishni murmured, then wandered off as though Wolfram had done nothing to save his life. A flare of anger scorched Wolfram's stomach for a second, but then he could think again. Whatever the Rat had in mind for the harm of their mutual enemy, it would have to wait until everyone else was asleep.

"You're alive!" Fredrik cried, running over to Wolfram. "I'd heard you were dead, just captured? Or did you manage to escape the field?" He embraced the half-Elf without restraint, planting a bristly spirit-scented kiss on either side of Wolfram's face. Simultaneously embarrassed and pleased, Wolfram gave him a brief squeeze in return.

"No, I was captured. I had to ransom myself."

"At least you could. Look, if you ever get stuck for ransom, send to me, all right?

Now that Sascha's gone, I can't think of anyone I'd rather have beside me in a charge." Fredrik's face tightened suddenly as he spoke Sascha's name.

"Did you see how he died?" Wolfram asked softly.

"I saw. By all the gods, I'd never have thought a man could stand two blasts of mage-fire. Only that crazy Kievian made us all look like little gnomes."

Wolfram put his arm around Fredrik's shoulders. If I've ever seen a man with a big chunk of sorrow he needs to puke up. "Come on. Let's find some spirits and we'll drink to him. I've heard that's the custom where he came from."

"Yes. There's not enough alcohol in the world to cure the way I feel but it'll help some. He deserves it. A warrior's warrior, by the gods!"

Wolfram only had half a bottle of wine left, but as they were finishing that, Mishni circled by and dropped a large flask into his lap.

"Little thanks," he said. "Careful with it." Wolfram nodded, sloshing Fredrik's mug full of the clear spirit and pouring a finger's depth into his own.

They drank late into the night, Fredrik recounting tales of Sascha while Wolfram listened carefully. This is how we keep the dead alive, Wolfram thought. The knowledge of who they were, what they were.

I barely knew Sascha and yet now I understand how much passed from this world with his death, what he gave to save me, for if he had fallen at the first blast, I surely would have been next. May the gods cherish him as I do, as I wish I could have done while he lived! To Wolfram's surprise, Mishni was not the only Forlorn Hope man who donated drink to Fredrik's memorial drinking. He would have sworn that the wretches he fought beside would have given up a limb before losing a swallow of possible oblivion and yet man after man came by with a bottle or a skin, toasting Sascha once before leaving his treasure to Fredrik. Even here, there is some decency in Men, Wolfram thought, amazed.

Who would have guessed it? But perhaps they are mourning their own deaths as well, hoping that some spark of memory or love will kindle from this raging fire when they, too, are fallen. Fredrik's capacity was amazing, but eventually the time came when Wolfram had to gently guide the Scandian to his tent, wrapping him carefully in his bedroll. Wolfram himself had drunk far less than his companion, but even so, he was amazed at how little it had touched him; no more than a gentle warmth in his belly and a general relaxed feeling. Have I been drunk since I, Wolfram thought back over his years in the Silver Eagle.

He had not dared drink more than a glass of wine every evening in his first wanderings, afraid of allowing himself to become vulnerable either to others, or to his own unknown nature.

Since then duty, the responsibilities of a Lieutenant, fastidiousness.

One thing or another had kept him from the traditional pleasures of a soldier. He should be at least unsteady on his feet now, longing for his quiet warm bedroll, but he felt as clear as if he had been drinking nothing stronger than wine watered to campaign regulations, one part to five. If I had known this, I could have cleared myself! Wolfram thought, suddenly angry. He knew why the other Elves in the Company had said nothing: an Elf-blooded who was so sundered from his heritage as to not even know its bone-bred language might be as susceptible to poisons of the mind as a Man.

But if Wolfram had been willing to trust himself, or another, even once I have been a fool. Over and over again. I may not have chosen this bargain but I have been a fool, throwing its good away while keeping the ill. Wolfram sat down by the low-glowing coals, picked up the last flask of spirits, and emptied it in a single draught. It prickled warmly down his throat and in his belly, but he felt no more from it than from a long swallow of water. Elves can no more be poisoned nor get drunk, than they can die of plague.

I can clear myself now.

Donmar willing, drag out the worm in the regiment's heart as well!

Wolfram sat and waited, watching the ash fur thick and gray over the last coals. The other fires had died down as well, men going to sleep one by one.

The Moon was down, but the hard silver light of the stars let Wolfram see as well as if it were day, watching the little scuttling shape of Mishni creeping closer and closer to him. Standing in the shadow of his own tent, the Rat beckoned. Wolfram rose, walking casually over to him.

"In here," Mishni whispered, his lips barely moving. Wolfram ducked under the flap; Mishni followed him in. "These."

To Wolfram's sight, the black letters stood out clearly against the pale ragged parchment, despite the smelly stains that blurred them. He read the letters carefully, then again. They would not have been proof by themselves but together with what Lieutenant Ludwig had told him and especially considering the man's disappearance.

"Enough to hang him," Wolfram whispered. "Why didn't you show me these before?"

The Rat's pointed features were downcast – ashamed? "Didn't trust. Couldn't. Especially, what their priest said."

What changed your mind? But Wolfram didn't have to ask. He had struggled with the answer long enough.

"Don't know what you are. Didn't have to save my life. No one know, if you leave me die. Whatever you are good."

Tears prickled hot behind Wolfram's eyelids. Graf Ulric would have undoubtedly hanged Mishni as a thief, not set him up as a judge over his sons' morals.

I know what the judgment is worth; what is the judge, to that?

"Thank you," Wolfram murmured. But there was no more time to think about his personal doubts. They had to act, and quickly.

"Fredrik won't be able to get out tonight, and Heinrich won't hear me again," he mused. "Mishni, is there anyone?"

"Rat has an idea. If you think proof strong enough."

Wolfram drew his dark hood around his pale face, letting the play of shadows in the starlight guide him. When the guard keeping the Forlorn Hope men in looked straight at him, the pale brown eyes did not widen, nor the slow sound of the man's bored heartbeat quicken. Wolfram was part of the night, letting the soft whisper of the breeze and the quiet darkness move him past. Even Mishni, skilled and silent thief that he was, sounded like a herd of horses thundering through the grass ahead of Wolfram's quiet gliding feet. The only danger, Wolfram realized, was that the beauty of starlight glimmering softly off the delicate angles of the tents and shimmering in the pale ostrich plumes on the guard's hat might lull him into still contemplation until the dawn came.

I am half Man, Wolfram reminded himself.

I do not have eternity; and I have a task to do. Once they had slipped past the guard posts, the chief danger was over. Wolfram touched Mishni's shoulder, pointing at the Golden Bear's Fähnlein.

The flag hung heavy in the damp night air, starlight glinting off the first pinpricks of gathering dew like a scattering of minute diamonds. Behind it rose Hauptmann Heinrich's pavilion. Wolfram's stomach twisted in fear, a coppery taste in the back of his mouth, but his hands were steady. If this failed, it would be the end: of his hopes of redemption, certainly, of his life, probably.

But at least I can do something now! He thought. The knowledge closed about Wolfram like armor on a wounded man, the comforting feel of leather straps tightening steel breast- and backplates to hold sprung ribs in place, steel greaves and vambraces pulling closer to splint injured limbs so that he could stumble to his feet and swing his sword for a little while longer. A temporary help, and one that only dulled the pain a little but enough. Enough, maybe, to turn the tide from loss to victory. Donmar, I shied from your judgment for honor's sake, not fear. Aid me now, god of the soldier, and if I win through I shall come to it if I can without forsaking my duties, and give you once more the trust I forsook. Heinrich awoke suddenly, his shout reverberating against Wolfram's palm as Mishni held his flailing limbs down.

The pistol he had left beside his bed was in Wolfram's other hand, its blued metal gleaming ominously as Wolfram touched the muzzle to his forehead.

"Quiet," Wolfram murmured to his former Hauptmann. "I'm sorry we had to do it this way, but you wouldn't have listened to me otherwise. We have proof of betrayal in this regiment, proof that I think will also clear myself, and Mishni. If we let you go, will you listen to us?"

The whites of Heinrich's eyes gleamed and shifted wildly, as if he were a horse hearing the cannons' roar for the first time. Wolfram felt the softness of his lips writhing above the hard edges of his teeth, trying hopelessly to bite at his captor's palm. He bent down to hiss into Heinrich's ear.

"We have written proof! For the sake of the Silver Eagle, will you listen? I will give your pistol back after you have heard everything; you can shoot both of us if you don't think this is worth bringing to the Herr Obrist. If we just wanted to escape Forlorn Hope, we could have done it already. Now, for Donmar's sake, will you listen?"

Heinrich's struggles subsided; his eyes narrowed. After a few moments, he nodded. Wolfram touched his temple with the pistol's muzzle again.

"I am truly sorry to have to say this, but if you shout for the guards when we let go of you, I will shoot you, and then we will have to run and leave the regiment to its traitor. Still willing?"

Heinrich nodded again. Wolfram took his hand away.

"This had better be good," the Hauptmann croaked softly. "The man you named last time never existed."

"Oh, he did. You didn't ask Gudrun, did you?"

Wolfram saw the faint flicker of doubt shimmering across Heinrich's face. "No. I looked at the records."

"You'll have your chance. It's all part of this Mishni, let him go and light a lantern so he can read the letters."

Wolfram heard the scritching and smelt the brief brimstone-puff of a phosphor-light, expensive, but no extravagance. A Landsknecht officer might need a reliable source of fire if his company were attacked in the night. A heavy wave of smoke from lantern-oil igniting then the little golden flame rose to cast wavering shadows through the tent.

"Let me see them, then," Heinrich said, pushing himself up in bed.

The Hauptmann went over each of the letters, squinting closely to make out the writing through the stains that blurred the ink. "Where did you say you got these?"

"Wilhelm tried throw them in fire," Mishi answered. "Thought might be worth look."

"Umph. If what Wolfram told me were true." Heinrich fell silent, staring at the soft ragged pages in his hands. "Give me the gun."

The weight of wood and metal trembled in Wolfram's hand. Heinrich had made his choice; but there was no way to tell what it was. *I have to trust. Or flee now. But if I die, I will do it with my honor whole.* Wolfram reversed the handgun, presenting it butt-first to his former Hauptmann. Heinrich took it and walked to the flap of the pavilion.

"Joachim, fetch the Herr Obrist here. Ask him for authority to summon Marshal Gudrun directly, now, without informing the Provost."

Wolfram heard the footsteps running off into the night as Heinrich walked back, seating himself by the small table and laying the letters down. "If this proves false," the Hauptmann said conversationally, "it will mean the wheel for both of you. I will turn it personally! Do you understand me?"

"Yes, sir," Wolfram answered. Mishni bobbed his head.

CHAPTER 24

Gudrun lay in the dark, weary, but sleepless. She had closed her eyes and practiced her breathing exercises, doing her best to breathe in power and sigh out the trembling dread in the pit of her belly; tensed and relaxed each muscle in turn; even opened her mind to the buzzing silence of the Chaos-flux in hopes of stilling the thoughts nibbling about its edge but nothing worked. Memories of her father shouting at her and her mother crying, her dreams of the night before, a face twisting in agony before her mage-flames charred its expression into coal tracked by the two white streaks of melted eyeballs. The insane urge to see if she could sneak out of the wagon and over to the Forlorn Hope encampment, to find out whether Wolfram were truly dead or alive, each possessed her in turn, a muttering near the edge of sleep rising to a roar in her mind.

Several times she almost rose to look for a cup of wine, in hopes that easing her clenching body would help her thoughts relax as well, but either fumbling in the dark or lighting candle or spell-lamp would awaken Wilhelm. Or, if he, too, were suffering a like haunting, it would confirm to him and to her, that the shrine was working against them. That certainty would weaken their magic in turn when tomorrow's assault began, which the Silver Eagle could not afford. War of the mind, or the spirit, Gudrun thought. She wondered briefly if everyone in the regiment were lying awake as she was, or seeking wine to silence their thoughts. Many soldiers, even experienced ones, grew nervous before battle, and had easier means at hand to soothe their nerves than she did. Wilhelm would lie with me, if I asked him to, she thought quite suddenly.

That expedient had never tempted her before; now it almost appealed. But the thought of the other mage's soft damp hands on her skin, or his body, clumsy bones beneath a thin covering of flabby flesh, made her shudder. Even if I were thinking of Wolfram at the time and if Wilhelm knew, and sometimes mages' minds do open when their bodies are so close, that would likely break his confidence forever. I'm sure there is a girl for Wilhelm somewhere, but not me. She sighed and closed her eyes again, going over the tables of planetary correspondences in her mind in hopes that the ordered ranks of memory would defend her thoughts like the well-built walls they were.

Earth. Stones. Black tourmaline, smoky crystal, black onyx. Colors, black and brown. Bright powers, alagrith, Froni, Waldrig and Waldriga. Dark powers, gurvethor. Peoples, Dwarves and Trolls. Beasts, Swine, creeping things, especially snakes and worms, the beasts that devoured the dead, except for those that specifically belonged to other realms, such as ravens and wolves, being animals of the air. At least, if Wolfram were dead, he would have been burnt with honor, having redeemed his crime, if he had committed it, with his life. If he isn't? What if he's captured and needs ransom? The Herr Obrist won't ransom Forlorn Hope men, but I have money. If that's the case, and I don't do something soon. What can I do without Alberich knowing? What? The sound of a man's voice calling out softly outside made her start sharply.

"Marshal Gudrun, you are to come with me at once, by the Herr Obrist's orders."

A piercing shock twanged through Gudrun's belly, like the shock she had felt once when, taking a step to get a clearer shot, an arquebus ball whizzed through the air just where her head had been. She could not tell whether the pang was fear or relief but her hands trembled as she pulled a heavy cloak over her shift and belted on her wand.

"What is this about?" She asked quietly when she was out of the wagon.

The young soldier shook his head, face pale in the thin moonlight. "Herr Obrist's orders, ma'am."

Why me? Where is Alberich? Fear twinged through her, a sharp lightning-ache like the metallic taste of uncontrolled chaos-flux sparking off steel. Could someone have gotten into our camp and killed him? His pavilion should be warded as thoroughly as the Black Wagon but even the best mage is vulnerable in sleep. Gudrun glanced about nervously, but saw nothing unusual. The soft glow of beds of coals ringed by tents, here and there, the dim light of a hooded lantern heading back from the sutlers' camp, men who had stayed out late whoring or drinking or gambling, and a few more lights circling steadily in the shadowy hands of sentries.

The night was chill and damp, a faint mist fuzzing the low red remains of campfires and the lantern beams. Gudrun wondered if the next day would be foggy. Not to the defenders' advantage, surely? If it were the shrine that raised it last time. The soldier led Gudrun to a Hauptmann's pavilion. She could not make out the image on the Fähnlein that hung limp in the still dank night air, but the heavy canvas walls shone faintly with all the lights within, as though the pavilion had become a giant lantern itself, an impression strengthened when the soldier pulled the flap aside, letting a beam of light fall straight in her face. Unnerved, she blinked the darkness from her eyes, trying to make out the figures inside.

The stocky shape of the Herr Obrist, wrapped like herself in a heavy cloak; when he moved, she caught the glint of chain-mail over a flash of long white nightshirt. Hauptmann Heinrich, small and dapper in his neat dark doublet, but his hair disheveled as if he, too had just risen from sleep. He held a wheel-lock pistol in both hands, aiming it at.

"Wolfram!" She gasped. The half-Elf stood with his hands tied before him, smiling faintly. There was something different about his face, Gudrun thought.

It took her a moment to place it, always, before, she had been able to see the little creases of tension tugging at his expressions, the tight binding of muscles that foreshadowed a Man's lines of pain and worry in age. Now, for the first time, the preternatural calm of an Elf had settled over him, a serenity that Gudrun would have thought impossible for anyone standing bound with a gun pointed at his heart and the Herr Obrist frowning at him. Unless, Wolfram's smile widened a little as she looked into his blue-green eyes, shimmering clear as turquoise water. *He trusts me. I am here for him and he is alive!* With a great wrench of effort, Gudrun forced her own face to calm. If the results of her spell were to be trusted, it would not do to fly her feelings on a banner before the Herr Obrist.

Instead she gave the Silver Eagle's commander a brief mage's bow and said, "Sir, I am here at your order."

"Indeed," Helmuth said. "We have some questions for you. Did Wolfram capture a Lieutenant named Ludwig in our first battle with the Sun Azure?"

"Yes, sir. I saw the man myself, and heard Wolfram speaking with him."

"Under what circumstances?"

Gudrun swiftly detailed how Wolfram had requested her to determine the truth of his captive's statement regarding the other regiment's pay rates.

"Why did you tell no one?"

"Wolfram said he had wanted to hold back until it was proven by my spell, presumably, which suggested to me that he had a plan in mind for after I had done so." Gudrun's voice slowed down as she spoke.

Suggested to me, an officer who failed to act, or acted, on such thinking would have deserved demotion. Perhaps this was another reason why mages were never in the line of battle command, save sometimes regarding the direction of their own. Alberich, too, would have torn strips off her for such muddiness.

"The Zauberobrist had previously chastised me for speaking to Wolfram. I was unwilling to bring the matter up to him without clear indication that it was necessary."

"What was the Zauberobrist's objection?" Obrist Helmuth asked. Gudrun looked at him for a long moment, trying to guess whether his heavy glare showed true anger, or only intensity.

"If you have only conjecture, you may report that, but define it as such."

"Sir." Gudrun paused again to gather her thoughts. "Two things. The Provost has mistrusted Wolfram for a long time, considering the contrast between his race and his behavior anomalous. He feared that Wolfram had become a distraction to me. I was increasingly convinced of his innocence. Because I am a woman."

Helmuth considered the two of them for some time, and Gudrun felt her heart sinking. The light of the lanterns hung about the pavilion, muted by the golden translucence of their horn panels, and the brighter flames of the candles glowed gold from Wolfram's hair, underscoring the perfection of his mouth and strong narrow jawline, gilding the fine lines of his high cheekbones and up-swept brows so that his blue-green eyes shone like crystalline jewels set in gold-washed silver. He was beautiful enough to quicken her breath and wring her heart. She had no doubt that it would be easy for the Herr Obrist to believe her deluded, or even a willing conspirator.

But all he said was, "Tell me the details. All of them."

Gudrun took a breath deep enough that she could feel her ribs shaking and let it out slowly, then began. Her doubt of the other mages' spells, her own effort, Alberich's explanation of the mind-skills of the Elves, the Zauberobrist's offer to search Wolfram's mind to its depths.

Obrist Helmuth waited until she was done, then said, "We require one more witness here. Hauptmann Heinrich, please send your man to fetch Arkoniel."

What does he need an Elf to tell him? Gudrun wondered. If Alberich was telling the truth about their ability to change the past in their dreaming memories? If so, why should he doubt? Or can one Elf read what another has done? She waited, caught between hope and fear, unable to look at Wolfram lest the certain truth of the distraction Alberich had warned about be read on her face. No one spoke until the full-blooded Elf entered the pavilion. The muted light that made Wolfram a vision made Arkoniel unearthly, as much frightening as fair, emphasizing the unnatural fierce delicacy of the Elf's fine-swept features. Gudrun could see the kinship between them but the difference was as a warm stone to a flame, one a comfort to the touch and one a searing, deadly danger. She hardly recognized Arkoniel's flowing gesture as a salute.

"Arkoniel," the Obrist said, "is Wolfram capable of re-dreaming the past well enough to confuse a truth spell?"

The Elf gave his half-blooded kinsman a glare of contempt that made Gudrun want to wither into ash, even Wolfram flinched beneath it.

"I doubt that he can so much as dream the past, let alone shape it. By his own will, he has no part in the soul of the Elves, though as Men count it, there has been ample time for him to rethink his choice. Is there anything more? Sir," Arkoniel added as an afterthought.

"I thank you. Please remain, with your weapons ready. We may have need of you."

What the fuck is going on? Gudrun wondered. Heinrich could shoot Wolfram any moment he wanted to, unless, the unspeakable suspicion was beginning to grow in her mind now, swelling from its depths like a huge, deadly gas bubble blistering up from the mud of a swamp.

Because if Wolfram is truly innocent, then Alberich.

"Marshal Gudrun," Obrist Helmuth said, "I have two documents regarding which I require confirmation. Can you tell me if they were sent between the same people, by the same mages?"

"Certainly, sir."

The Obrist laid out two pieces of parchment, both face-down. One was clean, curling inward at the edges as though it had been rolled and tied for some time. The other was ragged, smeared, and stained.

Gudrun pulled her wand free, letting its familiar tingle in her palm and the gestures deep-grained into her body draw her mind away from consideration of the unspeakable. The Chaos-flux glimmered in her sight, whirling colored sparks falling in a haze over the two documents.

Time and place set aside in the dance of Chaos, a dance anchored thinly on both ends by the random spattering of ink-droplets far tinier than the eye could see, a flickering of thoughts behind them that flashed closer and closer together until at last their flickering became a single matching shimmer between the two gates into the Void, the same dual shimmer falling perfectly into phase between parchment and parchment, arcing between the same spells, the same minds...the same places, even the same subject. The only slight tingle of difference lay in the runes of time, and, at the very bottom of the left-hand piece, two strange signatures.

"This one was written first," Gudrun murmured, letting her wand follow the infinitesimal flicker through her nerves to the right-hand document. "Otherwise, the same. All the same. Mages, places, subjects. All except the signatures on the left." Carefully she let the gathered power of the flux fade back into the Void, before the minute particles of Chaos could begin to gather and clump.

It left her looking down at the two pieces of parchment. The one on the right battered and limp as an ancient pouch; the one on the left clean and white, trying to spring back into its original roll. Obrist Helmuth was frowning ferociously now, his thick gray eyebrows drawing down and his head lowering like those of a bull about to charge.

"Will a truth-reading drain your powers?"

"Not, significantly, sir," Gudrun managed to say, still bewildered.

"Cast one on Wolfram, now."

Gudrun felt her arm raising, almost of its own accord, until her wand pointed straight at Wolfram's chest. Truth-reading was one of the easiest spells a mage could perform. It required no draw on the flux of the Void, only enough control to open the simplest pathway between mind and tongue, between what was known and what was said, and hold it free of the other flickering of the brain.

"Wolfram, tell us what happened the night you were arrested."

Gudrun listened numbly as the half-Elf repeated his story once again, a wondering smile growing on his face. There was no need for her to strengthen the barriers of truth's path, as there would have been had he tried to lie. It was as smooth and right as any spell she had ever cast. When Wolfram was done speaking, Helmuth looked at Arkoniel.

The Elf nodded. "As I said. Sir."

"No questions or difficulties, Marshal?"

"No, sir. The Zauberobrist must have..." Fouled his spell. Or:

"Must have?"

"Fouled his spell. Or lied."

Gudrun bit her tongue in shock, but the words were out, though she was beginning to tremble.

"Hauptmann Heinrich!" The Obrist snapped. "Unloose Lieutenant Wolfram and his comrade. We may require their assistance. Marshal Gudrun, are you capable of restraining Alberich's magic if he attempts to resist investigation or arrest?"

Gudrun's mouth fell open. My master, my teacher to raise hand against him? Like a squire taking a sword to his knight, or a vassal to his lord! But if he betrayed an innocent man to his death or worse. Even that would hardly call for all this. If Alberich has betrayed the Company. The pieces were falling together faster than she could give thought to them, gathering into improbable form like the minute ink drops of the letter-spell forming clean-edged words on white parchment. I swore to the Silver Eagle, as well and so did Alberich. If he has betrayed his oath, the choice must be mine.

"Can you or not, woman?" The Obrist roared at her.

"I must choose now." She glanced at Wolfram, then at the Silver Eagle's commander. Not for love's sake, but for justice. Landsknecht mages may not be part of the normal chain of command, but we are soldiers. This is not a knight's rebellion, but an officer's mutiny.

"I cannot defeat him in a duel of magic. But I can delay him long enough for a soldier to shoot, or stab."

"Good enough. Do you think Marshal Wilhelm was part of this conspiracy?"

"I don't know, sir. The truth spell he cast on Wolfram, he could have lied himself, or Alberich could have fouled it without his knowledge."

"Can't be risked," Obrist Helmuth snapped. "You're our magical force, Marshal. Heinrich, send for my Trabanten, Piriel, hmm, get your Fändrich as well. Orcs have some resistance to magic. I want everyone here, armed and armored, with hand-guns if they have them, in no more than fifteen minutes. Wolfram, Mishni, back to Forlorn Hope. Arm and armor, and get Fredrik if he's in any shape to fight. Move!"

CHAPTER 25

Wolfram's head was still spinning as he sprinted lightly back to Hauptmann Heinrich's pavilion in the dark. It had all happened so fast. The most dangerous part may still be yet to come, he reminded himself. He leapt over a guy rope, armor clanking softly. If Alberich tries to fight. For a moment, a great longing swept over him for Treuherz and the slight safety offered by a shield. Fighting in the Landsknecht lines was a very different thing from attacking a mage alone. I made my choice, I can only trust in Donmar and St. Hildebrand, and hope Gudrun really can hold Alberich back for a second.

The bastard! He had seen the stark agony on Gudrun's face when the Obrist asked her if she could restrain her master's magic. Graf Ulric had warned his sons never to forget that mages had their own honor, and the oaths between master and student far from the least of their bindings. But the betrayal was Alberich's. Why? Why me? There was no time to think about that now.

Mishni, quicker to armor if slower-moving in the dark, was almost to the pavilion. Wolfram caught up with him, and they entered together. The others, the big, hard-faced men of Helmuth's Trabanten, armed with the one-handed swords and large shields that could become a wall to protect their charge from Alberich's first blasts. Arkoniel and Piriel with bows strung; Kai with a long poll-ax, his snarling part-Orcish face ugly as any full-blood's in the candlelight, the Obrist and Hauptmann Heinrich together, the wheel-lock pistols they carried looking incongruously small and clumsy against suits of full plate as good as any knights could boast and Gudrun, bundled in her heavy cloak, frail and dainty compared to the armored men, but holding her wand with the sure ease of a long-experienced fighter, with a look of firm resolution on her pale face, were just moving into formation. Obrist Helmuth nodded.

"Arkoniel, Piriel, Wolfram, Kai, Mishni. You surround the pavilion. If he tries to escape back, top, or flank, kill him. If he comes quietly, fall in around us at twenty feet, with archers ready to shoot if you detect anything untoward. If Wilhelm attempts to interfere, stop him if you can, kill him if you must. When we get back here, Wolfram comes in, the rest of the outside troop surrounds again, striking to kill if Alberich manages to escape.

Arkoniel, Piriel, if I order you to stand down or otherwise pass, and you detect any sign of magic used on my mind, consider that an escape. All clear? Quiet march."

As they neared the Zauberobrist's pavilion, the outside troop peeled off, arranging themselves so that Arkoniel and Piriel had the two rear corners of the big rectangle with a clear line of fire across both the back and the sides. Kai, with his long reach and long weapon, took the back; Wolfram the left, and Mishni the right, not far from where the last glow of a fire pit would give him shadows to strike by at need. Though Wolfram suspected, from the way the Rat moved through the dark, that the Southerner's night vision was unusually good for a Man's.

A touch of Gnome in the blood, there? To Wolfram's surprise, he himself could see a faint glow starting about a foot from Alberich's pavilion, a deep purple, with ominous flickers of reddish-black creeping through it like dark lightning through a distant storm. The tiny hairs stood up on the back of his neck. He rotated his grip on his sword to circle its tip slightly, a trick Graf Ulric had taught him to keep him from choking up on his weapon when he was nervous. He knew that nothing short of life and death, or a direct order, would drive him to cross the boundary of that glow, he could sense, as much as see, the murderous force in it.

Wolfram waited, armor and body cooling in the thin dampness of the night mist hazing the lanterns coming up the path to the front of the pavilion. Even with his visor down, he could feel the soft cool stirrings of air and grass, standing in the stillness, not of stone, but of air and starlight and shadow, weaving into him until even the steel of his sword and harness were no more than part of the night. When his carefully scanning eyes flickered left, he saw that Arkoniel, was a fainter shadow still. Wolfram knew that no Man could have made the Elf's shape out even in full daylight.

He let that thought sink away, watching with the hovering stillness of a falcon, not just for the mage's body breaking out, but for the first disturbance in the ominous pattern of the flickering wards that might give him a split heartbeat's warning and heard Obrist Helmuth's battle-wrecked bass calling, "Provost Alberich, I require you!"

Gudrun's legs were shaking, but her grip on her wand was firm and steady. She could feel the power pressing against her, as if her flesh were a thin dam holding back the full strength of a river in flood. Alberich stepped out of his pavilion, his black-robed figure a tall gaunt shadow in the light of the lantern he held in his left hand. His wand was in his right, but not pointed; and, looking at the startle and worry on her teacher's bony face, Gudrun almost felt her legs fail her. *How can I betray him? Because I must,* she answered herself.

"What's wrong? Are we under attack?" Alberich asked.

Gudrun could see his blue eyes beginning to unfocused as he glanced about, as though he were looking for signs of hidden magic.

"Come closer. I don't want to shout this to the whole camp," Helmuth said bluntly.

Alberich walked towards the Obrist and his guards. *Of course,* Gudrun thought. *Helmuth doesn't want him dodging back into the warded pavilion, that's why he stopped so far away.*

"Halt!" Helmuth ordered when Alberich was about ten feet from them, raising his pistol to point straight at the mage's heart. "Toss your wand to Marshal Gudrun."

The surprised concern on Alberich's face hardened into startled anger, as though the craggy flesh of his face had turned to stone in an instant. His eyes blazed furiously, Gudrun could feel the wave of his wrath pressing against her, and had to bite the inside of her cheek to keep herself from taking a backward step.

"What, by the gods of Light and Darkness, is going on? Herr Obrist!" He snapped. "What do you think you're doing?"

"We have some questions to ask you. For Donmar's sake and yours, I hope you have good answers. If you don't surrender your wand and come peaceably, we will shoot to kill."

Alberich's wand was still pointed downward, but he made no move to surrender it.

"Herr Obrist, I am the Provost of this Company! I am responsible for Company law and trials. The Orders forbid my impeachment during my term of office. You cannot deal with me this way and as for you, Marshal Gudrun." His voice sent freezing shivers through the marrow of Gudrun's bones, as he turned that terrible gaze on her. "You are my oath-bound student. By all the laws of magic, you are sworn to my aid. Lower your wand from me now, or you will forever be oath breaker and forsaken to magic, your soul rightful prey to Gurthevor and Ravehild and the Dark Flame; and may they take you quickly."

A spasm of nausea and terror shook Gudrun as her teacher no longer! Spoke the names of the gods of Darkness. At least he had not called upon the Enemy by name, as only those who worshiped him would do but the Ravager and the Eater were terrifying enough in their calling. Gudrun shook her head mutely. Alagrith and Donmar protect me! She thought. Gods of Light, I hope. I pray, I'm doing the right thing!

"Do not threaten her," Obrist Helmuth said roughly. "You have to the count of three to surrender your wand. One, two..."

Alberich's arm swung back and forward as if to throw, but Gudrun had known when he named two of three on her that he would not surrender. The power burst forth through her, a bolt of lightning through her arm and wand, a fraction of a heartbeat before Alberich loosed his own fires.

Her lesser blast struck his just as it began to issue from the tip of his rod. For a moment, a corona of blue flames burned around a tall oval of darkness, bright enough to dazzle Gudrun's eyes. Redder flames leaped to either side of her, the shots exploding against her eardrums. She sucked in a choking breath of smoke and sulfur. A man was screaming, tinny and distant through the ringing in her ears.

Something pale seared a streak of lightning through the air over the pavilion, falling like a white-hot star in its light, she saw Alberich rising from his crouch to run, and pointed her wand again without thought, feeling her blow winging invisibly through the air. The impact as her strength slammed into the elder mage's legs staggered Gudrun as well but Alberich was on the ground, two of the shield men rushing forward to leap on him and pin him.

The power of the wand in Alberich's hand had felt like the heat of a great bonfire in front of her, when the little rod flew from his grasp, it was as though a thousand tons of snow had doused the fire suddenly, leaving only darkness and cold where a moment before house-high flames had raged.

"Gudrun, forward, get the wand!" The Obrist shouted. Flanked by two more of the shield men with their lanterns, Gudrun ran towards where Alberich lay writhing, scanning the ground desperately in the pale amber light.

It lay not a foot from the old man's flailing hand, rolling quickly back towards him. One of the shield men stomped his wide-toed shoe down on Alberich's fingers, and Gudrun dove for the wand, sweeping it up just before it could touch the mage's convulsing fingertips. She gasped as it sprang to life again in her hand, the polished wood slick and warm as a snake in the sun. He can still use the power in his flesh.Gudrun pointed her wand at Alberich with one hand, his own with the other, pouring strength through both of them. She could feel the churning where the two rivers of power met, rising over and around his struggling body, hardening into fetters to still his mouth, still his limbs, close his eyes, encompassing him like a torrent cold earth and stone pouring over a puddle of burning magma in layer after layer until the hot radiance could no longer seep upward to the surface.

Binding his power to his flesh, blocking the bond to his wand with her own until blood and wood no longer called to blood and bone, stemming the bright living flow of the underground channel to Wilhelm, silencing the empty horror of echoes resonating along the darkened underground channel to herself. Sick and exhausted, Gudrun slumped to her knees.

Alberich was barely moaning, a faint keen of pain, as the guards who had held him down efficiently gagged and blindfolded him, tying his hands with an elaborate wrap to keep him from moving his fingers and fettering his ankles as well.

She could see the black stains of blood seeping through the gag from his nose and mouth, the bruises swelling around his face and the darkening congestion of his fingers' flesh puffing up against the cat's-cradle of cords tying the hand the guard had stepped on.

"His condition, Marshal?" Obrist Helmuth asked. "Have you fettered his power enough for us to let him breathe?"

Gudrun blinked, then realized that, between the swelling and blood in Alberich's nose, his breath had already dwindled to a wheeze almost too faint to hear. *If he dies now, his last words were a curse to me. But not a ritual one and if he lives, he will try to do worse. I need to know why he tried to get rid of Wolfram, and to do, whatever the Obrist was so angered over. I need to know from him, or I will never be sure in my heart that his curse was not deserved, and it will eat me even if it was no more than words.*

"Yes, sir," Gudrun answered. "He is safely fettered. Please let him breathe."

"Remove the gag," the Obrist ordered.

Alberich drew in a deep bubbling breath, coughed a spray of dark blood out to mat in his little beard, and breathed again, each gasp a hiss of pain.

Donmar, he is an old man, after all! I never meant this, or expected. Yet Alberich had proven his guilt by his attempt to attack and escape. Gudrun could never have bound him, had he not been so battered. The fighters alone could not have killed or captured him without her, and she would have lost him if it had not been for the glowing object shooting over the tent. An Elf-arrow, or Elven spell, most likely. When he had chosen to resist, there was no hope of being gentle with him.

Nor would he have resisted as he did, if he were not truly guilty of something truly bad. Else-wise he would have law and custom completely on his side. At least Alberich was blindfolded. Facing the hate in his eyes would have been bad enough but what if he had looked at her with disappointment? *His praise was all lies, to keep me in order,* Gudrun told herself as the largest of the shield men lifted the battered old man and tossed him over his shoulder. Alberich did not cry out, but a faint keening noise escaped through his blood-bubbling nose. *If I could take part in the deed, I can watch it, there is always the chance he could surprise me still.*

CHAPTER 26

Wolfram hung back a moment as the Obrist's guard carried Alberich into Heinrich's pavilion. He understood the necessity, even the justice. If all were as it seemed, he had the right to do himself all that had been done. Still, it was like looking at the body of a woman slain on the battlefield, to some part of him, it was hard to see an old man, and no warrior, so battered. He was not unarmed, may not even be now. Helmuth looked sharply at him.

"Lieutenant Wolfram, you have a charge to lay as well. Why did you not bring your enchanted sword?"

"I had to give it up as part of our ransom," Wolfram answered.

"We will speak of that later. Come in."

The guard laid Alberich out on the floor, then drew his sword and stood with the tip of it leaning against the mage's breast, so that, if he fell down dead, his weight on the blade would nail Alberich to the ground.

Obrist Helmuth and Hauptmann Heinrich were calmly reloading their handguns. Gudrun stood with a wand pointed in either hand, her mouth wide and trembling and her face white and pained as if it had just been dusted with quicklime.

"Get the Marshal a cup of wine and a little food. Marshal, sit down. We shall need your services again shortly. Will poppy syrup make it easier to force the truth out, or harder?"

"The Zauberobrist. Alberich has endured worse pain in magic before. It may only strengthen his will. The poppy syrup should help."

"Good enough." Helmuth pointed at another guard. "Fetch Feldartz Falkenstein; tell him to bring poppy, a feeding funnel, and his tools. Marshal, calm yourself, you did very well."

A third guard brought Gudrun a chair. She was shaking so badly that he had to help her into it. The sight of the other man's big hands steadying the mage's cloaked shoulders woke a sudden fierce flare of anger in Wolfram. He had to clench his fists hard on his sword's long hilt to keep himself from striding over to push the guard away. But when Gudrun looked up, her gray-green eyes dark as agate in her white face, he smiled gently at her.

"You did what you had to, for all our sakes," he murmured. "And you heard what the Obrist said, you did it well. Just hold on a little longer, soon you'll know everything." Her answering smile was still shaky, but it warmed something deep in Wolfram's heart.

Still, we'll all know everything. He looked down at the mage's battered figure. Why? Mishni's documents, and Ludwig's cheerful boast, had made what clear enough. But why did you do it? Why me, even before the contract was settled? I would have known no more than I did in Forlorn Hope. But Alberich's plan had been to kill him, after all. No, to execute him, to avoid suspicion about his death.

It couldn't have been his Elvish blood. Arkoniel and Piriel were far more dangerous than Wolfram, in any way that an Elf could be dangerous. Save if he knew the truth of my blood. But if he did, there were other ways for him to get rid of me. Such as informing on him. The Obrist would have had the right to arrest Wolfram and hand him over to the civil authorities as a suspected enemy spy, or, at the very least, to throw him out of the company for his initial lies. Likely the former, Helmuth was intensely loyal to the Empire. It could still happen. Depending on what Alberich really knew.

Soon I'll know everything, Wolfram repeated to himself. At least I've redeemed my honor. Though doing so had cost Gudrun, maybe, more than it had cost him. He looked at her again. She was eating slowly, her hands trembling so that the lump of cheese was in danger of falling off the bread but every couple of bites, she glanced up at him. Skirting a wide path around Alberich, he walked over to stand beside her chair, close enough to feel the warmth of her body, and gazed down into her eyes.

Wolfram paused a moment before he spoke. She needed to hear what he had to say now. Or some of it. There were a few things that could wait until they were alone.

"Thank you," he whispered. "For believing in me. For everything. No one in the regiment could have met such a trial better."

"It's not over yet," Gudrun murmured back.

She took another bite of bread and cheese, visibly forcing herself to chew and swallow. Shock, he thought. But she's right. She does have the strength to do it. All I can do is stand by her and let her know I believe in her, as she believed in me. He grounded the point of his sword, his left hand releasing the grip and settling gently on her shoulder. He could feel her trembling through the fine bones and wiry strands of muscle beneath her heavy cloak, but the faint quivering began to ease beneath his touch.

Stroking her head would have been too intimate, there in front of officers and men, would have seemed as though he thought of her as a civilian woman to be calmed from the fright of war; but a soldier could touch another's shoulder in reassurance between hard battles, and no one think the worse of either. Just a slight movement of his hand brushed his fingers against a silken strand of dark auburn hair, a stolen pleasure that nearly took his breath away for a second. Gudrun finished her food, washed it down with a swallow of wine, and took a deep breath, her shoulders squaring.

Through his light touch, Wolfram could feel her gathering her strength again, almost feel the renewed current of the mage's trained will setting aside doubt and fear and exhaustion, compelling power and endurance back into her body. *If I had stayed in Löwenstein, I might never have known there were women like this in the world,* he thought suddenly. The shocked gasp of Feldartz Dietrich Falkenstein drew Wolfram's gaze back up. The field surgeon was staring at Alberich, his mouth open. Helmuth cut his questions off with a gesture.

"A large dose of poppy syrup, as large as you can give him and still keep him conscious to answer questions. Use the funnel, he may try to fight you."

Wolfram had seen Dietrich funneling medicines down the mouths of Landsknechts who were too badly wounded to realize the doctor was helping them, and fought as if against an enemy's tortures. Still, he was surprised at the vigor with which Alberich resisted the poppy syrup, his head thrashing until one of Helmuth's Trabanten knelt to hold it still, then sputtering and trying his best to spit it out. Gudrun closed her eyes for just a second, and Wolfram felt her wince, but she opened them again and watched the messy, undignified process to the end. *She feels it is her fault. Not without cause, St. Hildebrand, help her to know, in her heart, that this was her duty!*

After a time, the Feldartz said, "Is it safe to look at his eyes?"

"I must, but you were best not to," Gudrun answered. She had a wand gripped in each fist, pointed at Alberich again. She twitched her shoulder. Wolfram took his hand away, and she stood up by herself, walking steadily over to her former teacher.

"Take his blindfold off," she ordered the man who held Alberich's head. The wand in her right hand moved in a complex figure, and Wolfram saw its tip begin to glow a faint golden.

He lifted his sword again, and moved to where he could easily take the mage's head off again if the old man proved any threat to Gudrun. Alberich's eyes seared brutally into Gudrun's, scorching the gasp in the depths of her throat. She had seen men mad with battle and mad with pain, men who knew her for their killer and strove with their last heartbeat to take the step that would allow them revenge, and men near-mindless in agony, whispering. *"Mother"* as they stared at her with dreadful hope.

None of them had pierced her like the hate in Alberich's gaze, an acid of bitter loathing so strong that she could feel the pain like a blistering sunburn on her face and tear-stinging dust in her eyes. If the beating he had taken and Gudrun's grasp on his own wand had not distracted him and given her the power to bind him, she knew that his hatred would literally be searing the flesh from her bones and melting her eyeballs.

So strong, but she could feel the slight spillage of his last echo of power, too. The pain was helping Alberich resist the poppy; nevertheless, some of the drug was getting through, forcing him slightly out of focus. The knowledge strengthened her, aided her to open to the power of the flux and channel it through the wands, lines clean and straight as the edges of a spear-blade coming to a point in his heart.

"Curses." He whispered.

"No curses, Alberich," Gudrun said. "You broke your oath first."

"Not to you."

"Yes. You lied to manipulate my feelings when you should have been teaching me." Truth to truth. The lines brightened, the power pressed deeper. Each of his heartbeats trembled against it, his shields like the tough muscle of the organ resisting the first touch of the blade's point. Gudrun gazed steadily at him, a faint haze of light glowed in the middle of the long angle between her wands. I know the truth. "You wanted me to stop asking questions about Wolfram, and you lied to me."

Alberich gasped. Suddenly the barrier parted beneath her keen-edged pressure, the blade of power slipped in, and he was hers.

"The truth, Alberich. All of it. Why did you want Wolfram convicted?"

"Too dangerous. To me, to my plans. Old Elf, old enough, powerful enough, and trained to imitate a Man down to his gestures, even the sense of his mind." Alberich's words came faster, now that Gudrun had broken into the first link of the chain.

"The others keep their distance, but Wolfram, or whatever his name is, paid attention to everything the Men were doing. He was too good. He might have found me out. I used everything I had to knock him unconscious without him sensing and resisting me, and even then I was lucky. I had to, things were coming to a head."

"What things, Alberich?"

"Plans with Klaus. Get rid of Berthold, destroy his temples and defile his shrines. Here, towards the Empire's borders, is where the weak places need to be. Where Morbod and Gurthevor and Ravehild can work in like water into the cracks. Make sure the strongest regiments go to the right people. Sigfrid isn't one of us directly, but he suited our purpose. There's plenty of lords like that, willing to let their mages arrange things so they can get the best regiments and still afford what they need and target the ones we need destroyed."

"So you did interfere with the negotiations?" Obrist Helmuth growled sadly. "For the sake of."

"For the sake of our power and our gods." The fury still shone in Alberich's eyes, but diffused from a drill of white-hot fire to a vaguer glow.

"Get rid of the priesthood with its fingers in everything, an Emperor who keeps his lands by deluding his lords into fighting for him when they could fight for themselves, free strong arms and strong wills from the fetters of empire. The will is there, the highborn are always feuding anyway, it's just a matter of helping things along for the most part." He gasped for air, blood-crusted mouth opening and closing for a moment before he dragged a deep breath into his lungs.

"Is Wilhelm a part of this?" The Obrist asked. "Did he know about any of it?"

"No. Fouled his spell, easy enough, with his jealousy of the Elf and Gudrun. Made him think the papers that thief got from him were a pouch of money and get rid of both problems in Forlorn Hope. Had men paid to make sure neither of them survived their battles, but the incompetent bastards got themselves killed. Thought I'd managed it in the last one, should have gotten at least one, but the wretches both managed to ransom themselves somehow. Or some fool managed it for them. Shouldn't have been able to."

Alberich coughed again, a long deep rattle. "Feldartzt!" Helmuth snapped. "Johann, tell Arkoniel to go for Ruprecht, get him here now if he has to drag his arse naked through camp! Alberich, who else is in this conspiracy with you?"

Gudrun felt a faint pressure of resistance against her spell. It gave suddenly, and the two-edged blade of her power flared bright enough to half-blind her for a second with the unexpected discharge of magic. Alberich laughed an arching fountain of bright blood as thick as a man's wrist over Gudrun's face, his voice barely more than bubbles in the liquid.

"Morbod! Gurvethor! Ravehild! Queen Imrisi!"

"What Men in the Empire?" The Obrist pressed.

The noise that came out might have been, "...Klaus..." but the blood had drowned Alberich's throat. His lips curved into a grotesque smile beneath the slick red veil covering his face. Gudrun heard a sharper bubbling noise, and a heavier reek seeped into her lungs under the sharp metallic scent of blood: a sound and smell that every Landsknecht knew.

"Gods curse him," Heinrich whispered. "We didn't Marshal, what happened?"

"He was prepared," Gudrun answered, wiping Alberich's blood from her face with a fold of her cloak and spitting the copper-salt taste from her mouth.

"If I had any clue about the magnitude of what he was hiding, that it might be a conspiracy he'd rather die than give up, I might have been able to find it and stop it. But most likely not. Alberich was much stronger than I by himself. If he were working with someone like Klaus von Ludo, or another Magister of equal power." She shrugged unhappily. "I think if a Healer had plugged the one leak at once, he would have just kept exploding until he died. Nothing short of a miracle, or a much more skilled mage than I, could have helped."

"All right. You did your job, and did it well, Marshal. Are you in any danger from holding his wand?"

Gudrun blinked. The thought of channeling her magic through something tainted by Darkness was appalling but she had felt, could still feel, nothing evil in the wand. "I don't think so. Sir. It's a tool, more like a gun than a sword. If he'd made it for the purpose, maybe, but a mage usually keeps one wand all his life, and I think it seems to me that he shaped it before."

"Before he turned to the Dark? Maybe, but put it in the safest place you have and don't touch it for a while."

"Sir, we should worry about his pavilion. The spells he had must have been designed to work without him for a short time, not less than a couple of days or he wouldn't have been able to leave it for long, but perhaps not more than a week. When they fail, if there is valuable information in there, they may well fail catastrophically and spectacularly. The contents are likely to be trapped, as well."

Helmuth nodded thoughtfully. "Would the priests of the shrine here be able to counter the spells?"

"A team of skilled mages would do better in terms of retrieving information safely, sir. At least the priests should be able to make any dead-man spells of destruction harmless," Gudrun added reluctantly. "There are a few things in the Black Wagon we should get rid of tomorrow as well."

"You're in charge of that, Fräulein Zauberobristin," Helmuth told her.

Gudrun blinked. Zauberobrist had been Alberich's title, colonel of mages. Provisional? She thought. Just until we can get someone better, surely, after all, there's only Wilhelm and myself left.

The Obrist gave her a grim smile. "Not provisional," he said, as if he had heard her thoughts. "I'm not the best fighter in the regiment either, that would be Fredrik. I need someone quick-thinking and loyal, who knows how to direct whatever magic we have, in combat and out of it. That's you, unless you don't think you can handle it."

"I, Yes, Herr Obrist. I can handle it," Gudrun answered. I can. I've just proved it. I didn't beat Alberich by skill, but by seizing the moment and doing the right thing, in conjunction with fighting troops who knew their job.

"Excellent. You can give orders to your Marshals and anyone seconded to you. If there's something that involves the Company, see me directly, you'll also report to me at least once daily to keep me informed and receive your orders. Now clean yourself up and see to what needs to be done."

"Sir, we should start Alberich's body burning on the nearest fire straight away, and have Vater Franz watch by it. It may be difficult for things to get in, so close to a powerful shrine, but it's certainly possible."

"Peter, Bernhard, see to it. Tell Piriel to stay by the body until Franz gets there, and tell Kai and Mishni they're in my Trabanten for the rest of the night. For the rest of you, those two and Wolfram will guard me until sunrise, you're all seconded to the Zauberobristin until further notice."

Wolfram watched, quietly overwhelmed by delight, as the reality of Gudrun's promotion sank into her mind. She was rising to the shocks of the evening better than he would have guessed. A mage's training prepared the mind for such sudden changes better than a warrior's.

No doubt there would be times when she still felt twinges of grief or guilt over her choice to turn against her teacher, though his confession must have armored her against most of her sorrow and remorse or felt out of place in her new office.

Still, looking at the confident set of her delicate features beneath the smeared blood, and hearing the firm tones of her low voice as she looked Obrist Helmuth in the eyes when less than half an hour ago, she had been on the verge of passing out from magical exhaustion and rent emotions, and done battle twice with a stronger foe. You are worthy of your reward, Gudrun. I hope you still find me worthy of you!

"Gentlemen," Helmuth said when Gudrun and her guards-cum-aides had gone, "we have a great deal of work to do tonight. Heinrich, I need pen, ink, parchment, and sealing-wax. Then sleep while you can. At dawn, you will order your Fähnlein to strike camp and prepare to withdraw. Hmm, we had already promoted Martin to the office of your Lieutenant, and there is no other post empty at that level. Also, I dislike moving men out of a Fähnlein into which they are well integrated. I think I shall take Lieutenant Wolfram as my own adjutant for the time being."

"As you wish, Herr Obrist," Heinrich sighed in resignation. Wolfram knew that he had done a better job for Heinrich than Martin would, being much quicker with pen and sums.

But there was no way to disagree with the Obrist's reasoning. He himself would have made the same decision in the same circumstances. When the Hauptmann had produced the writing materials, Helmuth sat down and scribbled a brief note, pressing his seal-ring into a droplet of golden wax at the bottom.

"Kai, take this to whoever is in charge of the Forlorn Hope guard tonight. It states that Lieutenant Wolfram Longsword and Doppelsöldner Mishni the Rat have both been proven innocent of all charges by new information and reinstated to their ranks. When you have delivered it, come back to my personal pavilion."

Kai grinned widely as he saluted, showing all his thickened yellow tushes.

"Yes, sir!" He turned the grin on Wolfram for a second, black eyes gleaming red with reflected candlelight.

There was no time to speak, or even exchange handclasps, but Wolfram read all the other man's relief and delight in that one glance. The Obrist's own healer, Ruprecht, tried to rush in as Little Kai hurried out. After a brief confused scuffle at the entrance, Kai stepped aside with a courteous bow, holding the flap for the healer. Wolfram's smile widened, his heart warmed by the perpetual incongruity between the part-Orc's looks and his good manners. Seeing Kai acting like himself again seemed to wipe out all Wolfram's fears that Forlorn Hope had left an indelible stink on his name.

"Sir!" The healer said, straightening his tubby body and saluting uncomfortably. "Who am I here for, sir?"

"Too late, but no matter. You could not have aided: it was a matter of dark magic. I do need my full staff awakened and sent to my pavilion straight away. They should dress first, but quickly: there is much work to do tonight. Take Arkoniel with you to speed the process."

Ruprecht frowned, an offended glitter in his pale blue eyes, but either Helmuth's expression or the implications of dark magic clearly told him that meek obedience was the wisest strategy at the moment.

"Yes, sir."

"Come, gentlemen. Lieutenant Wolfram," the Obrist said as they walked, "I recall that you can not only write a fair hand, but compose a well-written letter. I shall require you to begin by composing such in brief to my counterpart of the Sun Azure, Obrist Arnolf von Lichtenfels, informing him that we are withdrawing due to, hmm, 'contractual difficulties', should be the phrase we want and that we have no idea what the remainder of Graf Sigfrid's forces will choose to do, but recommend that the shrine and village here." He frowned. "No, just tell Arnolf that I request a private meeting between himself, myself, Zauberobristin Gudrun, whoever holds Dr. Manfred's position as Zauberobrist at the moment, and one of the senior priests of the Bad Oberstein shrine."

"Sir, do you mean to give them a full account?"

"I think so." Helmuth smiled grimly. "The immediate evidence suggests that the Sun Azure is not directly involved with this dire matter."

Wolfram opened his mouth to ask, then realized, of course, the other regiment was fighting to defend one of the conspiracy's chief targets the more of us know, the easier it will be to guard against. While we can keep our knowledge between us. For if word went directly to the Emperor, he might well choose to strike the patents of all Landsknecht colonels in the Empire, perhaps even strike the laws that Maximilian I had written to create the Landsknechts from the books.

The Landsknechts have always dealt our own justice on our own. We shall do so again, and kill the rats before they can creep away to breed elsewhere!

"Yes, sir."

"Add a postscript requesting that he bring the sword which was taken as part of your ransom. There will be other thanks, but the least we can do now is to see the return of a portion of what you lost. Your full ransom-price will also be returned to you, and your pay back-dated to the time of your illegal conviction."

"Thank you, sir!" Wolfram said.

He had been able to lie to himself, to downplay the pain of his sword's loss compared to that of his self-respect but his relief at the prospect of its return showed him, hard and unmistakable as a two-handed weapon slamming full-force into his helm, how much of the feeling he had been blocking. "That is most generous."

"Barely a portion of what you're owed," the Obrist growled. "Have you the recall of an Elf?"

Wolfram was about to say no, then recollected his memory-dreams, so much sharper and clearer and, he was certain, more truthful than any memory or dream of his Man's life.

"Yes, sir."

"Good. When you have written the first letter, you will make a clean and perfect copy of everything that Alberich said in response to our questioning, save that you will not write the names of the Enemy and his kin directly, of course, but only indicate that he spoke them. Give that to my scribe and tell him that I want ten fair copies and must have them before we reach Graf Sigfrid's land, and we will be marching there at full speed."

"Yes, sir. Sir, may I ask a favor?"

"Ask away. I'll grant it if I can."

"I made a promise to Donmar that I would visit his spring if I survived this night's work, and were able to do so without forsaking my duties. If time permits, before we leave."

Helmuth's heavy brow furrowed. "That will depend on how swiftly we are able to set up the meeting I desire. It is a long climb up the mountainside to the shrine, and I am guessing that your prayer or penance is no simple one."

"No, sir," Wolfram admitted. "That is, I do not know." The god's judgment could come as swiftly as a lightning-bolt.

To be honest, well, given Wolfram's need to open and drain his long-infected heart, it could be hours. Or days.

"One man on horse or an Elf-blooded on foot could catch up with our column in good time."

The Obrist thought about it until they were almost at his pavilion. At last he said heavily, "I am sorry, Lieutenant. Graf Sigfrid's cavalry are too near. If there is battle, we will need you. If you are alone, I would not put it past them to take you and put you to the hard question, by means bodily or magical. Both for your own sake, and for the regiment's – the more so since you lack the Elvish skills which would guard your mind from the worst. I will not risk it.

Donmar hears prayers in battle and duty as surely as he does beside a stream. If the god wishes to listen to you, or speak, if you want a sign from him, or aid in some matter. There will be more than enough opportunity as we go. I myself would take it that he had a hand in this night's work, if not before. This night, we captured a rogue mage, with only one serious injury and that reparable. Before you and Mishni both survived one more battle in Forlorn Hope than most men do, even with your own linesmen trying to kill you in the confusion. You were brought together in the village of the god's shrine, and that in such a way that you put full trust in each other.

So the ways of the Enemy turn on themselves, for if you had not been in Forlorn Hope together, how should you have given up your prized sword for a rat on two legs?"

I wouldn't have needed to but I would never have spoken to Mishni at all under normal circumstances. I might not have been in a position to capture Ludwig,

"That bears much thought, Herr Obrist. Thank you."

CHAPTER 27

Gudrun and Obrist Helmuth rode back from their talk with the leaders of the Sun Azure and the Bad Oberstein high priest in silence, surrounded by the twelve men of Helmuth's Trabanten and the eight of Gudrun's own. The Silver Eagle was drawn up and ready for departure. When Helmuth reached the first unit of the regiment's Pfeifer, he called out, "Sound full march. Forward!"

The drums boomed into step, fifes shrilling out above them. All along the column, the musicians took up the rhythm, and the Landsknechts began to march, feet and hooves thudding on the dusty road like a more distant army of drummers answering as the wagon-wheels creaked into movement.

"Fräulein Zauberobristin, my staff is just behind the Black Wagon," Helmuth said quietly to Gudrun, his pale blue eyes staring intently at her from the shadow of his sallet's raised visor. "Would you do me the courtesy of returning Lieutenant Wolfram's sword to him and informing him of the fate of his captive?"

"I will, sir," Gudrun answered. Helmuth handed her the sheathed weapon, and she nudged her horse into a smooth rack, then a slow canter, hastening up along the column with her Trabanten falling into place around her again.

Wolfram was marching just ahead of the Obrist's wagon. Gudrun smiled to herself as she saw the ease and pride in the half-Elf's smooth gait, but her smile faded almost at once. *At least I have his sword for him.* She slowed her horse as she drew nearer, gesturing the guard who rode directly between herself and the marchers to pull aside.

"Lieutenant Wolfram," she called. "May I have the honor of your company in the Black Wagon for a time?"

"Of course, Fräulein Zauberobristin," Wolfram replied with a bow. He stepped out of line, running easily forward to match paces with the mages' wain.

Gudrun saw Wilhelm turn his head away as Wolfram came up
to the Black Wagon, narrow shoulders tightening beneath his dark
robe. If the Company had any other mages, she would have ordered
him off-duty that day. Her Marshal had taken Alberich's death, and
what she suspected he would think of as her betrayal of their teacher
for some time, almost as a physical wound, whey-faced and shaking
since she had told him of the late Zauberobrist's fate.

Wilhelm was fortunate, at that Gudrun had managed to bind
Alberich so thoroughly in his capture, else the elder mage would
likely have drained the younger in his struggle against Gudrun's
truth-spell, perhaps even to death. A grievous offense against the
bond of master and student but what would one more betrayal
have been to Alberich? Still, Wilhelm had not seen or heard their
teacher's end. Gudrun suspected that when he read the account of
the questioning, he would be in worse state for some time. Gudrun
pulled up beside Wolfram and swung down, passing her horse's
reins to Johann.

"If you would lift me up, Herr Lieutenant?"

"My honor, Fräulein Zauberobristin," Wolfram replied. His
visor was open to catch the light summer breeze. His smile down
at Gudrun, and the gentle strength of his gauntleted hands on her
waist as he swung her up into the wagon, were enough to make her
catch her breath.

The half-Elf leapt up beside her, waiting for her to open the
enchanted doors into the darkness. A spark from Gudrun's wand
kindled the lanterns; and then the two of them were alone in the
swaying wain.

"First, your sword, returned as Obrist Helmuth promised,"
Gudrun said, passing the sheathed weapon into Wolfram's hands.
A look of unbelieving joy spread over Wolfram's face as he stared
down at it.

It is far more than a fine weapon to him, Gudrun realized.
Something that matters enough that he had not dared hope for it
back, even with Helmuth's word on the matter. She waited, letting
him hook the sheath onto the empty hanging-loop of his narrow
gold-mounted belt. His right hand caressed the fluted ivory hilt, the
ball of his thumb brushing over the flat silver disk in the middle of
the round pommel as though it were the graven or enameled arms
that many noble men's swords bore there. Maybe someday he will
tell me its tale.

"Thank you," Wolfram said, his clear voice vibrating with feeling like a string answering to the tuning fork. "I had no doubt of the Herr Obrist's word, but it is still good to have this weapon at my side again."

"I am glad." Gudrun smiled up at him, but again her smile faded quickly. "Wolfram, I am afraid that I also have sad news. We asked after the fate of Lieutenant Ludwig."

Sorrow washed away the delight on Wolfram's face like a single clear wave scouring away a sand-sculpture. "Dead?"

"They found his body hidden in a clump of low bushes, a little way from the field. He had been partially scavenged by wild animals. They had believed that he had walked or crawled in blind agony, as some men will do, while the battle was still going on. Collapsed there where no one could see him, and died before the search for the wounded began."

"His name had vanished from our rolls as well, as you might have guessed. If we had not spoken to him. I would lay money that if we were to ask, we would find that Alberich had interfered with the minds of the other men who knew Ludwig was among us. If Alberich had not been afraid to try altering your thoughts without your knowledge, and had known that I knew, no one would ever have had any idea that matters were other than they seemed. Yes, if you had not been the one to take Ludwig captive, he probably would be alive now. You would still be in Forlorn Hope, with Alberich still seeking out men to stab you in the back on the battlefield and I would be aiding Alberich in his efforts to defile, or destroy, the Bad Oberstein shrine, to bring down a good and faithful lord, and to open a way for Darkness here near the Empire's border," Gudrun answered, her voice as gentle as she could make it when she, too, was seething with bitter anger.

"Ludwig's murder cannot be laid to our guilt. Save," she added with reluctant honesty, "as our orders and knowledge limited us. You, because he had been taken from your hands to the tally and you thought him safe in broad daylight with our mages watching over him. I because I thought my duty was solely to protect against trickery from our foe's side, not treachery from our own. So I suppose we are not wholly blameless. But neither do I see how you or I could have saved Ludwig.

Had I tried harder to deal with the matter, I would have gone to Alberich first. While you did the best you could, and that, I guess, was what betrayed Ludwig. Hauptmann Heinrich must have asked Alberich for permission to speak to me, and given the matter away thereby."

Wolfram nodded glumly.

"Had we any glimmer that our traitor could whisk a man away in broad daylight and make him vanish from minds and documents, we should have known who it was, and matters might have gone much differently. Worse, most likely. I would not have wanted to accuse the Provost without Mishni's letters in hand. But despite Alberich's worst efforts, I think we brought more good of what happened than ill. The innocent die in war. We have both seen that. But the results of not fighting are often worse."

Despite her staunch words, Gudrun could feel her mouth trembling. She had hardly known Lieutenant Ludwig, and would have killed him in battle if she could have. Yet there had been something she had liked a great deal about the wounded man's good cheer and honesty if Wolfram did not know what was all too likely to have happened to Alberich's enchantment-stolen victim inside the silencing walls of the dark mage's pavilion, she was not going to bring the matter up. Whether Wolfram guessed something of what she was thinking, or merely meant to reassure her of his own steadfastness, Gudrun neither knew nor cared.

When he lifted his hand to touch her shoulder, she let the sway of the wain move her a little closer, so that the half-Elf was suddenly drawing her into an embrace. Wolfram held her very carefully, her breasts barely touching the sun-warmed steel of his breastplate. It was she who, gazing into his turquoise eyes, had to pull his head down and lean forward under his open visor to kiss him. His lips were silky and hot against hers, the soft pressure of his mouth thrilling through her body as though she were a harp-string ringing beneath a skilled minstrel's hand. Distraction, oh, yes! Gudrun thought breathlessly, as far as she could think at all with Wolfram's mouth on her and his warm gloved palms pressing against her back inside the unyielding edges of his gauntlets.

Wolfram's head swam with indescribable delight as Gudrun's lips touched his. He had known a couple of women before his transformation, serving maids in Graf Ulric's castle, who bore charms made by the Graf's mage against conception but his most intense pangs of pleasure had been nothing to this. For a moment, he could not help joying in what he was, that he should be able to feel Gudrun's love so keenly, and that she loved him.

He kept her braced with one hand, lest a sudden lurch of the wagon bruise her against the fluted ridges of his armor or bang her face into the edges of his open helm, but the other traced over her shoulder, palm caressing the soft upper curve of her breast through his glove's thin leather and the heavy burgundy silk of her robe.

Gudrun's gray-green eyes, soft as sun-warmed lakes, gazed into his. He tasted a hint of spiced meat and watered wine as her lips opened against his and she murmured her pleasure quietly into his mouth. *I want to hold you like this forever, and more,* Wolfram thought. *No one would disturb the Zauberobrist in the Black Wagon, they could* but the same thought seemed to come to both of them at the same time, breaking the kiss.

"Graf Sigfrid's heavy cavalry is still out here," Wolfram said regretfully.

"There is no way of telling whether he will decide we are enemies when he hears we are withdrawing," Gudrun agreed, though she still nestled as close to him as he dared let her. "Or Graf Berthold may have sent out a force that doesn't know what's happening." She blinked water from her eyes.

"Still," Wolfram paused. *Is this what I want? Yes. More than anything, since I left Löwenstein.*

The Silver Eagle is my home now, and of all the women in the world and if I could go back and take my old place again, I would still want this. But she has to know the truth, or as much of it as is mine to tell. The priest at Bad Oberstein was right. A lie by silence is still a lie. If she found out later, she has already been betrayed by finding out she gave her trust to an evil man. If she were to discover that she had given her love, unknowing, to a Dark Elf, how should she dare to trust, or love, again?

If I gained my heart's desire for a time, and lost it again because of what I am, I might not be able to go on again.

"What's wrong, Wolfram?" Gudrun asked.

The tender worry on her face, looking up at him, no one had looked at him that way since his mother's death. She had always known, and still loved him, though she had every right to hate the rapist's bastard in her belly. She could have had him put down at birth. Instead, she had gone to great trouble to keep and cherish him.

"I," How do I say something like this?

"Gudrun, I'm not what you think I am."

Her eyes seemed to darken slightly, like clear lake water rippling beneath the shadow of a swift-moving cloud.

"What do you mean?" She breathed.

Wolfram released his hold on her, barely steadying her against the Black Wagon's movement with one hand.

"I'm partially of Elven blood, and a bastard, yes, but my father raped my mother. Or enchanted her, which comes to the same thing. He was a Dark Elf."

Gudrun blinked. "I thought Dark Elves looked different. That they had black skin and pointed teeth."

"Not naturally. They often paint or dye their skin dark for battle, since they raid at night, and many of them file their teeth. But beneath it, they look much the same as other Elves."

Gudrun nodded. "All right, but why should that matter here? Kai is part Orcish, after all, and no one cares."

"The difference, what Elves are, is born into them. Their language, their thoughts, their nature. The children of Dark Elves carry their parents' taint. If Arkoniel or Piriel knew what I was, I believe either of them would kill me. I've only passed by pretending not to speak Elvish at all, because they'd know the Dark Elvish accent at once, because it is bred in the bone. Obrist Helmuth would have me executed as a spy, or at least thrown out as a probable danger." Wolfram knew he was babbling, but couldn't stop, all his obsessive night-thoughts clamoring and forcing their way out of his mouth.

At last Gudrun put her hand over his lips. "Wolfram," she said softly, "if Dark Elves are born evil, tell me how you came to be as you are."

"I can't tell you everything. For the sake of the man who raised me as his son, and his heir who was my brother, I am bound to make sure that no one, not even the woman I love, finds out where I came from. What I will tell you will be as true as I can make it, but not the whole truth."

Gudrun drew in a soft breath, her eyes widening, but whispered, "Go on."

Wolfram told the tale he had told to Obrist Helmuth and Arkoniel on entering the Company. He added, "I do have a little more control of my Elven abilities than they know. I can speak Elvish, but only Dark Elvish. Though I never think in it.

It is a frightening tongue. I'm becoming more able to see magic and to feel power, the world around me. There is an Elvish word, but I don't know what the Bright Elves call it, and the Dark Elvish concept is unpleasant. But mostly I don't try to use any of it, except the night sight, because I'm afraid that, if I were to let myself become more Elvish, that the taint would come out, that I'd do harm without noticing, as I have accidentally frightened men with my gaze sometimes, or even that I'd come, more and more, to desire pain and blood."

Wolfram looked away, ashamed. Unfair of him, to burden Gudrun with this on top of her other sorrows and duties. He could have waited, he should have. Maybe pulled back from her company altogether, only speaking as one officer to another when duty required. If he truly loved her, how could he want to burden her with the befouled mess of his past?

"Wolfram," Gudrun said gently, "if there were more of Darkness in you than in other Men and I am very doubtful of that there must surely be more of Light as well. No one admires a man who tames a mouse. It is the man who tames a lion who deserves admiration."

"But,"

"But nothing. Wolfram, do you think every mage isn't tempted, often, to misuse her power? That's why we spend as much time studying ethics as studying magic. Often enough, as we've seen," she added sadly, "we fail nevertheless. Wolfram, I understand."

"You,"

She stood on tiptoes, carefully bracing her hands on the sides of his helmet to lean in and silence him with another kiss.

"If I could marry anyone now, I'd marry you today."

Wolfram felt as though, charging a great iron-bound gate with a battering ram, he had found it unlocked, unbarred, swinging aside before he touched it to leave him thundering into an empty courtyard. His feet, braced against the impact that had not come, sliding out from under him so that he flailed to restore his balance.

"You, will you? I was going to ask."

Gudrun closed her eyes in pain. "I, Wolfram, will you let me open my mind to you? I don't want to hurt you, or let you think that this has anything to do with your ancestry. You will, if you can't see for yourself."

Wolfram nodded.

Gudrun touched his face, her slim fingers cool against his cheek. Suddenly, he could feel her heart opening to him like a leaf unfolding to the sun. This leaf had a spine of steel and Wolfram knew, helplessly, that he loved her the more for it. *I love you. For all that you are. Wolfram, I have my commission, and my duties, just as you do.*

I can't be a soldier's wife. I might as well have stayed home. Wolfram had spoken of his great fear. Gudrun's was less easy to articulate, but he felt the complex weave of her life behind it. *The frustration of being put in a woman's place. Her parents' expectations of the nice quiet life of a well-off burgher's wife, husband and children and going to the market in a ruffled skirt and a bonnet with ribbons on it. The professors at the College who thought she should stick to magics suitable for a respectable woman, casting horoscopes and mixing little philtres. The cage-bars of a respectable life looming larger and larger in her future, until there was no escape left for her but to run off and join the Landsknechts.*

Terrified of battle, and of her fellow soldiers, at first; then growing accustomed to the life of the regiment. Now she is happy now, Wolfram realized. *She never knew it herself but this is what she was meant to do. Yet, we have hired women to cook and launder,* Wolfram argued. *You wouldn't have to give up anything. I'd never ask that. I love you for what you are. A fighting mage, a companion by my side.* Gudrun shook her head regretfully. *I can't be your wife. Or anyone's. Not yet, and especially not now, when I have to learn to be a senior officer. I do love you, and I'll be happy to be your companion, in everything, companion and lover, as our duties allow. I've seen your heart, or enough of it to know you understand that.*

"Yes," Wolfram murmured, with both his lips and his soul. It hurt to say it, when he had just let his hidden hope free of his own mind's depths but it was true, Gods of Light, so true!

"Yes, I do. I love you because you do as well."

"We'll share our love, then, and see what the future sends us. If we both live long enough, then maybe, in time."

It was enough for Wolfram's heart, though just barely. He kissed Gudrun again but he knew, as she did, that if they let it last too long now, there would be no stopping. Reluctantly, they let go of each other. Though it took a moment for him to disentangle a few stray dark auburn hairs from the tiny jointed gauntlet-plates over the hand bracing her back.

One more quick brush of lips, then Lieutenant Wolfram handed the Fräulein Zauberobristin out of the Black Wagon and boosted her up onto her horse before hastening back to his place by the Obrist's wain. Wolfram knew that it might be some time yet before he and she could consummate what they had begun. He might be free between setting up camp and the beginning of the dark-sighted watches, but there would be no off-duty nights for her.

Not in enemy territory, with the regiment so short-handed in magic and knowing that a mage of great power would become the Silver Eagle's enemy as soon as he learned of their withdrawal and even less so, given the need for Gudrun to search the Black Wagon as soon and thoroughly as possible for such secrets or traps as Alberich had left behind there. Still, to his surprise, for he was still painfully aroused inside the constraints of his steel codpiece - Wolfram realized that he could bear the wait as well as he needed to.

Perhaps four years of aging and abstinence had banked the burning urgency of his late teens, perhaps he had, in spite of himself, learned something of an Elf's patience in fulfillment. Or perhaps it is just different when the desire is heart and soul, not rampant body alone. Though in that regard, it was as well for him at the moment that the Landsknechts were infantry companies.

CHAPTER 28

The Silver Eagle approached the border of Graf Sigfrid's land by a different road than they had used on the way out, marching between fields of ripe grain. Many of the fields had been deserted half-harvested, Berthold's peasants fleeing news of the Landsknechts' coming. As they got closer to Sigfrid's land, the smell of old charring filled the air. A number of fields lay black and ruined in the sunlight. The small village on the horizon was burnt likewise, the houses' roofs fallen in and fire-stained walls jutting up black against the blue sky. Wolfram thought of the fisher village he had seen after a Dark Elf raid. Sigfrid's soldiers were only Men, but his keen nose caught the distant scents of old blood and rot, and he was still relieved that the Silver Eagle was far enough away that he didn't have to look at what they had done.

Wolfram understood the military sense of such quick raids. To distract a foe who cared about the defense of his small folk, to gain some of his supplies by theft or at least deny them to him by burning.

I should know better, by now, than to think of war as a matter of chivalry. Chivalric honor was a luxury between knights. War was simply to be won, as effectively as might be. Still, he liked Graf Sigfrid none the better for it.

"How long, Lieutenant?" Obrist Helmuth asked Wolfram. Wolfram pulled the map out of the case hanging from his saddle, unrolling it one-handed across his horse's golden neck. A quick scan of the road, comparing it with their travels in the last two hour.

"Another hour or so, sir. If Graf Sigfrid is in the appointed place for your meeting."

Helmuth's mouth twisted under his gray mustache.

"If, indeed. Well, we are steering as fine a course between honor and practicality as we can, we shall see how it comes out."

Wolfram looked at the map a moment more. The Silver Eagle had avoided the woods and rolling hills that would have offered concealment for an ambush, a precaution more than a real concern. Graf Sigfrid had nothing to gain from throwing troops away on a regiment of professional soldiers who posed no immediate threat to him.

And whom, in such an instance, might be expected to turn around and join his enemy for no more than maintenance-pay, the hard-faced Graf was vindictive, but not stupid. Under more normal circumstances, there would have been no reason for concern, but Obrist Helmuth and Gudrun were both uncertain as to how much control Magister Klaus might exert over his nominal master.

Wolfram would have preferred, they all would have preferred to leave without taking the risk. Graf Sigfrid had to sign to the voluntary dissolution of their contract, and carrying out the communication by magic, considering the traitor on the other end of the spells, was simply unacceptable. Arkoniel had delivered the Obrist's message to Graf Sigfrid, returning safely two days ago with the word that the Graf would meet them in the appointed spot. Perhaps, Wolfram thought, we shall see how deep the corruption runs by what Sigfrid says, and does, as a result of this.

Obrist Helmuth and his personal staff rode at the forefront of the column today, with Gudrun just behind them. Her dark auburn hair was braided up into a severe frame for her face; her expression was stern, remote with concentration. Wolfram looked at her as little as he could manage, lest her attention waver. The softening of her gaze when their eyes met melted his heart, but it was a distraction neither they, nor the Company, could afford at the moment.

The Obrist had filled out his normal Trabanten with the two Elves, lest Magister Klaus should manage to have infiltrated himself into the Graf's guard without Gudrun detecting his presence.

The Elves were resistant enough to the magics of Men that they should be able to meet any enchanter's treacheries with bow and sword. To protect the Obrist and Zauberobristin against traps involving more mundane violence, Fredrik had been summoned from his usual chosen place among the Forlorn Hope men. With Sascha dead, he was undoubtedly the best fighter in the regiment.

Wolfram had suggested that Mishni be nearby as well, thinking that no one else in the Silver Eagle was so likely to be able to detect sleights of hand and similar deceptions, but Helmuth had waved off the idea with a vague mutter about the Rat being more profitably employed elsewhere and when Wolfram thought about it, he realized that he hadn't seen the little Southerner for some time. Although that was hardly surprising, considering the amount of work the Obrist had for Wolfram.

He had only been able to snatch a few rare moments to spend with Gudrun, and most of those were by way of assisting her with her own work, as far as he could. At least Wolfram's Elvish blood gave him some ability to sense Darkness in magical items or workings. It still disturbed him that, while the tingle of evil felt different from that untainted power, he found its touch neither painful or distressing. He could recognize it, and that was worthwhile.

An open pavilion stood at the border-stone Obrist Helmuth had chosen as the meeting site, visible almost a mile away.

Graf Sigfrid's banner hung above it, there was not enough wind to lift the gonfalon, but Wolfram could make out the blue field and the hint of gold that would be Sigfrid's griffon.

Inasmuch as Wolfram had expected anything at all, he would have thought the Graf's pavilion would be made of bright silks, like those of the Silver Eagle's most senior officers. Instead, his keen eyes could make out only the dull coarseness of unbleached linen, brownish-gray as dead grass, such as might be used as a temporary shelter for soldiers on campaign. Wolfram stared searchingly at the area around, looking for any hint of concealment or reinforcements, but saw only a picket-line of horses. Sixteen, unless more were hidden behind the pavilion, enough for the Graf and a small troop of bodyguards.

Helmuth pulled up, holding up a gauntleted hand to signal a halt, the drummers struck the measure to carry the order back through the column. Gudrun's wand moved, its tip tracing tiny fiery patterns in the air. Her face was a blank marble mask. Though she was facing towards the Sun, her pupils swelled to drown her green-gray irises in darkness. Darkness lit by a faint blue glimmering, like a lake catching the last traces of light from the evening sky. At last her wand-hand dropped.

"Some traces of magic, such as might be expected in the gear of a powerful and wealthy man, sir," the Zauberobristin said, her voice strained. "No sense of concealments, or of a mage's presence. It is still possible that Magister Klaus could have woven protections for himself strong enough to deceive my abilities."

At the Obrist's glance, first Arkoniel, then Piriel, nodded.

"Even we are not infallible when it comes to the more powerful magics of Men," Piriel said quietly, "thus far there is no sign of such workings that we can see."

"Then we shall proceed." Helmuth nodded to his staff and Trabanten, nudged his horse into a walk. Wolfram moved forward to keep his place at the Obrist's left side. Hartmann fell back slightly, the Silver Eagle banner flapping above his head. Gudrun followed behind their commander, and the rest of the guards fell in around them.

Wolfram swallowed hard as they neared Graf Sigfrid's pavilion, his stomach tightening. This was a risk but Sigfrid would never have been willing to allow the Silver Eagle near his own fortress now, nor to come out into their midst. For a contract to be dissolved under such circumstances as these was virtually unprecedented. There was no clear procedure to follow, and there had been no real chance to negotiate safer terms on either side.

Wolfram was reasonably certain that the prickling of the little hairs on the back of his neck, and the cold feeling in his belly, came from nerves alone and not some subtle Elvish intuition of danger but only reasonably certain. I have only to serve as Obrist Helmuth's Schreiber, and defend Gudrun if fighting starts, Wolfram reminded himself. It is a simple enough duty.

The Obrist had chosen to leave his usual scribe behind, Arturus not being a fighter out of habit, Wolfram touched the sword at his side, making sure it was loose in its sheath. He could not help giving the hilt an additional slight squeeze, as if he had brushed his hand over Gudrun's fingers, just to reassure himself that it was really still there. Honorably regained. The pavilion was open at the front. Graf Sigfrid sat inside behind a small table, surrounded by large men in full armor with their visors down. Behind his own visor, Wolfram frowned.

He had never seen the Graf's mage, but Obrist Helmuth presumably had and anyone could be hiding behind those metal masks. I have heard that steel is supposed to hinder magic but it is no protection on the battlefield. Still, mages were rarely trained to move in armor. He glanced about the Graf's bodyguards, looking for any tell-tale signs of awkwardness or discomfort, but they all stood as still as any Imperial ceremonial guards.

Sigfrid glared at the Silver Eagle party as they dismounted, saying nothing. Wolfram noticed that his hands were out of sight beneath the table. A hand-gun? Would he risk it? He breathed slowly in through his nose, out through his mouth, feeling that odd combination of relaxation and readiness that Graf Ulric had once likened to a cat watching for a mouse to move, muscles loose, mind hyper-aware of everything about him, awaiting only the right trigger to explode into violent action.

Obrist Helmuth nodded to his company, and they dismounted, the fighting men with the quick whirling swing of leg that brought them to the ground in ready position, Gudrun slowly and carefully, never taking her eyes off the men in the pavilion for a heartbeat. Wolfram handed off his reins to Hartmann and took the case with the documents and writing materials from his saddlebag, then moved in closer to the Zauberobristin, where he could knock her to the ground if necessary, or, if nothing else, interpose his armored body between her and a bullet or blade.

Wolfram was not her only guard, there were three other men with no duty except protecting the mage but he knew that his reactions would be the quickest. Graf Sigfrid only waited, watching as Helmuth and his troop stepped beneath the pavilion's shade to halt in front of him. Wolfram could see the fury and hate burning in the nobleman's intense blue eyes, his broad face hard as a slab of steel beneath the raised snout of his visor.

"Explain yourself," Sigfrid grated.

"Your Excellency. As my message stated, due to the treachery of our former Zauberobrist, in conspiracy with your court mage Magister Klaus von Ludo, the bidding for our Company was interfered with to our detriment. We were played false to cause us to take this contract, we are therefore dissolving it. We understand that this is none of your personal doing. Nevertheless, we are not willing to re-negotiate."

"The contract is clear. Regardless of how the price was arrived at, you found it acceptable. I am not responsible for treachery in your own ranks. There is no justification for backing out simply because you found out that you might have gotten more money from the other side." Sigfrid bit each word off sharply. His expression did not change, but his face was reddening, with anger, Wolfram judged.

"Under more ordinary circumstances, you would have a case," Helmuth agreed. "As to what I would not trust to writing where your mage could read it, do you trust your men?"

Sigfrid's eyes did not so much as flicker to the armored guards about him.

"They will not speak against my will," he growled.

Graf Ulric might have said the same but Wolfram doubted that Sigfrid's men were bound by lifelong ties of love and loyalty. He wondered if any of the Graf's guards were the men whose gazes had so unsettled him, back at Sigfrid's fortress.

"Lieutenant Wolfram, read the account of Alberich's interrogation."

Wolfram took the parchment from his case, grudging every moment that both his hands were occupied. He straightened his back, reading in a good clear voice, watching Sigfrid's face as well as he could over the edge of the document. The Graf's face darkened with blood as Wolfram laid out the traitorous mage's confession.

"How dare you accuse me of working against the Empire?" He choked out savagely. "This is clearly a tissue of slanderous lies, slander against myself, and against Magister Klaus. It may well be that your Alberich was a traitor but I am well within my rights to seek to regain what is mine by force of arms when legal wranglings have not availed. Is having a shrine on one's land now as good as taking sanctuary in the High Temple?"

"Alberich was constrained by spells forcing him to tell the truth," Obrist Helmuth replied. "While a lord may not be granted immunity from war by the presence of a shrine on his land, the strategy desired by the compromised mages was specifically based on, not only the conquest of the shrines we discussed, but their actual destruction. Their defilement, in fact, Alberich was already preparing his Marshals for that task, which was unknown to me." He cocked his head, looking pointedly at Sigfrid. "As to you?"

"Berthold's priests would use that power to defend him," argued Sigfrid. "Those who choose sides in war must expect to become strategic targets.

We might as well have planned to leave clusters of mages unharmed as fail to deny our foe his chief unconventional asset."

"The priests of the Bad Oberstein shrine healed captives taken from our regiment, and informed those captives that if the shrine and its village were not molested, they would make no resistance. If I had not delayed to confirm that, my Company would already have furthered our mages' tainted agenda."

Wolfram could not help raising his eyebrows at that, although fortunately his closed visor hid his surprise. Gudrun kept her expression better controlled, but could not hide the sudden sick paleness of shock, as if the Obrist had driven a knife backhanded into her kidney. The half-Elf wondered what Alberich had told his students to prepare them for assaulting the shrine itself. The relationship between high magic and religion had always been notably uneasy.

"And you believed these assurances?" Sigfrid said. "Come, now, you are a man of experience in war."

"Indeed. Experience enough to know how those who are not soldiers behave. I have not yet seen a priest of Donmar, speaking in the very heart of a holy site, lie for the sake of expedience or military strategy.

There may be occasions when some priests would lie for their god's sake but not, I think, for an overlord, not even a favored one.

"Unless," Helmuth went on thoughtfully, in a more conversational tone, "the Bad Oberstein priests were aware that your war on Graf Berthold was guided by, and served the purposes of, a conspiracy of Darkness. In which case, I would be all the less inclined to pursue it and all the more likely to advise you to drop the matter."

The Obrist conferred with the priests himself after Alberich's interrogation, Wolfram thought. He must know whether they knew or not.

"It serves my purposes!" Sigfrid answered, his voice rising slightly. "Are you telling me that you are trying to evade our contract out of piety?"

Obrist Helmuth's voice chilled sudden and glass-hard as steel plunged glowing into the quenching bath.

"Out of loyalty to the Empire. For there is no question that this conspiracy, which both my former Zauberobrist and your court mage served, seeks its harm. The defense of the Empire is the cause of the Landsknechts' creation, and our duty above all others."

Sigfrid leaned forward over the table. "A high-sounding cloak for breach of contract! This flimsy weave of mage's madness and imagination has nothing to do with the defense of the Empire, or the Landsknechts' duty in that regard, which is to have trained pike men and gunners ready against real threats. Are you afraid to go on without a competent Zauberobrist?"

"I have a competent Zauberobristin," Helmuth replied calmly, "and if the Silver Eagle were accompanied by the Hohenzauberer of the College of Magics himself, that would make no difference in my decision. Moreover, I have already sent a full report of this matter to the Emperor. Because Alberich exonerated you of any knowing part in this conspiracy, I have presented you likewise. However, now that you are aware of Magister Klaus' portion in it and his true allegiance, you would be best to carry out the Empire's justice upon him, or at the very least secure him against the Imperial representatives' coming. Though I myself would be loath to try keeping a mage of such skill imprisoned for long without equivalent untainted magical resources."

"You," Sigfrid's face had gone white now, save for two burning spots on his broad cheekbones. "In the middle of a war? You expect me to get rid of my best mage, for this."

"For the sake of proving yourself both innocent and loyal, lest you find yourself matched against a far more puissant foe than Graf Berthold.

Whom, I suspect, would be willing enough to back off if you explained to him what has occurred. I gather that he is the sort of man who does believe that others may be motivated by piety, or concern for the struggle between Light and Dark. Else you would not consider him such a fool."

Sigfrid snorted, spat aside onto the grass. "True enough. Still,"

"If you do not deal with Magister Klaus yourself," Helmuth pursued relentlessly, before the Graf could continue, "you will have to explain to the Emperor's agents why you did not, when the evidence against him was clearly presented to you. Your position is endangered enough already, but you have a clear avenue of retreat if you use it soon." The Obrist nodded to Wolfram. Wolfram pulled the documents for the dissolution of the Silver Eagle's contract out of his case, laying them on the table together with quill and ink.

"Having realized how you were misled, your best choice now is to rid yourself of the Landsknecht regiment you hired before you have to pay us any more money, and as earnest of your willingness to protect the Empire's peace and defend the Light."

Sigfrid's gauntleted right hand curled into a spiky fist on the table, all the overlapping points of the little fluted finger-plates sticking out like a row of shining reptile crests raised in anger.

Certain, for a moment, that Sigfrid would strike Obrist Helmuth, Wolfram was poised and ready to catch the arm in mid-blow or to swing his sword from its sheath in a stroke that would end with its point stabbing through Sigfrid's face, if the Graf signed his men to attack. Then Wolfram heard the near-silent hissing of breath flowing out through Graf Sigfrid's clenched teeth.

Finger by finger, Sigfrid's clenched gauntlet uncurled.

If the Graf was not a good man, he was, after all, a practical one and tactician enough to know when his ground was lost. He reached for the quill, crumpling the parchments in his rough grasp as he dragged them across the table. Wolfram breathed slowly to keep his shoulders from tensing, but did not ease his vigilance. He had seen enough downed men suddenly curl up to stab a foe who thought too soon that the fight was over. Sigfrid signed the documents, crushing one into his belt-pouch and shoving the other back at Wolfram.

"Take it, and be damned to you," he said hoarsely. "And go where-ever you will but keep off my land. You will not be welcome."

"As you will, your Excellency," Obrist Helmuth replied with cold courtesy. "I trust, for your own sake, that you will take my advise regarding your court mage."

Graf Sigfrid gave him a searing glare of hate. "I will take it under advisement. You may find that your discovery has done the Landsknechts an ill turn."

"The Landsknechts serve the Empire above all," Helmuth replied. "If our ranks require cleansing, well, we have begun the process ourselves. We are not unfamiliar with the knowledge that some may have to be sacrificed to bring victory to all. Else we should not have a Forlorn Hope in our regiment."

"Go on as you have begun here, and the whole Silver Eagle is likely to end up as a Forlorn Hope," Sigfrid said.

"Perhaps so, but better forlorn hope than certain death or betraying the Empire to Darkness. May you fare well, if you have the wisdom to do what you need to." Obrist Helmuth turned on his heel, marching out of the pavilion. Gudrun followed him, the Trabanten falling in warily around them.

CHAPTER 29

Obrist Helmuth requested Gudrun and Wolfram to dine in his pavilion that night. His wife Lotte ate with them as well. Wolfram had seen her about, but hardly ever had occasion to speak with her. A tall, elegant woman, with silver streaks burnishing the rich brown of her hair, Frau Lotte's effortless poise and good manners made the camp's command center feel like the dining hall of a fine mansion or Schloss. She barely spoke of the campaign, except to very obliquely express her relief that the Silver Eagle had not been responsible for destroying Tilman Lindenschneider's art, and her regret that their new path eastward would give her no chance to see Graf Berthold's famous chapel.

"I recently saw the altarpiece that Herr Lindenschneider carved for the High Cathedral in Trevantum," Frau Lotte commented. "This peculiar technique he created is really most effective. Of course, ordinary sculptures are more lifelike from a distance, because of the color, but the shadowing and texture of the wood give Lindenschneider's faces a degree of expression that gesso and paint could never match. It seems peculiar to talk about the richness of monochrome work, but there it is. You find yourself wanting to touch the wood as much as look at it."

Wolfram held his tongue for a moment and then remembered that he was an invited guest at table, that moreover, he was one of the Obrist's staff, if only a Lieutenant, and much of the commander's business was spoken across the dinner table with nobles and the important men of cities.

"I saw some of Lindenschneider's works, a series of reliefs showing the miracles of St. Hildebrand, in a northern chapel some years ago," he commented casually. "It was most impressive. The man who had commissioned them mentioned that he had received a good deal of criticism at first, from those who thought that unpainted woodwork was more fitting to a peasants' hallows than to a Graf's own place of worship but now they are the treasure of his castle."

"Where was this?" Obrist Helmuch inquired lightly.

"Up on the northern coast, I was only there a very short time," Wolfram replied, trying to sound apologetic and forgetful. "The carvings made more of an impression on me than their owner did, I'm afraid."

"I am hardly surprised," remarked Frau Lotte. "You strike me as a young man with a fine sense of aesthetics.

Gudrun, my dear, are you interested in art?"

"I have hardly had the chance to be," Gudrun stammered. Wolfram wished that he could take her aside and hold her until she relaxed. He recognized her stiff shyness for what it was, a burgher's daughter's fear of embarrassing herself before her social superiors. My Gudrun, we are still in the Company: you have worth and rank in your own right.

Lotte smiled kindly. "Well, that is not surprising. I have heard that magic is an extraordinarily demanding subject, and you must have been an exceptionally dedicated student, to be doing so well while still so young. Do you, ah, here is the next course. I wonder if I shall have succeeded in convincing Frieda that simply because pepper is expensive, that does not mean that more of it in a dish is necessarily better?"

Frau Lotte excused herself when the sweets were served, saying, "There are some matters I have to see to tonight, unfortunately. Helmuth, I shall be in our wagon for a time, if you need me. Wolfram, it was a pleasure having a chance to talk with you properly. I trust we shall have many more occasions to do so. Gudrun."

The Obrist's wife pressed Gudrun's slender fingers in her own.

"I know some of the hardships of the road can be more difficult for a lady than for a man, or a woman who is, shall we say, less ladylike. If you ever have need of an old woman's advice, do feel free to come to me. I was never able to say that before, because Alberich," she shuddered, "became very sharp at the suggestion that he might not always know what was best for his students, and said that he wouldn't have me filling your head with silly feminine nonsense. I think that would be quite impossible with you but still, if you ever want to talk to me, do come find me."

"Thank you, meine Frau," Gudrun answered, glancing sideways at Wolfram and blushing slightly. Frau Lotte's warm brown eyes followed the glance, and she smiled benevolently.

"Goodnight to all of you, then."

Obrist Helmuth waited to speak until the strüdel made with the first sweet summer apples had been divided out among the three of them, and a small goblet of very sweet Rhenus wine poured for each of them. Gudrun took a sip of wine, momentarily overwhelmed by the rich flavors that floated into her nose and the back of her throat. It reminded her of Wolfram's kisses. Sweet and tart at once, subtle yet complex, gentle as the soft cool liquid on her tongue yet burning inside her with passion, she blushed again, hoping that the mellow amber lantern-light would hide her flushed complexion from the men.

Wolfram was looking at her, turquoise eyes clear and warm as the southerly waters of the Middle Sea in summer. Tonight, Gudrun thought, taking a bite of strüdel and letting the flaky pastry melt over her tongue. Then, more reluctantly, Or at least no more than two nights hence. If Sigfrid had his own troops waiting within a couple of miles, he could catch us without too much trouble.

A Graf's army could simply move faster than a Landsknecht regiment, with all the latter's encumbrances of sutlers and women, children and the amount of sheer baggage needed by those who lived on the road. Even if it was Alberich who warned me against becoming distracted, I should have listened! Gudrun said to herself in disgust, realizing that the Obrist had been speaking without any of his words sticking in her mind. Better to face up to it than risk missing important information, though.

"I'm sorry, sir? I was distracted for a moment."

"Indeed." Helmuth smiled, his graying hair and blunt features lending themselves well to the look of an indulgent grandfather. "I was saying that it appears that the former Zauberobrist was somewhat correct in his surmise about yourself and Lieutenant Wolfram."

"Sir!" Gudrun protested. "Neither of us has ever neglected our duties because,"

"Of course not," the Obrist soothed. "However, it is my duty to remain aware of the personal lives of my officers when it might affect the Silver Eagle. Therefore, are you planning to marry?"

Wolfram looked at Gudrun – hoping she would change her mind? No, he knew better.

He was keeping silence, letting her make the declaration, for fear of humiliating her otherwise. If he spoke first, the obvious inference would be that he thought her unworthy of marriage.

"We are not," Gudrun said firmly. "Lieutenant Wolfram asked me, he is an honorable man but I am not ready to take on a marriage in addition to my new duties. Sir, I am pleased and willing to be Zauberobristin for the Silver Eagle, but I do not delude myself that it will be easy."

"No. You have certainly been working hard to be worthy of your post. Still, I am concerned that if and when word of your relationship gets out, there may be a risk regarding your ability to keep discipline among your men, insofar as you are responsible for doing so."

"Any man who questions my capability, or thinks that I am a slut, may apply to me directly for correction," Gudrun said, looking Obrist Helmuth straight in the eye. "And as Wolfram is not my subordinate, nor am I his, there should be no question of untoward favoritism or impaired judgment."

The corner of Helmuth's mouth curled up in satisfaction.

"True enough, and well pointed out. Still, in the interests of maintaining general clarity, and to avoid causing any more offense than we must when we negotiate with more, hmm, conservative employers. Would you be willing to present yourselves as betrothed?

With no fixed date set for your marriage, of course! But the implication that you intend eventually to leave the Landsknechts and settle down, even if there is not the slightest shred of truth behind it and I hope that, even should you change your mind about marriage, you would remain with us. Would be greatly reassuring to those who look particularly askance at female officers, on the rare occasions that such ladies occur in Landsknecht regiments."

Gudrun looked at Wolfram, he looked at her. She could see the hope on his face now, alert and keen as a cat watching a rustle in fallen leaves. She almost feel his breath along her skin, shivering in anticipation.

"A promissory betrothal is not legally binding," the Obrist pointed out. "And it would save a good deal of unnecessary trouble, possibly for the whole Company."

Gudrun could not dismiss his logic. Faced with Wolfram's offer of marriage, with the sudden reality of his touch and the flooding delight of knowing her love returned, she had felt that she had to assert her independence completely before her heart drove her to do something her soul would regret.

I want him for my own, but not to possess; I want to give myself to him, but not to be owned by him. But a promissory betrothal surrenders no rights. Wolfram, gods, after the pain he has known, how can he not need the reassurance of something more solid than I offered?

"I would be willing." She turned to Wolfram, opening his mouth to object? He put a finger to his lips. "Not for appearance's sake, either. You startled me when you proposed, and I jumped farther than I meant to. If you want to be betrothed, with no wedding date or even year, knowing that our duties to the regiment come before our pleasure together, and that we're likely to be Landsknechts for a long time yet, it's what I want, us to each other."

"Yes," Wolfram whispered. For a moment it seemed as though Obrist Helmuth had faded into the shadows behind the lanterns, as though the two of them were alone in the pavilion. His arms went around her, so good, to be parted from his warm strength by no more than thin layers of velvet and linen, feeling his firm muscles move against her back! They kissed, their mouths sweet with apple strüdel and rich dessert wine.

"A toast to your betrothal," the Obrist said finally when they broke apart. Wolfram started, he had almost forgotten their commander was even there. He still could barely turn his gaze away from Gudrun, radiant and bright-eyed in the amber lantern-light.

Now that she had agreed to be betrothed to him, he was able to admit to himself how deeply disappointed he had been when she refused his proposal and how, even though he had heard the truth from her mind, part of him had still feared that his heritage had contributed to her refusal. *She knows, and still she loves me.*

She knows, and she wants to share her life with me. He wanted to weep with joy, or sing, but with Obrist Helmuth there, even beaming at them with what seemed to be genuine delight, all he could do was raise his goblet in turn, letting the sweetness of the wine flow across his tongue in a thick rich burst of summer fruit. *I will find her a ring, as soon as I can. Emerald, for Alagrith the Lady of Love, sapphire, for faithfulness diamond, the imperishable, the shield against all ill.*

"Now that is settled to everyone's satisfaction," Obrist Helmuth said, "we must return to more problematical issues. Fräulein Zauberobristin, your presence here is obvious. Lieutenant, you are here to learn and take notes for me, but I hope that you will also be able to provide certain insights. Both of you are here because I trust you; and I fear that complete trust will be in short supply for some time."

"Sir," Wolfram said, falling back on military courtesy to hide his confusion. Did the Obrist think, could he know about the taint in Wolfram's blood? Did he think the Dark Elf heritage could aid in untangling a conspiracy of Darkness?

"First, to answer some of your questions. Wolfram, I saw you start when I said I had sent a full account to the Emperor."

"Yes, sir. Sir, does this not put all the Landsknecht regiments under suspicion?"

Helmuth smiled. "What Sigfrid and you may have thought I meant by a full account may not have been the same thing I wrote, though the apprehension of it shall, hopefully, have discouraged Graf Sigfrid from doing anything ill-advised. We are going back to Mannerheim now, where I will speak to His Imperial Majesty myself, in full confidence. Yes, there is reason to be concerned but I think that Emperor Maximilian the Younger will find us more a useful tool than a risk in shoring up the Empire against this threat. For, assuredly, there is more to the conspiracy than Alberich was able to tell us, perhaps more than he knew. This war was an opportunity to be seized, no doubt, but feuds within the Empire, while not rare, are not so common nor so straightforwardly divided as to rest a plan of this nature and extent upon.

Even Graf Sigfrid, hard and limited of focus as he is, was not someone that could be trusted directly in the conspiracy. I hope," the Obrist added, aside, "that we have shown him that the risks of involving himself with it are more than he is willing to undertake. This is one of the Empire's great virtues. It gives lords who truly care nothing for Light or Darkness a self-interested motive not to declare for the latter when it seems more immediately expedient. I shall not be surprised if, for some years, we have Imperial agents joining the Companies. But that will do the better of us no harm, and we can rely upon them really being competent fighters, or mages, or whatever they are posing as among us." He turned to Gudrun.

"In fact, with your agreement, Fräulein Zauberobristin, I am thinking of asking for a couple of Imperial mages to fill out the ranks of your command. By that means, we can get sorcerers who will have the experience that you are still garnering, but who will have no ambition to supplant you, nor resentment at being commanded by a younger mage. By the time the Emperor is ready to withdraw them, your knowledge of the practice of magic should have reached the level at which such considerations are no longer a concern."

Gudrun nodded, wide-eyed. "Thank you, Herr Obrist. I had thought of the problem, but not the solution."

"Part of your training, Fräulein Zauberobristin. As one of my senior officers, you will have to grow accustomed to considering politics both outside and within the regiment. The next matter is a more delicate one. We know that Alberich recruited assassins for his own purpose within Forlorn Hope. That specifically does not concern me too much, since he is dead, and whatever inducements of money or compulsions of magic he may have employed to that purpose will no longer apply, is that latter correct?"

Gudrun shook her head. "Not entirely, sir. If he did use magic, and if he found a man, or men, who already hated Wolfram or, for that matter, Mishni, to use it upon, the compulsion could still lie hidden. Just a target who enjoys killing and doesn't care whom. It doesn't take much to make a man do what he wants to do, that's why even dog-mages can cast effective spells of seduction in most cases." She paused, then spoke reluctantly. "I think that was the method he used to foul Wilhelm's truth-spell at Wolfram's trial. I am not certain that he might not have laid other compulsions on Wilhelm. Compulsions to overlook suspicious actions, for instance, although that would be difficult to tell from the ordinary trust of student in teacher. I would have to perform a full examination of my Marshal's mind to be sure that nothing lingers, in any case."

"You have that authority, Fräulein Zauberobristin. Use it carefully, for if Wilhelm has not been compelled, it would be unfortunate to lose him. But if you think it needs to be done, do not hesitate. Better an empty office than one filled by a traitor."

"Yes, sir. It is even possible that Alberich might have deliberately left compulsions to be triggered by his death. By his death through betraying the conspiracy, since he took his risks in battle like the rest of us. If that were the case, you, or anyone in the regiment, might be in danger of assassination from certain of our own."

Helmuth sighed. "There have been times over the years when I found my care regarding the sort of men we recruit to be inconvenient. But now I seem to be reaping some reward, if I understand correctly that the men susceptible to the magic you describe are those with specific grudges, or pure killers by nature. Not that we lack the latter. The sweetest-natured peasant boy in the world may discover unexpectedly that taking life is his greatest pleasure after he has done it a few times but as a Landsknecht regiment goes, I believe most of our folk are guided by discipline and honor. Still, we shall require a constant vigilance. Lieutenant, please note the details and also select four men whom you know and trust to take turns as your own Trabanten, since you are the most likely target."

"And Mishni, sir?" Where is Mishni? Wolfram wondered again. Why haven't I seen him?

The Obrist smiled grimly. "Mishni can take care of himself. To the next matter,"

"Freimann Martin," Wolfram said suddenly. "Excuse me, sir."

"For your Trabanten?" Obrist Helmuth asked in surprise.

"No. But if we have one man, outside Forlorn Hope, who enjoys nothing more than the killing, and who was in constant contact with Alberich." Who likes being feared, as he walks about in his blood-red cloak with the hangman's noose dangling from his belt and beheading sword by his side. He was pleased to be the Provost's companion and enforcer.

"Ah. Note that a guard be set on Freimann Martin tonight and you, Fräulein Zauberobristin, will examine him in the morning. Now, do you think Alberich could have recruited any of the Silver Eagle's soldiers to his underlying cause?"

Wolfram thought about it, Gudrun's ruddy brows tightened in thought as well. "There were some men in Forlorn Hope who might have turned to Darkness by choice," Wolfram mused. "From what I saw of them, at least. Most of them are dead now, though. There may yet be a difference between a hardened criminal and a worshiper of the Three Gods of Darkness. Also, I can't imagine Alberich trusting so far in any of them."

"No," Gudrun agreed. "If he had succeeded in getting Wilhelm and myself to assist him in defiling the Bad Oberberg shrine, and perhaps others along the way, he might have slowly seduced us to his conspiracy without ever saying a word about it until we were fully committed." A look of dark sorrow passed through her eyes, like the sweep of a raven's wing-shadow over her face. There was more behind her words than she was willing to let on, Wolfram thought. "But Wilhelm was as disturbed as I by the plan to defile the shrine. Perhaps more so, in truth. In any case, Alberich had a great contempt for the mass of humanity. I cannot see him expecting the intelligence and self-will to understand his goals from anyone but another mage, save perhaps a great lord."

"Heh. That is one bright spot, in any case."

A great lord, or a Dark Elf? Wolfram thought. Alberich had spoken the name of Queen Imrisi, the ruler of Myrkheimr, after those of the Three Gods of Darkness when he was asked to name his fellow-conspirators. Wolfram, of all folk, should know how easily a Dark Elf could pass for one of the bright kin, at least as far as Men's recognition was concerned. Elves were very rare among the Landsknechts. Then, they were very rare, a Dark Elven spy might go unrecognized, but could never go unnoticed in a regiment, and only Wolfram's humanity had saved him from denunciation as soon as Arkoniel had seen him. Alberich was trying to foul the interrogation by naming the forces of Darkness. His conspiracy in the greater sense, perhaps but not what we meant by the question.

"Sir," Gudrun said after a few moments, "may I ask a question?"

"Of course, Fräulein Zauberobristin."

"I understand why we didn't try to demand Magister Klaus as a prisoner. It was difficult enough getting such concessions as we did from Graf Sigfrid, and we could not have succeeded in backing the demand by force." An understatement, given that the Graf's castle had been built to withstand foes significantly larger and more powerful than the Silver Eagle.

"I think that it would be easy enough for him to conceal himself from the Imperial investigators, when they come, and return to Graf Sigfrid's service afterwards."

"Ah. Wait." Obrist Helmuth grinned, a startlingly youthful expression on the older man's creased, blunt-featured face. He threw back his head and let out three extraordinarily realistic mastiff-barks. Even Wolfram's half-Elvish ears could hardly have told them from the voice of a real hound.

After a few moments, the pavilion's door-flap rustled aside. Wolfram was poised at once on the edge of his chair, ready to leap. Then he recognized the scarred features and scraggly dark hair of Mishni the Rat. A thick scurf of stubble shadowed the Southerner's hollowed cheeks; his leather jerkin was more stained and scuffed than ever, and a musty grass-scent hung about him, as though he had been sleeping on the ground or in haystacks for a long time.

"Did you succeed?" The Obrist asked him.

"All perfect," Mishni grinned. He reached into the neck of his jerkin, pulling out the leather thong with his skeletal, half-mummified rat. Next to the talisman hung a small leather pouch, from which Mishni drew a scrap of cloth. The pungent aroma that wafted from it was all too familiar to Wolfram from his time digging latrines.

"Great mage very careful with clothes, hair, fingernails, keep everyone out of rooms, even lowest servants. Even great mage have to use privy sometime. Could have stuck spear up his arse, but thought he might have spells telling him harm down there. Don't do no harm to take piss, though. Not then, anyway."

Wolfram glanced at Gudrun, shocked and embarrassed for her sake. A slow smile was spreading across the mage's face.

"That's brilliant thinking, Mishni!" Gudrun said. "Once in contact, always in contact, and a personal bodily fluid. Where-ever Magister Klaus goes, he can be found. A better mage than he might even be able to work an enchantment on him from a distance. A binding, say. Or possibly even a calling."

Wolfram stared at the Rat as he put the fouled rag away, untied the pouch from the thong, and passed it over to Gudrun. She took it with no sign of squeamishness, though her nose did wrinkle at the smell a little as she tucked it into her own belt-purse. Wolfram turned his gaze to Obrist Helmuth, then looked back at Mishni in time to catch his small nod to their commander. Wolfram began to wonder. He had barely had time to think about it that night, but the Obrist had responded to the accusations against his Zauberobrist and Provost with surprising speed.

Almost as if he had already known something, such as the contents of Mishni's jerkin and only been waiting for his suspicions to be proven true or unfounded. Wolfram had wondered before why the Rat would have filched a pouch of documents in the first place. Mishni met Wolfram's eyes as the first glow of anger began to kindle in the half-Elf's bowels.

"Truly not test for you," he said. "Would have died, for true, if you not ransom me. Obrist never know it me in Bad Oberstein. Alberich let him think I die in battle. Maybe think so self, till see us come back."

Gudrun hissed through her teeth, her jaw clenching, and Wolfram wondered what Alberich had told her. Had she thought he was dead, as well?

"Wolfram, I believed you were guilty until the last, there," Obrist Helmuth rumbled. "Grieved it, yes, because I had been keeping an eye on you as a promising young officer, considering that you had many of the advantages of your blood combined with the ability to understand soldiering as Men do.

I have seen promising young men break down before, and I knew you came with a heavily burdened past. I could only hope that you would survive your battles and return with your lesson learned and spirit whole.

As for Mishni, he had survived Forlorn Hope twice before, and, as you found out, its guards could not keep him in. Being there, out of the usual structure, gave him a better chance to look around unobserved.

"Keep in mind, that the suspect was our Provost as well as our Zauberobrist, an officer whose function is to make sure that there is one final and impartial judge who cannot be moved by force, rank, or command. It is not only legally almost impossible, but wrong, for a commander to turn his own power directly against the Provost, save when a clear breach of the Orders can be proven, or else something as heinous as had proved to be the case."

"But," Wolfram looked at the scruffy, smelly figure of the Rat looked back at Obrist Helmuth in his neat blue velvet Waffenrock with the broad bands of gold brocade ringing the heavy pleats over his golden silk hose. Gudrun, too, was glancing from man to man, her eyebrows arching incredulously.

Mishni cackled out loud. The Obrist smiled. "My dear young officers," Helmuth said. "By now, you should be learning that a Landsknecht regiment, which goes everywhere, asks few questions about a recruit's past, and usually fights for the highest bidder, is as much an opportunity for spies of various sorts as it is a home for the warlike and desperate. I was not jesting about the virtues of Imperial agents planted in one's regiment, but there are others as well, not all of whom have the Empire's best interests in mind. Seldom as dramatically as proved to be the case with Alberich, granted, but potential dangers nevertheless. Therefore, it behooves a man who would lead a Landsknecht company to have his own ways of watching over it, by night as well as by day. The Provost, walking around with the Freimann and bailiff by his side, is the controller that everyone sees. Even someone like yourself, Lieutenant Wolfram, on the one hand seeming to be a bright-eyed and investigative young officer clearly on his way up the ranks, and on the other, a half-Elf of unknown name and origins, well, Alberich thought you a likely enough spy, and enemy of his plans, to try to eliminate you. But a light-fingered Southern city rat, already in and out of Forlorn Hope twice? Who would suspect him of anything but looking to feather his own nest?"

Wolfram closed his mouth. For a moment no one said anything. Then Mishni threw the Obrist a vague salute, patted Wolfram on the shoulder, and bowed to Gudrun. He left as suddenly and silently as he had come, only a faint rustle of the pavilion's flap betraying that the Rat had passed there. Gudrun's hand stole into Wolfram's, pressing his fingers softly. He returned the gentle squeeze, looking down at her. Not tonight, not yet, with the Silver Eagle's other mage still of uncertain soundness and the possibility of Alberich's revenge lurking in violent minds, but soon.

"Fräulein Zauberobristin, I think it is time for you to call your Trabanten to escort you back to the Black Wagon," Helmuth said. "As for you, Lieutenant, stay a moment."

Wolfram waited to kiss Gudrun goodnight until her bodyguard had arrived. One, a Dwarf carrying a heavy pole-ax, raised bushy eyebrows at them, but Gudrun smiled joyfully back. "It's all right," she said. "We're betrothed."

The joy in her voice called up a wave of answering feeling in Wolfram's heart, like a spring rising beneath a torrent of warm rain. He kissed her again, and they bade each other good-night, the ache of the moment's regret and longing only sharpening the sweetness of the knowledge that they would be together soon. When Wolfram turned back to Obrist Helmuth, however, the grave look on his commander's face damped his glowing happiness like a shower of cold rain spattering black over a bed of fire-shimmering coals. What is it? Wolfram wondered. What couldn't Gudrun hear? Donmar, he doesn't mean for me to spy on her, does he? Surely, if he mistrusted her, he wouldn't have.

"May I have a look at your sword, Lieutenant?" Helmuth asked quietly.

The chill ran through Wolfram's heart like frost-rimed steel. He said he trusted me; but he must trust Mishni as well, and knows the Rat is a thief. Still, Wolfram unhooked the scabbard from his belt and handed the weapon over in silence. Helmuth held the scabbarded blade flat on his palms for a moment, his keen blue gaze running up and down it.

Carefully he touched the hilt, blunt calloused fingers tracing lightly over the blank silver disk that concealed the arms of Löwenstein. His hand folded over the grip, the Obrist raised an inquiring eyebrow at Wolfram.

"Go ahead, sir," Wolfram said, his voice rough with tension.

Obrist Helmuth drew the sword, holding it lightly and moving the hilt about a bit to feel the balance as he looked along one side of the blade, then the other. He re-sheathed it and gave it back to Wolfram.

"I founded the Silver Eagle twenty-eight years ago," he murmured, as if talking to himself.

"Our second contract was on the north coast, with Graf Ulric von Löwenstein, whose lands were suffering heavily from Dark Elvish raiders. He had reason, in fact, to think that the Dark Elves were planning to invade in force, which was why he hired us. He was right. I was blooded in war at fifteen and had been fighting ever since, against both Men and Orcs, but I had never seen anything quite like those battles or, worse, what happened when we failed to reach a village in time to protect it from the Dark Elves.

I lost nearly a quarter of my surviving recruits when that contract was done, and if I hadn't known that most wars weren't like that, I would have disbanded the regiment and gone back to living quietly on my lands. Hired someone else to fight if war ever came to me. In any case, I grew to know Graf Ulric fairly well through those black months. We fought together, sweated heaving logs into place for palisades together, yes, and drank and whored together, trying to kill the horror for a little while. I'm not proud of it; but I had left Lotte at home, thank all the gods of Light, and Ulric's wife had recently died of the fever, leaving him only one son.

Ruprecht? No. Rudiger, maybe. Something like that. There was one battle, the Dark Elves had swept around us, cutting through the back of the gevierte Ordnung. I was down on the ground, stunned. I thought my neck was broken, or my back. I still remember the face grinning down at me, that fair Elvish beauty lit by such malice. I could feel the joy he took in my pain, shimmering between us like heat-waves off a stove in winter, and those pale green eyes searing into my own like hot spikes. I felt everything go, piss and shit both, and the Elf took a deep sniff of it and laughed.

He or she, but I always thought he, stuck the tip of his sword through my right eye slit, probing a little until I could just feel it cutting into my eyelid, then he paused. Taunting me. Then I saw a sword shining against the dark clouds. Its light was green as well, but it was a pure green, not that unholy light in. The Elf moved damned fast, he managed to get halfway turned and lift his sword hilt-first to block the stroke to his head. But it left him in an awkward position. The next blow took his arm off, and the third went from collarbone to hipbone.

Graf Ulric leaned down from his horse; I grabbed his hand around the sword-hilt, and he pulled me to my feet. I hurt like three Hells, but I could fight again. You know how it is with battles, sometimes, looking back, everything is just a blur from beginning to end, but sometimes you come out with a picture in your mind, clearer than any painter could hope to match."

Helmuth fell silent, staring at the shadows. His heavy-featured face looked like a hollow mask. His eyes were the pale, fixed eyes of a ghost, looking through the empty darkness of the years at the battle that had ended before Wolfram was born. Wolfram had seen that look before.

Sometimes on Graf Ulric's older knights and men-at-arms, sometimes, though very rarely, on the face of the Graf himself, when he thought himself alone. Then Obrist Helmuth shook himself slightly and blinked, as though emerging from black water.

"So, you see, I knew your sword when I first saw it. I would never do such a thing against your will but I would wager any sum you like that, if I were to take it down to one of our smiths and ask him to pry the silver rondel out of the pommel, I'd find the arms of Löwenstein under it."

Wolfram sat mute, hardly daring to breathe.

"You look like him, you know. Oh, the Elven coloring and cast to your features hide the resemblance fairly well, to the casual glance. But if someone were to take that into account."

"I'm not Graf Ulric's son," Wolfram said, his voice thudding scratchily as sandstone beneath a hammer's blows. "The son of his second wife but not of the Graf himself. I left when it became known. If you were ever friend to Graf Ulric, I beg you to keep his secret."

Helmuth blew out his breath in a long, slow sigh, looking intently at Wolfram.

"There is a great deal you are not telling me. I hope you will find yourself able to, some day. But I have held my tongue since you joined my regiment, and I will continue to do so. For my old friend's sake and because I know something of that blade, and what it means to him. Had you stolen it, you would not live yet. Whatever your birth, he would not have given it to you, had he not judged you worthy to bear it. If St. Hildebrand grant that Ulric and I meet again where we can talk as men, in this life or the next, I will be able to tell him that you have proven his judgment good."

The Obrist swallowed hard, reached out to clap Wolfram on the shoulder. The rough warmth of the familiar touch brought tears prickling to the back of Wolfram's eyes: his father, foster-father might have reached through the other man's body to reassure him so.

"Go on," Helmuth said. "Pick four of my men to escort you to the Black Wagon. Yes, I know that you and Gudrun are terrified of letting your love interfere with your duties, but neither of you is completely indispensable through every single night. Consider this an order."

"Yes, sir," Wolfram replied, his heart leaping again.

He was almost through the tent-flap when he heard the Obrist's soft whisper. To himself, almost certainly, not thinking that Wolfram's half-Elvish hearing would pick up the barely-breathed words, "Still, Ulric, he is very like you."

HISTORICAL NOTES & GLOSSARIES

Forlorn Hope takes place in a world much like Europe's sixteenth century might have been – if our sixteenth century had been troubled by magic, non-human races, and the direct struggle between Light and Dark, Chaos and Order. Its progress was faster than ours to varying degrees in some respects: healing arts, aided by magic and the gods, are obviously much more efficient; the position of women is noticeably stronger, again because magical and spiritual power are more directly effective in both military and civilian contexts. In others, it was slower: noble society is closer in many ways to the fourteenth century than to the sixteenth, maintaining a much stronger emphasis on personal fealty, the chivalric education of young men, and so forth; the supremacy of the main organized Church remains unchallenged, etc.

However, the increasing development (and obvious efficiency) of a non-class-based military which might, for the first time, be described as "professional" (perhaps most importantly, in the capability to take a peasant boy and turn him, through constant and thorough drilling, into a full-time soldier who doesn't have to go home and harvest the fields every autumn, but continues to drill and fight as his career until he dies or retires), is coming more and more into conflict with those ideals.

The more so as the Landsknecht tactics, with their walls of trained pikes, are capable of defeating the noble heavy cavalry on most battlegrounds (a lesson which our world learned for the first time in the fourteenth century and slowly built upon until the day of the historical Landsknechts). The main directives of the Obrist (Colonel) were also set forward in a very clear form, suitable to professional soldiers of any day, e.g.. "The strength of the enemy, his number of horse, and his type of armor should be determined in advance and the lay of the land, the weather, the time of day, all taken into consideration before deciding on the type of battle formation to be adopted...Advantage should be taken of both the sun and the wind and the Landsknecht should be reminded of the more subtle ways of rendering the enemy pike effective by using sand or dust to disable them..." (Fronsberger, Leonhard: Funff Bucher von Kriegsregiment und Ordnung, 1555-56).

The Silver Eagle is based, with the obvious exceptions, fairly closely on historical Landsknecht companies. Such peculiar offices as the Hürenweibel (Whores' Sergeant), the unimpeachable Provost, and the Rumourmeister (whose duty was to separate quarreling women in the train by means of a truncheon) were a genuine and important part of these companies. Because the population of the Cimbrian Empire is significantly smaller than that of the historical Holy Roman Empire at this time, the size of the Landsknecht companies in this book is also comparatively smaller: about two thousand fighting men (rather than four thousand) and roughly the same number of sutlers, servants, prostitutes, children, etc.

The pay scales are the same as the original ones, which, together with the Orders, various descriptions of tactics and advice thereof (including the use of spies and agents in enemy camps), and overall arrangement of a regiment, have been well-preserved by documents of our sixteenth century. Cimbrian is actually a hybrid Celtic-Germanic language, but I have used German terms overall for the sake of familiarity. Remulan is a development from Etruscan interspersed with a good many loan-words from early Celto-Italic in much the same way, and for much the same reasons, that Germanic English is interspersed with loan-words from Latinate Norman.

Again, I have used Latin in its place, and substitute Latinate French for the pure Bretonic Celtic of Broceliande in order to convey a general sense of corresponding place and culture.

The lyrics to the song which begins "Death rides on a coal-black stallion" (Der Toten reitet ein kohlschwarzen Rappe) were actually written during World War I, when Germany was fighting in Flanders again, although the music is a Rhineland tune from much earlier. My Landsknechts have adapted it to where-ever they go to fight. Even though it is not properly historical, I personally love it too much to leave it out. The song Mishni sings while a captive is an actual historical Landsknecht song; his gross latrine-shoveling parody is, I am sorry to admit, my own. I owe special thanks to Obristen Gottfried and Ulric von Wolfsberg, who transmitted a huge affection for Landsknecht life and appalling color sense to me, and to all the Landsknechts of Drachenwald who have been a horrible bad influence on me.

GLOSSARY

LANDSKNECHT TERMS

Doppelsöldner – the men with two-handed swords whose duty was to cut through the pikes of the opposing forces in battle. Called "double soldiers" because they received double pay.

Fähndrich – the man who carries the Fähnlein banner into battle. The title literally means "ensign", but the Fähndrich was in practice the highest-ranking soldier in his Fähnlein except for the Hauptmann (captain). He would, for instance, occasionally give the flag over to someone else while going through the Fähnlein to keep it in order and good morale during combat.

Fähnlein – "little flag", the ten-foot unit banner. Also used as a name for the basic 400-man Landsknecht unit itself.

Feldartz – "field doctor", the primary physician overseeing the Fähnlein physicians.

Feldscher – the colonel's personal physician.

Feldweibel – sergeant major

Freimann – the company executioner.
Gemeinweibel – an elected position, changed monthly; the representative of the common soldiers.

gevierte Ordnung – "square order", one of the most common tactical maneuvers of the Landsknechts.

Hauptmann – captain; the commanding officer of each Fähnlein.

Hürenweibel – "whores' sergeant". The officer responsible for overseeing the civilian providers of food and services of all sorts who traveled with the regiment, making sure prices and quality levels were kept under control.

Igel – "the hedgehog"; a Landsknecht maneuver designed to emphasize the defensive capability of the long pikes. Particularly useful against cavalry.

Katzbalger – "cat-scrapper". A heavy, single-edged short sword or large dagger, used in the press of close fighting where long weapons such as pikes, halberds, and two-handed swords become unwieldy.

Lieutenant – "lieutenant", but actually functioned more as an adjutant to the Hauptmann. His pay was usually the same as that of the Fähndrich ("ensign"), but the latter seems to have been senior.

Marshal – an office not existing in our world; the title of the mages subordinate to the Zauberobrist.

Obrist – "colonel". The raiser and commander of the Landsknecht regiment, the Obrist would receive imperial permission to recruit what was, in effect, a small private army. He could hire it out pretty much where he pleased, although was responsible for fighting for the Empire when called upon.

Pfenningmeister – officer in charge of the regimental funds.

Proviantmeister – "provisions master"

Provost – as detailed here, a civilian post of amazing power.

Rotte – a sub-unit of ten ordinary soldiers or six Doppelsöldner.

Schultheiss – company judge, presiding over full trials.

Trabanten – literally "satellites"; a troop of personal bodyguards.

Weibel - Sergeant

Zauberobrist – "Sorcery Colonel"; the rank of the senior mage in a Cimbrian Landsknecht regiment. Zauberobristin is the feminine form.

Zweihander – the five foot-long two-handed sword used by the most expert Landsknecht fighters for chopping through pike shafts. The blade was most often straight, but flame-bladed Zweihänder were not uncommon.

CIMBRIAN RELIGION: PLACES AND RACES

Note: there are a number of other local, less well-known deities within the Cimbrian Empire and its environs. These are the most commonly worshiped ones. Some of them are also known by other names in different lands or among other peoples; some are not. The Elves, for instance (insofar as anything is known about their religion by Men), appear to be relatively monotheistic, worshiping a single Lady of Light who is unknown to most Men; whereas the Dark Elves' Queen of Night seems to be the same Person that the Cimbrians call Ravehild (and they also give lesser veneration to the other two gods of Darkness and various unwholesome spirits).

GODS OF LIGHT

Agwar – a "minor god", worshiped by the peasantry and generally honored in certain folk customs (e.g., "Agwar's Feastnight", a form of masked carnival). His worship pre-dates that of Donmar, but is found only in Scandia and the Cimbrian Empire. Often appearing as a wolf; his feast-day is in early February. A god of death, undeath, fertility, and (in Scandia), a type of folk-magic.

Alagrith – an Earth-mother goddess; Donmar's consort. Honored, but not to an equal or even near-equal extent by the organized Church. Her primary worship is carried out by the bands of priestesses known as Earth-witches, whose power has both religious and magical aspects; in folk religion, she receives a small cup of blood from the throat of every animal slaughtered, and the bodies of the dead are also considered to be offerings to her.

Donmar – the primary focus of the Church; sky-father, creator, and warrior-god, often perceived as the most direct personification of the Light. In Church theology, the Sun is called Donmar's Forge; he is often shown as smithing the universe.

Froni – Old Cimbrian or pre-Cimbrian fertility god; worshiped particularly on "May Day" and at harvest ceremonies, and by the agricultural peasantry for love and fertility. May originally have been a twin of Alagrith. In parts of Scandia, notably Svearike, he is still seen as the god who fills the land-king, bringing luck and good harvest.

Kunig – the smith-god predating Donmar. In official religion, demoted to Donmar's son and a very secondary figure; in folk religion, still primarily worshiped by smiths. Chief god worshiped by Dwarves, and portrayed (even by Men) as a red-bearded Dwarf; it is suspected that the worship of Kunig came to humans from the Dwarves with the knowledge of iron working.

Waldrig and Waldriga – twin patrons of hunting and game, largely relegated to peasant folk religion except for occasional conservative/isolated and hunt-mad nobles. In Church theology, Waldriga is the virgin daughter of Donmar; in folk religion, she is strongly sexed. Both official and folk religion indicate a strong sexual aspect to her brother, who is pictured bearing antlers.

St. Hildebrand – not a god, but the man who bore Donmar's power to drive back the allied forces of Darkness and Chaos over seventeen hundred years previously, inaugurating the new age (Era of St. Hildebrand), gaining the extremely rare title of "saint", and founding the Cimbrian Empire (he is also the line-father of the current Emperor, Maximilian the Younger). Particularly prayed to by warriors and those who need defense against Darkness.

Order and Chaos

Order is the only major force in the universe which is not personified in any way.

Chaos personifies itself as Arioris (also called "the Chaos" to distinguish it/them from the more generalized form), manifesting as either gender, both, or none as it/they choose. Its/their manifestations range in power from near-human (the Till Eulenspiegel type of culture-hero) to as great as, or perhaps greater than, the great gods.

Manifestations of Arioris may work with Light, Darkness, neither, or both, but generally appear when one side or the other has achieved enough power to bring about an excessive degree of Order.

Allied with Light, Arioris is/are the source of all freedom and creativity; allied with Darkness, Arioris is/are the source of havoc and horror.

Arioris is not normally worshiped, although mages, who draw their power from the Chaos-flux, reverence it/them; and occasionally someone seeking untoward power will try to use the Chaos personally, though this seldom goes well for the seeker.

Three Gods of Darkness

Gurvethor – represents particularly the terrifying aspects of nature, the medieval view of the forest/wild as the haunt of the Devil. Bringer of volcanoes, earthquakes, droughts, famines, tidal waves, hail, etc. Often portrayed as a black boar or bearing boar-like aspects; more rarely, appears as a nine-legged black stallion (the ninth leg proceeding from the genitalia and being comparatively exaggerated in size).

Rapists are branded on the face with a boar's head and a large G, as having been possessed by the power of this god. Folk names for him include the Black Boar or Stallion, the Ravager, the Trampler, Troll-Father, Nikki Big-Prick, Black Nikki, Tusker, and so forth. Worshiped as a general Father/Warrior god by the Orcs, and believed by them to be Ravehild's consort.

Morbod – never called by name except by his worshipers; referred to by everyone else as the Enemy, the Dark Flame, Master of Hells, Lord of Tortures, etc. In folk religion, most often called by more homely/apotropaic peasant names such as Coal-Eater, Him Below, Grandfather Hans/Old Hans, and so forth. Donmar's opposite in Darkness, most powerful and dreaded of the Three.

Worshiped only by the truly evil among men; some tribes of Orcs, most notably those currently or formerly under the direction of Dark Elves, evil mages worship him, while others do not.

Ravehild – the Crone; the negative of Alagrith as Morbod is of Donmar. Female sexual aggression/temptation, vagina dentata, devouring "Bad Mother", evil witch, etc. Sometimes portrayed as a three-legged black mare, sometimes as a black sow, sometimes as a woman with sharp teeth and the slick skin of a salamander reaching out of a bog or deep pool with the intention of dragging down a small child (variants of this exist in local folklore all over the Empire; in official theology, it represents her efforts to drag the soul down to the Hells of Darkness). In coastal areas, she also appears as a shark or shark-woman. Folk names for her include Katy Cold-Hands; Grandmother Snagglecunt/Old Snagglecunt; the Black Mare or Sow; the Eater, etc.

Called the Queen of Night by the Dark Elves, who revere her above the other gods of Darkness (like Elves in general, they are ruled by a Queen and have a slightly female-inclined culture); worshiped as a general Mother Goddess by the Orcs.

It is suspected by the very few who have had the opportunity to research the subject that Ravehild and Gurvethor may have been pre-Cimbrian deities demonized by the first wave of the peoples who later became the Cimbrians, and that the practices of those tribes of Orcs who are not devoted to Darkness as such could well preserve many elements of that original religion. Discussion of this topic is stringently forbidden (where it is even known to exist as a theory) by both Church and State.

BASIC GEOGRAPHY

Alba – Britain

Broceliande (roughly modern France)

Cimbrian Empire – the Cimbrian-speaking area (modern Germany, Austria, Hungary, Czechoslovakia, Poland)

Tir de Danann – Ireland

Kievia – Russia (Kiev maintained and enlarged its domination over the other great city-states and surrounding areas).

League of Cantons – the Alps from modern Switzerland southward; the buffer zone between the Cimbrian Empire and the South.

Myrkheimr – Estonia

Perkunan – Latvia/Lithuania

Scandia – a single kingdom. Gautríkr (West Sweden) was united with Svearíkr (East Sweden) to form the Twin Realms when King Bjólfr (known in English as Beowulf) married the widowed Queen Yrsa; some five hundred years later, Queen Sigríðr in stórraða of the Twin Realms married King Óláfr Tryggvason of Northroad (Norway), after which they conquered Sealand and Juteland together, but were stopped at the border of Suome by the power of the Suome shamans.

Southern City-States: the area of modern Italy, Spain, Portugal, and Greece comprise the South, which is divided up into quite a number of city-states.

Suome – modern Finland extending east into Russia

Twin Realms – Gautrike and Svearike (modern Sweden)

Races and Their Locations

Dwarves live in mountains, but are inclined to prefer more northerly climates. The Northroad part of Scandia is their favorite, although the excellent steel ores of the Twin Realms draw a good many of them to the lowlands there. Cities such as Milano, with its famous armoring industry, also tend to have large Dwarven populations.

Elves are found in large forests, but only when they want to be found. Broceliande, which has a very large and influential Elvish population, is the exception; almost all half-Elves active among Men come from there.

Dark Elves prefer northern climes and/or coastal areas: Myrkheimr and parts of Suome, Perkunan, and Kievia. There are rumored to be, or to have been, Dark Elf colonies in other mountainous areas such as the Alps, the Pyrenees, etc.

Orcs live where-ever the territory is rough enough that they can prosper and Men cannot easily drive them out.

The Children of Arioris (a general, non-literal term for all those magically-created races which appear to be a mixture of Man and some form of animal; does not imply that they worship the Chaos) live in appropriate environs: merfolk in the sea or large lakes and sufficiently large rivers; centaurs and cat-people in the woods; lizard-folk in the Sea of Sand (Sahara) or further south in the jungles; rat-folk in mountains and rough hills (they are often found either co-operating or competing with Orcs), and so forth. Nearly all of them are tribal; a loner is either a hermit on a quest of its own, or a dangerous renegade. They are generally intelligent and not disposed badly to humans, though individual groups may have unpleasant memories of the mage who created and attempted to use them.

Goblins, Trolls, Ogres, and Assorted Demi-Human
Thingies tend to prefer mountainous regions with few Men
or Elves and many caves. Trolls are generally found in
Scandia, where they have mostly driven out the others of
their ilk. Nearly all of these races are less intelligent than
Men or Orcs, with the exception of some individual Trolls.
Goblins are tribal in a rat-pack sense (as contrasted to
the sophisticated and organized tribalism of Orcs); Trolls
are solitary or live in small-family units; Ogres are very
solitary, meeting only to mate.

BIOGRAPHY

From his humble beginnings, Gundarsson would make his mark on the world by writing on the most rare and obscure myths breathing new life into them, for a new generation of readers. His fictional works written under Stephan Grundy focused on mythology and history and were met with international success.

Along with his fictional works, Gundarsson made a name for himself writing books on Germanic Paganism (also known as heathenry) and Germanic Culture. He is an Elder in the organization The Troth where he has dedicated a majority of his life influencing major changes in the organization, including the development of anti-racist and anti-sexist ideals.

He has fought for equality in trans-gendered communities, as well as fighting for the acceptance of Loki. Gundarsson has shaped heathenry through his numerous academic and fictional works as well as his extensive articles, thesis papers and his creation and sustainment of the lore program within The Troth. His hobbies included wood-working, jewelry making and gardening as well as historical re-enactment. He is currently attending medical school in Ireland supported by his loving wife Melodi where they maintain a local hof called The Tribe of Thor.

The Three Little Sisters

The Three Little Sisters is an indie publisher that puts authors first. We specalize in the strange and unusual. From titles about pagan and heathen spirituality to traditional fiction we bring books to life.

https://the3littlesisters.com